THE NOBODY PEOPLE

THE

NOBODY

PEOPLE

BOB PROEHL

TITAN BOOKS

THE NOBODY PEOPLE

Print edition ISBN: 9781789094619
E-book edition ISBN: 9781789094626

Published by Titan Books
A division of Titan Publishing Group Ltd
144 Southwark Street, London SE1 0UP
www.titanbooks.com

First Titan edition: September 2020
10 9 8 7 6 5 4 3 2 1

A CIP catalogue record for this title is available
from the British Library.

Printed and bound by CPI Group Ltd. CRO 4YY.

For Story and Alex,
who are growing up with strange abilities
I can only hope to understand

The earth keeps some vibration going
There in your heart, and that is you.
—EDGAR LEE MASTERS, *"Fiddler Jones"*

THE

NOBODY PEOPLE

PROLOGUE

THE INCIDENT AT POWDER BASIN

In the years before, when hateful men warned of the coming, crushing aluminum cans in their hands while their friends threw darts, or in rowboats tying flies, they spoke only of darkness.

—EVE EWING, *"Arrival Day"*

When reporters from the *Gillette News-Record* asked the survivors of the Powder Basin mine collapse how they survived, all twenty-three gave variations on the same answer: *It was an act of God. The will of God. God's own mercy.* Bruce Bennett, cornered on camera by the blond anchor from K-DEV down in Cheyenne, said it was the darnedest thing. Like the hand of God Hisself reached down and pulled them out of that pit.

The twenty-three survivors hadn't had time to confer. Once they were past the blockage, they trudged upward to the mouth of Shaft L in silence. They emerged, owls in the late autumn daylight. News vans were already there. Spouses with supervisors who let them off when the news broke or with baby-sitters who could show up on short notice waited within the circle of cameras, along with gawkers down from Gillette, phones ready to catch footage of miners or their bodies coming out of the tunnel.

The survivors had been underground nine hours. There was six solid feet of rubble between them and the surface, too much for God to cut through. God had nothing to do with getting them out. It was Tom Guthridge's oldest boy, Sam, whose forged employment papers said he was eighteen.

The Friday afterward, the Powder Basin mine was closed. All 140 employees were given the full day off with pay. The holding company went over maintenance records and noted how long since an inspector had seen the inside of Shaft L. The best course of action was to keep everyone happy.

The men who hadn't been in Shaft L gravitated toward the Chariot Lounge in Gillette that afternoon. Some said they'd had a bad feeling when they came in Thursday morning. Many claimed they'd heard the shaft go. They lied to feel like part of it. The lies were the way they understood the accident. True stories, made up after the fact.

Among the survivors, twenty spent their free day at home. They clutched their children more tightly than they had since the kids were babies. Dinners tasted better than anything the steak house in Gillette could grill up. That night, with the kids in bed, they made love to their wives the way guys did in the movies, knocking over lamps and tearing at clothes in a rush to get skin pressed to skin. As if they'd found something they'd forgotten losing and only now understood its value. All of them slept deeply and dreamlessly.

Sam Guthridge didn't leave his room the whole day, which wasn't unusual. He was a solitary boy, kind and gentle. His father, Tom, used to say Sam was too soft for this town. Not in anger or disappointment but regret that he couldn't offer Sam better. Tom and Lucy Guthridge had been socking money away for Sam's college. All that came to nothing when Tom got sick. Medical bills ate up the savings faster than the cancer ate through Tom's lungs. Lucy took it as a blessing that her husband hadn't lived long enough to see Sam go into the mines.

Sam didn't talk much to his mother about what happened. "We did what we had to, and we got out," he said. Lucy knew the truth and knew there would be consequences to come. There were times she wished she could take her kids out of the world. Hold them safe and away until the storm passed. But that wasn't the way of things, and as Lucy's mother once said, it rains on the just and the unjust alike.

Sam was a brave boy, but he carried too much. Tom had been the same way. A goofy grin covered the fact that he was holding the world up with his hands. Sam never knew that side of his father, but he picked it up all the same. You couldn't hide what was in the blood. When Sam didn't come to the dinner table Friday evening, Lucy sent his little sister Paige in with a plate. Sam thanked her quietly and kissed her on the cheek, because among his three little siblings, Paige was his favorite.

Joe Sabine, who'd never kept a woman around more than a week, and Danny Randall, whose wife had run off to Denver with an IRS auditor the previous year, burned Friday on Joe's back porch, both wearing their ratty varsity jackets against the cold of the November evening. They were a long time getting around to what needed talking about. They sucked back cans of Coors and threw the empties over the railing onto the lawn. Danny crushed his third on the armrest of his Adirondack chair, same as he did in high school. Joe followed suit, tossing the resulting disk away like a Frisbee. It was past dusk, and both of them were drunk before Danny mentioned the blue lights that had shot out of the Guthridge kid's eyes. The light cutting through the rock. The thin wisp of smoke, a serpent rising out of the stone. How the boy carved away manhole covers of shale. How the men heaved them aside as the light sheared them from the wall of rubble, edges hot to the touch. Down to the last one, the one that peeled away to show sickly sunlight. And air, air pouring out like beer from a tap, so the men crowded toward the opening, mouths gaping for it. Except Sam, who stepped back and let them, then started in again, widening the hole with his light.

"Wasn't normal," said Joe.

"No shit," Danny said.

"Wasn't any act of God either."

"No," said Danny. "Not God."

Monday, Danny Randall called in sick and drove up to the public library to use the computers. He had to wait in line. No one bothered to chase off the crazies and jerkoffs until the school let out. He was looking for context, a word for what Sam Guthridge was. There was something he remembered hearing on a radio show maybe a year before, driving back from the Chariot after last call. He tried a bunch of searches, but it was "strange abilities am radio late" that hit pay dirt. It was a radio show called *The Monster Report with Jefferson Hargrave*. Tinfoil helmet stuff broadcast on one of the Kindred Network stations to which his mother kept her car radio dialed. Danny borrowed a pair of headphones from the desk to listen.

Jefferson Hargrave reminded Danny of the Pentecostal preachers he'd been dragged to see when he was a kid. Sweaty men in starched white shirts railing on about the Lord and His wrath while Danny's mother swooned. Hargrave pounded words like nails into wood. "I've got reports here going back to the fifties," he said. "Government reports. And if you're surprised the government knows about these people, then you have not. Been paying. Attention.

"The thing is? The numbers are increasing. I've charted this, and it's, over the years, it goes . . . swoop, upward and upward. But what do I know? Maybe gamma radiation levels are on the rise, or it's hormones in hamburgers. I mean, the sun causes cancer. In a world where the sun causes cancer, anything is possible.

"This I can tell you. There's no links between these people that I can see. There aren't pockets or hot spots. You know, when some corporation leaks something awful and everyone on Shit River gets ball cancer? It's not like that. Their people, their parents, are normal, like you or me. Which means you could have a kid with gills or x-ray vision right out of nowhere.

"And then what happens to them? Because I can tell you, once one of these people gets spotted? They're not sticking around to talk to the press. They're not registering themselves as weapons. Which, from what I can tell, a lot of them are. They're *weapons*. And once they're found out? They disappear.

"So you're thinking I'm going to say it's the government. That these people are being rounded up and trained at black ops sites to fight the war on terror or come take your guns and your women.

17

"You know what? That's the best. Case. Scenario. That's what I'm *hoping* for. Because what's more likely? What, it seems to me, is the real nightmare? Is that they are organizing themselves. That they are forming, under our noses, their own army.

"And you have to ask yourself, to what end?"

Danny sat staring at the screen. He clicked the share button and sent the recording to Joe Sabine. After thinking about it another minute, he sent it to the other survivors. All except Sam Guthridge.

Tuesday after shift, the Chariot seemed like a safe place to talk, although who knew? Maybe the Guthridge kid could hear them from across town or read their thoughts like the sports section of the *News-Record*. That was the damnable thing. You could never know.

Danny bought a round of pitchers. He sprang for the fancy ones from the brewery in Jackson Hole even though it shot his beer budget for the month and left a taste in his mouth like sucking on a penny. Danny let the other men talk. He'd planted the seed and could tell it had found purchase. Alvin McLaughlin brought printouts of blurry photos and typed witness statements. Marc Medina fancied himself an expert on DNA and the effects of gamma radiation thereupon.

"Imagine a string of letters, except only four of them, repeating," he told Scott Lipscombe. "This radiation slices right through them. GTT slice! Like that. Then you've got two loose ends floating around. And they can join up again wherever." He laced his fingers together, then bent them into a tangle. "Genetic mutation," he said.

More rounds got bought. Troy Potter, the weeknight bartender, caught a couple of sideways looks and found things to busy himself with in the back. Talk turned to the subject at hand. What to do about Sam. They all made a point of saying they liked Sam. They acknowledged that they were indebted to him. They owed him their lives for what he did.

"With his *abilities*," Danny added, throwing it out there. "What he did with his abilities."

He let the strangeness of the word do its work on them. Some of the men nodded. Others squirmed.

Lowell Tyler, the oldest rockbreaker at the basin, met Danny's eyes.

"I don't like where you're taking this conversation, Danny," he said. "Even if Tom's boy hadn't saved your ass, which he did. This kind of talk doesn't go anywhere good."

"It's talk," Danny said. He held his hands up innocently. "Situation like this merits discussion, don't you think?" He gave Lowell his best "we're all friends here" grin. When it didn't work on Lowell, he turned it on the rest of the room. People were eager to chime in with agreement.

Lowell had lost a kid in Iraq and trained Tom Guthridge when Tom wasn't much older than Sam was now. He took Tom's death harder than anyone. In the weeks after the funeral, Lowell would show up at the Chariot spoiling for it, daring the young bucks to take a swing at him, like he needed physical pain to match what he felt in his gut. No one stepped up and decked the old man even though they would have been doing him a favor.

"I'm having no part of what you're talking about," Lowell said. "I'll tell you, Danny. Put it down. And you two—" He pointed at Alvin McLaughlin and Joe Sabine. "—don't forget this asshole talked you into breaking into Antelope Valley's locker room to shit in their helmets when you all were kids."

"We won that game," said Joe. His voice was a high whine.

"You two listened to it on the radio in county lockup," Lowell said. "And Danny got himself off without a hitch. The three of you forget that part." He held out a ten to Danny. "Here's for the beers."

"I got these," Danny said.

"This is for mine," said Lowell. Danny took the bill. He looked at it like Lowell had wiped his ass on it. They watched Lowell walk out, then turned to Danny. They weighed what Lowell said. They wondered if they ought to follow him out the door.

Danny slapped the ten down on the bar.

"Looks like Lowell stood us another round," he said. It got the desired laugh. More important, it put Lowell Tyler's blessing on them. Lowell said he had no part of it, but Danny had him buying the beers.

"The thing is," Danny said, "there's a risk this is the start of something. You can't know where something like this is going to lead. That's what we need to find out. The only way to do that is to go have a talk with Sam."

There would be time later for all the survivors to reconcile their actions and their consciences. Although, as it turned out, not much time. For now they were resolved. And as Danny Randall said, "It might as well be tonight."

Lucy Guthridge hadn't been to bed since the incident. She drowsed on the sofa or in the armchair after the kids were asleep. When she answered the door in her gray uniform from the diner, she knew this was what had kept her up. A vision of this assemblage, this mob camped out on her lawn. *It's a wonder you all aren't sporting pitchforks,* she thought.

These men had visited Tom in the hospital, where Lucy had held constant vigil. They took up a collection to help Lucy and the four kids, and they kept quiet when Sam, too young to grow a patch of beard if you gave him a month and a miracle, applied for a job in the mine. They'd been at Tom's funeral and come to the reception after at this same house whose lawn they were trampling over.

"It's awful late, Danny," Lucy said. She ignored the rest of them. "Is there something you're needing?"

"We came for Sam," Danny said, avoiding her eyes.

"Sam's earned his rest. Don't you think?"

Danny didn't answer. He stepped past her into the living room. The other men followed, crowding in until Lucy was pressed against the wall. Woken by the noise, the four Guthridge children stood in the hallway that led to their bedrooms. Sam was in a tee shirt and baggy shorts. He looked, Scott Lipscombe thought, like a boy. It was easy to miss that working alongside him, but now, thin limbs jutting out of clothes that were once his father's, Sam didn't look old enough to drive. His younger brother, Jeb, was in flannel pajamas, and the girls, Melody and Paige, were both in nightgowns. The three little ones huddled behind Sam, who held his hands stiff at his sides, fists clenched.

"Come with us, son," Danny said.

"Not your son," said Sam. He didn't move. Paige coughed, shaking off a cold she'd picked up at school. Little Jeb patted her back and rubbed it, then put his hands at his sides, fists tight like his big brother.

The room seethed with drunk energy. Marc Medina giggled nervously, and Alvin McLaughlin shushed him. Scott Lipscombe had his twelve-gauge hanging at the end of his arm, chambers full of rock salt. He felt a fat bead of nervous sweat roll down his temple, and he raised the gun to wipe it with his sleeve. That was when he saw it. He was sure he did. A blue glint in Sam's eye. He remembered the smell of rock burning as the light cut through it. He imagined himself sliced in two and wondered what burnt-meat smell his own body would give off. If the smoke would hit his nostrils before he died.

He emptied two chambers of rock salt into Sam Guthridge's gut.

Sam doubled over, the wind knocked out of him. Lucy pitched forward toward Scott, but Alvin McLaughlin grabbed her around the waist and spun her like a drunken dance partner. Paige, the littlest one, screamed. She held the side of her face where she'd been struck. She pulled her hand away to check for blood.

There was none. Where the salt crystals had hit, seven on her cheek and forehead, bright blue light shone through punctured skin.

"Shit," said Danny, "it's all of them."

When the fire burned itself out, the men dispersed. Most went home, where they lay awake next to their wives until dawn. Their minds were full of sounds that would wake them some nights for what was left of their lives.

A small knot, Danny and Joe and a couple of others, took bottles to the mouth of Shaft L. It was blocked off. The fence was a row of sickly teeth. It was the only time the men would talk about what had happened.

"Those lights in her head," said Scott Lipscombe. "They reminded me of a toy I had when I was a kid."

"Lite Brite," Danny said. "I thought that, too." He could picture the lights, the way they traced jagged lines in the dim room as Paige Guthridge's body hitched with sobs. Every time the men cut her, light poured out of the wounds. Danny Randall thought that when she died, the lights would fade like in a theater at the start of a movie. But they went out suddenly, like a candle

ONE

AN UNEARTHLY CHILD

There was a door & then a door surrounded by a forest.
Look, my eyes are not your eyes.
—Ocean Vuong,
"To My Father/To My Future Son"

A NULL SPHERE

The phone on the nightstand buzzes and pulls Avi Hirsch up from a dream of being tossed in the air and falling, tossed and falling. The arc his body makes in the dream becomes a loop. He flails awake. The dream is recurrent, felt in his body rather than his mind. A year out of the hospital and he can't remember on waking where he is. Kay has lost patience with this morning thrash of limbs and makes it a point to be up and out of bed before him. Avi grabs at the phone as it skitters toward the edge of the nightstand.

"I sent you something," says the voice on the other end. "A weird one. Take a look." The voice pauses, waits.

"Good morning, Louis," says Avi. Louis Hoffman is Avi's friend and occasional informant at Homeland Security. He works out of Homeland's Chicago office, but he and Avi have known each other since Louis's days as an army liaison. Louis hasn't called since Avi got out of the hospital.

"Look at it," Louis says. "Right on your phone. I'll wait."

"I'm in bed," says Avi, rolling himself up to a seated position.

"What happened to 'the news never sleeps'?" Louis says.

"That's not a saying," Avi says. "Besides, I'm not—"

"Put your eyes on it and call me immediately," says Louis, and hangs up. Avi sees the subject line on his home screen: *Roseland/Ballston Common Bombings.* His heart speeds up a little, that junkie rush. He thinks about opening it right now, before anything else. But Kay has let him sleep in, which sets them all behind schedule. He puts the phone on the nightstand, facedown. He picks up the sock from the floor and his prosthetic from its spot against the bed. The physical therapist says that over time, amputees start to think of their prostheses as part of their bodies. It feels like a foreign object to Avi. It looks like a plunger capped with a plastic foot. A half-witted piece of sculpture. He goes through the ritual of attaching it to his left leg below the knee. The process is boring while requiring close attention. A bad fit becomes painful as the day wears on, unbearable by lunch. In the beginning, Kay tried to help. The angles were better. It was easier for her to perfect the fit. But Avi was so angry in those first days home from the hospital. He yelled. Swatted her hands away. He apologized, and she assured him there was no need. It was important he accept his anger, understand it as justified. She knew that in time it would flow into the correct channel rather than spilling out at her like lava over its cooled levee. Eventually she stopped offering to help with the prosthesis. She stopped offering help with stairs or getting into the minivan in case assistance implied that she thought he was helpless. She leaves him this moment every morning. Alone with his leg.

He hears the first click of the pin into the socket and eases his weight on it. There's the deeper click, the one that echoes up his thigh. The one he can feel in his teeth. He rolls the leg of his sweatpants back down and examines his feet. The foot of the prosthesis is a shiny plastic foam, its color chosen to match Avi's skin tone. It's too pink, like cartoon flesh. The toes have toenails carved into them. He wonders if customers demanded this detail from the manufacturer or if the designers came up with it themselves. A little attempt at normality that makes the thing even stranger.

The floor is cold against the sole of his real foot. Avi puts on slippers and goes downstairs. Kay is at the kitchen table in the rattiest of her several bathrobes, the lavender one that offsets her dark brown skin. Her hair is up in a green silk wrap, a few tight curls escaping. She's reading a Nnedi Okorafor novel. The amount she reads amazes Avi. She works in immigration law, zeroing in on the minutiae of the government's shifting edicts and decrees, then fills her spare moments with science fiction and detective novels. She takes the train into the city rather than accepting a ride for the extra hour with her books. As he comes in, she gives him a bored grin that says, *oh, you're here.* It's what Avi feels reduced to this past year: the guy who keeps showing up every morning, wanted or not.

Their seven-year-old, Emmeline, is at the stove cooking eggs, standing on a stool to reach. She's wearing an old apron over her school clothes. It's so long on her that Avi worries she'll trip over the hem. Her hair, a riot of dark corkscrews, is pulled back into a tie, exploding out the back of her head.

"Did you teach her that?" Kay asks. There's an accusation

built into the question, and Avi is quick to defend himself. It will be a long time before he invites Emmeline near the stove. Kay doesn't cook. Avi taught Emmeline how to make toast, not much else. But here she is, flipping the eggs and folding them back on themselves, deft as a short order cook. Avi watches over her shoulder, then pushes her bangs back and kisses her forehead.

"Where'd you learn to cook, Leener?" he asks.

"They're for you," says Emmeline. "For your big day."

It's a smooth dodge of the question, put forth with Emmeline's strange assuredness. She fixes Avi with her eyes, blue made paler by contrast to her skin, darker even than her mother's. Then she goes back to work. Around the girl's icy irises runs a ring of navy blue. When Emmeline was born, Kay's mother said that this meant she'd have second sight. Kay told her to can it with that hoodoo noise. But there is something ethereal about their daughter. She seems to know things as if she's come prepared for all the big moments in her life, along with some of the small ones. On Emmeline's first day at kindergarten, when Avi dropped her off, he told her she was going to have a great day.

"No, I'm not," Emmeline said, not sad but factual. "But you'll come get me after I fall."

"Always," Avi said. He thought it was a testament to Emmeline's faith that he'd be there for her. *A verbal trust fall,* he said when he recounted it. After lunch, Avi got a call from the school. One of the other kids, *some racist little shit,* Kay called him, had pushed Emmeline off the top of the slide. Avi sped to pick her up. Emmeline wasn't hurt or upset. Avi told the story to other parents in the vein of *isn't it funny how prescient they seem sometimes.* No one ever responded with a similar story, and Avi stopped bringing it up.

"Big day?" says Kay. She doesn't look up from her book, but a smirk plays on her face.

"Not that I know of," he says.

"Who was on the phone?" Kay says.

"Louis at Homeland. He sent something. I'll look at it once I've got you all out the door. It's probably nothing."

Kay shifts her bookmark from its arbitrary spot near the back to where she's at and closes the book. "Is it about the church by my mom's?"

"I don't know what it's about," he says. "I haven't looked at it yet."

"If it's the church, you should pass it on to someone else."

"Yeah," he says. "I probably will."

"Avi," she says, hanging on that *probably.* She looks at him, then at Emmeline's back, then at him again. Her meaning is clear from the fact that she won't talk about it in front of Emmeline: *I don't want you writing about dead black girls in this house.* Avi wants to tell her it's not her business what he writes about and it's not her decision what he can and can't handle. He doesn't.

"I'll pass it off," he says. "If that's what it is."

Kay holds him with her eyes a second longer, then reopens her book.

Emmeline clicks the burner off. "Today," she says, half to herself. "Today things will start." She scoops eggs off the skillet and onto a plate, which she hands to Avi. A moment of reversal, the child performing the action of the parent with uncanny accuracy.

"None for me?" says Kay, trying to be playful, to wipe the tension away.

Emmeline shakes her head. "You had toast," she says. She points at the plate. "Try." He obeys. Kay prefers her eggs a gooey, amorphous mass, so that's how Avi cooks them. These are made for him, the way he'd make them for himself. Dry, overcooked so the snotlike quality that catches in Avi's throat is gone.

"They're perfect," he says. Emmeline nods. She knew they would be.

After he drops Emmeline off at school, Avi trudges up the steps toward his home office. Kay wants him to move his office out of the attic. There are no railings on the drop-down ladder, and she's sure he's going to topple. She imagines him lying on his back for hours like a stranded turtle, waiting for someone to get home. But the office is familiar. It's one thing that's remained normal in his life since he lost his leg, and he needs it. A place to return to even if getting there is hard.

This prosthetic, his third, is the best he's had for walking over flats. He misses the last one when it comes to climbing the ladder or ascending stairs. His doctor says he'll be ready for a permanent leg next summer. It takes time for the swelling to normalize. Avi reads up on prostheses the way some men shop for new cars. Kay says go all out. "Shoot the moon," she says. She imagines something robotic. She sees him as a comic book hero, a cyborg. Avi reads articles on the torsional strength of certain plastics. He visits online forums for amputees that winnow into more and more specific groups. Vets stick with other vets. Users with prosthetic knees don't have time for shin shoppers like Avi. Nested within every inclusive community is another whose losses are worse. Avi has settled into one of the outer circles of the group, his tragedy major but not as bad as it could be.

He makes it up the ladder and pulls the hatch up behind him. He drops heavily into the chair at his desk, the one Kay bought at a yard sale the month after they moved in. Everything in the attic is secondhand. Bookshelves at staggered heights. Mismatched rugs, some chosen for ugliness, covering the wood floor he's sanded but never finished. The computer is an ancient desktop, a glorified typewriter. It takes a minute for it to whir to life, another to open his in-box. Kay wants to buy him a new one. She wants him to know that they're doing okay moneywise even though he hasn't been writing since the hospital. Avi drums his fingers. The e-mail has been calling to him all morning, more loudly than he cares to admit. He turns on the space heater, and the room fills with the smell of toasted dust. The porthole high up on the western wall, opposite the desk, is the only place sunlight comes in, one octagonal shaft through the dust motes that creeps across the floor over the course of the day. If there's sunlight on his computer, it's time to stop working and return to the world.

The message from Louis is the only one in his in-box. Two videos, one dated last week, the other the month before. He recognizes the dates. The older one was the bombing at the mall outside DC. Nineteen killed. Homeland identified the bomber as some angry white male, killed in the blast. The more recent one was in Roseland, an hour's drive from here, near Kay's mother. Salem Baptist, a black church. Two dead. The black community in Chicago was livid, the mayor caught hell, but the national press didn't do much with it. These things happen too often to be newsworthy. Avi was surprised these fell into Homeland's lap: the agency rarely was let loose on white indigenous terrorists. Louis called Homeland's unrelenting focus on Muslims its "mandate for Mecca." Avi had gone out for beers with Louis and his coworkers. Off the clock, they said they were more scared of being shot up by an angry white male than by an imagined jihadi. They all knew guys like that or guys who were one bad day away from becoming guys like that.

Avi clicks on the first video. The mall. It's camera phone footage, grainy and jittering. It pops up in a small window on his screen. A girl, early teens. She's chubby and sweet-faced, ears newly pierced at the kiosk by the food court. She turns left, turns right. The stud catches the fluorescents and throws them at the camera. A flare, an x of bright pixels.

Here is the truth of all evidence: it hides in the ordinary. The moment believes you can't see it because it looks like everything else. Avi attends to backgrounds. He watches for glitches in the pattern. A van parked where it shouldn't be. A man in the souk who moves through the crowd more slowly than those around him. Avi wonders about the camera's operator. A boyfriend, maybe, or a best friend. His mind flashes to Emmeline, perpetually friendless, proudly alone. Then he focuses. A couple, boy and girl, argue in the corner of the frame. Escalating, drawing attention. The camera shifts. The glittering stud at the center of the shot hovers at its edge. The boy is shouting, but the audio is muddy. He's skinny, hatchet-faced. Sunken eyes and dirty blond hair. Avi leans in, searching for the vest. The belt. The detonator in hand. He expands the image until it covers the whole screen. The low resolution becomes more pronounced. People are stacks of squares. Colors move like storm fronts on a TV weather map. But there's nothing. The boy and girl wear tan polo shirts, uniforms from one of the franchise restaurants in the food court. With better resolution, you could read their name tags. The boy holds out his empty hands like he's begging her for something. His palms turn out, pushing her back. His hands are empty.

There is no bomb.

Then comes the blast.

The frame goes white. As if the glint off the earring had been a precursor, a trial run. From this distance, the blast wave of an explosive device should be enough to blow the camera backward. But the person who's filming holds steady long enough to show that the girl with the earring is gone. Everything that had been there is gone. The camera clatters to the floor. The screen goes black. In the dark, people scream.

Avi watches the footage nine more times. He pauses the screen on the whiteout and calls Louis.

"What did I see?" he asks.

"Did you watch both?"

"I'm watching the mall," Avi says. "There's no blast."

Louis chuckles. It's a grim sound. Louis took a job with Homeland after three tours with army infantry and a year as a military press liaison. When Avi met him, he was the kind of guy who'd get drunk and brag about the shit he'd seen. Now when he has too much, he gets a deep blank stare as if something in him has shorted out.

"Watch the other footage," he says. "I'll wait."

Avi clamps the phone between his ear and his shoulder and clicks on the other file. The one he was avoiding. It's similar. Shaky cell phone footage. The nave of Salem Baptist, shot from the back. A little girl zigzags through the pews in the methodical way small children play. The camera follows her. She has short hair in cornrows, and she's younger than Emmeline. Avi doesn't conflate the two girls. He doesn't put Emmeline in the picture. A boy, white, walks up the center aisle. The preacher, elderly, black, is at the pulpit. He's wearing reading glasses. Leaning in close, so he doesn't see the kid coming toward him. The preacher's name is Marshall Baldwin. Kay's mother talks about him even though she goes to First Corinthians. Baldwin was the pastor at Salem Baptist thirty-some years. Served on the Roseland city council. Started the community's meals on wheels program, along with a garden beautification initiative. Avi has read about the bombing, about Pastor Baldwin. In every article, he skims over the name of the girl, refusing to let it into his head.

The audio on this file is better. Avi can hear the boy talking, but he's facing away from the camera and Avi can't make out what he's saying. Pastor Baldwin looks up.

"You can't be in here, son," he says. Interviewed afterward, parishioners at Salem Baptist remarked on the deep basso of his voice, the way it resonated through the church, shook something in them. The boy continues his approach. "Miss Henderson," the preacher says. "Call the police." The boy turns to the camera. "Don't bother," he says. His voice is flat, emotionless. Then the flash. Again, white.

Avi scans back a couple of frames. The moment before the flash. A clear shot of the boy. Dirty blond hair. Eyes sunk into a hatchet face. Tan polo shirt.

"Jesus," says Avi.

"You want to see the scene?" Louis asks. "I can send a car over."

"I can drive myself," Avi says.

"Meet me there in an hour," says Louis.

Reporting on bombings is a low art among journalists. Information is tightly controlled. Reporters are left to paraphrase press releases. Avi has a gift for rendering these incidents in a way that can affect an audience that's numb to them. His old editor at the *Trib* called him the poet of the detonator.

Avi's obsession goes back to the first American bomb. Home sick from school, he watched coverage of the Oklahoma City bombing in 1995. There was no live feed, no footage of it happening. Only aftermath, the Federal Building sundered. Its face torn away revealed the rough structure beneath. Avi followed the investigation in the *Trib* and on the nightly news. He stared at pictures of the bombers, who looked like guys he went to school with. He read the descriptions of their grievances, their plans. He read stories of the victims, the survivors, their families. He read up on the bomb itself, cobbled together out of stolen blasting caps, fertilizer, and racing fuel. The bomb compressed the past of its builders and the futures of its victims into a point. Everything led up to it, and everything emerged from it.

Through college and grad school, bombs haunted Avi's dreams. It was a good time in America to dream about bombs. Old guard reporters were cold war kids. Their nightmare bombs were nuclear and bloodless. They imagined vaporization. An aftermath of ashes. Crowds reduced to a pile of powder. They were unprepared for broken bodies. Pieces of limbs without identifiable owners. They thought in terms of *blown away* rather than *blown apart*. A nuclear bomb was an end to all things. America had failed to dream about a bomb someone could survive. Worrying about smashed atoms, they forgot about fertilizer and racing fuel.

Avi got his first embed in 2003, a year before he met Kay. It was where he met Louis, whose company he was stuck with for two months. Avi was in the market in Kandahar when some idiot blew himself up. He spotted the bomber before it happened. People at the market meandered or darted. Buyers moved slowly, sellers dashed. The bomber plodded, unrushed but deliberate. Avi saw him open his jacket to reveal the bomb. Ethylene glycol dinitrate, a clear liquid. It registered for Avi as a belt made of water bottles around the man's waist as the bomber raised his cell phone like a tourist taking one last selfie in the souk. Avi was far enough away from the blast to remain standing and unscathed, mentally recording people's frenzied reactions. He saw the smoke within the blast radius settle and the destruction it revealed. He saw the chaos around it, people frantic to get away from an event that was already over. Surrounded by panic, Avi was a calm eye.

The *Washington Post* picked up the piece he wrote. It won the kinds of awards that were being given to well-written war journalism at the start of things. Other assignments and embed offers came in. Sudan. Aleppo. When he started dating Kay, trips to war zones were part of the rhythm of their relationship. If anything, it sped things along. Avi was away so often, it made sense for her to move into his apartment. Any time the annoyances of cohabitation built to near the point of rupture, Avi was off to the other side of the world for a month. When he got back, they were both so relieved he was alive, the counter was set back to zero. In their wedding photos, he has a black eye from the butt of a Ugandan military rifle.

He stopped when Emmeline was born. When he looked at his daughter's face, the risk and the adrenaline were ridiculous. He threw himself into parenting, spending all day with Emmeline while Kay studied for the bar. At night, he'd lie awake half hoping to hear her cry. Needing a reason to spring out of bed. A minicrisis. A dim echo of sirens and blasts. A few days after Emmeline's second birthday, he got a call from *Newsweek* about an embed in Damascus. Kay had landed a job. There was no financial justification for him to take dangerous work. She was making more than he had in his best years, and foreign journalism paid shit money. No one cared about a decade-old war. It was background noise. Page 10 fill. Avi knew all this and took the job like a dry drunk convincing himself he can handle one beer.

When he got back, they had the talk. Kay proposed that once a year Avi could accept a foreign assignment. The rest of the year he'd cover domestic terrorism, school shootings, and subway station gas attacks. He'd pick up local murder stories for the *Trib*. Mostly he'd take care of Emmeline and the house. Kay gifted him those terrible vacations because she understood something in him that Avi couldn't articulate. His need.

A year ago, embedded with Joint Terminal Air Controllers outside of Mosul, their JLTV hit a roadside IED. A garden hose across the road for a trip wire, triggering buried paint cans packed with triacetone triperoxide. You could make it from nail polish remover, hydrogen peroxide, and battery acid. Three of the men in the JLTV were shredded when the blast went up. A column of flame lifted the eight-ton vehicle fifteen feet and dropped it. Avi's left leg was burned away to nothing below the knee, the stump cauterized.

The next day, doped up on pain meds in a military hospital in Kirkuk, he thought how he'd been chasing this bomb most of his life. *You couldn't even wait for it to come to you,* he thought. *You had to go get it.*

Salem Baptist is right off the interstate. Homeland has it tented, wrapped like a present. If the intention is to discourage curiosity, it fails. Traffic crawls by. Even in the cold, drivers roll down their windows and crane their necks as if they can peek behind the curtain. Only the locals remember what's underneath. The bombing made the news, but people don't keep track of the locations of these things unless they're nearby. What difference does it make where this one went off? Where those kids were shot? The important thing is that it wasn't your town. Wasn't your kid. You wait for one you can connect yourself to second- and thirdhand so you can talk about it at parties. You heard it from your house. Your friend's cousin is in a wheelchair for life. The other details blur into the next incident. As long as you and the people you love remain intact.

Avi takes the right up the drive. Someone from Homeland is on him immediately, shooing his van back onto the road. His attire, thrift store parka over a ratty cable-knit sweater, does not scream professionalism. Avi rolls down his window and holds out his driver's license.

"Avi Hirsch for Agent Hoffman," he says. The kid from Homeland snatches the ID. The department is less than twenty years old, and no one's been in it since the beginning. They come in clean cut and young and leave broken and scruffy. Louis says the life span of a civilian recruit into Homeland is five years. They burn out and transfer to a desk job at the IRS, and no one ever hears from them again. The only people who stick around are ex-military. Those are the guys who bust doors down in a cloud of tear gas and flashbang, never the kids checking IDs at the gate. This kid sizing Avi up, comparing his picture to his driver's license. He's hard now, fixing Avi with a stare designed to reduce a suspect to tears. Avi'll bet the kid didn't see this scene until it was cleaned up. Somewhere down the line, something is waiting for this kid. A bloody mess. A dog's dinner. Something he won't be able to unsee. The hard will go out of those eyes, and he'll put in for a transfer to somewhere safe.

"You're the gimp expert," the kid says. Faked military contempt for outsiders. Rookie badassery.

"Expert gimp is better," says Avi. The kid waves him through. Avi catches a look of envy from the drivers left in traffic behind him. As if Avi's been ushered through the velvet rope into an exclusive club. The tent opens around the back, away from prying eyes. Louis rushes to help him out of the car. Louis knows other amputees, but he treats Avi as fragile, an invalid. Avi imagines what he looks like stepping out of the minivan. The mechanical plant of his left leg on pavement. The slow, careful shift of weight. He moves quickly to preclude assistance and has the door shut behind him by the time Louis reaches the van.

"You're early," Louis says.

"Lead foot," says Avi. It doesn't get a laugh. None of his jokes about the leg do. Kay laughs sometimes but won't make jokes on her own. The forums online are full of jokes. *The Endolite Elans are nice, but they cost an arm and a leg. Did you hear what the kid with no hands got for Christmas? I don't know; he hasn't opened it yet.* Jokes soften the reality of it, but they also assert ownership. *This pain is mine, and I will do with it what I choose.* Avi wonders how he'd react if Kay did make a joke about it.

Louis leads him into the tent. The white fabric amplifies

the sunlight, turning it fierce. The whole space is a slide on a microscope. An array of spotlights hangs from the corners and edges. Light from every direction. Every shadow blotted out by light from a different vector. Louis puts on dark aviators. They make him look like a G-man in the movies, broad shoulders and dark blue suit, eyes obscured.

"It's ridiculous in here during the day," he says. He gestures at the lights. "Techs say we can't shut them off."

Avi squints up at the building. What's left of it. It looks like God came down and took a bite out of the church. Half of it clipped away. *A rapture in miniature*, Avi thinks. *His terrible swift sword.* It's an old church, one of those Black Baptist churches where they planned rallies against Jim Crow. How many bomb threats did Salem Baptist get over the years? How many bricks through the window? How many times did they have to paint over hateful graffiti on the front doors before Sunday service? How hard and often did they fight to exist, only to have some white kid blow it up?

He approaches slowly. Destruction at this scale demands respect. It holds you in a sick sense of awe. He takes out his phone and brings up the footage, playing it back in slow motion. He holds up the screen and moves around the edge of the blast crater. He steps behind the last row of pews. When he gets to the point where the picture overlaps the reality, he stops.

"Anyone else in the press seen the footage?" he asks.

"You think I'd double deal on you?"

"The woman who shot it," says Avi. "Was the girl her daughter?"

Louis shakes his head. "Preacher's granddaughter. Her parents died when she was a baby."

That's good, Avi thinks. He's relieved there are no grieving parents for him to think about, empathize with. He walks forward toward the blast crater. He puts his left foot in and slips. The surface is slick. Louis is there to catch him, holding him at the elbow.

"Everyone here's gone ass over teakettle at least once on this thing," he says. "It's smooth as glass."

Louis guides him along the curve to its nadir. The blast ate two feet into the ground. At the edges, techs scrape and peer. This has become familiar. Not just to Avi but to the world of viewers. A building ripped open, its guts exposed. Rebar severed and pipes idiotically leaking fluids into midair. This one is different. There are no jagged edges. Once he notices this, Avi starts to notice the other things he isn't seeing.

"You sanitized the site?" he asks.

Louis shakes his head. "This is how we found it."

"Where's the debris?" says Avi. "Where's the scorching?"

Louis shakes his head again. It's as if someone carved a sphere out of the world. There's a symmetry to it. A perfection. The movement of a blast aspires to this, but the real world gets in the way. The blast expands haphazardly. Nibbling here and feasting there. It's a collection of vectors moving at different speeds, each with a life span of nanoseconds, spending themselves in a race away from their point of origin.

This is different.

"Let me say that if you have anything on this," says Louis, "it would be a huge help to me. Because a week in and I have whatever is less than zero as regards ideas."

"Is that why you asked me down here?" Avi asks.

"You're good with this stuff," says Louis. "I thought you'd pick up a vibe."

"I'm not a hotline psychic." Avi climbs up the other curve and lays a hand on the severed wall. Concrete, a foot thick. He traces a line from inner edge to outer. The barely detectable curve. The edge of a spheroid of lack, of void. "Tell me about the bomber."

"Are we going right to that?" Louis asks. "Are we skipping over the tonnage of debris that doesn't exist?"

"It's the same kid that blew up the mall," says Avi.

"It would appear to be," Louis says.

"You think it's, what?"

Louis shrugs. "Twins? I like the idea it's twins. Gives it a real murder mystery feel."

"It's not twins," Avi says.

"The boys with the facial recognition software swear it's the same kid," he says. "They say telling twins apart is consumer-grade shit. It's the same kid. Owen Curry, eighteen, of Seat Pleasant, Maryland. Perfect overlap of boring and crazy. Lived with his mother, who we haven't been able to find. Worked as a fry cook at Planet Chicken in the Ballston mall food court. Bottom third of his class in school. No girlfriend. No friends. We ID'd him from witness statements. And the footage."

"But he didn't have a bomb on him in the footage."

"Certain people were willing to overlook that in favor of having a shut case."

"You find supplies at his house?" Avi asks. "Bomb-making instructions? *Anarchist's Cookbook*?"

"Nothing," says Louis. "Makes no sense. For one thing, angry white males tend to be shooters, not bombers. Bombing's for believers. But then also, his place is clean. No bottles, no stray wire clippings. If you're going to blow yourself up, why clean up afterward? Leave a mess, I say. Fuck, help us out and leave a note."

Sunlight from the porthole window creates a glare on the top of Avi's screen as he watches the video from the church again. His brain picks it apart, like watching a magician do a trick to figure out how it's done. He can't be seeing what he's seeing: a dead boy blowing up a church without a bomb. He tries to see something else, something that makes sense, but the reality of it persists.

There's a banging from the hatch. Kay keeps a broom in the hall for when she needs to roust him from work. It hasn't been used in a year.

"Avi!" she yells. "Where the fuck are you?"

Avi jumps out of the chair, nearly toppling. He goes over to the hatch and gives it a push, too hard. It drops fast, swinging toward Kay. She catches the edge and lowers it.

"Where the hell have you been?"

Everything clicks into place. Avi returns to the world. The sunlight on the computer screen. Hunger growling in his gut.

"What time is it?" he asks. He eases himself down the ladder. Going down is harder.

"Six-thirty," she says. "The school's been calling you. I've been calling you. I had to get a cab from work and go pick her up."

"My phone—"

"It's in the living room," she says. "Doing no one any good."

"Shit, Kay," he says. "I'm sorry. This stuff Louis sent me—"

"You said you were going to pass on it," she says. She stands with her arms crossed, watching to be sure he doesn't fall but not helping him down. He doesn't have anything to say. Once he's off the ladder, she turns away from him. "We stopped at McDonald's. You're on your own for dinner. You should go apologize to her."

Kay goes into their bedroom and closes the door. The argument feels like a relic, something left over from the time before. Avi doesn't want to be the person who forgets anymore. The one who climbs out of a bomb crater to discover he's broken a promise. Tomorrow he'll call Louis and tell him he's got nothing. He'll call Carol at the *Trib* and ask for assignments. School boards and common council meetings. Double homicides. Something local, safe.

He stands outside Emmeline's door. She'll be over it by tomorrow. An apology is meaningful only right now. Inside, she's talking to herself. He can hear the tone but not the content. The high musical cadence and bounce of his daughter's voice, broken up by long pauses. Emmeline has always had imaginary friends. She retreats to her room to talk with them. There's another pause, then she says, "I know you're out there, Daddy. Come in."

Avi opens the door. Emmeline is sitting cross-legged on the floor, drawing a blackbird in crayon. She looks up at him. "You haven't eaten anything all day, have you?"

Avi sits down on the bed. He's most aware of his handicap around Emmeline. She is of a size to be occasionally lifted and carried and tossed. She isn't too old for them to play together on the floor. But he hates needing her help to get up.

"I wanted to get you a hamburger," she says. "But Mom was mad at you."

"She was right to be mad," says Avi. "Are you mad at me?"

Emmeline shakes her head. "Where were you?" she asks.

"I was upstairs," he says. "There's a person who hurt a lot of other people. I was trying to figure out how he thinks."

Emmeline nods as if taking in information she already knew. "I bet his brain is a mess," she says. "I bet a bad idea got pushed in and grew. Like roots." She presses the heels of her hands together, fingers curled, then extends her fingers out until they are tree branches, antlers. Roots.

THE ONE-LEGGED DETECTIVE

Avi should have called Louis right away, standing outside their bedroom door so that Kay could hear his performance. *Look what I'm giving up for us. Look at how I'm being better.*

But he waits until morning. Kay is on to a Chester Himes novel with a smoking pistol on the cover. Emmeline attempts a series of gambits to trick Avi and Kay into talking to each other.

"I think our yard is big enough for a dog," she says. "A small one. A yippee dog."

"If Daddy got arrested, Mom, would you defend him? Or would it be a conflict of interest?"

None of them catch.

Kay gives Avi a dry kiss on the cheek and hugs Emmeline long and deep before she leaves. In the car on the way to school, Emmeline says, "I'm not mad, Daddy." Avi thanks her for saying so. "Are you going to catch the man who hurt people?" she asks.

"I'm not trying to catch him, Leener," says Avi. "The police will catch him."

"You think they will?"

He pauses. He wants her to live in a world where the bad guys get caught and little girls don't get turned into nothing while they're at church. But he decided a long time ago to trust his daughter with the truth, no matter how unpleasant.

"No," he says. "I don't think they will."

"Do you think he's going to hurt someone else?"

"Yes."

Emmeline nods and looks out the window. "If they were trying to catch me, they would look at all the places that serve French fries," she says. "Even if I was hiding, I would eat a lot of French fries. You could check the hotels near French fries and you'd find me."

He watches Emmeline go up the school steps, then fishes his phone out of his coat pocket and plays the church video again. His head spirals back into the mess. He goes home and examines the photos Louis sent him of Owen Curry's room in Seat Pleasant, Maryland. The room looks more like a proper bomb site than the bomb sites. There's chaos in how boys that age exist in the world, as if they're flinging themselves at it, hoping to break through to something better. Avi was that way when he and Kay met even though he was ten years older than Owen Curry is. He took a new assignment every month. He crashed back into Chicago in a mess of booze and drugs, trying to scrub his mind of the horrors he was writing about. He hired someone to clean his apartment while he was away, then let it degrade into squalor again, sink full of dishes, air rank with weeks of old takeout.

Avi wonders about the smell of Owen's room. It would

be feral. It would hit you the minute you walked in. A trigger scent. Body odor and the grease off discarded fast-food containers. He thinks of what Emmeline said, about finding her eating French fries. His daughter on the lam, trailing ketchup packets in her wake.

Avi takes another look at the pictures. Containers and wax paper from fast food lie around the room. Each one has a plump smiling chicken orbited by a star. Planet Chicken. The place Owen Curry worked in the mall food court. He was wearing his uniform in the footage from Salem Baptist. Avi thinks of Owen's complexion, the flurry of zits on his cheeks.

"Kid's an addict," he mutters. He googles "Planet Chicken Chicago."

Two results. One is out in Cicero. The other is in Roseland, within walking distance of Salem Baptist.

Avi wonders who would laugh harder, Kay or Louis. Louis would laugh. Kay would worry for his sanity. *Avi Hirsch, invalid investigator. Gimp gumshoe. One-legged detective.* He parks the minivan in the parking lot of a strip mall a half mile past Salem Baptist, in front of Planet Chicken. He has a printout of Owen Curry's senior high school photo, unsmiling, and a flip notepad to make himself look legit.

It's too early in the day for much of a lunch crowd. Three young black employees stand behind the counter. They're wearing the beige polo shirts Owen Curry is wearing in the footage. On the chest, the fat chicken with the orbiting star, bright yellow and red. They make themselves look busy even though they've already done everything there is to do.

"Welcome to Planet Chicken, can I help you?" asks the girl. The other two flank her, looking at Avi. He's self-conscious about how long it takes him to make it to the counter, worried he's hobbling.

"I'm looking for someone," he says.

"You a cop?" asks the taller boy.

Avi shakes his head. "Reporter," he says.

"If you're a cop, you've got to tell us," the boy says.

"I do," says Avi. "Except I'm a reporter. Like I said."

"Who're you looking for?" the girl asks.

Avi offers her the photo, and she takes it. The boys lean over her shoulders to look.

"Oh, shit," says the shorter boy. "It's Employee Discount."

"You know him?" Avi asks.

"He came in a couple times," says the girl. "He's got a shirt from another location. Looks like it hasn't been washed all year. Every time he comes in, he asks me if he gets an employee discount. Like I didn't already tell him no ten times."

"Kid can't tell black people apart," says the taller boy. "He pulled the same shit with me three times last week."

"How long has he been coming around?" Avi asks.

"Week and a half?" says the girl. Two days before the church bombing.

"Any chance he paid with a credit card?" Avi says.

They all shake their heads.

"Crisp bills, every time," says the taller boy.

"Paid with a hundred one time," the girl says. "You could cut yourself on the corners." She hands the picture back.

"What'd he do?" asks the taller boy.

"I'm not sure yet," Avi says, avoiding eye contact.

"Fucker did the church," says the girl. The other two look at Avi for confirmation.

"Yeah," Avi says, staring down at his notepad. "Fucker did the church."

"So he's blown to shit?" the shorter boy asks.

"We saw him in here fucking yesterday," says the taller boy. Avi looks up at him to confirm that he's not bullshitting, but the taller boy's not even looking at Avi. He's reminding his coworker. Avi gets the rush of excitement and dread that comes immediately before something huge happens. It's the feeling of seeing the bomber in the souk, of spotting the white van pull up to the curb. A coppery taste floods his mouth, one he hasn't experienced since he felt the JLTV begin to lift into the air underneath him. He's disturbed to realize he's missed it.

"You see him with anyone?" Avi asks. "You see him in a car?"

"He walks out of here," says the girl. "Heads that way." She points away from Salem Baptist, down the road.

"How do you know?" the shorter boy asks.

"I knew he was a sketchy motherfucker, so I kept an eye on him," she says. "Cops come around looking for somebody, you want to have someone to give them."

"You guys have been a huge help," says Avi. He fishes out his wallet and takes out two twenties. He hands one to the girl and one to the taller boy.

"What about me?" says the shorter boy.

"You didn't know shit," the girl says.

OWEN CURRY AND THE SHIMMERING ROOM

In stories, when people find out they're special, part of them already knew. Owen Curry didn't have that part. His mother made a point of telling him how not special he was. How he was lucky to even have a job and to stop with his retarded talk about college. She sat at the kitchen table, smoking Parliaments and listening to James Taylor on the tinny speaker of her phone, expecting Owen to stand there until she finished running him down. When she started wheezing and coughing, he went upstairs to his room with a Dozen Bucket from the Planet and stared at the bubble gum–pink ceiling. His mother had painted his whole room pink, like a womb. Calming, she said, but the pink crept into his dreams. Owen was having weird dreams. He was in a room, a big shimmering room, like Cinderella's ball. The room was full of people. He could hear them talking, but it was like background party noise in a movie. No words, just *blah blah blah*. No one noticed him. No one ever noticed Owen, even in his fucking dreams.

No one trusted him either. In part because he couldn't sit still. He was twitchy. He fidgeted. Also clumsy. Especially around girls. Even ones who weren't superattractive, but more in his league. Amanda Smoot, who worked with him at Planet Chicken, was not a ten by any means. Nice, though. She spent her whole break driving to Starbucks down in the plaza for salted caramel lattes. One day, Owen decided to be nice. Not flirty or sexual. Nice. He stopped by on his way into work and picked one up for her. He brought it to her, and as he was holding it out to her: *bam*. Spilled all over Amanda's uniform. He practically pitched it at her. Twenty ounces of hot sweetened milk over the front of her shirt and her jeans. Everyone laughed except Amanda. Amanda screamed at him. In the concourse, in front of everyone in the mall.

Owen whom no one noticed, Owen whom no one trusted lost it.

"You think you're so fucking special?" he screamed at her. "You think you're hot shit?" His insides were a tangle of anger and sadness. His stomach roiled with something that wasn't different from hunger. He held his hands out to Amanda, who stepped back from him. "I was just trying to be nice," he said, pleading.

Amanda was three feet away when it happened. It came pouring out of his gut, white and cold. Time slowed, dilated, and Owen watched the edge of a sphere of nothing expand to include Amanda Smoot. It nipped away the tip of her nose, leaving a dark red circle like she'd dipped it in the Blast-Off barbecue sauce. The circle got larger, covering the whole nose, the high appley rounds of her cheekbones. It shaved away Amanda the way the mandoline they used to make the Planet's fresh-fried chips sliced at a potato. It exposed bright red layers of her insides, leaving less with each pass until there was barely enough of Amanda to press against the imaginary blade. Owen saw the heel of her sneaker on the tile floor, a nub of bone, skin, and blood inside it, then only rubber and leather. Then that was gone, too. Then the tiles. Then the food court.

Owen came to a second later in the first-floor hallway, between a Pacific Sun and a Build-A-Bear. Above him, he could see a circle cut through the food court, through the ceiling above it. The sky was milky with clouds. He scrabbled to his feet and bolted for the nearest exit. In the parking lot, he sat in his car, listening to sirens approach. His heart raced, but he felt drowsy, like after a big Thanksgiving dinner. A heavy downward pull. Owen Curry's mind tumbled backward. He fell through the shimmering room, with its endless ghostly partygoers, and landed like a feather in a different room. It was as small and cramped as his bedroom, but it was clean. Instead of pale pink, the walls looked like they'd been carved out of black bone. A man sat in a chair made out of the same stuff, leaning back as if he'd been waiting for Owen. He looked like radio static sounds, like a plastic bag full of wasps. When he spoke, his voice bounced off the walls. It echoed in Owen's skull.

Owen Curry, he said. *You are so important. You are so special.*

"No, I'm not," Owen said.

You are, said the man. *That's why you're here. Only special people can come here. Only people with a certain vibration in them. Not many people have it. One in a thousand. But you do. It's what gives you your ability.*

"I don't know what you're talking about," Owen said. "I don't know what just happened."

Tell me something, said the man. *Are you hungry? Are you always hungry?*

Owen had to admit he was. There was something inside him, a void.

That's it, said the man. *That's your ability. You take the emptiness inside you and let it out.*

The man laid his hand on Owen's cheek. It felt like a rubber glove full of beetles, but Owen held it there, savoring the way the surface of the man's palm twitched against his skin. Then he fell again, upward, coming back to his car. Police cars and ambulances raced by, headed to the other side of the mall, the hole that Owen Curry had ripped in the world. Owen drove home with the radio off, hearing his friend's words.

You are so important. You are so special.

When he got home, Owen looked at his house as if it had appeared from nowhere. It was neither important nor special. Another shithole in Seat Pleasant, Maryland. Shitty house in a shitty town, home of Owen's formerly shitty life. The back door slammed shut behind him as he went in, a cue for his mother to start in on him.

"What'd, you get lost?" she said. "It doesn't take half an hour to get home from that fancy-assed mall. If you can't come straight ho—"

Conscious of it this time, reaching a decision and acting on it, Owen fed her to the null. He found it in his gut and brought it forth, an egg-shaped void that extended from his midsection and swallowed everything where she and her chair had been. A bite was missing from the Formica table. Owen was alone in the kitchen. James Taylor's thin treble still sang about going to Carolina. Owen fed his mother's phone to the null, a quick blip of nothing. The house was finally quiet. He went into the living room and sat on the couch, enjoying the silence. Then he turned on the news. They were at the mall, talking about terrorists and bombs.

The television clicked off.

"You've done an amazing thing, Owen," said a voice from the kitchen. "I am so proud of you."

Owen jumped off the couch. The man was more solid than in the black bone room, but his face was like the surface of the grease in the deep fryer waiting for an order to drop. It wavered and bubbled, iridescent. "You can't stay here," he said. "They'll find you. I have a place you can go to hide."

"Why are you helping me?" Owen asked.

"Because I'm your friend," said the man.

His friend gave him gifts. A bus ticket to Chicago. A stack of money: crisp twenties and even a couple of hundreds. And one other thing.

"So we'll never be apart," his friend said. He put his hand on Owen's cheek the way he had in the black bone room. This time it was a cool liquid thing on Owen's skin. A drop rolled upward into Owen's ear. He could feel it moving, burrowing. Owen thought about the scene in *Wrath of Khan*. The Ceti eel. It used to scare him when he was little, and his mother would call him a pussy. This was like that, but it wasn't scary. He trusted his friend. He accepted the gift.

On the bus ride to Chicago, the little piece of his friend in Owen's head spoke to him. It talked about plans, about the black bone room and how important people like Owen were. *We're here to be shepherds*, his friend said. *And if we're the shepherds, what does that make* them?

"Sheep," Owen whispered. The person in the seat next to him snored as the bus plowed through the night somewhere in the country's flat midlands.

They're livestock, his friend said. *Cattle. It's important that you learn to think of them that way.*

He told Owen he wanted him to use his ability somewhere particular this time. There was a church near Chicago. He wanted Owen to feed it to the null.

"Why a church?" Owen said, whispering. A thin needle of pain shot through his head. He felt something warm and wet in his ear, and when he swabbed it with his pinkie, the finger came away bloody.

First Corinthians Church in Roseland, said his friend. *Tomorrow night. Take the whole church for me.*

The bus dropped him in Roseland, on Chicago's south side, after the sun had gone down. He asked the driver for directions to First Corinthians, but the driver had no idea. He wished he'd kept his mother's iPhone with the maps on it. An old black lady at the bus station gave him directions. She smiled sweetly at him. Owen tried to suss if she had vibration, but she was cattle, like his mother, like Amanda Smoot and everyone he'd fed into the null at the mall.

Owen found his way to First Corinthians, a ten-minute walk in the cold. It was a church for black people. There were kids practicing for a Christmas pageant. Owen sat in the back of the church, rubbing his hands together to warm them. He listened to those kids sing about angels. There was a black lady down the pew from him who was a little younger than Owen's mother but pretty. She was watching the kids, rapt. He couldn't tell which one was hers, but he could tell how much she loved whichever one it was. He reasoned that he had a job to do and that someone had loved Amanda Smoot and all the other people in the food court. What Owen was part of was bigger than love.

When he reached down to find the empty spot in his guts, he felt something strange, like an echo. Someone in the church had vibration. It screamed at him from every direction. He went into the black bone room, letting his head loll on his shoulders as if he'd fallen asleep in the pew, and he could feel it. Owen was sure his friend wouldn't want him to null out someone like them. Someone special. He came back to. The pretty black lady was looking at him. She probably thought he was a drug addict. She had no idea what he was.

Owen snuck out the back. He walked back toward the bus station, near the middle of town, and got a room at a motor inn. The next day, he found another church nearby, called Salem Baptist. It was mostly empty, just the preacher and a secretary and some kid. Cattle. The preacher yelled at Owen to get out, and Owen dug the null up, tugging it upward from the center of him. He imagined it growing big enough to engulf the whole church, but he stopped it. He pulled it back before it took the secretary. He left her as a witness to what he'd done, to what he was becoming.

He walked back to the motel room. Lying on his bed, he waited for his friend. He knew he shouldn't stay here, so close to the church, but he didn't want to leave without instructions. He waited all night and the next morning, but his friend never showed. Owen tried to wake up the little piece of his friend that was in his head, but he didn't know how. It wasn't like a phone you could call out on. He had to wait. He bought a marble composition book and a bag of Bic pens at the convenience store and started writing down everything he remembered his friend telling him. He felt like the men who wrote the Bible must have, fumbling divine thought into clumsy words on paper.

After a few days with no word, Owen was worried. He had taken the wrong church. He hadn't done what he was asked. He wanted to beg his friend for forgiveness, but how could he if his friend wouldn't even talk to him? He sat at the window, peering out through the blinds at a man getting out of a minivan. There was something about him Owen didn't like, something in the way he walked. He wondered if he could reach across the parking lot and feed the man into the null. He'd never done anything like that before, and it excited him, thinking about new things he could do with his ability. He needed his friend to guide him, to show him who he was going to become.

Owen thought about the dreams he'd had before they met. The shimmering room full of people. Something in the dream felt like the black bone room. Owen wondered if the two were connected, rooms in the same house. Maybe the shimmering room was where his friend was from originally. Owen tried to remember what it felt like to be in the shimmering room, and as easily as dropping backward into bathwater, he was there. It was different this time. He knew it immediately. People could see him.

"I'm lost," he shouted. "I need to find my friend."

Before anyone could answer, he felt the needle of pain in his head again. It was distant, because it was in his body and he wasn't. As soon as he felt it, he crashed back into reality, back into the chair at the motor inn, waiting by the window. He scuttled up to attention, looking around the room, listening with his ears and with whatever in him heard the voice in his head. There was nothing. A trickle of blood ran out of his ear, and he got up to wash it off in the sink.

Over the sound of the water running, he heard a door opening in the other room. There were three people in his room, people he didn't know. Two women and a man. One of the women wore one of those head scarf things. Owen had no problem with Muslims. Vibration was more important, and she had it. All three of them did. Owen's heart leaped.

"Did he send you?" he said. "Are we going to be a team?"

"No, Owen," said the head scarf lady. "We're the opposing team."

Something was very wrong. Owen panicked. He reached inside to null them all out, but the other woman, the blond one, put her hand on his forehead, and his thoughts scrambled, words skittering out of order like spilled Scrabble tiles. *Null feed into them. Touch don't me.*

"You're fucked, Owen," said the head scarf woman.

Owen tried to scuttle away from the blond woman's touch, but his legs wouldn't listen. Moving on their own, they walked him forward, through an open door. It didn't matter that he didn't want to go. It didn't matter at all.

ROOM 152

In the office of the Roseland Rest, a white woman in her seventies wages war on flies, watching infomercials at deafening volume. The Roseland Rest is a half mile from Planet Chicken. Owen Curry would have to be incredibly lazy or ballsy to hole up here, but Avi's plan is to stop at every lodging in the direction the girl pointed him, and this is the first. It takes three rings of the service bell to get her attention. He shows her the picture.

"You a cop?" she asks. Her tone is exactly the same as the boy at Planet Chicken.

"Reporter," he says.

She looks unimpressed. She examines the picture. "What'd he do?"

"He won a prize," says Avi. "All expenses paid."

"Hell he did," she says. "The nasty little shit." She turns around and takes a key off the hook. "Room 152," she says, handing it to him. "Don't kick the door down."

"Why would I do that?" Avi asks.

She shrugs. "People do."

Louis and half the Chicago Homeland office are at the

church, five minutes away. One call and they come down like the wrath of god. Owen Curry goes into the system, and no one ever sees him again. Louis won't be able to answer any of Avi's questions afterward, even on deep background. They're friends, but Louis is a company man. The story will be dead, and Owen Curry will be packed off to some government warehouse with UFO fragments and the Ark of the Covenant. The only way Avi will know what happened is to find Owen Curry and ask.

The room is on the second level, so Avi makes his way up. The stairs are metal, narrow. Avi is careful not to hook the prosthetic under the edges as he goes up. The upper balcony is Astroturf over concrete. Avi inches along toward 152. He can feel the pull he's missed. The rush of knowing he's near something terrible. An awful end. There are things about himself he's had to pass through to get to this point. He's walked through the dark room full of snakes. He's looked at everything hateful in himself and said *yes, come with me, let's all step into the fire*. The last words he said to Kay were a promise to call Louis. The last thing he said to Emmeline was a promise to pick her up from school. If he dies, they'll remember him as a liar.

It matters less to him than what's behind the door.

I thought I was cured, he thinks. *I thought I burned it out of me and all it cost me was my leg. But it has to cost everything. It can only ever cost everything.*

He slips the key into the lock of 152. He turns the knob slowly, but the latch clicks as it frees itself from the plate. He presses his shoulder against the door and pauses. He's unarmed, but so is Owen Curry. Except Owen Curry can vaporize a whole building, whereas Avi has a flip-up notepad.

He enters like he's coming into a surprise party he already knows about. The faucet is running in the bathroom, but there's no one in the room. He moves along the wall and peeks around the edge of the bathroom door. Empty. The lights are harsh fluorescents, the shower curtain pulled back to show a lime-speckled tub. The motel room looks like a staging of Owen Curry's room in Seat Pleasant, Maryland: clothes, papers, Planet Chicken containers. On the bed there's a journal, a marble composition book. The blue-lined pages are scarred up with words, half of the journal full. Avi glances through it, catching certain phrases that repeat. *The cattle. Vibration. The null.*

He takes out his phone to call Louis and stops. He can't explain being in the room. He should have called six steps back. He pockets the phone, grabs the journal off the bed, and walks out.

"Did you see him go out?" he asks the woman in the office as he gives her back the key.

"Who?" she says.

He hands her the printout again.

"I'd've told you if he wasn't in there," she says.

"How's he been paying?" asks Avi.

"Crisp twenties," she says. She rubs her thumbs roughly along the edges of her index fingers, miming the difficulty of separating fresh bills. "Fucking things stick together."

THE DOOR THAT WASN'T THERE

Nothing comes together. Owen Curry's journals are babble. Each page is titled in block letters: "VIBRATION = GODHOOD?" "THE TRUE LOCATION AND MEANING OF THE BLACK BONE ROOM." Owen Curry has built an entire world in his head. Diagrams of nonsense science, treatises on imaginary physics. When someone's mind breaks off from the world as cleanly as Owen Curry's, the writing takes on an alien aspect that is flat and opaque. Curry's sentences are grammatically correct but unintelligible. Avi feels as if he needs a cipher key, a Rosetta stone, to begin to make sense of them. He keeps coming back to the word *vibration*, but it's gibberish to him.

In the morning, after he drops Emmeline off at school, Avi heads out to Roseland. Homeland is wrapping up the scene at Salem Baptist, making room for the church to start the slow work of rebuilding. They'll put it back exactly the way it was. No modernizations or improvements. Erasure of a wound is a form of healing. One of the things that bothers Avi about his prosthetic is that it reasserts its difference from what was once there. He'd prefer a less comfortable prosthesis that looked more "lifelike," one that wouldn't remind everyone of his handicap. From his phone, in the parking lot, Avi makes an anonymous donation to the Salem Baptist reconstruction fund.

He checks back at the Roseland Rest and at Planet Chicken. No one's seen Owen Curry in days. Out of ideas, Avi drives home. He calls Louis to see if Homeland has had any luck finding him.

Louis laughs. "I can barely get permission to go looking for this fuck," he says. "Officially, Owen Curry died in the Ballston mall bombing and we are looking for an identical suspect in the Salem Baptist bombing. The whole thing's gone cold."

"Until he blows up something else," Avi says.

"I'm having trouble selling that argument to my superiors," says Louis. "Maybe if there was some sort of public outcry."

"You want me to publish?"

"It would move things on my end," Louis says.

"The *Trib* won't take it without a verified source," says Avi.

Louis pauses. There's no way he'll go on record. No one from Homeland ever goes on record. Homeland speaks in press releases.

"Fuck it," Louis says. "Use the footage. Don't run it, but you can show it to an editor to verify."

"It'll be obvious it's from you," Avi says. Part of him doesn't want to keep at this story. Maybe it's the dead girl in the church, the fear that she'll come to haunt him. That he'll start to see her running around the living room furniture, playing in the backyard. Shadowing Emmeline. Maybe it's something else. Last night he dreamed he was back in Mosul, in the JLTV.

In the dream, Owen Curry hoists the vehicle over his head like it's nothing. The other guys in Echo Company disappear, blinking out one by one.

"If this shows up in the *Trib*, it forces my boss's hand," Louis says. "I get to go find the kid. Right now he's a ghost."

Avi thinks about the Roseland Rest. The feeling that Owen Curry had been in the room a second before Avi opened the door. Maybe the kid is a ghost.

"I can't guarantee the *Trib* will take it, even with the footage," Avi says. He can't guarantee Carol will pick up the phone. He hasn't talked to anyone at the *Trib* since the sympathy calls dried up. He's a ghost himself.

"Do what you can," Louis says.

He gets up from the desk and puts a record on, laying the needle down gently. A stumbling drumbeat floods the attic space, one leg dragging behind the other, followed by the opening guitar and keyboard flourish of Bowie's "Five Years." The Ziggy Stardust album should clear his head, but as soon as it starts, he thinks of something Bowie said in some stoned interview from the seventies about the mythology behind the album. Bowie's starmen were black hole jumpers. Creatures who leap from universe to universe. They come on like saviors, but they're tourists. They can't save anyone. He thinks of Owen Curry at the center of a blast, disappearing into nothing, popping up somewhere else. He wonders what that would feel like.

The side ends. He never minded the inconvenience of records until the first time he sat in his chair listening to the needle scratch along the label edge, unable to make the walk across the room. It was a motivator, a reason to move. Every second the needle scraped was a rebuke for his self-pity and laziness.

Avi flips the record and goes back to his chair. He picks up Owen Curry's journal:

The entrance into the null is through me, and through my vibration. The null is not me. I am the gate that opens. I am the mouth gaping to swallow the world.

Black hole jumpers, Avi thinks. He wonders where Owen Curry goes the moment after the flash. Where he disappears to in the split second after everything around him blinks out of the world.

There's a knock on the door.

His first thought is that it's Kay pounding on the ceiling with the broomstick. That he's drifted again, lost the day, and stranded Emmeline at school. But the album marks time, breaks it into pieces of twenty minutes a side. He looks across the room, checking for the sun in the porthole window.

Under the porthole, there's a door that doesn't belong. Dark wood and a burnished brass knob. The jamb stands out against the pale wood paneling of the attic, highlighting the door's not-rightness. Its unbelonging. Avi closes his eyes and opens them again. The door is still there. He thinks of the Winchester House in San Jose, its metastatic architecture spawning staircases to nowhere, rooms inaccessible from anywhere in the house. This door would open to the outside, fifty feet above Jarvis Avenue. On the record, strangled saxophones fade out and die. Avi stands up, steps toward the door as if he's approaching a rabid animal. Sidesteps. No sudden moves.

The knob turns. Under the music, a creak of metal hinges as the door opens inward. A young black woman looks out. Her face is round with high soft cheekbones. She has dreadlocks heaped precariously on her head, tottering to the left.

"Good, you're here," she says. "Last time we came by, you all were out. I'm Kimani Moore. This is all going to be a little strange."

Through the door, where there should be only open air, Avi can see a living room that is not part of his house. The walls are bright orange with blue trim. Warm lights make the room glow behind her.

"Come on in," Kimani says. "I've got coffee up."

Avi walks to the door as if he's under a spell. This is fairy tale stuff. A door in the air. A room that can't exist. Kimani pulls the door open, and Avi thinks of Dorothy stepping into Oz, the burst of Technicolor scarring the sepia of her little world. He steps across the threshold, fingers trailing along the surface of the door to be sure it's real, as if touch is truer than sight. The wood is smooth but solid. Kimani shuts the door behind him, and the music goes silent, not muffled but cut off. A blond woman sits on a couch, teasing a German shepherd with a knotted rope. Behind her, a tall white man with dark hair browses a bookshelf. Neither looks at Avi or greets him. Standing next to Kimani is another man, older, with a trim salt-and-pepper beard, round wire-rimmed glasses, and a pained expression he's worn long enough to carve lines into his face.

"Mr. Hirsch," he says. "I'm sorry to come into your home like this."

"This isn't my home," Avi says, looking around. Avi's house is furnished to be soft. Every piece of furniture was bought when Emmeline was small for her to bounce off unharmed. This room has clean lines and abrupt corners. There's a Stevie Wonder poster on the wall, a concert from his *Talking Book* days. A print of a William Eggleston photo, the back of a woman's beehive shot in a Los Alamos diner, the turquoise of the bench and tiles psychedelically bright under the lights. On the floor, there's a bone-white rug, shag pile. No one with children owns a rug that white.

"There's a lot we have to tell you," says the man with the wire-rimmed glasses. "You should sit down."

"I'll stand," Avi says. As soon as he says it, he becomes aware of the ache in his leg: a low thing that will expand.

"Here, sit," says Kimani. "You're making me nervous." She takes his arm and leads him toward an oddly angled chair. Avi sits, looking from one person to the next.

"He's spooked," says the tall man by the bookshelf.

"Of course he's spooked," Kimani says. "He just stepped out the side of his house."

"You came very close to being killed the other day, Mr. Hirsch," says the man with glasses.

"That should calm him down," says the woman on the couch.

The man with glasses shakes his head and smiles. "You're right, Sarah. I'm going about this all wrong." He puts out his hand. "My name is Kevin Bishop," he says. Avi leans forward, takes his hand, and shakes it. It's an automatic action, a script the body carries out reflexively when given the proper signal. The part of Avi's brain that observes and reports notices that his hand is sweat-slick against this man's cool, dry palm, while another part, frantic and barely coherent, shrieks that this man cannot even be here, that the room they're standing in does not and cannot exist. Bishop lets go of Avi's hand, and it hangs in the air, shaking nothing, before Avi becomes aware of it and tucks it under his leg. "This is Patrick and Sarah Davenport. They work for me. They're teachers."

"Siblings," says Sarah. "He's older."

"And Kimani is . . ." He pauses, searching for the word.

"I'm your driver, Kevin," she says. "Call it what it is."

Bishop winces. "I don't love the visual of me being *driven* around by a young woman of color."

"You've also got me serving coffee," she says.

"That visual is going to be the least of our problems," Patrick says from the corner.

"Do you take cream?" Kimani asks. Avi shakes his head. The question is too normal, a leftover piece of some other conversation. Avi tries to retreat to that conversation as he takes the coffee from her. The heat of the cup startles him, and he drops it. He sees motion in the far corner of the room. Patrick reaches for the falling cup. His arm stretches across the room, elongating like pale taffy strung from shoulder to wrist. He catches the cup before it shatters. Avi stares down into the coffee cup, which is cradled in Patrick's hand at the end of an impossible arm. Silver dollar drops spatter the white rug and bloom like time-lapse flowers.

The German shepherd nuzzles Avi's knee, trying to get his attention. Avi looks down at the dog.

"Mr. Hirsch," the dog says in the blond woman's voice, "my friends and I are very special people. And we want you to tell the world about us."

The dog looks at him quizzically as if Avi is the thing out of place here. Which he obviously is. The problem isn't talking dogs or floating rooms; it's dull, ordinary Avi Hirsch, spilling his coffee on the rug, with nothing to say to a talkative German shepherd. Avi lets out a high-pitched sound, something between a nervous laugh and a panicked yelp.

"If the two of you are done showing off," Bishop says, wiping his glasses on his shirt. The dog trots back to Sarah's side. Patrick places the coffee cup on the table next to Avi. His arm retracts into the sleeve of his dress shirt, and he shoves his hand in his pocket as if embarrassed.

"I've read several of your articles, Mr. Hirsch," Bishop says. "I liked the piece about the bus bomber in Tel Aviv. I liked that you interviewed his family. Not a lot of reporters bother with that kind of thing. It's not the normal way to cover an incident like that."

Avi remembers the boy's mother. She was so hurt and so ashamed. *What god was worth doing this to me?* she asked Avi, sobbing. She showed him pictures of the boy when he was younger, playing soccer in the same square where he'd blown himself to pieces. At the end of the interview, she gave him the picture. *Take it*, she said. *That boy was never real. That boy was a lie.*

"Most people save their sympathy for the victims," Avi

says. He feels comfortable talking about his work. It's a reflex response, no different from putting out his hand to shake. By the couch, the dog huffs and lies down to sleep.

"But not you," says Bishop.

"The boy was a victim, too," Avi says.

"What about Owen Curry?" Patrick asks.

Avi pauses, trying to summon up sympathy for Owen Curry. It doesn't work that way. Once he has to try, he's playacting, fooling himself into thinking he's a better, kinder person than he is. He tries to imagine Owen Curry as a boy deserving of love, but he sees the girl zigzagging through the church pews. The flash of white.

"Owen Curry is like us," Bishop says, gesturing to the others with an open hand. "He has abilities. He's also a very sick young man. We've worried for a long time that someone like Owen Curry would be the first the world would hear about us. If he became the public face of our people, we'd all be branded monsters."

"We *will* be branded monsters," Patrick says. "You think a nice write-up in *The Atlantic* means they won't come for us with pitchforks?"

"Let the grown-ups talk, Patrick," says Sarah. Another yelping laugh slips out of Avi at the thought that he's one of the adults in the room. He has the childhood feeling of being adrift in a sea of incomprehensible things.

"It's become apparent that it's time to go public with who and what we are," says Bishop. "It's increasingly difficult to keep our existence a secret, and it's only a matter of time before some other Owen Curry is exposed. Before that happens, we'd like to provide the public some context. We'd like your help."

"What *are* you?" Avi asks. He stares at Bishop, trying to see what strange ability he's hiding. Bishop smiles as if he knows what Avi is thinking.

"We call ourselves Resonants," says Kimani. "We can do things, but we're people. Like you."

"When you talked to that boy's mother," Bishop says. "The bomber in Tel Aviv? Were you surprised how normal she was?"

"I had no reason to think she'd be anything but normal," Avi says.

"We're normal, Mr. Hirsch," Bishop says. "We have families and jobs."

"Owen Curry has killed twenty-one people," Avi says.

"You would have been twenty-two," Patrick says, "if we were two minutes slower."

Avi remembers the hotel room. The feeling that someone had just left.

"You know where he is?" Avi asks.

They all look at one another, assessing the weight of a secret.

"He's off the board," says Bishop.

"We need to show Avi," Kimani says. "Demonstrate some trust."

"Based on what?" asks Patrick. "He's working with Homeland Security. What makes you think he won't turn us in?"

"I don't work for Homeland," Avi says.

"He won't turn us in," Kimani says.

"We should wipe his memory and throw him back," Patrick says.

The idea they could erase his memories of this conversation hits Avi for the first time as a possibility. A vertiginous panic unsteadies him, makes the floor waver out of focus under his feet until he's sure he can see the snow-flecked lawn one story below. The possible is defined by its limits, with everything that can happen bordered by another, scarier world of things that can't. *What can I know now?* Avi thinks. *What can I be sure is real?*

Bishop nods to Kimani, and Patrick slumps his shoulders, defeated. Kimani goes to the same door she brought Avi through and opens it into somewhere completely new.

THE BOY IN THE BOX

The lab is brightly lit. The stark white walls are covered in tacked up pieces of paper. Schematics and notes and equations on graphing paper, cocktail napkins. Tables full of wires and takeout containers. The ceiling is lined with hexagonal chicken wire, like a metal honeycomb. Avi notes that there are no computers, a trend he's heard about in people's offices, a pushback against the encroachment of constant access. A dam against rivers of information. The clutter reminds Avi of Owen Curry's hotel room. In the corner, a woman is hunched at a workbench, wearing a lab coat and dark goggles over a red hijab. The blue spark of her welding torch sputters.

"Fuuuuuuuck," she says, drawing the profanity out. "Kimani," she yells over her shoulder, "did you know when you door in, it fucks with the air pressure? My fucking ears popped."

"Avi," Bishop says, "this is Fahima Deeb. Our resident genius."

"Your beleaguered tech support," Fahima says. She swivels on her stool. She takes off her goggles and rubs at her eyes.

"I told you not to door into my lab, Kimani," she calls. "Use the fucking elevator. Or the fucking phone." Kimani smiles at her from the doorway. "This is the reporter?" Kimani nods, and Fahima swivels again, pointing at Avi with the acetylene torch. "You have any experience in science writing?"

"No," says Avi.

"Physics, genetics, nothing?"

"No."

"Fuck," Fahima says, slouching her shoulders. "I'll have to translate my notes into idiot."

"We need to show Avi something," Bishop says.

Fahima glares at him, unsure what he means. When she figures it out, she frowns. "That seems like a terrible fucking idea."

"That's what I said," says Patrick.

"Fuck, now I'm agreeing with Patrick," Fahima says.

"He needs to know what's at stake," Bishop says.

"Why do we trust this guy?" Fahima asks.

"You know why." Bishop gives her a thin smile. Avi may have misread him as the kindly uncle of the group. His smile has a threat in it, and it's effective.

Fahima sighs, resigned, and turns to Avi. "Come meet Prince Charming."

She goes to one of the room's actual doors. They're heavy steel, in contrast to the rich wood door Avi came through. She punches in a long string of numbers on a keypad, and the door cracks open with a hiss.

"Take him in," says Bishop. It has the unmistakable tone of a command.

"I'm not going in there," Patrick says. "Those lights make my eyeballs itch."

"Scaredy-cat," Fahima says, smirking.

"Come on," says Sarah. "Let's get this over with." She takes Avi's arm and moves him toward the open door.

"Let the ladies handle this," Fahima says.

They enter a short hallway, and immediately Avi knows the kind of place he's entered. His first time in a makeshift jail was in Kirkuk. Army intelligence was holding two dozen suspects in the basement of a school. *Charges pending* was the euphemism, but none of the men would be charged. The platoon threw up cinder block walls to separate the prisoners, with sheets of chicken wire in place of bars. Nothing physically kept the prisoners from breaking out. The structure of a jail, the word *jail,* and the idea behind it held them in place.

This room has the same shape and feel, although it's permanent, better built. The walls are glass, and there are empty cells behind them. Everything is lit with a sickly green light that pulses like an artery. The lights buzz loudly, more organic than mechanical or electric. Sarah makes a noise when she steps in like she's going to be sick.

"Fuckwit's at the end," Fahima says, pointing to the one occupied cell in the hall. Owen Curry sits cross-legged on the floor, rocking back and forth. He has on the brown polo shirt, which is filthy from a month of wear. He has the patchy stubble that curses blond boys that age, more like an accumulation of pale dirt than a beard. His sunken eyes float over deep, bruised bags. He stands when he hears them come in. He steps to the glass and presses his hands against it. Clouds of condensation form around the points of contact: the meat of his palms and the pads of his fingers.

"I won't talk to *him*," he says. He snarls at Avi, showing rows of uneven teeth. "You've given me time to think. And I am only talking to people like *us* from now on. If you want to have a conversation, get him out of here."

"No one wants to talk to you, fucker," Fahima says. "No one needs to hear anything you say. We're here to gawk at you. Like an animal in the zoo."

But Avi wants something more, something so big he can't name it or speak it out loud. It's what pushed him up the stairs at the Roseland Rest, pressed the door of Owen's room open when he knew an ugly, meaningless death might wait inside. It was the thing that drove Avi to tour army munitions factories to see bombs being manufactured. For context, he told himself, but it was for this feeling. Proximity to something that could destroy him. Standing close to a bomb was a way of being judged, although it was forever unclear to Avi who a bomb found wanting, its victims or its survivors. That was what he saw in Owen Curry: a bomb that spoke.

"I want to talk to you, Owen," Avi says. His voice is soft and cajoling. He steps closer to the glass. Owen is sheened in sweat. He looks sick, as if they have him in quarantine rather than a jail cell. "Where did they go, Owen? All those people, where did th—"

"Shut off these lights and I'll show you where they went!" Owen screams. Spit flies from his lips. He bangs his forehead onto the glass, and it cracks, a spiderweb spreading from the point of impact. Sarah jumps back.

"They're nowhere," Owen screams, blood trickling down his forehead like the roots of a tree. Avi shivers when he makes the involuntary association, a flash of Emmeline dancing in his vision. "They're in the null, where nothing lives. Where all the cattle go."

"Let's get out of here," Sarah says. She tries to pull Avi back, but he shakes her off. He stands against the glass, annoyed that she's even there. He's the one who worked for this, hunted this moment across war zones and killing fields. This moment is his by right. Owen Curry is his.

"Why did you do it, Owen?" Avi says. His voice is calm and even. "Why did you kill that little girl in the church?"

Owen flinches. There's something human in him. It flickers in his eyes, guilty, then is gone. "Because it's a war," he says, baring his teeth. "And we won't win until we kill every last one of you. My friend told me all about you. You'll kill us if we don't kill you first. He told me what I had to do."

Owen turns away, slumps hard against the glass, and starts sobbing.

"You don't understand," he yells. "I could feel him in my head, and now I can't feel him anymore. It was so beautiful. You put these lights on me and you killed him. You killed my imaginary friend, you fuckers."

"Any other burning questions for our guest?" Fahima asks. Owen looks like a bag of broken sticks. In the video from the mall, there was a way he reached out to the girl, a way his hand stopped short of touching her. Avi knew that gesture and the feeling behind it. He felt that way with Kay sometimes, as if he were holding his hands out to her, waiting for her to bridge the rest of the gap between them. He imagined he could understand Owen Curry. Seeing him now, there isn't enough of a person here to understand. Owen Curry isn't a bomb. He's just a monster, the kind you can find anywhere. The thing that's in him, that Avi is actually hunting, can't be questioned any more than he could interview an IED or an atom bomb. Owen Curry is the shitty container it walks around in.

"Let's go," Avi says.

Fahima leads them back into the lab and locks the door behind them. "Sweetheart, isn't he?"

Avi takes a deep breath, trying to reset himself. There is mercifully familiar ground he can stand on here. He can be a reporter, run the professional script. Everything is easier to handle if you have someone to be. He slaps his back pocket, wishing for the notepad that's sitting on his desk, in his office, in another world. "How long are you going to hold him here?" he asks.

"Indefinitely," Bishop says.

"You can't keep him locked up," says Avi. "You can't keep him in there."

"We can't turn him over to the police," Bishop says. "The lights are the only things inhibiting his ability."

"Thank you very much," Fahima says, taking a little bow.

"They're hurting him," Avi says. With grim pride, he realizes he's managed to sympathize with Owen Curry.

"Good," says Patrick.

"There's no jail that could hold him other than this one," Bishop says.

"We should kill him," says Patrick.

"No more killing," Bishop says.

Avi stares at Bishop, registering the implication of the word *more*. Something vague and dangerous about Kevin Bishop is confirmed. Out of the group, the only ones Avi trusts are Patrick and Kimani. Her because she seems kind and honest. Him because he seems like an asshole. You know where you are with assholes.

"Someone is moving pieces around," says Bishop. "I doubt Owen Curry was an angel before, but someone's been in his head. He was pushed to do those things. Even if he wasn't pushed very hard."

"Why?" Avi asks.

Bishop shakes his head. "To force us out in the open?"

"Worked," says Patrick.

"There's no reason for me to be involved," Avi says. "I write about wars and school shootings. This is . . . I don't even know what this is."

"We are trying to preclude a war," Bishop says.

"We're busing ourselves to the killing fields," says Patrick. Avi can sense the longevity of this argument, the way it's been buried only to rise back up.

"We need your help," Kimani says.

"I haven't written anything in a year," Avi says. "I'm not on staff anywhere. I have no platform. Walk into the newsroom at the *New York Times* and say, *Hey, we've got superpowers. Who wants to interview us?* They'll line up."

"We don't say superpowers," says Patrick.

"There's something else," Kimani says from the

doorway. Bishop shakes his head, but Kimani ignores it. Avi recognizes the sadness in her face. He's never gone on a death notification, but he's seen military officers prepare for them, readying to deliver the worst news a family can get. The mix of solemnity and compassion is how Kimani looks at him as she says, "When we came to your house the first time, you weren't the one we were looking for." Avi stares at her, his face blank.

Bishop sighs. "Your daughter is one of us," he says.

"She can't be," Avi says. As he denies it, he knows it's true. *That's them*, he thinks. *That's them in your head making you believe them.* But it isn't. It's everything he's ever known or suspected about Emmeline confirmed. What they're telling him is the answer to all the things he's wondered about her, and it turns out he didn't want answers. He wanted to keep her strange and ethereal without it ever needing to mean something larger. As the mystery of his daughter ossifies into something definite, he's grieved by the death of the mystery. He clutches at that uncertainty, begging it to come back and replace this awful new knowing.

"How could you know that?" Avi says. "You've never met my daughter." He doesn't say her name, as if he can keep it from them. *They know*, he thinks. *They know everything in your head.*

"It's difficult to explain," Bishop says.

"Try," says Avi, a panic welling in his chest. None of them speak. Then Fahima clears her throat.

"You and I are going to be having a lot of conversations that don't make any sense," she says. "So why not start?

When someone begins to resonate . . ." She trails off. She sounds like a parent trying to have *the talk* with her kid but unsure what the most basic building block of the talk should be. "There's a space, like a shared psychic space, that all of us have access to. It's like a chat room just for people like us. We call it the Hive. When someone's abilities manifest, they start to show up in the Hive. Usually they can't talk to anyone else. It takes a while to learn how to communicate in Hivespace. But we can see them. Like a blip on a radar. Emmeline showed up maybe two weeks ago. She may not even know she's going there. But she was there."

"And you saw her?" Avi asks. "You saw the blip?"

"Fuck yes, we saw her," Fahima says.

"Emmeline isn't a blip," Bishop says. "She's more like a flare. Your daughter is very powerful, Avi. Or she will be."

Avi looks at the steel door that contains Owen Curry, a broken boy who disappeared twenty-one people out of the world with half a thought. He thinks of all the words he would use to describe Emmeline and how incompatible each is with the word *powerful*.

My little Emmeline, he thinks. *What will she become?* It's a thought any parent might have about any child, but now, with nothing left as impossible, its implications are bigger than Avi can fathom.

KEPT LIKE A SECRET

When Emmeline was a baby and Avi had her with him at the park or the food co-op, people remarked on how she never cried. Avi assured them that when he got her home, all hell broke loose. It was a thing to say to other parents that said *yes, I am in the parenting trenches like you, fighting to survive*. But it wasn't true. Even at home she was preternaturally calm.

She used to follow Avi from room to room. She climbed the big red chair in the attic as he read through editor's notes. She played on the kitchen floor while he made dinner. One day, when she was three, Avi put water on to boil and turned away from the stove to wash dishes. Emmeline snuck behind him and pulled the pot of boiling water off the stovetop, spilling it down her arm. Avi ran around the kitchen like a cartoon character with his ass on fire. Emmeline sat in a puff of steam as if she were floating on a cloud. Avi snatched her up off the floor and plunged her arm into the cold water in the sink, casting the scalded flesh of her forearm into the whorls and dunes it's been set in since. Emmeline looked at the scarred arm quizzically, observant.

Days later, when Kay could register anything other than fury at Avi for letting it happen, she worried that Emmeline might be one of those kids who didn't feel pain, who had to be trained to understand the dangers of heat and sharp edges in the abstract. Avi countered with a list of Emmeline's childhood injuries and their appropriate squeals and crying jags. While they argued, Emmeline sat on the couch, gazing through the cling wrap the doctors had put over the burn at the new alien landscape of her skin.

Avi often thinks about Emmeline, sitting with the steam dissipating around her. He imagines the control and the strength it took to remain calm. It was the kind of thing he'd read about in mystics and fakirs. People whose faith let them stick their hands into fire, walk across coals. And there it was, possessed by a three-year-old child. Avi wonders what his daughter is.

Kay calls to say she'll be late. She's calling to remind him to pick up Emmeline, but she doesn't say it out loud. Emmeline is quiet in the car, staring out the window at the bare trees that line the streets of Rogers Park. She mumbles something about homework and goes straight to her room. Avi stands in the foyer with his jacket in his hand.

The minute he goes upstairs, something will end. He thinks about his life in terms of turning points. Rubicons. Marrying Kay. Emmeline's birth. The burn. Mosul. They took on their importance afterward. Even with marriage and Emmeline's birth, things he knew were coming, he hadn't conceptualized their impact on his life. He hadn't understood the extent to which his old life would become a country to which he could no longer return. This is bigger. The whole world pivots on a point. The point happens to be his daughter.

He stands outside Emmeline's door. There's no sound from inside. He knocks gently, and Emmeline tells him to come in. Emmeline's walls are bare, and her room is cluttered without being messy. There are books in piles and drawings everywhere. A blue car, the circular heads of two girls sticking out of the windows. One is obviously Emmeline from the spiraling curls. A city block with a towering black building at the center. Emmeline is lying on the floor, drawing concentric circles. She's started with a dot, and now they tangent the edges of the page. She has changed into a tee shirt, which she wears only when she's gotten to her room at the end of the day with no intention of leaving. She never comes downstairs in short sleeves.

"How was your day, Daddy?"

"It was a tough day," he says. "Strange."

"Oh," she says. She sits up and crosses her legs underneath her. She looks down at her hands. With her index finger, she traces a path through the maze of her scar. It winds and loops from her elbow to her wrist.

"Leener," Avi says. "Are you—" He can't locate the words. If he says them aloud, he'll make them true. Emmeline looks at him, then back down at her arm.

"Today's the day you find out," she says. Her voice trembles.

"Find out what, honey?"

"I'm like the people you met today," Emmeline says. "I can do things."

89

Avi is scared. This is the dark room full of snakes. This is the bridge in the movie, made of ropes with slats missing, suspended over a river of crocodiles. He was less afraid as the IED went off, the moment he knew what was happening and knew he couldn't stop it. He felt less afraid stepping across the threshold of the door in the attic into what should have been open air.

Avi looks at his daughter. When she was a toddler, he understood that she would always be small to him. He would see the baby she'd been even when she was an adult. Her past would echo off her present.

Resonate, he thinks. The word becomes capitalized, scared out of its former meaning.

"What can you do, Leener?"

No answer will make it all right. No strange ability his daughter can possess that can be ignored and forgotten. Avi braces himself for what comes next.

"I don't know yet," Emmeline says. "I'm sorry, Daddy." She tosses herself at him, crashes like a wave. She's crying, little hitched breaths. "Do you still—am I still yours?"

Avi's arms come up from his sides slowly, in shock. He wraps them around Emmeline. Downstairs, the front door bangs against the wall. "Hey, guys, I'm home," Kay calls. Emmeline inhales deeply, a snuffling sound against Avi's shirt. She wipes her eyes with the heels of her hands.

"Hey, Momma," she calls, leaving Avi alone in the bedroom. Her question hangs in the air. For the rest of his life, Avi will regret not grabbing his daughter immediately and saying *Yes, Emmeline, yes, always.*

o

Kay holds Emmeline aloft, swishing the girl back and forth like a wiper blade. She sets her down and smooths the short sleeves down over Emmeline's shoulders, her hands stopping at Emmeline's elbows.

"You must be cold," Kay says, pushing the door shut with her foot. A wedge of snow has blown in with her, but it's not the cold she's remarking on. After the accident, Emmeline wanted to keep her scars covered all the time. Avi argued that they should discourage this, but Kay shot him down. "Let the girl feel normal," she said. Avi wonders when the last time Kay saw Emmeline's arms bared was.

A white box sits by the door. Avi recognizes it as a comic book long box, the kind he used to keep in his closet at college.

"I have a present for your dad," Kay tells Emmeline. "You want to show it to him?" She points to the box.

Emmeline strains to pick up the long box, then carries it in front of her to the base of the stairs, and Avi sits on the bottom stair to inspect it. Kay walks behind Emmeline, hands resting light on her shoulders. She's going to be tall. She'll get her height from him, although she's gotten everything else from Kay. Except those blue eyes. Her inexplicable eyes.

"I had something weird today," Kay says, taking off her coat. "Leenie, hon, open the box."

Emmeline takes the lid off the long box. "It's comics," she says.

"Pass one to Daddy," Kay says.

"Which one?" Emmeline asks.

"You pick," Kay says.

Emmeline flips through a couple, pulling some up out of the box to look at the covers. She settles on one and carries it over to Avi, pinched between two fingers by the corner like a dirty Kleenex.

It's bagged and boarded, the way Avi used to keep his comics despite Kay's cracks about it. Avi was better at taking care of things than he was at taking care of himself. He inspects the cover. "The trial of the Perfectional," he says. "This issue's a classic, Leener."

Emmeline looks at him, questioning. He knows what the look is asking, and he nods. What he needs to say to Kay, what they need to share with her, is too big to put into words. With this look and this nod, they seal it away. He hands the comic back to Emmeline, and she carefully puts it back in the box.

"You would not believe my day," Kay says, heading for the kitchen. Emmeline trots behind her, giving Avi one last look over her shoulder to confirm their pact.

"You went binge buying at Alleycat?" he says, forcing a smile. She grabs a bottle of white wine from the fridge and deftly uncorks it. They used to hit up the comic book store on North Clark together once they'd cautiously told each other that they were fans, a revelation no less intimidating than the second time they'd seen each other naked. The first time, they jumped into bed. The second time was a series of nervous uncoverings. Finding out about their mutual love of comics was the same. Avi was more shy about his fandom than about his body and never would have brought it up if Kay hadn't found the long boxes in his closet after she'd moved in. He came back from an assignment to stacks of comics laid out around the living room as if she'd found a stash of pornography or busted a drug ring. "You were a Timely Zombie?" she asked him. He nodded sheepishly. "More of a National fan," she said. "When I was a kid." She was, if anything, a bigger fan than he was, picking up new issues on Wednesday and stowing them at her office. On their first Wednesday "date" to Alleycat Comics, all the clerks knew her name. They gave Avi awkward nods even after years as a regular.

"Those are from a new client," Kay says, pouring him a glass. "This guy, I am not joking, hired me to read comic books." Emmeline sits at the kitchen table, paging through an *OuterGirl* comic older than she is. Avi leans heavily on the counter, and Kay comes up behind, slipping her hands around his belly. His body tenses when she touches it. "This guy comes in, first thing this morning, with this box of comics. He says he's interested in the legal issues around superpowers."

Wine catches in Avi's throat. "That's weird," he says. "What does that have to do with immigration?"

"He said he was a friend of one of the partners," Kay says. "Mr. Salazar told him I would be perfect for this project he's fiddling with."

"What's the project?" Avi asks, too casual.

"Unclear," Kay says. "But he put me on retainer to read a bunch of comics and just think about them."

"He paid you?"

Kay produces a check from her back pocket, trifolded and snow-damp. She presents it to Avi.

He should note the amount first. There's that sound the van makes when he takes a hard left, and the other day when he finally took the bins of summer clothes down to the basement, he was sure he saw a leak under the hot water tank. They could use some extra cash. But what he sees first is the signature line. *Kevin Bishop.*

He holds the check, one more impossible thing thrown into his day. Once the borders fall, everything can come through. Kay, not noticing how he's staring at it, takes the check and tucks it back in her pocket.

"What's for dinner?" she asks, looking around at the bare counters, the empty table.

"I got caught up with some work," Avi says.

"We'll order in," Kay says, scrolling through her phone. "Which one's the good Indian place? Dinner is on Mr. Bishop."

They spread out a buffet on the living room carpet and pass comics around. Avi opens another bottle. He tells Emmeline about the Ferret, the R-Squad, and the Freak Phalanx. He's evangelical, although he's never tried to rope Emmeline into his habit. Music, yes. He's played records for her since she was an infant. "This is the Beatles," he'd say. "This is Aretha Franklin." As if the baby were filing these things away. He'd take her up to his office and play records for hours, giving Kay a chance to sleep. She preferred to sing to Emmeline, whispering songs into her ear. When Emmeline started making sweet atonal mumbles, it was the songs Avi played that she regurgitated. "Under My Thumb" rather than "Row Your Boat," "Trouble Man" instead of "Mary Had a Little Lamb."

When Avi pauses to breathe or eat, Kay tells Emmeline the stories as if they were ancient myths or Just So stories. How the Astounding Family got their powers. How Red Emma swore revenge. How the Visigoth ended up in space and how he fought his way back to earth to discover centuries had passed.

"What happened to all his friends?" Emmeline asks.

Avi side-eyes Kay. They forget how little Emmeline is. They forget to shield her from sadness because she's so able to take it in stride.

"He makes new friends," Kay says. Emmeline pretends to be interested, but it's a show she puts on for them. By the time the food is eaten, it's close enough to her bedtime that Kay doesn't bat an eye when she asks to go to bed. Avi wonders if she's tired or needs to get away.

"Sure thing, Leener," he says. "Who do you want to tuck you in?"

"Momma," she says. Avi pretends to be hurt to cover up his surprise. He expected that Emmeline would take this chance to give them a moment to debrief, to finish the conversation they'd been having when Kay got home. Kay, a little drunk, holds her fists up like a victorious prizefighter. She does a victory dance and hoists Emmeline onto her shoulders, teetering. As they start up the stairs, Avi struggles to get up off the floor, scooting backward so he can use a chair for support. He catches Kay looking back at him, wanting to help, knowing it's not what he wants from her.

Avi puts the comics away. He moves all the superheroes from Timely Comics to the front of the box. These are the characters who are, in their grand ridiculous way, human.

They can fly but also have to pay rent. They can shake the earth under them but can't hold together a relationship. Kay prefers National Comics. Icons and archetypes. Gods in the shape of humans. He shuffles those toward the back. By the time Kay comes down, he's got the Timely Comics in rough chronological order.

"She's asleep?" he asks.

"She's a brick," says Kay. "We done with superheroes for the night?"

"I found some good ones," Avi says. He takes one of the comics out of the box. An old issue of *OuterMan*. "This one, OuterMan is on trial for de-aging the Ruminator with a, what is it, it's like a—"

"It was a ray," she says. "It was the Ruminator's device. A de-aging ray."

"Right, right," says Avi. He hands it to her and pulls out another. "This one has Medea sued for using her psychic powers to rig the New York mayoral election."

"She was dating the candidate," Kay says.

"Who turned out to be an evil time traveler," says Avi.

"Eternus," Kay says. Her voice goes dreamy. Before Emmeline, they'd lie in bed together, stoned, recalling details of old comic book plots. The reveal of Red Emma's father. Iota body switched not with OuterWoman, as Avi remembered it, but with She-Savage. They built on each other's knowledge, filling in their gaps.

Avi pulls his phone out of his pocket. "I need your help with something," he says. Kay looks at the phone, wary. "Something's not clicking in my head on this. I need your eyes."

It's something they used to say to each other. When Kay was stuck on a case. When Avi couldn't get a piece to read right. They were careful not to overuse it. They both dealt with terrible things. They both trucked in horrors. It was important to protect each other. Sometimes you needed to get out of your own head. They developed a code, a safe phrase so they'd understand when it was truly important: *I need your eyes.*

On the screen of the phone, there's the church, midday sun streaming through the stained glass. Pastor Baldwin in the front. At the right edge of the frame, the little girl. A triangle inscribed in a circle hung over the middle of the image.

"I can't," she says.

"I wouldn't ask," says Avi, "but I need something to break open on this, and I've lost my eyes."

He intends it as a way to get her to the other thing. To start the conversation that will lead them back to their daughter. Kay puts her wine down on the coffee table. She puts her hand over her face. "Avi, I can't," she says. "If I put that shit in my head, it's going to rattle around in there forever. Don't ask me to." What she means is, *Don't ask me again. Don't call this promise in; don't hold me to it.*

"No, it's fine." He pockets the phone. He tells himself he will try again tomorrow by some other route. But he knows he won't. He had another obvious way in, through the check, the comic books, Kay's new client. But that would make all this about Kay. Her story instead of his. It's also possible he picked the path he knew Kay would refuse so he could tell himself he tried without risking success. "I think there were some old *Red Emma* issues in there," he says, pointing to the box. "You used to love her."

They spend an hour reading the adventures of a prosecutor who swears revenge on organized crime after her entire family is gunned down. They each hold one side of the comics, reading them together like children's books, each of them pressed gently into the other's side, until Kay yawns and Avi follows her upstairs.

When she's asleep, her body leaden heavy with wine, Avi slips out of bed. He goes to Emmeline's room and eases the door open. A wedge of light from the hall falls across her sleeping face. Every decision he makes has become weighty and permanent. It's felt that way since she was born, a change, the introduction of consequence. It's what people mean when they say *there's the kids to think of.* But that implies the option of not thinking of one's kids. When Avi made the worst decisions for himself, he was thinking about Emmeline, if only with guilt that even she was not enough to get him to stop or that it was in part the responsibility of her and to her that necessitated the bad choices.

He wonders about Owen Curry's mother. What decisions had she made that produced him? Was it that she couldn't love what he was? Or understand it? Did she fail to give him a context in which to see himself? A word for what he'd become? *How do I save my daughter from becoming like him?* he thinks.

He takes out his phone and enters the number Kevin Bishop gave him. It was not, he noticed, the same as the one on the check to Kay. Avi takes some pride in this, graced with the direct line.

I want her to meet you, he types. Then adds, *all.*

TWO

ACADEMY FOR THE ARTS

Liberating education consists in acts of cognition,
not transferrals of information.
—Paolo Freire,
Pedagogy of the Oppressed

THE TOUR

Monday morning, Avi offers Kay a ride to the El station, and she accepts because it's viciously cold out. At the station, Kay leans over the emergency brake and kisses Avi good-bye. They understand that this must be done. Neither can leave the other without a kiss even if they're angry. Even if they're not speaking. A marriage runs on love initially, but as it gets polluted with battles and betrayals and resentments, it relies on rules. Rituals. Parts of their life together have a workmanlike quality to them, but it works. It holds them together on days when they don't share a grand passion and gets them through to the times when they feel that again. Drive and structure. Fire and skill.

Kay gets out of the car and goes to Emmeline's window. Emmeline's been quiet since she got up. She stared into her cereal bowl, then went upstairs to get a sweater. She sat on the bench in the front hallway, waiting for Avi and Kay to be ready to leave. She rolls down her window and kisses her mother, a loud smack. A stage kiss.

I made it through the morning without lying to my wife, Avi thinks as she dashes through the station doors. It's a teenage thought, relying on technicalities to absolve him. His omission is so large that it can't be called anything but a lie.

"You want to hop up front?" he asks Emmeline. She's too slight to ride in front, but the car is one area where he and Kay have both adopted a *we did it that way and we grew up okay* approach to parenting. Settled in the front seat, Emmeline looks like a toy.

"You want to talk?" Avi says. Emmeline shakes her head. Avi turns up the radio, the classic rock station whose scope includes bands Avi listened to when he was a teenager. A song comes on he hasn't heard in years, "Drain You" by Nirvana. Avi remembers the first time he saw them on television. Cobain's sullen magnetism. A charisma that shone through all the singer's efforts to cover it up. *Maybe he was one of them*, Avi thinks.

He makes the turn onto North Clark, heading home.

"I'm not going to school, am I?" Emmeline says.

"You can if you want," Avi says. "Some people are coming by the house who'd like to meet you. People like you."

"Are they going to take me away?" she asks.

"No, honey," Avi assures her. "No one is going to take you away."

It isn't a lie or an omission on his part. Simply a mistake.

Emmeline hasn't been up to the attic since she was tiny enough Avi could strap her into the baby carrier and climb the ladder. That magical time he could set Emmeline down in a circle of toys and books and the girl would exist there, happy, for hours.

Avi sits in the red chair and watches as Emmeline, still wearing her puffy purple coat with the mittens attached to the cuffs, investigates the space. She flips through his records. She plays with the orange tassels along the edges of a rug. She opens a drawer on the file cabinet, peers in, and shuts it. Seeing it through Emmeline's eyes, Avi is aware how shabby his office is. What he thinks passes for kitsch might be junk. The threadbare furniture. The ugly rugs. How do you explain ironic furnishing to a seven-year-old?

"Leener," he says, "they'll be here in a minute."

"Should we go let them in?" she asks.

"Wait," says Avi. "Come here." Emmeline climbs into his lap, and he swivels the chair so it faces the western wall. "Watch," he says.

The first time Kimani arrived, Avi hadn't seen it coming. Now the two of them watch the spot where the door appeared. Avi imagines a point of light at the floorboard, a sparking little star, rising up like an acetylene torch burning through sheet metal, tracing a molten line six feet into the air then turning, traversing, descending.

It's not like that at all. There is no door. Then there is.

Emmeline gasps like it's a magic trick, and Avi is relieved. He needs all of this to be strange to her, too. If they can't discover it together, if Emmeline has come preloaded with the ability to make sense of all this, he's lost her already.

Kimani opens the door and pokes her head out. "Is this her?" she says.

"Leener, I'd like you to meet a friend of mine," he says. "Kimani, this is my daughter, Emmeline." Emmeline hops out of his lap and helps him up, then shrinks back, hiding half behind him. Nervously, she takes one step toward Kimani.

"I've seen you before," Emmeline says. "In the shiny room."

"I saw you, too," Kimani says. "Out on the edges. You should've come and said hi."

"I didn't know how."

"You'll learn," Kimani says. She beckons Emmeline into the room, and Emmeline follows. For a split second, Avi is sure Kimani will close the door and take off without him, but he crosses the room and joins them.

"Where's everyone else?" Avi asks.

"They're meeting you there," Kimani says. "I'm sure Kevin's got your whole day planned out."

Emmeline examines this room as she had the attic. The room is different from the day before. Avi might not have noticed if Emmeline wasn't exploring it. All the furniture has been replaced. The harsh, knifelike corners on the tables are smooth, unthreatening curves. The couch is plush, cushy. The walls have been painted, a cooler blue, calming. Emmeline touches one of the silver sculptures lightly, and it shifts its shape, wriggling like a fish on a line. She gasps and pulls her hand back. The sculpture stops moving, held in a strange shape halfway between what it was and what it was trying to become.

"They don't bite," Kimani says. "My friend makes them. She's a kid not much older than you. Look." She lets the palm of her hand hover above the silver, and the sculpture reshapes itself, straining upward to form a ring around Kimani's hand. Kimani removes her hand and holds it up to show Emmeline it's unharmed. "I've got to tell you, though, it's pretty disgusting to watch Isidra make them." She leans over to Emmeline like they're sharing a secret. "She pukes up all the silver stuff."

"It's a puke sculpture?" Emmeline asks. Kimani nods. "Gross."

Kimani gets down to one knee and puts a light hand on Emmeline's shoulder. "Some of us have abilities that aren't too nice to look at," she says. "They can't all be as good-looking as the two of us, huh?" Emmeline smiles. "I wish you could spend all day with me here. But Mr. Bishop gets very upset when I'm late."

"Where are we going?" Emmeline asks.

"New York City," Kimani says. She opens the door again, this time onto an alleyway, behind a Dumpster. "Not the most scenic drop-off spot," she says. "But it's right out the alley and down the block: 136. Doesn't look like much."

"It was nice to meet you," Emmeline says. Kimani smiles at her, and Avi is aware of an instant bond, something forged by unity in difference. Something he's on the outside of.

Avi hasn't spent much time in New York, but one of the things he loves about the city is the way every block is a mishmash of architectural styles, of eras. Chicago holds on to its past, keeping pockets of time preserved. New York discards yesterdays as soon as they're useless. It molts, revealing shiny new skin beneath. Situated on 57th between Third and Lexington, the Bishop Academy for the Arts is one of those throwaway bits, a piece of late-sixties optimism that didn't pan out. It sits, nondescript, sandwiched between two newer, sleeker dreams. You wouldn't notice it unless you were looking for it. Which must be the way Bishop wanted it.

A tall set of revolving doors lets Avi and Emmeline into the lobby. Doric columns line the walls, and the Deco tile floors have waves of dried salt tracked in from the sidewalks. The front desk is staffed by a broad-shouldered man with a body-builder physique and a name tag that reads SHEN in large gold letters.

"Can I help you?" he asks. He steps away from the desk, forming a second door between them and the rest of the building. Avi wonders if it's possible he had increased his size. All things are possible here, he reminds himself.

"Avi Hirsch," he says. "We're here to see—"

"Shen, this is the gentleman we've been talking about," says Bishop, hurrying across the lobby, straightening his tie, half the collar of his blazer folded up. The temporary disarray feels like an affect, a way to make himself seem softer. Avi thinks of military men he's known, the two faces they keep for war and for family. The impulse is to try to determine which one is real, but the truth is always that both are real in equal measure. The best of them can switch on a moment's notice. This is Bishop's face for family, but Avi's seen his war face.

"Avi, glad you could make it," Bishop says, patting him on the shoulder with false chumminess. "And Emmeline." He turns to her as if he's forgotten Avi is there. "I'm so happy to have you join us." With obvious discomfort, he lowers himself to one knee and extends his hand. Emmeline takes it. Avi imagines a rapid, massive flow of information between them. A mutual download. A Vulcan mind meld. Bishop lets go of Emmeline's hand, and Emmeline continues to watch him, unsmiling. "This is a school I started for people like you and me," Bishop says.

"It's very nice," Emmeline says quietly.

"This is only the lobby," he says. "This is the part anyone gets to see. We keep all the best parts hidden. Would you like to see more?"

Emmeline nods, and once again Avi finds himself trailing behind, an afterthought, as Bishop leads them across the cavernous lobby. He can't help but think about Willy Wonka opening up his factory to the public for the first time. The most memorable parts of the movie, the reasons Kay's deemed it too grown up for Emmeline, are the ones in which Wonka's facade of genial showman falls away to reveal something frightening underneath. Avi goes to put his arm around Emmeline, but she's a step ahead with Bishop.

Before they get there, the doors of a brass Deco elevator open. A teenage girl bounds out and past them, floating a few inches off the ground, a pale aura of purple around her.

"Marian," Bishop says quietly. "No abilities below the second floor."

"Why is that the rule?" the girl asks, hovering in the air, arms crossed defiantly.

"No abilities below the second floor," Bishop repeats.

"This is bullshit," the girl mutters. She settles to the ground, and her aura goes dim before she exits the building.

"It's amazing we've kept this place a secret this long," says Bishop. "Five hundred teenagers. It's like herding magical cats." They step into the elevator. "We're having breakfast with some of the staff," he says, "then a little tour of the facilities. Just something to start off, to give you a sense of the place."

The doors close in front of them, leaving the normal world behind, and Avi is sure beyond any doubt that Bishop is talking to Emmeline and not to him.

ACADEMY FIGHT SONG

Carrie Norris busts into the boys' dorm room.

"Headmaster Bishop is a dick," she proclaims.

Waylon Winans drops the lit joint Miquel Gray just passed him. The cherry fractures on the hard industrial carpet and dies in pieces. The boys sit cross-legged on the floor. Miquel holds the toilet paper tube capped with a dryer sheet Waylon thinks deadens the smell of smoke. He's wrong: the eleventh-floor hallway is rank with the skunky odor.

"Shut the door, shut the door," he says.

"What are you up in arms about?" Miquel asks.

"About she doesn't get to talk to the reporter guy," Waylon says, relighting the joint.

"Get out of my head, you creep," Carrie says, shoving her thick, half-combed brown hair back from her face and snapping her fingers to call for the joint.

Waylon holds up his hands defensively. "It's like a neon sign on your forebrain," he says. "Miquel could see it if he wasn't staring at your ass."

"Fuck you," says Miquel, taking the joint and passing it to Carrie along with a lighter.

"Why are you even here?" Waylon asks. "You have a room, right?"

"Hayden and Jonathan are practicing in there," Carrie says. "They get to perform a special little concert for our guest."

"Practicing," says Waylon, putting annoying air quotes around the word. "Those two are totally fucking."

"Shut up, Waylon," Miquel says. He made out with Hayden at a party last summer while Carrie was back home in Deerfield. Both of them texted Carrie to apologize the next day. Neither made it explicit why it was necessary to apologize, although Carrie obviously knew. "Hayden's a good choice," Miquel says. "Nonthreatening."

"I am nonthreatening," says Carrie.

"You could sneak up behind somebody and kill them."

"She could sneak up in front of somebody and kill them," Waylon says.

"Hayden can look like anyone they want," says Carrie.

"But they don't," Miquel says. "They look like Hayden."

"Well, I haven't snuck up behind anyone and killed them."

"Yet," says Miquel, smirking.

"What if you were fucking Hayden and she switched back into a guy?" Waylon asks. "You would be instantly gay."

"You are instantly gay," Miquel says.

"Hayden would never fuck you, Waylon," Carrie says, not bothering to correct his pronouns and instantly feeling bad about it. "And they don't switch. Ever." She tokes hard, leaning back against the door. She holds the joint out to assess it. Waylon spends an inordinate amount of time worrying about becoming gay. Boys like Waylon have to put up a front of masculinity for some imagined audience all the time. It must be exhausting. But he is a deft roller. The joint looks like a chrysalis.

"Bryce grew this?" she asks.

"Mmm hmm," says Waylon.

"So it grew, like, on him?" Carrie asks.

"It's gross, right?" says Miquel.

"It's amazing," Waylon says. "You're both such prudes. Why don't you fuck already?"

"We're essentially smoking his body hair," Carrie says.

"His body hair that gets you completely fucked up," says Waylon. "Give it back if you don't want it."

"No," Carrie says, taking another hit.

"So why is Bishop a dick?" Miquel asks.

"I wrote that article *last year* for the paper about how we should go public," she says. "And now it turns out I'm a hundred percent right, and they're bringing in a reporter to write about us."

"And they don't want Carrie anywhere near him," says Waylon.

"So what the actual fuck?" Carrie says.

"It's not just you," Waylon says. "No one's supposed to talk to him. No one's allowed to use their abilities all day. It's basically like when the board of ed inspectors come." He makes gimme-gimme gestures for the joint, which Carrie ignores. "We're supposed to look like Juilliard. They want our best face forward."

"I'm a great face!"

"You're a volatile agitator."

"I have opinions that could—"

"So go," say Miquel.

"What?" Carrie says.

"You're like a fucking superninja spy thief and you're complaining you're not on the guest list? Go. Get in there next to this guy and tell him what you think."

"She doesn't know what she thinks," Waylon says.

"Get the fuck out of my head."

"She'll know once she says it," Miquel says. Waylon snatches the joint from Carrie, taking one more mighty puff.

"Late for Ethics," he says, chest puffed out. He exhales and grabs a stack of textbooks off the desk. "Light a candle when you two are done banging. I don't want to come back and have it reek of fucking in here."

"Dick," Carrie mutters.

When the door closes behind him, Carrie climbs up and sprawls out on his upper bunk. The sheets have never been washed and hold the deep fug of concentrated teenage boy. Salt and earth. Goat stink and vegetables going to rot. Miquel says the reason he gave Waylon the top bunk is that smell rises. Miquel is meticulously clean; he smells like soap and a candle that's been put out.

He plays music through the tiny speakers on his desk. Sleepy vocals fill the room, and Carrie starts laughing when she recognizes the song.

"Please tell me you don't always listen to Pink Floyd when you smoke," she says.

"It's good," says Miquel.

"It's a stereotype," she says. "You're like the cartoon of a high school stoner."

"So put on something else."

Carrie pulls the iPod out of her pocket. It's an old one, seventh generation, objectively the best. Last model with a click wheel. She scrolls through artists' names, trying to find one that's safe, something she knows he'll like. But she keeps coming back to a song that feels unsafe, too weird. It's one of her favorites, but she's never played it for anyone, not even Hayden. She hops down and plugs the iPod into Miquel's speakers, then clambers back up as the song starts. A cello line trips through the air, spirals downward, and recovers. The singer's voice trembles as if he's making up the words.

"What's this?" Miquel asks.

"Arthur Russell," Carrie says. "He's good."

The song fills the room with negative space pinpricked with cello and horns. Carrie waits for Miquel to say something smart-alecky about whether this even counts as music, but he doesn't. He listens, and she wonders if he hears the same magic in the song she does.

"It's good," he says as the song fades. "Sad somehow."

"Yeah," Carrie says. When she's high, she flickers. It's difficult to keep a clear picture of herself. She starts to think of herself as an echo, the idea of herself more vague until she's in her resting state: barely perceptible. The next song starts, and her heart speeds up because she's secretly thought of it as *their song* and it feels like Miquel will know. "I should get ready for class," she says. "I've got History of Revolutionary Thought with No-Fun Novak."

"Get ready how?" he asks. "You look great. Want to hang out here? I've got a free period anyway."

"I guess," Carrie says, trying to sound casual. First period is breakfast, but upperclassmen use the unsupervised time for sleeping, fucking, and recreational drug use. *Wanna come over first?* is a crude pickup line at Bishop. Miquel asking her to stay carries an implication even if it's there only because Carrie wants it to be. She examines the stuccoed ceiling, each little stalactite of it looking as if it might drip down onto her.

"You're not angry anymore," Miquel says.

"Don't do that," she says, blushing. "It's as bad as Waylon." Sometimes Carrie works so hard to keep how she feels from Miquel. Other times it's like she's silently screaming at him, wanting him to hear.

"Waylon goes into people's heads," he says. "That's fucked up. This is how I see. You were all red when you came in. Now you're like a light orange. Sad, a little. Like this song."

When Miquel is high, he takes deep breaths and blows them out like he's thinking the deepest thoughts. His breath is out of sync with the music. She likes listening to him breathe. She thinks of his chest rising and falling, and it seems impossible that he doesn't know what she's feeling, that she hasn't turned the neon equivalent of whatever color Miquel sees as desire, want.

"I should go find the reporter," she says. *Ask me to stay,* she thinks. *Keep me here with you.*

"You should," says Miquel.

"I don't know what to say if I find him," Carrie says.

Miquel lets out one more deep breath, and Carrie can almost feel it passing through the air between them, through the stink of Waylon's mattress and into her lungs, filling her with calm, confidence.

"Tell him something that only you could know, that only you could tell him," Miquel says. "Tell him what it feels like not to be seen."

Third period, and the reporter is visiting Sarah Davenport's Artistic Expression class in the black box theater on the fifth floor. Carrie knows because Hayden told her. Not to make Carrie jealous but in a sincere effort to help with whatever Carrie has planned. Sometimes Carrie pretends she's resentful of Hayden because Hayden is prettier, more confident. Because Hayden makes music and Carrie just consumes it. But the resentment isn't real. Hayden is someone else to imagine being, but only because Hayden imagined themselves into someone better to begin with.

She sneaks in before anyone else arrives and takes a seat by the door. There are two microphones set up in the center of a circle of chairs, along with a stereo on a cart and the odd collection of AV equipment that accumulates in any room that isn't regularly used. Carrie has Sarah for Psychic Defense last period, and she knows there's a risk that Sarah will spot her mind in the room. Carrie pushes herself way down, basically invisible. Invisibility is a strain. It's like screaming *I'M NOT HERE I'M NOT HERE I'M NOT HERE* as loudly as you possibly can. The cloud of weed lingers in her brain, and she flickers back into visibility every now and then.

A dozen students file in, and Carrie recognizes each of them, even the younger kids she's never spoken to. Bishop isn't that big, and they're all trapped in one building together. An island floating in the middle of Manhattan.

There's Isidra Gonzales from Carrie's year. She makes metal sculptures that respond to touch, or time, or light. They're made of a silvery substance Isidra literally spits up from her guts. Last semester, she made a semi–perpetual motion sculpture: shiny silver koi that circled the fountain in the front lobby for two weeks before slowing like a dying watch and losing definition. By the end of a month, amorphous blobs of mercury traced a zombie circle in the water, then sank.

Darren and Lynette Helms, twins, both with the same jet-black, ruler-straight hair, file in behind Isidra. They're arguing about their weekend plans, something involving skiing. The Helmses come from money, and their parents are both Resonants. Lynette is sort of useless, but Darren is actively the worst. He's a drinking habit away from committing date rape. They're a year ahead of Carrie. After fifth year, students can opt to leave or can stay for two "postgrad" years. She hopes if one of the Helmses decides to stay, the other one will leave. The best thing Lynette could do is to get far away from her brother.

Maya Patel is a third-year, a heavy-set Indian girl. She speaks only when absolutely necessary. Ask her a question and the image of the answer appears in your head, stamped on your thoughts like a photo negative. Neal Byrd, pale and spotted with acne, doesn't talk to anyone either. He goes directly to a pile of scrap metal in the corner and begins spinning a piece of rebar by twirling his finger at it, but Maya snaps at him and he lets it clatter to the ground. Jovan Markovic is a second-year and can make slightly amorphous shapes out of water.

Jonathan Mazur comes in with Hayden Cohen. Half the kids at Bishop believe Jonathan and Hayden are not just fucking, not just dating, but destined to be one of those star couples you see in magazines. He's good-looking in an outdated way. Seventies hot, like a low-rent Jim Morrison. Long, wavy hair, bronze skin, and thick lips. In the cleft of his Paisley silk shirt, a triangle of bright orange throbs in time with his pulse. He has to wear heavy turtleneck sweaters whenever he leaves the academy to cover it up.

And there's Hayden, Carrie's roommate for the last three years. It makes sense that someone who could look like anyone would look like Hayden. Their beauty comes off as effortless because it's the result of so much effort. Hayden's ability is constantly engaged for the purpose of, as Hayden puts it, keeping up appearances. Hayden winks at Carrie as they come in. Hayden can always find Carrie no matter how far down Carrie tries to hide.

Once the whole class is seated, Sarah arrives. Behind her, the reporter and his kid, who's got Sarah's dog, Cortex, trotting along with her. When Carrie first got here, she assumed Cortex was a service animal: one of those dogs that can smell an oncoming seizure or an emotional support dog. Waylon says the dog's like an external hard drive but then won't explain what the fuck that even means. It follows Sarah everywhere. The kid is vigorously petting Cortex, which none of the students are allowed to do.

The reporter is not that impressive. Carrie and Miquel had tried to imagine him, thinking he'd look either like Robert

Redford in *All the President's Men* or like Dustin Hoffman in *All the President's Men*. The latter was closer to the mark. He looks like he used to be muscled and let himself go. *Dad bod*, thinks Carrie, even though it's one of those awful phrases adults come up with to sound like teenagers. She tries to guess his age, but mostly what she notices is that he looks stunned, as if he's been smacked. She thinks of reporters as having a keen eye, but Avi's eyes are wide, trying to take in everything at once but unable to. When he smiles, it's too taut to be genuine.

Sarah calls the class to attention with a golf clap. She comes from money, too, although she doesn't reek of it the way the Helmses do. Sometimes she comes off like the matron at a finishing school.

"Today we have some guests," she says. "This is Avi Hirsch; he's a reporter with . . ." She turns and looks at Avi.

"Freelance," Avi says. Sarah looks at him like he's used the soup spoon to stir his tea. She's such a priss.

"He's a *noted* reporter," she says, putting weight on the word to see if it holds up. Unsatisfied, she adds, "Award-winning." This pleases her, and she moves on. "As you know, there's been an initiative to go public about the existence of people like us. Mr. Hirsch has been asked to help us with that. He may write about the academy, but he won't be revealing any personal details of students or any details about its location. We want you all to know that you're safe here."

Carrie lets out an annoyed burst of breath loudly enough that Lynette looks over at where she is to see where the sound came from. Bishop goes through all this effort to instill pride in who they are, to make the students feel good about being different, and then hides them from the whole world. It's hypocritical bullshit, done in the name of safety.

"And this," says Sarah, "is Avi's daughter, Emmeline. Emmeline is a Resonant, which some of you may have sensed. She's new to all this, so I hope you'll welcome her and make her feel that she's found a home here."

The students, who nodded and mumbled when Avi Hirsch was introduced, all say warm and cheerful hellos to Emmeline. She smiles back, then shrinks into Avi's side. She's so young. Carrie has never heard of someone that young resonating. She has dark skin and amazing corkscrew curls, and her eyes are like pale ice. From behind her father's leg, she looks right at Carrie. Emmeline holds eye contact with her, then hides again.

"Today we have presentations," Sarah explains to Avi and Emmeline. "In this class, we work on ways to use our abilities to express creativity. So much of what we do at the academy involves teaching *essentials*." Sarah puts the word in air quotes and rolls her eyes. "*Control. Defense*. But it's important that students engage their full selves not as Resonants but as human beings."

This line is so overused, it's become a joke among the students. Any time students use their ability to do something they could just as easily have done without it, someone else will rag on them for failing to engage their full selves.

"Now," Sarah says. "I think Hayden and Jonathan have a song for us."

Hayden and Jonathan go to the center of the room to

a smattering of applause. Jonathan intently tunes while Hayden adjusts the mic. When Hayden and Carrie first met, Hayden was into pure pop music, and their interest in being a singer had as much to do with fame as it did with music. Hayden and Carrie found a few singers they both liked, and once Hayden got a sense of how into music Carrie was, they adopted Carrie as their personal tour guide. The only trouble with them was that they wanted to try emulating everything as soon as they heard it, not giving it a chance to sink in. Lately, they'd been listening to a lot of early Leonard Cohen and writing songs with the same murky cadences. There was such a sonorous quality to Hayden's voice that even their strained metaphors seemed deep. It was as if Hayden shaped their vocal cords into a perfect instrument, an internal echo of their physical attractiveness.

"That was great, Hayden," Sarah says when the song is done. "Really lovely. And because I wanted to give you a little taste of how abilities and the arts can intersect, Lynette has something for us."

Lynette Helms stands up.

"I have something, too," her twin brother, Darren, shouts. It's awful enough that Lynette has a brother as unlikable as Darren, but Darren hangs on her like a stink. He has no interest in artistic expression. He's here to make sure Lynette doesn't have a moment she can enjoy. She has no female friends at the academy. None of the girls are willing to put up with Darren. Lynette doesn't say anything. She walks to the middle of the room and stands with perfect, practiced posture.

"Since I knew we'd be having guests today," she says,

giving a little bow toward Avi and Emmeline, "I wanted to do something that would involve all of us."

"Get on with it, Lynnie," says Darren. The corner of Lynette's mouth twitches, but she carries on. She turns to Avi and frowns. She looks like she's about to tell him he has cancer.

"I should say, though, Mr. Hirsch," she says, "I've never tried this with a . . ."

"A Damp?" says Darren.

"Darren, that's enough," Sarah says sharply. Darren smirks. Carrie watches Avi. Even if he doesn't know the word, he knows what it means. There's an instant understanding when someone calls you a name meant to tell you you're other, less.

Lynette produces a stack of note cards from her pocket and hands them out. Carrie stands up and looks over Maya's shoulder. Hers says VIOLIN.

"What about me?" Emmeline asks. She hasn't been given one.

"Your part is the most important," says Lynette, smiling. "I need everyone to think about their card. You can think about the word, or you can imagine the instrument or how it sounds. It shouldn't matter which." She goes over to Emmeline. "Emmeline, since you're our guest, you get to pick the song. Think of it in your head." Emmeline closes her eyes. "You got it? Okay, I'm going to . . ." Lynette puts her hands on Emmeline's head. Carrie's head floods with music, a descending line played on the violin she has pictured. It catches her off guard, and she flickers visibly. She fights the urge to hum along.

"She's gotten into your record collection," Sarah says to

Avi. "Or mine." She's smiling, and her eyes are closed, so she can't see how frustrated Avi looks. He strains to hear whatever's written on his card. He must be visualizing the instrument, imagining the sound of it, but getting nothing. Lynette opens one eye. Her shoulders slump.

"You can't hear it, can you?" she says to him. "I'm so sorry. Here." She crosses the room and turns on one of the three stereos. It's an old silver tank like the one Carrie's dad has back in Deerfield, Illinois. It comes alive with static. Lynette lays her hand on it, and at her touch it blasts noise. "Dammit," she mutters. "Levels." She closes her eyes again. The noise takes shape just as the song hits its swell, spinning off into orbit as an astronaut speaks back to ground control across a void. Even without the lyrics, with the melody line rendered by a tenor saxophone, it rings of spacemen and glitter.

"Nice choice, Leener," Avi says, looking around, embarrassed. He ruffles his daughter's hair. Emmeline smiles at him, but there's a sad quality to it. She's thrilled with what she's seen, and Lynette was smart to choose a manifestation of her ability that let the girl be a part of it. Along with the excitement of realizing she's like these other kids, there's the understanding that her father is not, can't be. She's found her place in the world, but it means she'll have to leave him behind. He must know that, too. Carrie wonders how long he's known that the kid is a Resonant. She's glad things went the way they did with her abilities and her parents. She faded out of their minds, as if they'd heard a song called "Carrie" on the radio once and hummed it for a little while, then forgot it.

"That was very interesting, Lynette," says Sarah. "And your transfer to electronics has gotten much stronger." Lynette smiles, delighted by the teacherly praise. Darren stands. He has no intention of letting her enjoy the moment.

"Mine's better," he says. "Want to see?"

"Darren," says Sarah, "today is not the day."

"Lynette got to do her party trick," Darren whines. "Hayden got to sing his little song."

"Fuck you, Darren," Hayden says.

"Pass, thanks," Darren says. "I have something I want to share. I think I should be able to express myself."

Sarah is about to come down on Darren, but Avi, without any context for what's happening, says, "It's fine." Fidgeting in her anger, Sarah spins a finger in the air to indicate that Darren should make it fast. He struts to the front of the room and turns on one of the televisions. He draws a full breath into his chest, ready to proclaim. At that moment, Emmeline raises her hand and clears her throat. Darren deflates.

"May I go to the bathroom?" Emmeline asks. Carrie smiles. It's possible the girl needs to go, but she timed her request exactly to poke a hole in Darren's moment. The reporter might not be much, but the kid was all right.

"Of course," Sarah says. "Cortex will show you the way."

This must be exactly what Emmeline hoped for, and she follows the dog out of the room. On her way out, she reaches out her little hand and rests it, just for a moment, on Carrie's. Carrie jumps, visible for a flicker, but the kid is gone before Carrie can read anything off her face. Darren puffs his chest back up and begins.

"I've been working on 3D projection," he says. "It's tough, because video is already so much more information than audio." He shoots Lynette a withering look. "And for 3D you need two different camera angles. You need to find two people with a shared experience. I've been fishing around, and I finally found one." He smiles, a terrible wolf grin. "Jovan and Maya have an experience they've shared."

Jovan and Maya go pale as an image appears on the screen. It's fuzzy but resolves, rising out of the static the way Lynette's song did. It's a hand stroking an erect penis, seen from above.

"This is Maya jerking Jovan off," Darren says. He sounds like he's narrating a nature video. "The reason I chose it is they must have their heads very close to each other. Like, Maya is sitting right next to him in his dorm room and stroking him off. But there's enough distance between the two points of view that you get this great depth of field. Wait till he comes; it's like it's shooting right at you."

The class reacts with a mixture of shock and giggles. Carrie doesn't join in. She thinks about sneaking up to the front of the class and punching Darren Helms right in the dick. Hayden's already on their feet, about to do just that, when Sarah shuts the television off and turns on Darren. "You think it's funny using your abilities against people who can't defend themselves?" She reaches out, rests her fingertips on his forehead. Her eyes glaze over with a milky whiteness, and Darren's whole body shudders. His posture straightens, and he turns to the class.

"My name is Darren Helms, and I'm a spiteful little shit," he says. His voice is even, affectless, as if he's reading off a teleprompter rather than processing the words he says. "Other than the occasional unlucky medical professional, the only person who will ever touch my sad micropenis is me."

Carrie has to stuff her fist in her mouth to keep from laughing. Even Maya and Jovan laugh, if only to hide how mortified they are. Carrie's a little horrified by the class's willingness to turn on their own, to pivot at the scent of fresh blood in the water. Darren's body shakes like he's come up from a bracing swim. Sarah's eyes return to their normal green. Darren drops to his knees, clutching his head in both hands.

"You can't do that!" Darren shrieks. "There are rules against—"

"You want to cite rules as soon as you think they'll protect you?" Sarah towers over him, and Carrie regrets ever thinking of her as a priss. "Here are the rules. What a person can do to you is limited by their ability and constrained by their ethics. If I were you, I would pray the people you meet have a higher moral code than yours, which is a fairly low bar to set."

"I'll report you," he says. "I'll go right to the headmaster."

"Report yourself while you're there," says Sarah. "Get out of my classroom."

He brushes by Carrie as he gathers his things from his desk, stomping the whole way. On his way out the door, he nearly knocks over Emmeline, who's returning from the bathroom with Cortex behind her. She looks around at the faces in the room as if to ask what she's missed. Avi gathers her up protectively.

"Please don't put this in your article," Sarah says to Avi. Avi shies away from her, pushing Emmeline farther back.

Carrie knows what he's afraid of and why this is exactly what they wanted to keep hidden from him. They're all towing the line of *look how normal we are*, but now they've given him a glimpse of how powerful some of them are.

Carrie smiles. If she was writing about Resonants, introducing them to the world of normal people, that's the first story she'd tell. *You don't have to worry*, she'd say. *Sure, a couple of us are total dicks. But we police our own. We won't let people like Darren Helms hurt anybody.*

THE PHYSICAL KIDS

Things get shuffled, changes in a schedule Avi isn't privy to. After the debacle in Sarah's class, they sit in on a high school English lecture that's indiscernible from any other high school English class in America. The same picking apart of themes and symbolism. The same vacant, sleepy looks on half the students' faces as the other half passionately discuss the relevance of Octavia E. Butler's *Mind of My Mind*. *They want me to see all this as normal*, he thinks. *They want to lull me into forgetting what they are.*

At lunch in the teachers' lounge, Sarah embarrassedly recounts the incident with Darren Helms to the engrossed faculty, all of whom agree that Darren Helms is the worst. There's debate whether he is the worst *currently* or the worst *ever*, with older teachers reaching back in their memories to find truly abhorrent alumni. Whenever Avi tries to ask a question, he's put off: *The headmaster will go over that with you* or *Mister Bishop will want to discuss that directly*. They've been media trained, and they're hewing to it.

Sarah hands them off to Kimani, whose door appears next

to the vending machine in the teachers' lounge. Emmeline looks happy to see a familiar face.

"Have they had you sitting around classrooms all day?" Kimani asks Emmeline.

"It wasn't too bad," says Emmeline. "Everyone was nice. Except the boy that wasn't. I helped play a song in everyone's heads." She looks at Avi apologetically.

She's handling all of it so well, he thinks. *So much better than I am.*

"Kids your age can't be cooped up all day," says Kimani. "You need time to run around. Blow the stink off, my mom used to say. You like gym class at school?"

"Not really."

"Maybe you'll like it here. It's a nice day out for it."

"It's snowy," says Emmeline.

"Well, it must be a nice day somewhere," Kimani says. She opens the door, looking down from the top of a hill onto a deep field of green. The air that comes through isn't warm, but it's nowhere near the chill of December in New York. Kimani hunkers down next to Emmeline and points upward. "Look, up in the sky."

Two teenagers fly overhead, swooping in a double helix pattern across an expanse of blue. Leaving Avi and Kimani behind, Emmeline chases after them like they're a flock of pigeons, waving her arms in the air as if she could take flight. As he steps out into the field, Avi wonders what keeps Emmeline on the ground.

At the bottom of the hill, there's a boy skinned in pale birch bark, talking to a flower. Avi can't hear the conversation, but the flower begins to grow, spiraling around the boy's body like an affable snake. Caught in its coil, he laughs like a little kid, an unselfconscious sound that's strange coming out of a teenager. Nearby, a girl holds rocks the size of basketballs in each hand. She hurls them at the head of a boy in a Beastie Boys tee shirt. Avi is about to scream, but the rocks shatter and the boy grins, unharmed, brushing chunks of stone off his shoulders.

"This is the only place they can do this," Patrick says, coming up behind Avi. At their first meeting, Avi hadn't noticed his lankiness. It's as if his body, once stretched, has never pulled back into its correct shape. It gives him the look of a convincingly animated scarecrow. "I'd love it if we had a training facility on campus, but there just isn't space."

"This isn't the first-year class, Patrick," Kimani calls from the doorway.

"I thought this would be more enlightening," Patrick says. "Show Mr. Hirsch the full scope of what we are."

"Did you clear this?"

"Are you going to report me?"

Kimani shakes her head in the universal sign for *I don't have time for this* and recedes from the doorway, which remains at the top of the hill, casting no shadow in any direction.

"So where are we?" Avi asks.

"Oregon," says Patrick. "There's a place out here for Resonants who can't pass as human. They call it the Commune. I'm sure you'll get the tour before you write your little story."

"You don't like this whole idea," Avi says.

"I don't like that we're doing it, and I don't like that we're doing it in half measures," Patrick says. "You must see it. Trying to pass ourselves off like any other school. We're not. We're something else entirely."

"So why participate?"

"I recognize the necessity," Patrick says. "The world's too small for us to hide in anymore. Fringe nut jobs have already put together that we exist. People who spout off about UFOs and the New World Order. You just have to be willing to believe in impossible things. We're the next conspiracy theory."

"Why not stay that way?" Avi asks. "Those guys are a joke to most people."

"It's getting easier to connect the dots," Patrick says. "An incident here and there. The right search term and they're linked together."

"Then what?"

"Then someone reputable figures it out and does a story exposé-style, and it looks like we're hiding."

"You are hiding," Avi says.

Patrick smirks at him. "The week before we had to go hunt down Owen Curry, I was in Powder Basin, Wyoming," he says. "Ever heard of it?" Avi shakes his head. "There was a family that died there last week. The Guthridges. Lucy, Sam, Paige, Melody, and Jeb. Single mother, four kids. Local newspaper said they died in a house fire."

"I didn't hear about it," Avi says.

"The mom and kids were beaten and stabbed to death before the fire was set," Patrick says. "The local paper didn't mention that. We were tracking the oldest boy and the youngest girl. Both energy projectors from what we could tell. Sometimes a person's Hivebody indicates how their ability will manifest. I approached Sam, the older boy, about coming to the school. He said he couldn't leave his family. Bishop was going to offer financial support for the mother and the other kids. The middle kids were baseliners. Sam's ability had already manifested, so I was tutoring him in the Hive. After work for both of us, when we could find the time. There's a disconnect, teaching people to use their abilities there instead of in person. It's like reading a book on the Maillard reaction without ever putting a steak on the grill." Avi thinks of Emmeline at the stove cooking eggs. It seems like weeks ago. "A couple days before the fire, he came to me and told me he'd used his ability to dig out of a mine collapse. He was so proud of himself. Scared, too, because all the men he worked with had seen him use it. Those men killed him and his family."

"They were lynched?" Avi says.

Patrick shrugs. "No charges," he says. "Police put it down as an accident. Bad wiring, maybe. These things happen."

Avi's great-grandfather had come over from Germany before the war started. He said that by the time there were official pogroms, grassroots violence had become commonplace. A mob would burn down a Jewish-owned business on the main street in the middle of the day with half the town watching, and the next day the papers would say it had burned as a result of *Missgeschick*. Misadventure. As if sometimes cobblers' shops and tailors simply burst into flames. *There was no conspiracy*, his grandfather said, *but a consensus that the truth was not a thing to be spoken.*

"The Hive's not a perfect way of finding new Resonants," Patrick says. "It takes time. I'd guess a fifth of the Resonants we pick up have had the shit kicked out of them before we get to them. Usually by someone close. Boyfriends, mothers. A big part of their first months at Bishop is convincing them they aren't freaks or demons who deserve to die. Some we don't get to in time. Fahima has numbers on that. She always has numbers." Avi doesn't want to see those numbers for fear he'll imagine Emmeline as one of them. He thinks of every incident she's had at school in which her behavior or some kid's reaction to it necessitated a call home, an awkward conversation with a parent who, while apologetic, clearly agreed with his or her kid that the problem wouldn't have come up if Emmeline had been normal. How long before it escalates? Before Emmeline moves from mixed-race oddity, to superpowered freak, to number?

Patrick cups his hands around his mouth and shouts to one of the fliers. "Eli, keep your ankles pressed together to cut your drag. You look like a goddamn pinwheel."

"You think coming out is going to get more of you killed," Avi says.

"Bishop thinks they kill us because they don't understand us," Patrick says. "Their kid or their sister starts glowing, and they shriek 'demon' and beat them to death with a bat. He thinks if they have a word for us, a concept, we'll be safer."

"But not safe," says Avi.

"I don't think naming a group of people has ever kept them safe," Patrick says. Avi's been thinking the same thing.

He wonders if he's helping create a label that constitutes a target, only to slap it on his daughter.

"Why not quit in protest?"

"Somebody has to teach these kids how to fight," Patrick says, looking out at the students playing grab-ass in the field.

"Who will they have to fight?" Avi asks. He imagines Emmline on the front lines. Emmeline in a foxhole. Emmeline in a JLTV, lifted in the air by a blast.

"People like you," Patrick says. "Excuse me." He strides across the field toward the girl hefting boulders, warning her not to lift from the shoulder. *You're wrong*, Avi thinks. *I'd fight with you before I'd let her.* It's the sprawling, empty pledge fathers make to keep their children safe against all threats, to swing blindly at the world as it comes for their kids.

Avi wanders down the other side of the hill, half looking for Emmeline. He finds Fahima lying in the grass, massive black bug-eye sunglasses covering most of the exposed parts of her face.

"Patrick give you the doom-and-gloom speech?" she says.

"Something like that," he says, carefully lowering himself to sit next to her. He stretches his legs out in front of him, relieved to have the weight off.

Fahima waves it away. "He's a kitten," she says. "Bishop's going to be pisssed he went off script and showed you the upperclassmen. We're supposed to be putting our best faces forward. Whenever he brings his jocks out here, he gets it in his head that we're training an army."

"You're not?" Avi asks. "Training an army?"

"It'd be a pretty scraggly army," Fahima says. "We've

got fliers who can't dunk a basketball. Kids whose strength is usable only when they're throwing a tantrum. But if we were, these kids would be the front line."

"Even the tree kid?" Avi asks.

"The tree kid supplies ridiculously potent weed to most of the upperclassmen," says Fahima.

"No shit," Avi says.

Fahima nods. "I had to confiscate some once," she says. "Fucking incredible."

"You didn't kick him out?"

"We don't kick anybody out," Fahima says. "It's a sanctuary as much as it's a school. We keep our people safe for as long as they need to feel safe."

"So you're a teacher, too?"

"I'm a lot of things," says Fahima. "But yeah, I teach."

"You split your time between the lab and the academy?"

"The lab is in the basement of the academy," Fahima says, popping a long blade of grass between her teeth and grinning.

"You have Owen Curry around a bunch of kids?" It's the first threat to Emmeline that's concrete, and in Avi's head the worst, the thing he's been avoiding, happens. He sees Salem Baptist Church in Roseland, Emmeline zigzagging through the pews as Owen Curry makes his way up the center aisle like a bride.

"Owen Curry's not going anywhere," Fahima says.

"Because of the lights?"

Fahima makes a gesture between a nod and a shrug. "It's tough to explain."

"I'm already tired of that as an excuse," Avi says.

"I know. I'm trying to throw a lot at you all at once to see what sticks. So far you are the Teflon of reporters."

"I think I'm doing pretty well."

"We need you to do better," Fahima says. "Now that things have started, they are going to move very fast. No one is going to have the time to make sure you're keeping up. If we don't do this exactly right, every single one of us is going to be in a box like Owen Curry. Or worse. Even your girl."

"I'll do better," Avi says, resolved. He turns back to watch Patrick's students hone their abilities. "Are all the kids at the academy like this?"

"These are the physical kids," she says. "Their abilities tend to be, I don't know, showy? And these are upper level. Best of the best. But even these ones, when we get them back to Bishop, they'll be slightly less impressive. That's why I come out here." She taps her temple. "Up the ol' abilities."

"What changes?"

Fahima lowers her glasses so she can glare at him over the tops. "There's fewer of *you* around."

"Me?" Avi asks.

She scratches an itch high up on her forehead, under her hijab. "Have you heard anyone use the word *Damp* yet?"

"Darren Helms called me a Damp," Avi says. "I assumed it meant someone who's not like you all."

"Most of us call you guys baseliners," she says. "Damp is kind of a shitty thing to call someone."

"I got that impression," he says. "Reminded me of when kids used to call me a kike at school."

"No one ever called me anything but Muslim," she says.

"Sometimes the name of a thing is bad enough. But yeah, Damp is of that proud tradition. Standard exonym. Some of the kids think having baseliners around dampens their abilities."

"And you're saying it does?"

She shrugs. "I'm saying Kevin Bishop is a smart man, and there has to be some reason he put a school packed with 500 very powerful teenagers in the middle of a city of 20 million people." Avi thinks of dynamite sticks packed in boxes of hay. In the movies, when one character assures another it's safe, the audience knows the explosion's coming. He pushes the image away.

"So," Fahima says after a pause, "have you figured out what Owen can do?"

Avi remembers the smooth edges of the blast radius, the lack of debris. He sees the little girl running through the pews of Salem Baptist.

"He negates matter," he says. "Destroys it outright."

"He *nulls* it," Fahima says. "That's the kid's favorite word other than *cattle* and maybe *fuck*. Except you can't negate matter. It's a basic law of physics. In any closed system, the amount of mass and energy is conserved. At first I thought he was moving it somewhere. But from what I can find, no one's reported a mall food court showing up in their backyard."

"What if he teleports it out into space?" Avi asks.

"That's not bad," Fahima says, nodding. "But via what medium? Even an Einstein-Rosen bridge requires an extra dimension. And as much as I hate to believe it, this is what I have come to conclude. That there is an extra dimension out there. And resonating is us connecting to that."

"So you're getting your powers from the fourth dimension?" he asks. He can't keep the skepticism out of his voice.

"We don't say *powers*," Fahima says. "We say *abilities*. You have to think of them that way. Extensions of what humans can do. That's all they are. Otherwise you start thinking of us as something other than human."

"You call yourselves something other than human," he says.

"It's our endonym; we get to decide. But it's a bullshit position to be in. Deciding what you want to be called. If I call myself a Muslim American, I'm marginalized. I call myself an American and I erase my heritage. I call myself a Muslim and I'm labeling myself as a threat. All the choices fucking suck."

"Resonant Americans," Avi says. He tests the words out. He sees them in 48-point type on the cover of the *Trib*.

"Most Americans," Fahima continues, "the first Muslim they ever heard of was Osama bin Laden. But the first openly queer person they encountered was on *Will & Grace*. That's what we need. One of us to show up on a sitcom. We need to be the wacky neighbor or the sassy best friend. Before they meet people like Owen Curry."

"You think there are more like him?" Avi asks.

"He's not the first," she says. "Bishop's usually better at finding them before they cause trouble. I think that's what's got him shaken. Like someone was hiding the kid."

The flying duo swoops down close enough to ruffle Avi's hair and flap the ends of Fahima's hijab. Emmeline, giving chase, stops near Avi and Fahima. She's out of breath from laughing and running.

"Daddy, they can fly," she says.

"I know, Leener," he says. "It's pretty amazing."

"Do you think I'll be able to fly?" she asks Fahima. Avi leans forward, hoping for a definite answer even if it only winnows down the options. Of all of them, Fahima seems like the only one who's telling him anything.

"I think whatever your ability is, it's going to be fucking amazing," says Fahima.

"Fucking amazing," Emmeline says. She laughs and sprints off after the flying kids.

"Thanks a lot for that," says Avi.

"Swearing's the least of your problems," Fahima says. "Can I ask?"

"Ask what?"

"What happened to your leg?"

"Lost it."

"You check under the couch?" Fahima asks. "Sometimes when I lose something, it's under the couch."

"I checked," he says. He's grateful to her for the joke. It makes him feel a little more normal.

"I could build you a better one," Fahima says.

"This one's all right."

"Bullshit," she says. "I bet it chafes something awful. And how does it respond when you don't have your full body weight on it, when you're pressing from the knee? Like on stairs? For shit, right?" Avi shrugs. These are downsides he's come to accept. "I swear I could build you a better one," Fahima says. "That's what I do, by the way. I build things. If that hasn't been obvious. I could splice the wires into your existing nerve endings. It could have intercoordinated muscle groups."

He's not sure what some of the things she's saying even mean. Nothing like that ever comes up in the forums he visits. There's something scary about it, like the early parts of a science fiction story. A robot leg that slowly takes over the amputee's whole body. "Maybe some other time," he says.

"Whatever you say," Fahima says. "It's your fucking leg. But listen, this shit is only as strange as you let yourself think it is. Telling yourself it isn't real, that this isn't your life, it'll fuck you up. You and the kid both."

At the bottom of the hill, Emmeline lies in the grass, arms folded across her chest. Bryce, the tree kid, kneels down next to her. He whispers to the ground, and flowers begin to sprout and blossom underneath her. It reminds Avi of the time-lapse nature films they used to watch in school in which a dead raccoon putrefied in seconds. The stems of the flowers grow thick. Collectively, pushed by Bryce's will, or his words, or his fourth-dimensional energy, they lift Emmeline a few inches toward the sky.

FADE AWAY AND RADIATE

The bell rings for the end of ninth period, and Carrie knows she's missed her chance. She's shit as a spy. But it's like Waylon said: What does she have to say to him anyway? What makes her opinion so all-fucking important? She puts in her earbuds and clicks on a Sleater-Kinney album that blares into her ears, sweetly obliterating all thought. She's about to head upstairs to self-recriminate when she spots the reporter in an empty hallway on the sixth floor. He leans back against the wall, looks both ways, then puts his head in his hands and sinks down into a crouch. She yanks the earbuds out. She can hear him breathing in deep, panicked breaths. She comes up to fully visible and squats down next to him.

"Mr. Hirsch," she says. "Are you all right?"

Avi jumps, then turns to her, wiping his eyes. He examines Carrie's face.

"You were in Sarah's class," he says. "I kept . . . I kept almost seeing you."

Carrie shrugs. "That's my thing," she says.

"You were invisible?"

"More like 'relatively nonperceptible,'" she says. "Where's your kid?"

"She's with Sarah," he says. "She's getting a tutorial in Hivesomething." He takes out a manila folder full of papers and pamphlets. Some of them Carrie's seen before. The dull, information-heavy documents about the school given to prospective students, the shiny brochures given to their parents. The truth and the half-truth. It's interesting they've handed Avi both sets. "I've got it in here somewhere. I feel like I'm learning a foreign language."

"They're teaching her to form a Hivebody," says Carrie. "It's so she can talk to people in the Hive. It's good. It'll keep her connected to us after she leaves."

"I'm wondering if she should leave," Avi says.

Carrie looks around. Posters for field trips to the Met, movie night in the common room on the tenth floor, Spanish club. Sometimes Bishop is exactly like any other high school. Then Lloyd Tynion's face phases through a sign-up sheet for choir auditions. He looks both ways down the hall, then emerges from the wall and runs toward the cafeteria.

"It's a good place," she says. Avi nods, though he looks skeptical. Carrie knows this is her moment, the spotlight waiting, the microphone gleaming. She doesn't have a thought formed, so she decides to start talking, to learn the road by walking it, just as Miquel knew she would.

"The first thing anyone asks when you start here is, *What was your first time like?*" she says. "First week, you answer that a hundred times. The best thing is to get an audience. Tell everyone in one shot. Savvy noobs hold out their whole first day and spill in the student lounge postdinner. Or they wait until after lights-out, when anyone who's not fucking or getting high meets up in the Hive to shoot the shit.

"If you're real lucky, you have a first-time story so bizarre that it spreads on its own. My friend Leticia, her first time was during her first time. Her other first time. She levitated the bed she was fucking on until her boyfriend's ass was bumping the ceiling fan of her room. He screamed, then she screamed, then the bed came crashing down. Her mother was downstairs saying her rosary and busted in on them. Everybody knows that story. I think it'll stay here after we're gone. Like the way third-graders are always telling the same jokes you told when you were in third grade. You ever notice that?"

Avi nods, but Carrie's talking not so much to him as through him. He's a line out, a conduit to the larger world she's been quietly coerced into hiding from. "My first time is less racy, but it's different enough that Fahima Deeb uses it as an example in her Ability Theory class," she says. "Like a thought experiment. *Can you have your ability fully manifested and not know about it?* Your first time is an event. A bird talks to you. Your hand bursts into blue flames. You sprout a second face on the side of your regular face, and it starts singing show tunes."

"Wait, is that real?"

"Huh?" says Carrie, broken out of her trance. "Oh, yeah, Francis? He lives at the Commune. Obviously." She watches Avi nod again, although the look on his face is still confused. "So after it happens, you react. You freak out. Or the people around you freak out. Maybe you get beaten. Maybe you go nuts. And then someone in the Hive spots you and tells you what's happening. You're saved.

"I didn't notice. Not all at once. I was thirteen. I lived in Deerfield, Illinois. It's sort of near Chicago but not near enough. I started to notice people were paying less attention to me. I stopped getting called on in class or picked for teams in gym. I wasn't superpopular or anything. Sort of in the middle. These things happen, and I didn't think much about it. Then my so-called boyfriend ghosted me in the hall between classes. I texted him right from the next class. He said *didn't see you*, but that was bullshit because he looked right at me. I thought *at*. I guess *through*. Anyway, I didn't want to come off like a stalker. I texted *k*, and I didn't think about it for a while.

"It got worse. My parents started leaving me out of conversations at dinner. My brother stopped pestering me all the time. It was nice at first. Everything was quieter.

"And there were the dreams. At least I thought they were dreams. Every night I dreamed I was at a huge party. It was packed with people, but none of them could see or hear me. The dreams wouldn't come just when I was asleep. I drifted to the party in class or listening to music in my room. It made things worse, the isolation. Even in my dreams I was invisible."

Carrie pauses, remembering just how bad those weeks were. The worst parts get lost when you're telling a story. The lesson of a story is that you lived to tell it. If that's the end, how do you communicate the point where you were pretty sure you wouldn't or didn't even want to? The time in the middle when surviving was unlikely or even hateful? For weeks Carrie knew what was happening but didn't have a name to put to it. She was fading out of the world and couldn't find a way to stop it. And she gave up. She became convinced that she would disappear entirely and that this was the best outcome. The alternative was to stay as she was, a ghost, haunting her own life. Unable to voice that to Avi, she picks her story up on the other side.

"Fahima and Sarah found me in a diner," she says. "I used to go there because there was one waitress who would always see me. I used to try to figure out when she was working. Not because I was going to starve otherwise. It just felt good. Having her see me.

"She wasn't there that day, so I was just sitting. Fahima and Sarah stood out right away. Sarah had Cortex with her, which is a total health code violation. But they walked right in and sat down in the booth across from me. I remember Cortex snuck under the table and lay down on my feet.

"Sarah said they'd been looking all over for me. *We knew you existed*, she said. *We kept looking in the wrong place.* Then Fahima said they had to look at all the places I wasn't, and when they ruled those out, they knew I'd be here, in this booth at the diner."

"That doesn't make any sense," Avi says.

"No," Carrie says. Being found was a miracle. The fairy tale quality of it, the dreamy strangeness of that day in the diner is precious to her. She never thinks to interrogate it, to make sense out of it. It's enough that it happened. "They told me about what I was. That there were others like me. That *they* were like me. They told me about the Bishop Academy. Fahima said there was a place for me there if I wanted it. You grow up reading fantasy novels where some poor girl in a drudging life finds out she's a princess. The whole world makes you ready for a moment like this to happen. Even before I started to disappear, my life felt ill-fitting, maybe, designed for someone else. I was attached to it because, you know, it was mine. Watching my own life from inside it, I saw its limits. My boyfriend was cute, but he didn't give a shit about music or books or anything. My parents were nice, but they just ended up with kids, like you do. If they wanted them, they hadn't wanted one like me. Fahima and Sarah offered me a way out. I never wanted anything more."

"So they just took you away?" There's a look on his face somewhere between fear and anger. Carrie never thought about how it might feel from a parent's point of view. No one worries about the farmer whose daughter, secretly a princess the entire time, finally is whisked away to the castle.

"They didn't just kidnap me," she assures him. "They came to my house the next day. They were wearing business suits. They looked like salespeople. My mom let them in and told my dad to go make coffee. Fahima gave her a brochure."

"Like these?" Avi asks. He fans out brochures like he's about to do a card trick.

"Yep," Carrie says. She's starting to see why they brought him here. It's not about him; it's about the kid. They could have picked any reporter, but they picked this guy. It's got nothing to do with him. He's the get-one-free that comes with the buy-one. Carrie feels bad for him.

"The Bishop Academy for the Gifted and Talented," he reads.

"That's the one they used," Carrie says. "Some kids' parents get the Academy for the Arts pitch, but I've never been all that arty. My mother even asked what my talent was, and Fahima said, *She falls more on the gifted side.*" Carrie laughs, although it isn't funny. It hurts to remember her mother essentially asking a stranger, *What's so special about my daughter?* Weren't parents supposed to know? Shouldn't she have had a list? Just as bad is remembering the look of surprise on her parents' faces when Carrie's name was brought up. It was as if they'd forgotten her completely and were mildly inconvenienced to be reminded.

"My mom asked how much it cost," she said. "Nothing about college placement or extracurricular activities. I don't even know if she asked where it was."

She clears her throat, pushing the worst parts aside. "I spent the rest of the week wrapping up things at my old school. There wasn't much to do. I'd slipped off the radar of my friends. My teachers had to be reminded they had me in class. Boyfriend was dating someone else. My last day at Deerfield Middle, I walked through the halls, trailing my fingers along the lockers. Like I was trying to make good memories to come back to later. But it was just the place I went to school because my parents got jobs in Deerfield and bought a house in that school district. It wasn't special. So I stopped.

"At the end of my last day, I sat in a stall in the girls' bathroom and wrote Carrie Was Here and the date on the door in red Sharpie. It was a stupid thing to do. I watched the ink, thinking it would fade. When it stayed, I started to cry."

I should stop, she thinks. It's all so fucking embarrassing, and she's lost the point somewhere. There's something in her story bigger than her, something that should matter to him, but she hasn't found it. She can tell by the way his eyebrows are pinched together. Maybe the only way is to keep telling.

"My parents drove me to Chicago for the flight to New York. I had one suitcase. They were supposed to mail me my books, but they never did. While we were waiting at the gate, my dad kept forgetting why we were there. My flight got called, and I hugged my parents and my brother. They all seemed relieved. Like it was hard work to notice me and they were glad they didn't have to do it anymore. They could just let me go."

"It must have been better for you here," he says. It hovers between a statement and a question. He needs to know that this place is the right choice for his kid, that the minute she arrives, everything will be fixed. She considers lying to him but doesn't.

"It was Deerfield Middle all over again. At first. Fahima promised we'd start training together, but she forgot. I got thrown into classes. People looked past me in the hallways. Teachers didn't notice I was there. Then Miquel, he's my friend. He's an empath. He got a feeling when he walked by me in the hall. He stopped and looked right at me. He was the first person who did. And he said, *I'm sorry. You've been here the whole time, haven't you?*

"It was special," she says. "It meant a lot."

What she doesn't say is that she threw her arms around him and cried into his shoulder, and he hugged her back without hesitation. She keeps that part to herself. Carrie's never been able to separate her feelings for Miquel from the relief she felt in that moment. Sometimes she hears it thrumming underneath their conversations, a bass line: *Thank you for seeing me. Thank you.*

"I want to make sure you know what you're doing is important," she says. "Superimportant. It's going to decide how I live the rest of my life. I don't want to go through my life hiding. I don't want to worry every day someone will figure out what I am. It's not that much to ask to be able to be who you are. To go through the world as a whole person without keeping a part of yourself back. But it's important. I think." She hates herself for adding this, for pulling something she knows to be a fact into the watery realm of opinion.

"I want that for Emmeline," he says. "For my daughter." He shifts forward, peering down the hall as if she's coming back. "Do your parents know? What you are?"

Carrie stares at her shoes. She thinks about her parents' befuddlement the month she went vegetarian. How they thought she was a lesbian because she went out for JV volleyball. "They didn't know what I was before," she says. "They weren't those kinds of parents."

"Did they love you?"

"That's different from understanding me," Carrie says. "They loved me even if they didn't understand me."

"Do you wish you could tell them?"

"I could tell them," Carrie says.

Avi nods. "So you don't want to tell them."

Carrie thinks about it every time she calls home, which isn't more than once a month. Her parents set up a debit account for her, and sometimes they need to be reminded to put money in. Other than that, they don't talk much. She can't imagine what she'd tell them. Her parents wouldn't have the language for what she is.

"I don't want to give them more than they can handle," she says.

Avi glances back toward the faculty cafeteria. "I don't know how to talk to her about it."

Carrie laughs. "She doesn't know how to talk to you about it either," she says. "I guarantee it. Be there for her when she's ready. That's the best you'll be able to do."

A trample of feet heralds the kid's arrival, barreling down the hall toward her dad.

"Daddy, I almost did it," she says, throwing her arms around him. He totters but rights himself with his hand. "I can't talk in there yet, but I can hear what people are saying instead of just wah wah wah wah."

"That's great, Leener," he says. "You ready to go?"

"I guess. If we have to," she says. She stops, noticing Carrie for the first time. "You're the invisible girl from the art class."

"I was being superinvisible," says Carrie. "And you saw me anyway."

"Maybe I have x-ray vision," Emmeline says. She narrows her eyes down to little slits and stares hard at Carrie, who grins at her.

"Anyway, welcome to Bishop," Carrie says. "Glad you survived the experience."

"I had fun," says Emmeline.

"I hope I see you around sometime."

"I hope I *see* you around sometime," Emmeline says, pointing from her eyes to Carrie with two fingers. Then she grabs her dad's hand and hoists him up off the floor, steadying him when he momentarily wavers.

THE INTERVIEW

Kay brings home two plastic bags heavy with Chinese food and sets it out for them. When Avi asks what's the rush, she says she wants to take Emmeline Christmas shopping, which is not a thing they ever do. The fact they're keeping secrets from him is less troubling than the idea of Kay and Emmeline spending the evening together without him there. He worries she'll slip and say something that hints at where they went last week. As if she knows, Emmeline gives him a smile of feigned innocence. Whatever they're scheming, it's minor and harmless.

"I'm meeting someone later downtown," he says, "but I can take a cab."

"Hot date?" Kay asks.

"It's for this piece I'm working on," he says.

"I noticed you're working this week," Kay says. What she means is that the house is a mess. "What's the piece?"

"It's for the *Trib*," he says. "Nothing big."

"That's the way to get back into it," says Kay. Dinner is friendly, full of small talk, but they're dancing around each other like boxers at the start of a bout. Kay and Emmeline are out the door a second after the fortune cookies are cracked, and Avi heads to the attic to go over his notes one more time. He's just gotten the ladder dropped when his phone rings. He stares at Louis's name on the screen, wondering how he'd managed to forget about the Homeland agent this entire time.

"I wanted to check in," Louis says. "I've got a department meeting tomorrow morning, and I was hoping you had something for me."

"Nothing's adding up," Avi says. "I don't think I'm going to be any help."

There's a pause. "You sure?"

"It's that girl," Avi says. "The girl in the church. She was Emmeline's age. I can't have that in my head right now. I can't get close enough to this to be any help."

The pause is longer this time. Avi's lie hangs on the line between them.

"What's a Resonant, Avi?" Louis asks.

"I don't know what you're talking about." Avi's pulse speeds up, and his palms seep sweat, making the phone slippery in his hand.

"The attachment I sent you had a Trojan horse," Louis says. "We don't let information like this out without keeping tabs on it. I'm remote into your computer right now."

"What the fuck, Louis?"

"It's the job, Avi," says Louis. "You're not a virgin, so stop acting like it. What's the academy? What the fuck kind of cult is Owen Curry part of? Have you been contacted by members of his group?"

"I haven't been contacted by anyone," Avi says.

"Did they threaten you?" Louis asks. "Did they threaten Emmeline and Kay? We can bring you in. We can protect you. You can't deal with people like this, Avi. You can't trust them. They don't think like we do."

"You don't know what you're talking about."

"We can protect you. You need to let me help you on this."

"You can't," Avi says.

"Do you know where Owen Curry is?"

Avi hangs up the phone and turns it off. The call came from Louis's office number. It's a half-hour drive from here to there. Avi wonders how likely it is that Louis will hop in his car and drive out to Rogers Park to arrest him or that he made the call with a team already waiting outside. He listens to the house on Jarvis Avenue. Sometimes he thinks of the house as an extension of himself, like a snail's shell, something he's grown to protect his fragile body. He knows the spots under the hallway carpet that have too much give and the stairs that protest when you step on them. He knows how it sounds when the breeze batters it, the creaks it makes as it settles in for the night. He listens for a knock at the door, for the sounds of them breaking it down. After a few paralyzed minutes, he goes up the ladder and prints out everything he has about the Bishop Academy, about Resonants, then deletes the files. He prints the half-finished article and the e-mail exchange with Carol at the *Trib* and Richardson at *The Atlantic*. He shuts the computer down.

Tomorrow, he thinks, *I'll buy a laptop and transcribe the article. I'll buy myself a gun.*

o

Bishop let Avi pick the bar, but there's a difference between choosing the setting and being allowed to choose the setting. Avi chose the Magician, a crowded hipster cocktail bar in Wicker Park. Everything about this sit-down is dictated by Bishop. Every move he makes broadcasts that Bishop holds the power in their relationship. Journalists have nothing to do until their interview subjects show up, and most savvy interview subjects intuit this. The fact that Avi's had to wait a week for a one-on-one meeting is testament to the fact that this is Bishop's world Avi's wandering around in. The man holds no office more imposing than high school principal, yet Avi thinks of him as a representative of all Resonants, their leader.

Avi's late, but Bishop's a half hour later. He steps out of the men's room and stands at the end of the bar, assessing the place rather than looking for Avi. As with every time Avi's seen him, he wears a suit coat and jeans, dress shirt open to the second button. He has the taut skin Avi associates with ascetics and long-term prisoners, and it makes it difficult to place his age except as anywhere between fifty and seventy. Kimani must have dropped him off in one of the stalls. Insisting Bishop come "all the way to Chicago" was a power play on Avi's part that amounted to nothing.

Bishop steps out of his office to wherever he needs to be, Avi thinks. *Not all doors connect to the room adjacent.* He wonders if the lines are worth writing down. He files them in the part of his memory that stores fragments, where they float detached like half-remembered snippets of melody.

"This is such a relief," Bishop says as he sits on the stool next to Avi. "Do you know how long it's been since I've been to a bar? When you're away so long, they seem magical. You speak the name of the thing you want, and it appears before you." He turns to the bartender, who smirked through this speech. "I'd like a gin martini. Something middle shelf. Dry, up, with olives, please." The bartender sets to making his drink, and Bishop grins like a kid about to get ice cream.

"Isn't it like that for you all the time?" Avi asks. "Do you have much trouble getting what you want?"

"Have we started?" Bishop asks.

"I was thinking we'd get a booth," Avi says.

"No, let's stay here. I'm worn out on cloak-and-dagger meetings. Let's be overheard." The bartender delivers Bishop's drink, then disappears. "And no," Bishop says. "It isn't like that for me all the time. It could be, but it isn't."

"Why not?"

"Do you go around punching everyone in the face to get what you want?" Bishop asks.

"Of course not."

"But you could."

"I could."

"Exactly the same thing," says Bishop. "A difference of degree rather than kind."

"So what is your ability?" Avi asks.

Bishop leans over the bar and sips from his drink. "It's rude to ask," he says. "It's *considered* rude. We have an etiquette about these things. You develop for yourselves etiquettes and ethics. The closest I can think of would be it's like asking someone flat out if they're gay or pregnant. It's just not done."

"The benefit of being ignorant is you get to ask rude questions," says Avi.

"But not necessarily get them answered," Bishop says. "For you, I'll make an exception." He plucks an olive from his glass and slices it in half with his front teeth. Without any warning, all movement in the bar stops. Men making important points sustain hand gestures while their dates keep gazing off past their ears. The bartender pours a glass of wine until the glass overflows, the bottle emptying onto the back bar. The piped-in electrojazz in the background is the only sound that continues except for the whir of ceiling fans.

Avi swivels on his stool. The woman next to him has her drink halfway to her lips. The glass is tilted. The liquid sloshes gently, short of the rim. He reaches out to touch her, wondering if she'll be cold or hard. He puts his hand on her bare arm. It's warm flesh, nothing unusual. He grips it and can feel her brachial pulse, steady. He lets go and turns back to Bishop.

"I'm in their minds," Bishop says. "All of them at once. At the academy, we split telepaths into readers and writers, although most can do a little of both. Some writers can only suggest. Others can command. I am, strictly speaking, *not* a telepath. I'm an omnipath."

Bishop chomps on the remainder of his first olive. Motion returns to the bar with a lurch. Only the bartender notices the pause, cursing the inexplicable puddle of wine dribbling onto his shoes.

A drop of blood falls from Bishop's nose into his drink. It expands into a pink nebula and hangs suspended. Bishop's hand goes to his nostril. He wipes away the trickle that runs down to the edge of his lip. He turns his hand outward, two fingers up like a Boy Scout pledging. The fingertips are smeared with a pale pink liquid. "Too light to be blood, right?"

"What is it?" Avi asks, leaning in to look.

"The closest correct answer would be to say it's my thoughts, running down my nose like snot," Bishop says. "Another answer would be to say it's my Resonance. My ability." He takes the spear that impales his olives and stirs the drop of blood into his drink until it's no longer discernible. "Or you could say it's Resonance. Not mine specifically but ours in general. The shared source of our abilities."

"Running down your nose like snot," says Avi.

"With some old-fashioned blood mixed in for color. When you find out how the magic happens, it's never as magical as you hope."

"How *does* the magic happen?" Avi asks.

"I'm not entirely sure," Bishop says. "It's a frustrating thing for a scientist not to be sure."

"You're a scientist?"

"I was," he says. "I was a mechanical engineer."

"There're no records of you anywhere," says Avi. "It's like you don't exist."

"Yet here I am, existing," Bishop says, holding out his hands as proof. "I worked for the government during the war. When we were done, some of us became public figures. Oppenheimer. Fermi. Bethe. Some of us disappeared. It's likely I would have disappeared afterward anyway. Taken an academic job somewhere. Pined for the bomb like an ex-lover. Many of those men and women went on to lead very sad, very dull lives."

"You worked on the Manhattan Project?"

Bishop nods, and Avi's heart leaps. This is the mother of all bombs, the God bomb. He's read book after book on the Manhattan Project, biographies of all the major scientists, memoirs of women who did computation at Los Alamos, transcriptions of the security lecture Robert Serber gave to new arrivals. He has a hundred new questions for Bishop, but none of them relate to the story at hand.

"How old *are* you?" he asks.

"Too old," says Bishop. "We should die when our ideas become obsolete. A red jewel in your hand should blink, and someone takes you off the board. It'd be a mercy."

"Did the bomb give you your abilities?"

"I assumed it was radiation for a long time," Bishop says. "It was the fifties. We had no idea what radiation could do. We thought it would mutate ants and scantily clad women until they were monstrously large. We thought it would make us glow in the dark. Why couldn't it give me abilities? I taught myself genetics so I could comb my genes looking for the glitch. I expected to find something entirely new. A fifth nucleotide. Gene X. I spent years looking before a friend of mine pointed me in another direction."

"Who was this friend?" Avi asks.

"A colleague. A close friend," he says. "Another scientist on the project. He was a physicist. Theoretical stuff. Beautiful man, like a film star. And brilliant. Maybe not as brilliant as Feynman or Szilard. But beautiful. It happened to him, too.

His abilities were similar to mine. Moving things around in people's heads. But his thinking on it was different. He thought the bomb was like a tuning fork struck against a glass. That it set certain people in tune with something elsewhere. There was a vibration that served as a connection. A conduit. Once there were more of us, this made more sense. There was no genetic link between, say, me and a kid in the Ozarks who could produce perfect duplicates of himself, like an amoeba dividing. If the genetics were insufficient, the biology was even more so. Where did the *matter* come from to produce those duplicates? Where did the energy come from that shot out of Sam Guthridge's eyes?" The name startles Avi: the dead boy in Wyoming Patrick told him about. He sees pain pass over Bishop's face mentioning it, and he wonders if Bishop remembers the names of all of their dead. "The human body can't produce that on its own. It would burn itself up. We had to be drawing it from somewhere."

"A source," says Avi.

"With a capital *S*," Bishop says. "I've always capitalized it. We thought of it as a place. A physical location outside of our current dimension. We tried to access it directly with no luck. That's how we created the Hive."

Avi notices the repeated use of *we* but decides he'll dig into it later. "I don't think I understand the Hive," he says.

"It's a place. Something like a place," Bishop says. "It's between here and there. There are things I won't tell you about it and things I can't because I don't know. A long time ago, I stopped trying to figure out where our abilities came from and focused on what we could do with them."

"What about your colleague, what was his name again?" Avi asks, knowing Bishop hasn't mentioned the name. "Did he keep trying to figure them out?"

"My friend's investigations into the Source led him far afield," Bishop says. "Eventually it got him killed."

"How did he die?"

"I killed him," Bishop says. Bishop signals to the bartender for another drink, then turns back to Avi with a face that indicates he's finished with this subject. This is the reason to be afraid of him, thinks Avi. Not because he's someone willing to kill. Because he believes every decision he makes is justified. Avi's met true believers. Government agents. Insurgent leaders. The object of belief is irrelevant because ultimately the object of belief is themselves. They can be incredible forces for good, but they're easily suborned, led wrong by their self-confidence. He wonders if Bishop is a man he can hand the care of his daughter over to, then realizes with a chill that even if he doesn't send Emmeline to the academy, the rest of her life will be spent in a world populated by Kevin Bishop's disciples.

"Why did you hide?" Avi asks.

"It was what I knew," Bishop says. "I moved back to the city after the war. Lived there most of my life, when I wasn't traveling. People forget or they have trouble imagining it, but people were being arrested for being gay well into the seventies. In New York. We had to keep ourselves secret, but also we had to be able to recognize one another if we didn't want to be alone. We developed languages, ways of seeing and signaling. We had to be legible to one another and illegible to everyone else. We built a world within the world.

"The way Resonance works, the way we can instantly know our own, combined with the implicit threat we present to others. It seemed to me the only answer was to hide. We could have one another. We could be loved without being afraid."

"Why not change everyone's minds?" says Avi. "Why not take over the world?"

Bishop laughs, a bold thing that comes from deep in his chest and spreads out into the room. After a few seconds, it breaks into coughing. He recovers in time to thank the bartender for his second drink.

"I can barely keep the school in order," he says. "Why the fuck would I want to rule the world?"

"You could be a philosopher king," says Avi. "A benevolent god."

"At best, I'm a gardener," he says. "I tend to my charges. I bend them a little toward the light."

"You pull out the weeds," Avi says.

"Owen Curry," Bishop says, looking down at the bar. "Will Owen be in your article?"

"I haven't decided."

"I'd rather you didn't. Not right at the beginning," Bishop says. It isn't an order, only an expression of preference, but Avi feels the force of it. "We're learning how to police our own. For a long time, my methods were less humane."

"There were others who were bad?"

"Some," says Bishop.

"And you killed them?"

"I did," Bishop says. His voice is bright, as if Avi had

asked him if he was enjoying his drink. "Part of me thinks I should have killed Owen Curry. I lie awake in my quarters, thinking I could go into the cell and end him and no one would blame me. What would your friend in Homeland Security do if I dumped Owen Curry's corpse on his desk?"

"He'd give you a fucking medal," says Avi.

Bishop nods. "Fahima told you about the effect baseliners have on our abilities," he says. "Being around people who aren't Resonants dampens them. It reduces what we can do. But the opposite is true, too. The more of us there are, the stronger we get. The school sits in a kind of balance. The students are stronger for being together but are held back by being in the middle of the city. The risk of one of us being too powerful frightens me. I was out hunting monsters, but I was also a population control. Which, when I say it out loud, sounds monstrous."

"You were culling?" Avi asks. It's not exactly the question he wants to ask, since he already knows the answer. He needs to know the circumstances under which Bishop would take a life. Would it have to be someone who'd gone bad, irreparably evil? Might it be someone who made a mistake? Or someone who was too powerful, as powerful as Bishop and Fahima believe Emmeline is going to be?

"I was willing to yank out a seedling that might grow to be a weed," he says. "Abilities like ours in the hands of teenagers is a terrifying thought on its own. With the idea that those power levels would increase as the Resonant population increased . . . Well, I was more preemptive than I should have been. Too many of us would be too much."

"Fahima says there are more of you."

"Every day," he says. "It's a slow curve upward, but it's speeding up. Maybe that's good for the world. Maybe that's what the world wants, if you can think of the world as having desires. My friend used to talk about the Source as if it were sentient. I don't know that I ever believed it, but I had the sense I'd been picked for this. Even before it happened. Before the Trinity test. I remember putting my hand on the Gadget and feeling it wanted something from me. There was some plan in place that I was part of." Avi thinks about the IED that took his leg, the feeling that that particular bomb had been waiting for him, that they'd been moving toward each other his whole life. "Planning indicates sentience, the existence of a plan. Why couldn't the world be sentient, too? I'm not going to stop it by executing every thermic teenager who torches his middle school. It's not for me to decide."

"What about the decision to go public?" Avi says. "Why do you get to decide that?"

"I was the one who told them to hide," Bishop says.

"And they listened?" Avi asks. It's something he hasn't been able to make any sense of. These people, these Resonants, have existed for almost seventy years. And in all that time, not one has gone rogue, not one has gone to the press and announced himself. You could argue that Owen Curry had, but Owen Curry only proved the point. He'd blown up twenty-one people, and the public didn't know about him or that there were more like him.

"I'm going to tell you this because I don't think you'll understand it, which makes it safe to say," says Bishop. "The

Hive is *like* a place, but it's not a place. It's also like a conduit through which the energies that provide our abilities pass. It's not necessarily transparent. That's not exactly the word, but maybe you get my meaning." He holds up his drink between himself and Avi so that the Christmas lights behind the bar twinkle inside it. "Light can pass through glass, but it's bent in its passing. A lens carver knows this and can use the properties of the glass to shape light."

"You're right," says Avi. "I have no idea what you're talking about."

"I like to think I've been a good influence, is all," Bishop says. "I like to think that I've bent our light toward the good." He lowers his glass. "Any other questions?"

"What's Emmeline's ability?"

"I can't answer that any more than you could have guessed what she'd grow up to be on the day she was born," Bishop says. "We look at them for hints. We jump to conclusions at each developmental milestone. *He walked at eight months, he's going to be an Olympic runner. She knows so many words already, she'll be a novelist.* But in the end, they turn out to be themselves and we can only sit by and watch. Anything else?"

"Do you have kids?"

Bishop smiles. "Hundreds. Thousands."

"Why are you paying my wife?" Avi says. He expects it to be a question that stops time, but Bishop rolls over it as if it were nothing.

"I wanted her involved in a way she'd understand," he says. "Same as you. I made a promise a long time ago to keep the two of you in the fold."

"A promise to whom?" Avi says.

Bishop tips his glass all the way back, gulping the last bit of gin. His head clicks to the side, and he smiles, contented, then returns to the conversation, staring into the bottom of his glass. "Emmeline."

"What does that mean?" Avi asks, setting his glass down harder than he intended. Of all the advantages Bishop holds, this one is the most unfair. Avi would trade every other answer to know what Bishop knows about Emmeline. But before his anger can build, he feels a cool wave wash over his brain. It's as if he's gotten his answer even though he doesn't know what it is. It's the first time Avi is aware of Bishop using his ability on him. It's like being shoved away from the things you actually think while also being made to feel completely at ease with being shoved. Later he'll understand what's been done, and he'll question every interaction he's had with Kevin Bishop.

"These glasses are very large," Bishop says. "The ones I'm used to are half this size. I think I'm a little drunk. Let's pick this up again tomorrow or next week. I'm assuming we have time."

"My editors think it should wait until the new year," Avi says. He's nagged by something he's forgotten, a question he meant to ask. "They're worried if it comes out around the holidays, it'll read like some hokey Christmas miracle story."

"These are the editors at the *Tribune*?" Bishop says.

"The first piece will be in the *Trib*," says Avi. "The in-depth stuff will be in *The Atlantic*. First issue of the new year."

Bishop slides his glass across the bar and signals for the

bill. "That's good. I like that," he says. "Beginnings. Fresh starts and that kind of thing. It's strange, knowing that people out there know about us. Not bad. New."

The bartender arrives, and Bishop covers their drinks. Avi hasn't asked him where the money comes from. How he bought a building on 57th and Lexington, how he pays faculty and staff without apparently charging tuition. There are so many questions left.

"What about the academy?" he asks. "Will you keep it hidden?"

Bishop smiles: an old New York grin full of slightly crooked teeth. "I haven't decided," he says. "I'm thinking it might not be my decision to make. Have a good night, Avi. Happy holidays if I don't see you." He signs the credit card slip and excuses himself, disappearing back into the men's room and the door that waits for him there.

THE PAGEANT

Kay tells him they're going to meet her mother out. It's unusual for Kay to drive, but she plays this off with a half-truth. "You're too responsive in the snow," she says. "You start to slide, and you slam the brakes and try to correct. You have to go with it."

"Fine," Avi says. He spends the drive fiddling with the radio, trying to find a station that isn't playing Christmas carols. When Kay pulls into the parking lot of First Corinthians in Roseland, her mother's church, Avi glares at her.

"What is this, Kay?"

"It's not a big deal," she says. The moment they're inside, Emmeline is whisked away by one of the church's numerous old ladies, who separates children from their parents and herds them to the back of the church. Kay and Avi take seats next to her mother, who is buzzing with excitement. As the preacher starts in on the nativity story, Kay finds Avi's hand and squeezes it reassuringly. He doesn't respond, doesn't return the ping she's sent him. She has him trapped, with no way to express his anger. So he seethes, bolted into the pew.

A couple comes to the front of the church dressed in robes.

His brown, hers blue. She holds a baby. When Emmeline steps out of the choir entrance, clutching a shepherd's crook, a stuffed sheep tucked under her arm like a football, Avi's hand gives Kay's an involuntary squeeze. They will always be joined by the live wire of their daughter.

A dozen shepherds, none taller than Emmeline, mill about the front of the church, singing "Angels We Have Heard on High," followed by "O Come All Ye Faithful" and "Hark the Herald Angels Sing," flanked by taller kids in brilliant white robes and paper wings. The sound they create, thirty kids without a tenor or baritone among them, has weight and light. It's a physical thing, a new presence in the church, and for a moment, watching his daughter become part of it, Avi feels a calm settle over him, a thin sheath of joy protecting him from the world and the world to come.

After the pageant, families flood into the cold. Kay's mother makes the three of them pose for a picture in front of the church. Kay and Avi huddle around Emmeline as if they can protect her from the cut of the wind. They close ranks on her instinctively, and the naturalness of the motion makes Avi think, *We're going to be all right.* They should have been better than all right. On some parallel earth, versions of Kay and Avi lead fantastic lives. They communicate through telepathy rather than hand squeezes and glares. They have flaws, but they don't feel broken. They don't exhaust each other. When Avi smiles for the picture, it's with resentment of and resignation to the state of being all right.

"I'm sort of hungry," Emmeline says as they reach the van.

"It's late," says Avi. "We should get her home."

"There's a place right up the road," Kay says, stepping around him to unlock the driver's side and take the wheel. She drives them past the wreckage of Salem Baptist. In the dark, it's only a lump of scrapped wood, but Avi wonders how Kay can fail to notice it. It glows in his awareness, a site that's taken on such importance in his life that the last month feels as if it's emerged from that crater, a new and stumbling thing fallen to earth. They pass the Roseland Rest and pull into the parking lot of a strip mall where the neon of Planet Chicken bleeds under the streetlights.

"I'll wait in the car," Avi says.

"It's zero degrees out here," Kay says. He's earned some points with her by not complaining in front of her mother, but her threshold for annoyance with him is set low.

"Daddy, barbecue sauce," Emmeline says as if Avi were unaware of the invention. Kay shuts off the car, and they go in. Planet Chicken is brightly lit, white fluorescent lights verging on blue. Emmeline orders nuggets, a mode of conveyance for barbecue sauce. The girl behind the counter slips Emmeline two extra packets, then looks up at Avi to take his order.

"Hey," she says. Avi gives her a quick chin up of recognition and orders a wing combo, looking down into his wallet as he pays.

"I was disappointed you weren't an angel," Kay says in the booth. "But you were the most amazing shepherd I've ever seen. That sheep didn't make a peep."

"You have to whisper to them," Emmeline says. She spoons deep crimson sauce into her mouth via nugget. "Quiet in their ears. Especially in front of big crowds. Sheep hate crowds." Avi was so caught up thinking about the pageant as an attack against him, he failed to register its effect on Emmeline. The girl beams in a way they rarely see at home, where she usually only glows. The little candle of her happiness becomes a flare.

Emmeline isn't a blip. She's more like a flare.

Avi excuses himself and walks swiftly toward the bathrooms, his mouth swimming in saliva. He dry heaves, then checks himself in the mirror. His eyes are glassy with tears, the way they get when he smokes pot or throws up. Kay gives him a *what the actual fuck* look when he gets back to the table. He sits down and puts a napkin over the remainder of his wings. He doesn't speak for the rest of the meal.

They wait until Emmeline's asleep to have the argument. Whoever moves first decides what the fight will look like, what will be the terms and the limits. Generally this is Kay, but tonight it's Avi.

"Was that supposed to be some kind of ambush?" he says. "Dragging me to church like that?"

"To see your daughter," Kay says. "It was a surprise."

"Bullshit it was a surprise," he says. "You and your mother and your evangelical shit."

"What are you even talking about?" Kay says.

"How did Emmeline know all those songs? Those hymns?" Avi says. "You've been indoctrinating her."

"I've been taking her there to practice once a week all month," says Kay. "Not that you fucking noticed we were gone. Besides, everyone knows those songs. *You* know those songs."

Avi thinks of a Seder they took Emmeline to last year at the home of one of the partners at Kay's firm. Avi, empty-stomach-drunk, tried to teach Emmeline the words to "Dayenu" even though he barely remembered the rapid-fire Hebrew lyrics. They laughed about it on the way home, the three of them shouting gobbledygook to the song's bouncy tune.

On a parallel earth, he thinks, *Kay and Avi are doing better than all right. On Earth-X, they are fantastically in love.*

"What happened at the restaurant?" she says.

"Food poisoning," says Avi, turning away from her.

"Bullshit it was food poisoning," she says. He can tell she gets a little charge out of turning his phrase back on him. "Instant salmonella?"

"I felt sick," Avi says. "Figure it was something I ate."

"It's what you put in your head," she says. "It's dead girls and bombs creeping out of your head and rotting your guts."

"You sound like one of those books you read," Avi says. He flicks his wrist at the paperback pile on her nightstand.

Kay picks up Avi's phone from the nightstand and holds it out to him.

"Call Louis," she says. "Tell him you've got nothing. Have you even talked to an editor about this story? Are you even getting paid? Or are you chasing ghosts on your own dime?"

"You don't know what you're talking about."

"Call the *Trib* and tell them you don't need the money," she says. "Tell them your marriage is more important than—"

"You don't know what you're talking about," he shouts at her. It echoes in the sleeping house, and they both stop, shocked by the volume of it. They wait to hear if Emmeline wakes the way they did when she was a baby and some loud noise ran the risk of startling her. The shared response strengthens a sense of their history together, but it doesn't mean anything anymore. If Kay presses now, he'll fold. He has to. She could dig until what he's hiding is revealed, until she's won. But she has no interest in winning with him anymore.

"Go write your fucking story," she says. Not knowing what else to do, Avi starts toward the door.

"You know you're not going to solve this, right?" she says. "Whatever fucked up mystery case Louis dropped in your lap, you're not going to figure it out. Even if you did, it wouldn't save that girl in the church. Even if you did save her, she's not Emmeline."

It stops him, because all of this is an effort to save her. Even if Kay can't see it, even if Avi doesn't know what he's trying to save his daughter from, the goal, the dream end product now is Emmeline, safe.

"I'll be in in a little bit," he says. He closes the door gently behind him.

Avi takes a few steps down the hall and stands outside Emmeline's door. *Can you hear me?* he thinks as loudly as he can. He holds the sentence clearly in his mind, like it's printed on a page. When he doesn't get an answer, he knocks quietly so Kay won't hear. Again there's no response. Avi eases the door open.

As soon as he steps into the room, he knows something is wrong. The sound of Emmeline breathing in her sleep is written into the base code of his thoughts. A hundred nights he's stood in her doorway in the dark, listening to it, marveling at the fact she even exists, much less breathes. He's sat up with her nights when her breathing was labored and hitched, struggling to draw through snot-clogged sinus passages, or when it rattled through inflamed bronchioles. He knows how it speeds up when she has fever dreams, the change in its cadence when she moves from one level of sleep to another, like a stone dropping through wet tissue paper into waiting water. Her breathing is shallow and quick in a way he's never heard. He shuts the door behind him and crosses the room in the dark, crumbling her drawings underfoot. Standing by the side of the bed, he puts a hand on her forehead. She's cool and clammy, like granite in spring. He tries to shake her awake, but she won't stir. He knows this is not within the normal scope of illness. This is something to do with *them*, with the thing that's strange and new about Emmeline. He fumbles his phone out of his pocket and calls Bishop, but there's no answer. He calls Kimani's number. She answers after four rings, long enough that he almost hangs up and calls again.

"It's late, Avi," Kimani says, sounding sleep-fuzzy and annoyed. "What'd you need?"

"She won't wake up," he hisses, trying not to be heard. "Something is wrong, and she won't wake up."

In the middle of the wall the room shares with Avi and Kay's bedroom, the door appears, visible in the dark by the warm light that seeps from underneath it.

ABSCESS

Fahima Deeb puts the kettle on and washes up in the kitchen sink. She lays out her prayer rug, deep emerald with gold cross patterns. Watching out the window as bundled pairs brave a December night in Prospect Park, Fahima hurries through the rakat on autopilot. Isha'a is more about slowing the gears of the Rube Goldberg device of her brain than communing with the divine. She likes the mechanics of it. She turns her head to the right, to the left, murmuring her As-Salaamu-Alaikums. She makes dua, palms up as if she's about to be handed a brimming cup. Nearly inaudible in the empty apartment, she asks for the same thing she asks every night: more time. *Allah, slow down the world for me.* She stands. The water hasn't come to a boil.

Clearing off the kitchen counter, she stops at an odd bit of a drawing she'd made, scribbled over with notes. Her handwriting is a scrawl, illegible even to her. She examines the drawings, trying to make sense of them. An obelisk wired to a series of thrones or electric chairs. Something to gather energy from a group of Resonants, focus it.

"Those handheld things with the blue lights guitar players use," she mutters. "Like bowing one string at a time. Long monotone whine. Induced vibration on the string."

Her brain shifts, and she effortlessly imagines the inner workings of a device she's only seen. A feedback circuit with a sensor and driver coils. A signal that moves something otherwise inert. Makes a dead string resonate. Connections begin to form, implication of the smaller thing upon the larger. If you could induce vibration in a string, could you induce Resonance in a baseliner?

Alyssa arrives home from her shift at the hospital in a clatter of opened locks and kicked-off boots and breaks Fahima's reverie. She comes up behind Fahima, wraps her arms around her waist, and kisses her neck. She's half a head shorter than Fahima, and her kisses often land there, where shoulder becomes neck.

"Working on a death ray, babe?"

Fahima smiles and leans back into Alyssa. The buzz of the idea is gone. The kettle whistles.

"Could be a freeze ray," Fahima says. "Too early to say for sure."

"It looks like a very awkward vibrator," Alyssa says. "I'm going to go clean up." She and Fahima have been dating for three years, living together for one. Alyssa believes that Fahima works for a think tank downtown, a blue-sky idea factory with a mission statement about inventing the future now. Fahima never explicitly told her this, but she's never disabused her of it either. Alyssa doesn't know her girlfriend dreams of machines that don't exist. She doesn't know

Fahima can hear the kitchen appliances lovingly telling one another good night.

The day the FBI came to arrest Fahima Deeb's father, there were still bootprints on the rug from the Homeland raid that took her uncle.

Fahima and her family lived on a block in a Polish neighborhood on Buffalo's north side. A handful of Lebanese families happened to live there, drawn together the way immigrant families often were in a new place, like droplets of water on glass. Her parents and uncle co-owned a kebab stand at the Polish market, a run-down building on Broadway and Gibson that once had been the province of Polish Catholic vendors but now housed soul food diners and halal butchers along with the standard kielbasa and pierogi. Fahima worked at the stand from the time she could walk. She'd chat with the babcias who ran the bakery and called her the Angel of the Market, or with Eva, who sold ropes of hair extensions and gave Fahima a leopard print shawl that Fahima's mother wouldn't let her wear as a hijab. Most of her time was spent in the kitchen, shaping ground lamb into patties and laying them on broad metal sheets.

When she was ten, an idea came to her for a machine that could scoop lamb from the plastic tub and mold it into a patty. She'd been dreaming of machines for weeks. In the dreams, one piece of a mechanism floated in a field of white. Other pieces swooped in and attached themselves until they completed an elaborate apparatus. Fahima didn't know the function of those gadgets. They faded when she woke up.

She looked forward to the dreams. They were better than the others, the dreams of the big, crowded room. Those dreams felt like drowning to Fahima, who was already prone to social anxiety. But the dream of the meat machine stuck with her long enough that she drew a schematic on the classified ads while she chomped on dry Cheerios. Her uncle Muhair, who lived with them, performed a late and hasty fajr in the corner of the kitchen.

"What're you working on, habibi?" he asked, looking over her shoulder. Fahima covered up the drawings with her hand, then moved it to show him.

"For the shop?" Fahima nodded. "You'll put yourself out of a job!" He shook her shoulder and left her to finish. That night, after isha'a, her parents settled in front of the television, she showed Muhair the completed drawings. He was like a second father to her, sometimes kinder than her own father. He agreed to help build this dream thing of hers.

They worked on the device in the shed in the backyard. Fahima told Muhair what they needed, and Muhair acquired parts. Auto junkyards in the suburbs, mail-order catalogs, the appliance repair place down on Hertel Avenue. Anything Fahima asked for materialized and was slotted into the meat machine, which came together as it had in her dream, piece by piece.

When it was finished, it looked like a car engine with spider legs. Exactly as she'd dreamed it. This was the first of the dream machines Fahima had seen made real, and it was beautiful. More beautiful than a person could ever be. Muhair made Fahima promise not to tell anyone the device's purpose until it made its debut at the market on Palm Sunday. It was the busiest weekend of the year, when all the babcias in the city descended on the market to buy butter lambs and crown roasts. It was the perfect moment to show off Fahima's dynamo. The device sat in the shed for two weeks, covered by a half dozen old prayer blankets Fahima's mother had deemed unfit for use but too dear to be thrown out. Muhair brought half the neighborhood, Lebanese and Polish alike, around to see it. He'd lift one sajjada for one group, exposing a single arachnid limb, and another for a second group, showing a complex of gears. Within the neighborhood, the meat machine was like the elephant assayed by the three blind men. People argued and speculated about its purpose, its appearance, and the likelihood it would burn the whole market down come Palm Sunday.

Maybe it was Mr. Pryzborowski, who ran the appliance repair store on Hertel and sold Muhair odd bits of wire and gear over the previous month, who called Homeland Security. Or one of the neighbors who hadn't been invited to preview the device but watched from behind curtains as Muhair and Fahima went out to the shed day after day. It was 2003, and people were wary of Muslims tinkering in sheds and garages and basements. Regardless of who made the call, Homeland Security agents, bulletproof vests over their dark blue suits, broke down the Deebs' door one night in April as the family rolled up their prayer rugs after Maghrib. The smell of cumin was thick in the air from the pot of fuul her mother had on the stove all day. The men dragged her uncle out the front door; his heels left trenches in the living room carpet. In the morning, her mother pitched the contents of the pot out the back door into the yard, killing a patch of grass the shape of a tulip blossom.

Her parents met with a Yemeni lawyer from the suburbs. Muslims had developed a cross-national immune system for random and senseless arrests. An envelope of cash appeared in the mailbox: donations collected at an Iranian mosque on the north side. Egyptians and Turks and Pakistanis Fahima had never met showed up on the doorstep with Tupperware containers full of food. Every 'amme on the block had a theory about who had sold Muhair out, although no two agreed. They drank endless pots of tea with her mother while Fahima finished homework in the living room, convinced that the women could read the guilt on her like the tea leaves in the bottom of their cups.

Not long after the machine dreams started, Fahima began to hear the appliances around the house and at the market. They weren't precisely talking, but she could sense feelings coming off them along with their radiant heat. The industrial mixer that blended the lamb, egg, and spices pined to be used each Saturday morning when Fahima and her mother arrived. The aging fridge understood that there was no rest coming for it and wanted only to die. In the days after her uncle's arrest, a voice rose out of the soft clamor of the house. It was the desktop computer in her father's office, which he used to keep the stand's accounts and e-mail family members in Beirut. It called to Fahima. It said it could help.

Her parents off with the lawyer again, Fahima sat at the computer in the empty house. It didn't tell her what to do, but it guided her hand like the planchette of a Ouija board. First to the public website for Homeland Security and then, through a series of log-ins, deep into the site's working guts. From within, you could access everything. The computer urged her toward her uncle's name. Fahima marked Muhair Deeb as FOR IMMEDIATE RELEASE.

In their flirting days, Fahima told Alyssa a version of the story that left out the machine voices and painted Fahima as a gifted inventor and hacker. "It was poor timing," Fahima told her. "By 2006, everyone at Homeland was so bored, they would have let something like that slip. Paperwork says let him go, let him go. But it was 2003, and they all had raging hard-ons to fuck brown people."

Homeland caught the change in Muhair Deeb's status and called in the FBI to investigate the hack. They traced the IP address to Fahima's father's computer. As soon as the Deebs heard the knock, interrupting dinner this time, Fahima knew what it was.

"Baba, I made a mistake," she said too softly to be heard as the newly replaced door came down. The men, this time in black suits, grabbed her father out of his chair. Fahima screamed, "It was me! It was me!" Her mother, worried that the FBI would believe her, held Fahima around the waist with one arm and clamped the other hand over her mouth.

With the second arrest, the outpouring of community support ceased. It was impossible that the government had erred twice was the consensus. Even if it had been a mistake, the family was bad luck, likely to be catching. The Deebs, now only Fahima and her mother, were ostracized.

With the house empty and the kebab stand without customers, the machine voices got louder. Fahima's ability to filter them diminished. She broke down in the lunch line at school, yelling at the soda machine to leave her alone. The ambulance came directly to the school, and Fahima was paraded into the back of it in front of her classmates by paramedics who held her by the arms. The scene resembled the one she'd seen twice before, and Fahima felt a moment of kinship with her father and uncle. Prisoners, all three.

At the hospital, medical devices were a cacophony in Fahima's head. They existed in a constant state of panic, their beeps and bells external signs that these monitors and defibrillators and imagers were undergoing a barrage of people's pain. In oncology, two floors above the psychiatric ward where Fahima was housed, a husband flatlined. His wife picked up the heart monitor and threw it on the ground, kicking at it in a blind rage as nurses tried to resuscitate him. Fahima felt each blow as if it were delivered onto her own body. She cowered on the floor while upstairs the new widow savaged the hapless piece of equipment.

Fahima was sent to Lakeview, an institution in central New York. She was catatonic by then. Lakeview was the best her mother could afford, which blessedly meant it hadn't been able to purchase technology since the late 1980s. In the quiet, Fahima's mind began to heal. It was three years before her thoughts felt coherent again, before she could keep all voices but her own out of her head.

While she was unresponsive, the orderlies had taken her hijab. She asked Ms. Gudrun, the facility's director of youth therapy, if she could have it back, and Ms. Gudrun told her the other patients found it "strange and upsetting." The next day in the common room, when one of her fellow patients switched the television to an evangelist station at defeaning volume, Fahima shrieked, "Turn it off!"

"Ms. Deeb, there's no need to shout," said the orderly on duty.

"I find it strange and upsetting," Fahima said.

"It makes them feel safe," the orderly said, gesturing to every patient who wasn't Fahima. Fahima swallowed hard and nodded.

"You're right," she said. "I'm sorry." She went to the bookshelf, which contained only dated magazines. After a pause to give herself plausible deniability, Fahima told the television to shut off, and it did. The room erupted in cries. Fahima buried her smile in a copy of *Good Housekeeping*.

Her best days were spent in a vegetable garden on the Lakeview property. Ms. Gudrun, convinced that Fahima suffered from claustrophobia, arranged for her to work, supervised, in the slim window of hospitable weather upstate New York provided.

Late spring, when Fahima was fifteen, she was putting up wire rabbit fence around the cabbages. Because the wires were sharp, Ms. Gudrun was seated on a stool nearby, wearing a jacket and scarf against the chill. An orderly led a man through the garden, careful not to trample any of the sprouting plants. The man was in short sleeves despite the chill, pale skin over cables of stringy muscle. He had a beard like a cumulus cloud and little wire-rimmed glasses.

"Can you turn your cell phone off?" Fahima called when they were twenty feet away.

"Of course," said the old man. The whisper that nagged at the edge of Fahima's mind went dead. "Is it the signal?" He adjusted his glasses. "What you're hearing?"

"Fahima isn't hearing anything," said Ms. Gudrun. "Are you, Fahima?"

What she'd heard was a chirrup, like a bird in the man's pocket, telling her it was coming.

"Interesting," the man said. "Do you get a sense of an object's history? Maybe you pick something up and you know things about its owner?"

Fahima paused. Words swam in front of her like the blobs you get when you press the heels of your hands into your eyelids. *You're safe*, the words said. *My name is Kevin Bishop. I'm like you.*

"It's not like that," said Fahima. "Also, I dream of machines. Machines that don't exist."

It was the first time she'd talked about the dreams to anyone. Even when she'd showed the schematics for the device to Muhair, she hadn't told him she'd seen them in her sleep.

Ms. Gudrun placed herself between Fahima and Bishop, a great wall of a woman. "I'm not sure who you are," she said, "but we've been working very hard to help Fahima understand that these voices—"

"You've been trying to shut her down," he said. "You don't understand what's happening with her, so you want to make it go away. Make her dull like you, Ms. Gudrun."

"How did you—"

"You wear your name and job title on your forebrain like a badge," he said. "It's all that holds your identity together. A mantra. *I am Michelle Gudrun, director of youth therapy. I am Michelle Gudrun. Chugga chugga chugga chugga.* A little train going around and around." He was getting annoyed. The orderly standing behind him was limp, like a sleepwalker. His head lolled drowsily on his thick neck. "I'm constantly finding our people in places like this. Under the ostensible care of people like you. Now please, be quiet a minute." Ms. Gudrun crossed her legs, sat down in the dirt between the cabbages, and fell asleep.

"Ms. Deeb," said Bishop, "I'm very pleased to have found you. I'm sorry it's taken me so long."

Fahima approached Ms. Gudrun and carefully removed her scarf. The cloth was nubbly and cheap. She folded it into an approximate triangle, draped it over her head, and wrapped it around her chin. It wasn't quite right, and she could feel air on the back of her neck. She made a triumphant huff and followed Bishop back toward the main building.

Fahima Deeb left Lakeview that afternoon with transfer paperwork to an institution downstate, one that offered more opportunities for outdoor therapy. This made Ms. Gudrun happy because it confirmed her diagnoses. Neither the therapist nor the orderly remembered the encounter in the garden.

Alyssa screams from the shower, a quick shriek of surprise. Fahima rushes to the cry, throwing the bathroom door open. Alyssa has grabbed a towel and is using it to cover herself. The water is running, soaking the towel to a dark shade of purple. Across from Alyssa, in the sliver of vertical space between the toilet and the vanity, there's a narrow door, barely wide enough to be a broom closet.

"Where the fuck did that come from?" Alyssa yells. "I heard a pop, and I looked out, and there was a door."

"It's okay, Lys," says Fahima. She shuts the shower off and wraps the wet towel properly around her. "Wait in the bedroom. I'm going to figure this out."

Kimani calls from behind the door. "We need your help." The sound of a voice from inside their bathroom wall further spooks Alyssa, but what worries Fahima is that Kimani is panicked, too. She's the most cool and efficient person on staff at Bishop. Her room is a sanctuary and shrink's office because even in a crisis, Kimani doesn't shake. But she's shaken now. "Fahima, please," she cries.

Alyssa's face changes when she hears Fahima's name. "You know what this is," she says.

Fahima has wanted to have this conversation from the start of their relationship, but it's been impossible. When they decided to go public, Fahima vowed she'd out herself to Alyssa. It was going to happen tomorrow or next week. There was always more time. Until now, when there's none.

"There are things about my work that I haven't told you," Fahima says.

Alyssa is scared, shaking. Fahima wants things to pause. Whatever the problem behind the door is, she can deal with it. The situation with Alyssa, she can deal with it. But she can't do both at once. Something needs to stop.

"Lys, we can talk about this later." Alyssa gives her a look that indicates that this will not be happening. Fahima sighs. "Get dressed quick," she says. "I'll explain as much as I can."

Alyssa hurries into the bedroom, and Fahima opens the door. The room is stark, walls hospital white, floors harsh tile. It looks like an apartment someone's moved out of. Kimani stands behind Avi, who holds Emmeline cradled in his arms, a pietà in reverse.

"She won't wake up," he says. "She's breathing, but she won't wake up."

Emmeline looks peaceful except for the way her head, arms, and legs dangle like those of an unstrung marionette. Fahima takes the back of the girl's head in one hand and jabs at her neck with two fingers, looking for a pulse.

"Let me," says Alyssa, shouldering Fahima aside. She's in her scrubs, her face set in the way she gets at work or doing the crossword. She has things under control, and the best thing to do is to stay out of her way. Fahima steps aside, taking a moment to marvel at this woman who may very well be out of her life by tomorrow.

"Pulse rate and temp feel normal," Alyssa says. She peels the girl's eyelid back. "She's in REM sleep."

"She's resonating," Fahima says to Kimani.

"What does that mean?" Alyssa asks.

"How is this her fucking ability?" Avi shouts. His eyes are full of tears, and Fahima thinks it's possible they've broken him before he could finish his job. "Is she . . . doing something in her sleep? Is it safe? Why won't she wake up?" Alyssa looks at Fahima, wondering the same thing.

"Someone's holding her in the Hive," Fahima says,

speaking to Kimani, using code words and jargon that leave Avi and Alyssa in the dark. "Someone's got her trapped."

Kimani collects Patrick and Sarah, closing the door and then opening into each of their apartments in turn. Patrick is wearing his teaching clothes: a pair of pleated khaki pants and a pale blue polo shirt. Sarah is in a thick flannel nightgown, Cortex at her heel. The dog positions himself between Sarah and Patrick the way he always does when the three of them are together.

Alyssa focuses on Emmeline and on keeping Avi calm. *She's a better person than I am*, Fahima thinks. She's having trouble keeping her mind from straying away from the girl and into the implications of Emmeline's current condition. What it means about the Hive.

The Hive bothers the shit out of Fahima. If she'd never been there herself, she'd say it couldn't exist. She never properly found her way to the Hive on her own, although it was later explained to her that the dreams of the crowded room she had as a kid were early fumblings at its edges. She had to be guided to it once she was at Bishop. She doesn't have the sense of wonder about it that other Resonants do. They call it things like the Shiny Place and the Shimmering Room, like it's something from a fairy tale. For Fahima, it's one more odd-shaped piece in the ongoing puzzle of what she is. What they all are.

Avi grabs her wrist. "Tell me what's going on." He and Fahima both look at his hand clamped around her arm, and the anger goes out of him. He lets her go, leaving pale ghosts of his fingers behind. "Please, tell me anything."

"Someone attacked Emmeline through the Hive," she says. "It shouldn't be possible, but I think they're holding her hostage."

"She's not a hostage; she's right here," he shouts.

"That's just her body," Fahima says. "I think Emmeline is somewhere else."

"Why would anyone—"

"I don't know," Fahima says, cutting him off. *It's because we dragged you into this shit,* she thinks.

"Let me check her," says Sarah.

"Are you a doctor?" Alyssa asks, holding her ground in front of the girl.

"No." She puts her hand on Alyssa's arm, and Alyssa steps aside. Sarah kneels and places her palm on the girl's forehead. A beat passes, two. "She's not in her head," she says. "You're right; her consciousness must be in the Hive." Fahima turns away, concealing a smile. Impossible things are happening. You can always learn something new when impossible things start happening.

"We'll have to go in and get her," says Kimani.

"What do we do?" Avi asks.

"We should all go in," says Kimani.

"We should call Bishop," Fahima says. "You should have gone to him first."

"He doesn't like it when I show up unannounced," Kimani says.

"Yeah, and I fucking love it," Fahima says, glancing at Alyssa, who's taken back her spot at Emmeline's side.

"We can call him from in the Hive," Patrick says.

"We need to drop them off first," Kimani says. She looks at Avi. "You need to go home."

"I can't go home."

"Take us to my apartment," Alyssa says. Kimani nods and opens the door back into their bathroom, steam lingering in the corners, fog on the mirror. As Avi wedges himself and Emmeline through, Sarah touches him on the shoulder. "Take care of her," she says. Fahima sees him relax a little, as if there is no one here but him and his daughter, clutched in his arms. Sarah must have pushed into his mind enough to calm him. The ethics are questionable, but Fahima can't fault the result.

So much of the Hive has to do with attention. The things you're not looking at fuzz out of focus and into nonexistence. The things you're attending to become clear and crisp, regardless of distance. You can hide yourself, create a bubble of privacy. It's not difficult; most people aren't singling you out anyway. Fahima went through a phase of wild sexual experimentation in the Hive when she first got to Bishop. The Hive offered the freedom and anonymity that Internet chat rooms once promised, but with sensation rather than words. Hivebodies made of pure consciousness pressed up against one another without the mediation of language. Psychic ghosts fucking psychic ghosts. You didn't have to be yourself, which, for a girl still in the closet, was like salvation. Fahima could be with women in the Hive without admitting to herself that she liked women. Selves were not necessarily involved. Hivebodies were ideas about selves, fiction suits you could try on and discard, although the Hivebodies calcified over years until they appeared in the Hive as approximations of their owners' physical selves. Fahima ultimately found her trysts in the Hive insufficient, recipes without food. But they led her to a truth about herself, and they helped her understand something about how the Hive works. It responds to what you want. It's shaped by desire. If Emmeline wants to be found, she should be findable. If the Hive is fluid and responsive to personal desire, there should be no way to hold someone against her will.

"Is it possible she's hiding from us?" Fahima asks.

"Us maybe," says Sarah. "But why would she hide from her father?"

"There's lots of reasons to hide from your father," Patrick says. His Hivebody is smaller than his real one. It flickers like a bad television signal.

Bishop materializes next to Patrick. Most people blip into existence in the Hive, but Bishop crafts his Hivebody. It's shapeless, then expands, as if it's being birthed through a plastic bag. A puff of smoke becomes a man. A white beard forms on his chin like frost on a window, and two lines trace themselves around his eyes, wire-rimmed National Health glasses. In the Hive, he looks exactly like he does in person, if a decade younger, less careworn.

"What's this about?" he asks.

"It's Emmeline Hirsch," says Kimani. "Someone has her trapped."

"That's not possible," Bishop says.

"A cage," says Fahima. "Someone built a cage."

"That's not the way this place works," Bishop says. "No one can build here. This place resists permanence. Anything structural would have to be pushed through from the Source."

"Or pulled through?" Fahima says. Bishop glances at her, and she knows she's guessed right.

"Can that happen?" asks Patrick.

"It can't just *happen*," Bishop snaps.

Fahima hangs on Bishop's every word. He knows more about the Hive than he's told her, but the idea that it exists in a liminal space between the physical world and wherever Resonants draw their abilities from, the Source, is something he's confirmed. That the Source can physically intrude into the Hive is news to Fahima and will require some reconsideration of certain theories.

Bishop's Hivebody becomes translucent. It diffuses. He calls this casting, and it's nearly impossible. Sarah, on a good day, can cast her Hivebody into a sphere about ten feet across. Fahima can barely puff out her cheeks. Even in the psychic space of the Hive, an individual consciousness stays focused at one point. Bishop now exists spread out like a net across the Hive, searching. After a few seconds, he coalesces back into a solid, becoming opaque again.

"It's like a cancer on the skin of this place," he says. In his face, Fahima sees the righteous anger of the man who plucked her from the garden of a mental asylum. "Come with me."

In the all-at-once way travel happens within the Hive, Fahima and the others follow.

As they approach the thing, Fahima thinks of the words Bishop used: *a cancer on the skin of this place*. It's a mass of black stone, shifting in shape, alternating between presence and absence. *Abscess*, she thinks. Not a building: a hole. The more she looks at it, the more frequently it changes. It's a box, then a wound. Its edges are geometric, angles sharp, and then it's fractal, a Mandelbrotian mess, a biomass of jet-black bubble and tendril.

"This can't be here," says Bishop.

"How do we get her out?" Kimani asks.

Fahima can't stop looking at it. She steps forward, past Bishop, and lays her hand on it.

"Don't," says Bishop, too late. The black surface is cold to the touch. Fahima has never had a perception of temperature in the Hive. It's one of the things lacking from sexual encounters here: no heat. But the abscess sends a numbing chill across her palm and up her arm. The surface seethes and roils under her hand. *It doesn't feel organic*, she thinks. *But it feels alive.*

As she's tallying these observations, a feeling washes over her, a memory boiled down into its emotional content. Her father dragged away by the feds. Her mother holding her back, shoving Fahima's confession back into her mouth. Fahima feels angry and ashamed, the outsized emotions of a panicked child. They threaten to pull her down into them, the boundless dark space of them where logic and rationality are easily drowned. A small, ugly piece of the emotional complex expands, blotting out the others. It's a feeling of relief and escape. It's the sense she's gotten away with something. *Better him than me*, she thinks. *What good would he have done the world, the kebab-selling nothing he was? How much good have I done already?*

Bishop grabs her wrist and pulls her hand off the surface.

"It wasn't like that," she says. "I never felt like that. I never thought that." Maybe she had that feeling, so inchoate it couldn't rise to the level of thought, to be seen and named and spoken. She stares at the spot on the surface where her reflection ought to be. It's nothing but flat black.

"What did you see?" Bishop asks.

"I didn't see anything," she says. "I *felt* something. I felt bad."

"This shouldn't be here," he says.

"Kevin?" Kimani shouts. She's the only person on staff who calls him by his first name. She points at the crest of the hill behind them. Shapes emerge out of the ground, a dozen, more. They look like fingers on a corpse, black and bloated. In seconds, they become roughly human-shaped, lumbering golems made of the same shifting black substance as the abscess. Like it, they flicker, as if they're trying to exist in two places at once. They encircle Fahima and her friends, trapping them with their backs to the abscess. They move in slowly, unspeaking.

"Back the fuck off, people," Fahima says.

"They can't hurt us here," says Patrick. "We can't be hurt here."

"Ten minutes ago you couldn't trap anyone here," Fahima says.

"They're not people," says Bishop. "We push into this space from our side. These are pushed into this space from the other."

"Why do they look like people?" Fahima asks.

"Someone's doing it," Bishop says.

One of the golems puts the bloated slab of its hand on Patrick's shoulder. It's a gentle motion, brotherly, but Patrick shoves the golem away with both arms. Undaunted, it starts toward him again.

Kimani is up against the abscess. Two golems come at her slowly, almost patient. Their hands are extended as if to calm her, but she steps away from them, looking back into the shifting hole, terrified.

Sarah is trying to read the one coming at her like a panhandler on the street. *It would be less scary if they charged*, Fahima thinks. Their slowness makes them feel inevitable. Before the golem gets near her, Sarah blips out, her Hivebody ceasing to exist for a second before she reappears, outside the narrowing circle, staring helplessly as the shapes close in on her friends.

"What do we do?" Fahima asks. One of the golems lumbers toward her, a child's drawing of a movie zombie.

"Keep them back," Bishop says. Fahima turns so that she can face the oncoming golems but keep Bishop in the corner of her vision. He lays both of his hands on the abscess. His face contorts in pain and concentration. Fahima feels energy pouring off him. He's pushing something into the abscess or drawing something up from the ground of the Hive into it.

White lines rise up along its base like vines. They expand, webbing its entire surface. The abscess stops fluctuating. It takes a solid shape, a dark cube shot through with veins of bright white. It becomes fully real, and in the next moment it shatters. Shards of black glass fly in every direction, forced away from the explosion of the abscess. Others move of their own accord, fluttering off with the erratic flight paths of bats.

Emmeline stands where the abscess was, her Hivebody bigger than her actual body. It looks as if echoes of her older self are laid over the image of her as a little girl. The effect is holographic, producing a sensation of depth, like seeing her reflected in a hall of mirrors, an infinite regression of images on a flat surface. Emmeline's hair is a dark corona around her head. Her eyes blaze pale blue. A little girl surging with power. Even Bishop stands back, in awe of her.

The golems continue their approach, and Emmeline's Hivebody disappears in a liquid flash. Fahima can feel her with them, everywhere now. She's casting the way Bishop did but more strongly. Emmeline infuses the Hive with herself, becoming a thunderstorm. Bright lines of energy blaze toward the golems from the spot where she was. The lines spiral around them and constrict, squeezing them into the ground, shrinking them like the Wicked Witch melting into smoke, into nothing. They go soundlessly, without protest. Never alive, they're not dying, only returning to wherever they came from, like a glass of seawater poured back into an ocean.

Emmeline's Hivebody reconfigures in the air. She looks at what she's done, a goddess surveying her work. Her hands go up to her face, pressing through the future echoes, condensing her Hivebody into one opaque thing, and then her face goes slack and she falls. Patrick stretches out his arms in time to save her from crashing onto a pile of black shards. He reels her in, clutching the girl to his chest. She mutters something about the stove being on. "I can smell it," she says. "The blue flame's not there yet, and I can smell it."

"What the fuck just happened?" Patrick says.

"We saved the girl," Bishop says. "That's what matters."

"Seems like she saved us," says Fahima.

Bishop shoots her a look she's never seen from him. He's never tried to shut her up. This is the look that does it. Then his Hivebody dissolves, aspect by aspect, until there's nothing of him left.

Fahima can hear Avi crying in the next room. Emmeline says, "It's all right, Daddy. I'm okay." Bishop once told Fahima that the Source wasn't sentient but responded to sentience.

Whatever the fuck the Source is, it's a big fan of you, kid, Fahima thinks.

She looks at the others. Bishop isn't with them. Sarah and Kimani look exhausted. Fahima must look just as bad. Patrick looks like Patrick: smug, bored. But Fahima saw it the moment the shape had its hand on him. The horror and repulsion on his face.

"Go talk to her," Kimani says, interrupting Fahima's thoughts.

Fahima stands in the doorway, looking on as Alyssa checks the girl's vitals, Avi cradling her, rocking her back and forth.

"She seems fine," says Alyssa. "But she seemed fine before, except for being—"

"Brain dead," Fahima says. Avi winces, and Fahima regrets saying it.

"Emmeline," Sarah says, "did you see who took you?"

"No," says Emmeline. "I was there in the shiny place, like you taught me to. I heard someone call me. It sounded like when the radio in the van is between channels. I didn't like it, but it knew me. I went toward where I heard it. I went down. Then the ground went all black and reached up and grabbed me."

Sarah gets down on her haunches and holds her hands out. "I'm going to try something," she says. "I'm going to look around in your head—"

"Get away from her," Avi says, pulling Emmeline closer to him.

"Sarah, no," Patrick says. His arm shoots across the space between them and pushes Sarah's hands down before she can lay them on the girl.

"We need to know," Sarah says, shaking free of his grip.

"You can't go into her head right now," Patrick says. He's spent more time with Sarah rattling around in his head than anyone else. He knows the disorienting underwater feeling of having her go into your mind. "Let her rest."

"He's right," Fahima says. She's had Sarah in her head once or twice. She isn't a big fan.

"Latent memories decay," says Sarah. "Tomorrow there are details that could be gone. Details we need to figure out what's happened."

"We'll figure it out some other way," Fahima says. "Emmeline gets the night off."

Emmeline smiles at her, then at Patrick. Then she smiles at Sarah, too. *She would have let Sarah do it,* Fahima thinks, impressed by the girl's bravery.

"Is someone going to tell me what happened?" Avi asks. There's so much to explain to him. Everything that happened in the Hive is a violation of rules, of laws he's never known existed. They have to be careful not to overload him. Not to break him.

"Someone tried to take her," Fahima says. "Someone incredibly strong." Even this isn't entirely true. Fahima's not sure it was some*one*. She puts her hand lightly on the girl's head, her fingers swallowed in twists of hair. "Emmeline was stronger. She's fucking amazing."

"Let's get this fucking amazing little girl home," Kimani says from the doorway. Emmeline jumps out of Avi's arms and runs to her. Avi looks after Emmeline, stricken. Too exhausted to fight, he goes to follow.

Before he can step through the door, Fahima grabs his arm and pulls him close. "It'll happen again," she says. "She needs to learn to protect herself."

"I'll teach her to—"

"You can't," Fahima says. She sees his face fall as something breaks in him, a hope he'd held on to. Fahima drops his hand, letting him go back to his daughter.

THREE

THE TOWER

Falling from the tower are broken figures of the garrison.
It will be noticed that they have lost their human shape.
—ALEISTER CROWLEY, *The Book of Thoth*

THE DAY THE STORY BROKE

Everything is set into place, a great Rube Goldberg device of information, waiting for its first domino to be tipped. Fahima sends documentation to the networks, giving them time to confirm. She uses Avi's contacts and elicits promises not to run with anything before the *Trib* article. She's been working with scientists across the country for years to prove that Resonants can do the things they do. He's hurt that he wasn't the only baseliner brought in, but he understands the need. A flood of scientific papers is in the pipeline, held back by nondisclosure agreements that will be lifted once Avi's pieces go public. The science is opaque to him. His job is to communicate who they are, not what. It's to make them people rather than biological oddities, rather than freaks. He's confident he's pulled it off. The next few days and weeks and months will tell. He thinks about what will happen to Emmeline if he hasn't.

The *Trib* article is written as a trumpet blast. The *Atlantic* piece, scheduled to come out three days later, is the culmination of the last two months of Avi's life. It's a sprawling 10,000-word article with Bishop, Patrick, and a glowing girl named Marian on the cover looking like the cast of a summer blockbuster. It maps out more of Resonant culture and delves into whatever science Fahima could explain to him. It wasn't everything. Avi signed NDAs protecting the locations of the academy and the Commune, along with the identities of Resonants who wanted to speak off the record and watch the dust settle before outing themselves. Avi pointed out that there was enough information about Kevin Bishop in the piece that a savvy reporter could find the school with a reasonable amount of digging. Kimani told him they were taking care of it.

On the February morning when the headline on the *Trib* reads "They Walk Among Us" with Avi Hirsch's byline below it, the article simmers. The biggest news stories have context, a connection to the previously known. Bombshells about the president assume that the reader knows who the president is. Celebrity shockers are built on a base understanding of a culture of stardom and familiarity with the famous person in question. The *Trib* story comes out of nowhere, science fiction intruding on the real world.

The world doesn't wake with the knowledge that everything has changed. The realization settles in gradually. In the house on Jarvis Avenue, where they've let their subscription to the *Trib* lapse, the morning routine goes on as usual. Avi fixes breakfast. Kay reads her book. Emmeline half sings a Stevie Wonder song they heard on the car radio yesterday, filling in the words she doesn't know with tuneless nonsense sounds. Every so often she catches Avi's eye. They haven't talked about what happens next.

Publication means a hard stop for the secret they've kept from Kay. It will be good to be rid of it. It's become a fourth person in the house, a lodger who's never seen but whose presence is felt in another room, listening at the door. Once the secret is out, their lives will return to what they were before, as if by becoming public and shared, the facts he's hidden from Kay will cease to be.

Avi puts it out of his mind as he cooks breakfast, as he drives Kay to the station and kisses her good-bye. He's relieved when she bypasses the news vendor in her rush to catch the train. He drops Emmeline off at school and watches her puffy purple coat blend into a scrum of soft, round bodies. He wonders how long before the story trickles down to these kids. How many will recognize Emmeline instantly as one of the people the story is about.

He picks up a copy of the *Trib* on his way home but doesn't bother to read it. He's worked on it for so long that he can recite all fifteen hundred words. At home, he sets up a Google alert for the word *Resonant* and for his own name. Not a Twitter user, he looks up #Resonant and mentions of the *Trib*'s Twitter handle. He waits, uselessly refreshing pages that auto-update if they have anything new to show. He hates the phrase *go viral*. It converts language and thought into biological weapons. But he is waiting for his story to do just that. He's the epidemiologist watching for red spots to appear on a map, waiting for the screen to flood while worrying about what will happen when it does. He knows the screen is only the map, not the territory. Behind it, there are lives about to change, Resonant and baseliner. Emmeline's. His.

Around lunch, the story begins to move of its own accord. It looks nothing like a virus. It looks like fireworks. Someone with a significant number of followers posts the story, and there's a burst. Another over there, in some fiefdom of the Internet. Responses are stunned or mocking. *WTAF?* and *Did you see this?* Posters ask if the *Trib*'s been bought out by *Weekly World News* or if it's possible for a newspaper to straight up lose its collective mind.

Then people start to post sightings, confirmations. To give a thing a name is to call it into being, bring it forth into people's consciousness. Avi read an article once about Homer's persistent description of the Aegean as "the wine-dark sea," referring to the sky as bronze no matter the time of day. A linguist theorized that at the time the *Iliad* and the *Odyssey* were written, there was no Greek word for blue. In most languages, blue is one of the youngest color words. Without a word to describe it, the ancient Greeks didn't perceive things as blue. Their sky *was* bronze, their sea a deep and frothing purple. The word *Resonant* illuminates a blank space in people's minds, and #Resonant begins to yield results. A little girl in Omaha who flew away from schoolyard bullies and never came back. The man in Durham who was arrested for simultaneously robbing two banks on opposite sides of the city, then bailed out by an identical twin records showed he didn't have. A schoolteacher in Cincinnati who healed a kid's broken arm by the laying on of hands. People had seen things, but without a word to attach to them, a conceptual hashtag, they filed them as miracles and hallucinations. Now they know better.

Another strain arises along with the sightings. People coming out. People admitting who and what they are to the world. Some of the responses to this are terrible, hateful things, death threats and rape threats. Those who step forward are called freaks and monstrosities. But there's support, too, and something like religious awe. And there are aspirants, wannabes. *You're amazing,* they say. *How do I become like you?*

Avi's first call is from CNN. They want him on the air that night or the next morning. It's clear they're settling for him. What they want is an actual Resonant, someone to do tricks live on air. "Can you bring anyone with you?" the segment producer asks. *Not yet,* Avi thinks. All of this has been planned out, timed. First him, then them. He does a phone interview with Lakshmi Rameswaram, an NPR host he knows from Chicago media functions back when he attended such things. Her questions are vague. Most of them amount to, *Is this happening*? He assures her he's met dozens of Resonants and they are very much real. *We should have laid more groundwork ahead of time,* he thinks. *We should have been more prepared.* There was no way to know. Anything done for the first time unleashes a demon.

It turns out other people were ready. The Kindred Network, a consortium of right-wing television and radio stations, bumps one of its AM radio wingnuts up to the television side. Jefferson Hargrave has a camera ready in his studio, which looks like it's been set up in a supply closet.

"I've been warning people for years," he says in the frothing patter of a manic street preacher. "You can check the archives on my website. I've devoted hours of my

program. I wasn't *collaborating* at the level of this reporter."
He slaps a folded copy of the *Trib* he's using as a prop.
It's yesterday's edition, but the effect is the same. "I didn't
know there was a fancy name for it. I didn't have the kind
of documentation he does. But I had the knowledge. I had
the testimony of honest Americans about what they saw.
And I think the thing left out of this little article is what do
they want? Why step forward now? I saw the piece in the
paper with that headline, 'They Walk Among Us,' but what
I read was 'We Come in Peace.' And we've all seen movies
where the aliens who look just like us show up and claim
they come in peace. When they claim they want to work
alongside us for the betterment of humanity even though
they themselves aren't human. We know the two ways that
movie ends. It ends up with the humans in concentration
camps and cattle pens. Or it ends with a group of humans,
maybe only a couple, rising up to stop whatever these
things are from taking what's ours."

Avi opens his in-box. It was empty a week ago, but
the number of messages is climbing through the low
thousands. He goes downstairs to fix himself something to
eat before diving in.

Kay's in the living room. She looks surprised when
he comes down the stairs. "I called for you," she says.
"I thought you were out." She has a copy of the *Trib* in
her hand, rolled like she's about to swat something
with it.

"I must not have heard you," he says.

She nods, collecting herself. Avi sees what's coming

before she speaks. *Maybe I'm like them,* he thinks. *Maybe I can see the future.*

"You need to tell me about this," she says, tapping the newspaper. "You need to tell me about our daughter right now."

"I know," says Avi.

"Did you think you could keep it secret?" Kay says. "It's on the front page of the fucking *Trib.*"

"She's not mentioned—"

"Anyone who's not an idiot can read her in here," says Kay. "My *mother* will know."

"I didn't know where to start," Avi says.

"Start with Emmeline."

"She's one of them," he says. "A Resonant."

"How long?"

"I think they're born that way," he says. "But Emmeline—"

"How long have you known?"

"A month," he says. "Two months."

"You both kept it from me," Kay says. "I'm assuming you discussed keeping it a secret. How did you not tell me?"

"The day I found out, we just didn't say anything," says Avi. "We didn't know how. Every day we didn't tell you became one more thing we'd have to explain." He's aware that saying *we* over and over is a way to protect himself, to use Emmeline as a shield. He needs every defense. "Not telling you became easier."

"Oh, good," she says. "I'm glad it was easy for you."

"It wasn't—"

"What can she do?" Kay says. "What's her superpower?"

"They don't say *superpower*," Avi says.

"What can she do?"

"We don't know yet," says Avi. "Sometimes it takes a while for abilities to manifest. Emmeline is young. But Kevin Bishop says—"

"This is the person who bribed me with a box of comic books."

"He runs a school," Avi says. "An academy."

"I read the article," Kay says.

"It's in New York," says Avi. "That's not in the article, but it's in Midtown. Emmeline and I have been talking, and we think—"

"You have a plan, Avi?" she snaps. "Because we're still recovering from your last plan. We're paying medical bills and waiting to see if you climb out of the pit you've been in since your last plan. Do you even recognize what this is? It's one more war zone. It's all the excitement of Darfur and Mosul right in our living room. And you get to bring Emmeline with you." She rubs her hand over her face. "Fuck, this Kevin Bishop saw you coming. I mean, he piqued my interest with a fat check and a box of back issues. But they had you at go, didn't they?"

Avi stands under her glare, waiting for it to cool. Silence is no better than yelling. He puts his hands up, patting the air between them. "I want us to talk about what's best for Emmeline."

"You don't get to decide what we talk about," she says. She slaps the newspaper again, the same way the man on television did. "What does this have to do with the church bombing? There's nothing in here about Salem Baptist."

"It was one of them," Avi says. "They asked me not to write about it."

"They can blow up buildings?"

"They caught him," says Avi, as if her question is about Owen Curry in particular and not the dangers of the new world she's watching dawn, the sharks their daughter might swim among.

Things become awful between them, but quietly. Silently. Kay speaks to him when it's absolutely necessary. She finds reasons to stay late at work. When she comes home, she pours herself an overfull glass of wine and sits in the kitchen, reading old comic books, taking each out of its sleeve and holding it so it obscures her face. She eats dinner on her own, reheating whatever Avi and Emmeline had. Emmeline goes in to talk to her sometimes, and Avi strains his attention toward them, hoping to hear something. From what he can tell, they don't discuss Emmeline's ability. They talk about books and television shows. They make small talk like they're on a first date or a layover in an airport bar. They tread neutral ground.

This goes on for a week, each of them retreating to his or her own area of the house as early in the evening as possible. Emmeline puts herself to bed. Kay sets the box of comics in front of her on the couch, a glass of wine on the end table. Avi ascends to the attic, going over his notes on Owen Curry. A piece he's promised himself he'll never publish. The hatch to the attic rattles. It does this in the winter when the front door opens, a shift in the house's air pressure he's learned to ignore.

It's after eight, so Avi climbs down to investigate. At the bottom of the stairs, Kay holds the door open for Kevin Bishop. He's standing in the cold, brown paper bag tucked under his arm, while she decides whether to invite him in, hand on her hip. After leaving him in the cold a while, Kay steps aside.

Bishop looks up at Avi. "The articles have been well received," he says. "Congratulations."

"I'll leave you to it," Kay says. She turns to go.

"Stay," Bishop says. Kay stops abruptly, as if she's forgotten something.

"Are you in my head right now?" she says. "Did you—"

"A reflex," Bishop says. "I'm sorry. It's disrespectful, and I won't do it to you again. It's you I came to speak with. I need to talk to you about Emmeline."

"She's the only reason I let you in this door," Kay says. Avi catches her glance as she says this, spreading her anger around without thinning it one bit. "I don't want you in my head or in my house. I don't want your money or—"

"We can talk about that," Bishop says. "Is there somewhere we can sit?"

"Kitchen," says Kay.

Bishop hands the paper bag off to Avi. Inside, two glass bottles clink together. "Would you mind?" Bishop says. Exacting instructions for making a gin martini appear in Avi's head, along with a specific craving for one. The craving is recognizably foreign to him, a thought that is not his own. It's like having something on the surface of his eye that affects his vision, except it's on his brain, overlaying his thoughts. He goes to the freezer to get ice as Bishop and Kay sit at the table, well within earshot.

"I've made every possible misstep with you," Bishop says to Kay. Avi searches the cupboards for their martini glasses, which are tucked deep behind a legion of wineglasses. They are not cocktail people. "I'm usually so good at reading people."

Kay laughs, a tight exhalation of air. Avi sets three glasses on the counter and drops ice cubes into each one to chill it. *A chilled glass is an important and often overlooked part of the drink*, he thinks. It's not something he knew a minute ago.

"My impression of you was that you needed to find your own way to discovery," Bishop says. "In my defense, I believed I had more time. I've been trying to determine the best way to approach you since the beginning of summer."

Three ice cubes clink loudly into the shaker. Avi is disappointed with the quality of the ice. He doesn't know what good ice would look like, but this isn't it. Within the script for cocktail construction he's playing out, another thought emerges. Bishop was thinking of approaching Kay in the summer. She was the first choice. He was a consolation prize, the one who didn't need to be finessed. He measures out the gin and pours it over the ice.

"Your daughter is powerful," Bishop says.

"Is she going to blow up churches?"

Bishop folds his hands and rests them on the table. "Avi's talked to you about Owen Curry."

"That's his name?"

Bishop nods. "The young man is strong and badly damaged. But the ability to destroy matter at whatever level is something we can manage. It's within our purview. There's something different about Emmeline. If we had a scale for these things, I would say she is off it. She is also very young. Do you understand why this combination made me nervous?"

Avi glances over his shoulder and sees Kay shaking her head. He digs through the silverware drawer, looking for a long stirring spoon they don't have. He can see what one would look like, but they don't own one.

Try a butter knife, says a voice in his head that doesn't sound like his own.

"A child is a creature made of will and want," Bishop says. "The world provides or denies them what they want. Think about a child's demands for ice cream or television. They don't respond to reason. They are pure desire butting up against the limits of their own agency."

"You're talking the long way around the barn," Kay says. Avi tosses the ice out of the martini glasses into the sink. He drizzles vermouth into each one and carefully swirls it. It coats the inside of the glass. *It's the residual sugar in the vermouth that does it.* This is a thing he knows now.

"Imagine that same child with those limits removed," Bishop says. "Imagine a child with the power to shape the world into the thing the child wants it to be without ever realizing they're doing it. The world complies with the way they believe it should be, instantly, with the tiniest exertion of effort. Imagine a world shaped by the whims of an all-powerful child god."

" 'It's a Good Life,' " says Kay.

"I'm sorry?"

"*Twilight Zone* episode," Kay explains. "A kid isolates his whole town from the rest of the world, holds them hostage because he can read their minds and turn them into jack-in-the-boxes and whatever."

"And in the end he makes it snow," says Bishop. "I remember that one."

"And that's Emmeline?" Kay asks. "She'll be able to read minds? Send anyone she doesn't like to the cornfield?" Avi stirs the drinks, counting each revolution of the knife in his head.

"No, but I was concerned it could be," Bishop says. "When an ability manifests in a younger child, it's important that the child's home life is stable. We approach the parent the child feels more bonded to so they can be there for the child. A support."

Avi pauses, shaker over the glass, tilted but not pouring. He was the second choice. Not just Bishop's. Emmeline's.

"With the two of you there to support her and with our guidance, Emmeline is going to be something wonderful," Bishop says. "As a parent, you might feel there's no place for you in our world. I wanted to create that space. A way for you to be an integral part of Emmeline's life even as she goes through these changes. I can't literally make you one of us. But I have a role for you that will make you feel a part of who we are."

Three olives plop into each drink. Avi takes two glasses and sets them on the table in front of Bishop and Kay. Bishop looks up at him, surprised. "I forgot you were there," he says. It's a lie. This conversation is for Avi's benefit as much as Kay's. Bishop wants him to know he's important only as he relates to Emmeline. Even then, he's not that important. "This is very good," Bishop says, smiling over the rim of his glass. "Well done." Always susceptible to praise from the teacher, Avi blushes.

"I'm going to take mine to the living room," he says. It's like hearing himself say it. He watches himself pick up the last of the three martinis, the one that poured short, and walk out of the kitchen. He sits on the living room couch and sips the drink. It tastes awful and leaves a cold burn going down. He tries to hear them in the next room, but he can't. He has no urge to read, to turn on the television. He sits, waiting, like a child put in a time-out. Grown-ups are talking.

He's finishing his martini when they come out. Kay doesn't look any happier than when Bishop arrived. Her drink, barely touched except for the olives, dangles from her hand; she's gripping it by the rim, fingers spread.

"Take a look at the literature about the academy," he says. "And promise me you'll think about my offer."

"You going to *make* me think about it?" she says.

Bishop smiles at her, abashed. "The work matters," says Bishop. "The things I said to you in your office, I stand by them. I think you'd be excellent."

"I'll think about it," she says. He shows himself out without saying good-bye to Avi.

Kay sloshes her drink into Avi's empty glass and heads to the kitchen to wash hers. "Tastes like chilled paint," she says over her shoulder.

"What did he want you to do?"

"He wants to teach me the secret handshake, like he did

with you," Kay says. "Little late for it."

"He's a good person," says Avi.

"He's a fucking liar," Kay says. "Same as you. If I take his job, it won't be for him. It'll be for her."

There's a thread hanging from this, a loose bit of yarn. Avi's smart enough not to tug at it. The gin sluices through his brain, moving him forward when he knows better. He pulls.

"Will you stay with me?" he says. "For her?"

It's cheap and low. As soon as the words are out, he wants them back. Kay shakes her head.

"Not even for her," she says.

They never have a conversation about it. The literature Bishop left with her disappears from the kitchen counter. It included not just the glossy bullshit meant to comfort parents and hide what their children had become but stuff Avi believed he'd been given special access to for his work. Once it's gone, he expects they'll have the talk. He looks forward to it. He and Kay have so much in common now. So many of the same fears. Together, they can weigh the dangers of sending her to Bishop against the dangers of not sending her. They can assess what they can give her and what they're able to protect her from. *She'll have to forgive me now that we're both terrified,* he thinks.

But they don't talk. Avi gets caught up with interviews and other things. There is an entirely new world to explore and report back from. People look to him to tell them what to think and how to feel. And Kay's work is ceaseless. He remembers when she was deciding whether to take the job at a firm that handled immigration cases. *Shouldn't I pick a fight I can win?* she asked him. He loved that about her, her willingness to engage in a never-ending battle.

One day he gets home and finds a letter on the kitchen counter in with the bills and the mortgage statement and every other insignificant thing that shows up in the mailbox like trash pitched up on shore by the tides. It's open, addressed to Emmeline: "Dear Miss Hirsch. We are thrilled to welcome you."

Kay comes into the kitchen and watches as he reads it. Her glass of wine is half empty. They have nothing to say to each other. It's already done.

A WALK IN THE PARK

Bright winter sun through the hotel blinds casts a ladder of shadow and light across them, and the Hirsches take their waking slowly. Avi stares at the ceiling, listening to his wife and daughter breathe. It's like a race: Emmeline a constant step behind. Kay slips out of the bed she and Emmeline slept in and sneaks into the bathroom. When the door shuts, Avi puts on his prosthetic. Emmeline rolls onto her elbow and watches from the other bed. She studies him, a little Buddha. Avi thinks of father-son stereotypes, the things you're supposed to teach a boy-child. If Emmeline had been a boy, would she have stood next to him, examining his reflection as he shaved? Would Avi have shown her how to tie a tie, struggling to mirror the ingrained motions as he formed the knot around her neck? When Emmeline was two days old, lying between them in the bed, Avi whispered to Kay, "There's nothing she can learn from me." Kay assured him it wasn't true. But Avi's been proved right. There's so much she needs to know and so little Avi can give her except to leave her in the hands of those more capable.

"You ready for this?" he asks her.

"No," she says. "I want to go home."

They haven't told her how impossible that is. She doesn't know the negotiations that went on while she spent her last few days at her old school in Rogers Park. The house on Jarvis Avenue is up for rent. Neither Avi nor Kay can afford to buy the other out, and Avi refuses to sell. His refusal isn't based in faith that this will work out so much as inability to accept that it won't. His dreams are haunted by bombs in reverse: fiery shrapnel reassembles itself into a car, broken bones knit, and rent skin heals, scarless. He called Fahima in the middle of the night to ask if it would be possible for a Resonant to move time backward.

"That's not how time works," she said. "Everything that's happened has happened." He could hear her girlfriend breathing in the background. Whatever fight they'd needed to have had been weathered. At least some wounds could heal.

Avi crosses the divide between the beds. The prosthetic gives an extra click, the leg setting into the socket at an angle that's not quite right. He ignores it and sits down next to Emmeline. He promised Kay he won't tell her anything. They haven't sat down to talk with Emmeline together. Kay insists that Avi wants to tell her so he can seem like the one who's open and honest when he's been lying the whole time. She's right. The saddest part is that their marriage is reduced to winning and losing. Their language now is silences and secrets.

"You'll make friends," he says.

"You always say that, and I never do."

"You'll be with kids like you," Avi says. He wonders if Emmeline will have things in common with the students at Bishop because they all have abilities. The other kids may not read as often or as deeply as Emmeline. They may not love to draw. Regardless of the fact that they can move objects with their minds or create protective shells around themselves, the girls may be into dolls or makeup, things in which Emmeline's never shown interest. What keeps Emmeline apart from her peers may not be her abilities but the person she is, the million ways she's different. Everything Avi loves about her may make her a target. Bishop Academy may be full of kids with fantastic abilities who are otherwise dull as paint, perfectly normal.

"Maybe my ability will be I can fix everything," she says. This stabs at Avi. He's hoped Bishop Academy might teach her to repair the broken marriage, the broken trust. The last manifestation of her ability could be to let itself go, a djinn freed by a generous third wish, leaving only their daughter, never normal but not special like she is. Special to them, not to the whole world.

Avi hugs his daughter tightly because it's a way to hide his face from her as it trembles and falls apart.

Kay suggests they spend the morning in Central Park. Avi can't help thinking that proposing a long walk is a *move* on her part: a way to physically hurt him. Kay's mind doesn't work that way, but the idea is there, thrown on the pile of awful things between them. Before Kay and her mother moved to Chicago, they lived in New York, and Kay loves

Central Park. She wants to be somewhere she feels safe now as all possibility of safety falls away.

By the time they get to the entrance on Fifth and 79th, the low friction of the prosthetic's cup chafes against his leg. Despite his best intentions, he thinks of it as Kay's fault. She links arms with Avi, leans into him a little. Emmeline runs ahead to investigate a yellow drift of ginkgo leaves. She approaches a klatch of geese. All of this feels scripted. They're putting on a play for Emmeline. Tomorrow they strike the sets. They abandon the roles of people they used to be. The performance is important. They don't have the classic divorcing parent line to fall back on. They can't tell Emmeline it's not about her when it so obviously is. The ossification of their marriage was gradual: it took time to reach the point where it could shatter under one hard strike. But there's no question what the blow was. Kay won't allow this. She won't let Emmeline know it's her fault.

Kay's phone buzzes in the pocket between them. She frees her arm and checks the screen too quickly for him to read the caller's name.

"I have to take this," she says. She walks down the path. Her shoulders relax as she starts talking. The burden of faking affection for him drops away. Avi wonders if she's having an affair. Or if the possibility of an affair is becoming actual as a result of all of this. After the hospital, in the worst depths of his depression, he told her she should. "It would make *me* feel better," he said. "I'd know you're getting what you need even if you're not getting it from me." He could see how badly the offer hurt her even if, in his emotional state, he couldn't bring himself to care. It was an attempt to push her away, no different from swatting her hands as she helped ease his stump into the cup of his prosthesis. He felt like a terrible person, and her refusal to see him as terrible made him angry, determined to convince her how awful he was. If he could have left, he would have for Kay's own good. Maybe it would have made things better. What of their last year was worth having him around? Who benefited except for him?

Emmeline buys feed from a coin op dispenser by the lake. It pours pellets into her cupped hands, and the geese take a sudden interest. *They're as big as she is*, Avi thinks as they encircle Emmeline. He is ready to step in, battle them off to protect her. When she was born, he started seeing the whole world as a threat. Emmeline throws the handful of pellets into the air so they rain down on her and the geese. Avi expects a melee, Emmeline pecked and nipped bloody by creatures with brains the size of a spun dime. They froth and fight around her in a perfect circle, a hurricane with Emmeline at its eye. Avi wonders if Emmeline holds them back, keeping herself safe with her ability. Or if luck cast the pellets up in exact arcs so not a single one lands on her coat to tempt their lizard brains. Emmeline spins at the center of them, laughing. Kay rejoins Avi, slips her arm back into his. For a moment they are exactly who they're pretending to be: two parents walking in the park, desperate in their love for their daughter.

Emmeline stops, looking across the lake at the city. The geese pause, leaving a slew of pellets on the ground. Avi thinks they're following Emmeline's gaze, but then they scatter. She shakes her head, her hand raising up to point to something on the skyline. Avi and Kay rush to her. Avi reaches her a second late and ends up holding on to Kay, who is holding Emmeline.

"Why is it here now?" Emmeline says. "How did they build it already?"

Avi and Kay look where Emmeline is pointing. Blocks away, rising over all the other buildings, is a shining tower, an obsidian spire stabbing into the sky.

"Can you hear it?" Emmeline asks. "It's talking to all of them at once. It's sending out hurt."

Avi looks at Kay, and the horror on her face tells him she can see it, too. He thinks about newspaper photos of the New York skyline after the attacks. The absence of the World Trade Center buildings made it feel like they'd never been there, like he'd been remembering the city wrong the entire time. This tower has the same effect: it threatens to become a permanent part of the way he sees New York. He tries to orient himself within a map of the city to understand where the tower is. *It's where we're going*, he thinks. *It's the Bishop Academy.*

Then it's gone.

Emmeline's breathing returns to normal. He can feel it slowing through Kay's body, which rises and falls with every breath. The image of the tower becomes vague in his mind until he can summon only the words he attached to it, not the image itself. Shining tower. Obsidian spire. The fear, too, fades quickly with nothing to hold it in place.

"What the fuck happened?" Kay asks Avi. She's stiff with panic. Until this moment, she hasn't believed any of this.

She may have let herself understand that what Avi told her, what he wrote, was true. That there were people in the world who had these abilities. But she hadn't believed their daughter was one of them.

Kay lets go of Emmeline as if the girl is red hot.

THE ORIENTATION

Avi's relieved there isn't a throng of reporters in front of the academy. They'll be here soon, but they respected the details in the press release. They'll wait to be let in. If they rush the doors, they'll be locked out forever.

Sarah is there to meet them in the lobby. Emmeline runs to Cortex the second she sees him, nuzzling into the deep fur of the dog's neck. Avi introduces Sarah to Kay. He wishes it were Bishop or Patrick meeting them rather than an attractive young white woman. The optics of who he's been spending his time with are bad. Kay's beyond caring.

"I'm sorry everything's so disorganized," Sarah says. "It's a weird day here."

"You get normal days?" Kay says flatly.

Sarah smiles patiently at her. "I was thinking you'd want to see the place."

"I want to get Emmeline set up," Kay says. Her hand rests on Emmeline's head, fingers lost, twined into her curls. "Get her all squared away."

"Of course," Sarah says. "First-year residences are up on the eighth floor. Follow me." Shen nods at Avi and smiles broadly at Emmeline as they head to the elevator.

Emmeline's room is in a hallway of identical rooms. Her soon-to-be roommate's bed is overpopulated with stuffed animals that spill onto the floor. She's papered her side with pictures of movie stars and boy bands. This decoration ends abruptly at the room's midline, where it gives way to bare cream-colored walls. There's a desk for Emmeline and a twin bed made up with crisp hospital corners and a thick comforter folded at the foot.

"We'll have to get pictures for you to hang up," Avi says. "Some of your drawings, maybe."

"You can send some from the old house," Kay says, then winces. "The house," she corrects.

"It's okay," Emmeline says. She presses down on the edge of the bed with her hand. She opens and closes the empty drawers of the desk. "I like it like this."

"Is this her?" asks someone in the doorway. She's older than Emmeline, with straight mouse-brown hair and a spatter of freckles across her chubby face. "I know I'm supposed to let her get settled, but I had a break between classes and I couldn't wait!" The girl bounds across the room and hugs Emmeline, who stands and suffers it awkwardly before softening, placing her arms delicately around the girl's waist.

"Emmeline," says Sarah, "this is Viola Wilkerson. She'll be your roommate."

Viola releases Emmeline and turns to Avi and Kay. "Hi, I'm Viola," she says. "I'm a thermic." She says this the way someone might give her astrological sign. She holds out her hand to Kay, who recoils. The girl is crestfallen for a second, then shifts her attention to Avi. He takes her hand. It's as warm as freshly baked bread. "Can I steal her?" she asks. She pivots back to Emmeline. "There are a ton of people waiting to meet you in the common room."

"Why do they want to meet me?" Emmeline asks.

"Because you're new, silly," Viola says.

"You going to be okay?" Avi asks Emmeline. It's been half an hour since whatever they saw in Central Park, but she's fine now, or she's remembered to look like she's fine. Avi wonders if the brave face is for him or for Kay. He and Emmeline have been protecting each other from how scared they are, how much they're each worried about what the other one is becoming. There was comfort thinking they had time to work it out, to find new selves and fit them together into something that could hold. It was a silly thought. Emmeline realized it sooner than Avi.

"I'll be fine, Dad," she says as Viola drags her away by the hand. It's the first time she's called him *Dad* rather than *Daddy*, and the lack of the last syllable feels like a dropped note, a skipped heartbeat.

Sarah is called away to deal with two students involved in some kind of psychic tussle, leaving Avi and Kay hovering awkwardly outside Emmeline's room. Kay folds her arms around herself, pulled into a knot. The last time they visited Emmeline's school for a teacher conference, standing in a hallway like this one, Kay's hand twitched up every time a kid passed by, as if she wanted to touch them, pat them on the head, and reassure them they would be okay. She said she wanted more kids, then said the time was never right. The problem was that Avi was never right for it. He never committed enough to being the father of one child for her to make him the father of two.

"I'm supposed to meet my photographer," he says, looking down the hall toward the elevators. "Carol sent someone from—"

"Go," Kay says. "I'm going to find Emmeline and say good-bye."

"You're leaving?" Avi asks.

"I'm meeting someone about an apartment in an hour."

"An apartment here?" Avi asks.

"I'm taking the job," says Kay.

"What job?"

"The one Bishop offered," she says. "There are already cases being brought against people who've come out as Resonant. Since your article." Her look says this is all his fault. "He's paying me to take them on."

"This is what the comic books were about?"

"I gave my notice at work," she says. "There's a couple of stays of deportation I'm in the middle of, then I'm done."

"Why didn't you tell me?"

Kay shrugs to tell him it isn't important. *He* isn't. This is what the phone call in the park was about. He's relieved it wasn't an affair. He wants to hold on to all the blame. Even here at the end, agency has power.

"I'll be back and forth a lot," he says. "They'll want me around as a media liaison." He hasn't talked to Bishop yet about what his role will be moving forward, but this seems likely. "I was going to take her to lunch afterward if you want to—"

"I've got apartments all day," she says.

"Next time I'm in New York we can—"

"You should go meet your photographer," Kay says. She puts her hand on his elbow, gives him a gentle shove.

"Right," Avi says. "I hope it goes well."

"Yes," says Kay.

Avi steps toward her, unsure whether he's offering a hug or a handshake. What happens is somewhere in between, a collision of bodies, arms squashed between stomachs, as clumsy as their first night together. They're like magnets with the same polarity: pushed together by outside forces, they repel each other and stand, held apart.

The next week, Kay files divorce papers in Illinois. They never get around to signing them. It isn't a priority, and the world changes too much for it to matter. In any way that truly counts, this is where their marriage ends.

DEBRIEFING

The library of the headmaster's quarters on the fifteenth floor had been like a home to Fahima. When she started at Bishop, she thought she was special because the headmaster had personally recruited her. She soon found out that Kevin Bishop spent most of his days away from the school, gathering new students. He had very little contact time with them after that except for occasional broadcasts into everyone's head through the Hive, the Bishop Academy's equivalent of a public address system. What got Bishop's attention was her persistent and pointed questions on the nature of Resonance. Apparently most teenagers, when told they have incredible abilities and access to a globe-spanning psychic network, blithely accept that they can push the limits of what's possible. Fahima was obsessed with figuring each ability out. She analyzed her fellow students like math problems. How could a body produce superhuman levels of energy without consuming massive amounts of fuel? If someone's ability caused permanent physical change, was that ability constantly engaged, or did the initial manifestation result in a new base or resting state? The human body was a machine like any other, and all around her she saw late-model Chevettes racing like Ferraris. Something didn't add up. She was angry that none of the teachers had answers for how Resonance worked or even seemed to care. *Would knowing change anything?* they asked. *Of fucking course,* Fahima shouted. After Fahima derailed Mr. Duncan's Energy Manipulation class with a barrage of questions, he sent her to Bishop's office, ostensibly as a punishment. Instead, it became the first of many bull sessions held weekly in that office, then among the old wood and soft leather of Bishop's library. At some point, he started drinking martinis during their meetings, sipping as he pondered whatever paradox she brought up to the top floor with her that week. Eventually, he offered her one.

As the elevator deposits her on the top floor, Fahima hears music coming from within, the complex guitar wail of a Prince album. Bishop's record collection tends toward classical, with a particular affection for mid-twentieth-century Russian composers, but he also has a shelf full of funk, soul, and rhythm and blues records and is a religious Prince fan. "Part of the American songbook," he told Fahima once, "Darling Nikki" grinding away on the speakers. It's an aspect of his charm, an effortless, unassuming cool. One of the myths of cool is that it involves not caring when it actually requires very deep caring. Bishop chooses objects and ideas precisely and loves them with devotion.

She knocks and lets herself in. Bishop is lying on the couch, reading an old comic book. On the cover, a scantily clad woman with her spine impossibly twisted fires energy bolts out of her fist at a shadowy figure.

"Is that Patrick's new syllabus?" Fahima asks.

"Did you ever think about the fact that superheroes showed up in the culture around the same time Resonants did?" Bishop asks. "OtherMan was created seven years before I was. And then the flood of them in the sixties, when our numbers started to rocket."

"You weren't created," Fahima says.

"Before I *became*?" Bishop says. "How do you talk about it?"

"Before I resonated," she says.

"Well, yes," he says. "But you had context."

"I had you."

"We had no idea, when it happened," Bishop says. "It felt like being born as something completely new."

"You're feeling philosophical," Fahima says.

"It's that kind of day."

"I brought treats," Fahima says, holding up her bag. She sets it on the coffee table and extracts a bottle of gin, then one of dry vermouth. She takes a metal flask out of the bag. It's wide at the base and has a thin neck, and the silvery metal surface flows like liquid. She pours in five counts of gin, then one count of vermouth. She takes the bottle by the neck and begins swirling it.

"You could be curing cancer," Bishop says.

"Where's the fun in that?" She pours out two glasses of ice-cold gin. "Fuck. Forgot the olives."

"We'll make do," Bishop says. He picks up the drink closest to him, raises it. "I'm glad you came by."

"Feels like a day to celebrate," she says. "It's been a long time coming. And it's time we talk about what happened with the girl."

He glances up from his drink, directly into Fahima's eyes. He's older than he looks. After the liberation of Europe at the end of World War II, he toured the camps. His wartime work with the Office of Scientific Research and Development earned him some favors. "I knew I had become something different," he told Fahima. "I needed to see firsthand what people did to those who were different." He never told her specifics. He said any telling made it less than what it was. But she's watched a look settle into his face that said he was back there, seeing it all again. Something about Emmeline Hirsch triggers that look.

"I never thanked you for building the cell downstairs," he says. "The inhibitor is a piece of genius. Did it come to you in a dream?"

"More or less," Fahima says.

"It's strange when something comes along you didn't know you needed. I'm thinking of having you build one for me in my house up in Maine. As a quiet room. A respite. Are there negative effects?"

"I wouldn't keep anyone in there permanently," says Fahima.

"Keeping Owen Curry locked up isn't a permanent solution anyway. But I'm tired of permanent solutions." He gives her a painful, tight smile that reminds Fahima how much of his story Bishop hasn't told her. He leans forward and sets his glass down on the table. "So let's talk about the girl."

"We should talk about the thing in the Hive," says Fahima.

232

"I'm more concerned about Emmeline Hirsch," Bishop says.

"She's a sweet little kid," Fahima says.

"You're giving me opinions," Bishop says. "Start from what you know."

Fahima sighs. When she was his student, she was so easily cowed by him. She used to wonder if he was using his ability against her, bringing her down a notch. He swore he'd never do that to her. He pushed her to think deeper, work harder. *Remove anything but facts so you can see the thing clearly,* he told her. *Start from what you know.*

"She's an early bloomer," Fahima says. "But her abilities haven't manifested in the real world yet."

"Any sense of what her ability is?" Bishop asks.

Fahima thinks of the file she has on Emmeline. Report cards and school forms. Teacher evaluations, a psychological assessment. She thinks of the way the girl's Hivebody manifested, a stack of layered images. She remembers thinking it was as if the girl called in future versions of herself for help. None of this amounts to anything definite. At most, there's an indication of a prescience, an eeriness about the girl.

"Not yet," she says.

"Keep eyes on her," he says. "And keep me updated."

"Why all the interest in this one?"

Bishop shrugs. "What she did in the Hive was impressive."

"What she did was impossible," Fahima corrects. "But you were looking for her before you knew what she could do."

"The girl is powerful," he says. "She's demonstrated the ability to manipulate Hivematter, which is within my area of interest. I have thoughts about her, but I don't *know* anything." He sips his drink, purely for effect. "Is that enough for you for now?"

"It's all I'm getting, right?"

"I trust you to handle it," he says. It's Bishop code for *I will continue to monitor you very closely and possibly without your awareness.* "You want to ask me about the abscess."

"You knew what it was," Fahima says.

"I have thoughts on that, too."

"You need to share them," she says.

"I don't *need* to do anything," says Bishop. "The Hive is a special place. It's what unites us, connects us to where we draw our abilities from. Without it, we're a scattered collection of accidents. We're a coincidence rather than a people."

"So no one gets to know you built it," Fahima says.

"Most of them don't need to know," he says. "You know. Patrick knows, and Sarah."

"What if you can't control it anymore?" Fahima asks. "What if someone else can build things like that abscess in there? The Hive could be dangerous."

"The Hive will always be safe," Bishop says. "We built it to be inviolable. If someone was able to manipulate it, I'd know."

"Someone did, and you didn't know," says Fahima.

"We saved the girl, Fahima," he says. "Take the win. Today's not about that." He looks down onto the street. People are gathering on the sidewalks, lining up.

"You should be out there with them," says Fahima.

"Today's not about me either," he says. "Come to the window. It's about to start."

OWEN CURRY AND
THE FRIEND WHO CAME BACK

They forgot to feed Owen Curry this morning. His stomach grumbles and growls, and the emptiness there feels like the null, but not enough. Not nearly. An echo of a roar. Shadow instead of void. The *almost* of it makes the lack worse.

When the door slides open, he's sure it's the Islam bitch with his slops. Everything they feed him is so fucking healthy when what he wants is grease and fat. Vegetables leave him full but never sated. He wants to rip into food with his hands. Tear and rend.

But it's not her or the blonde. Whoever the fuck it is isn't carrying a tray. Pressing his face hard against the glass, Owen can see his visitor. He's tall, lanky. His face is blurred like a television screen full of static. Owen's heart leaps.

"You came," he says.

"I told you I'd come for you, Owen," says his friend. "Did you lose your faith?"

"I couldn't hear you," Owen says, clawing at his temples. "They put me under these lights, and you weren't in my head anymore."

"I was always there, Owen," his friend says. He flips off the green lights. Then he punches in a key code, and the glass slides back. Owen can't believe it. He's afraid to step through the opening. He summons his courage and crosses the threshold, into the hallway.

"I'm going to null them all," he says. "I'm going to wipe out this whole fucking building." He reaches into the part of himself where the null lives and gets ready to let it out, all of it this time. He'll null the entire world. There's a stabbing pain in the middle of his head. Brain freeze times a thousand. It drops Owen to his knees, and he can feel the null pulling away from him, shriveling like a scared animal.

"Not. Yet," says his friend. "I have a sentimental attachment to this place. And if you're going to be my sword, you need to remember who holds the hilt." Owen hears the words wrong and has to sort them back. What he hears initially is *be my dog*. What he hears is *who holds the leash*.

"I'm sorry about the church," Owen says, sounding like a whiny child even to his own ears. "I know you told me First Corinthians. But there was a girl there who's like us. And I thought, *He wouldn't want me to kill our own*. But I was so hungry."

"I know what you *thought*, Owen," says his friend. "But I need you to *trust*. Do you trust me?"

"Of course," Owen says. *I love you*, he thinks. "I'm sorry."

"Stop sniveling," says his friend. "We don't have time. There's an opportunity to get you out, and we have to take it. They're distracted. It's a big day for them. For you, too. Today everyone walks in the light. But Owen." He grabs

Owen by the chin, his grip strong but fluid. "Disobey me again and I'm going to hurt you."

"How am I going to get out?" Owen asks. He assumes there is security, armed guards ready to shoot him dead.

"Up the elevator and out the front door," says his friend. He holds the outer door open. "Fall in with the other children. Speak to no one. When you get the chance, peel off from the crowd. I'll be with you. To guide you." He steps to the side to let Owen pass. As Owen squeezes by him, out into a cluttered lab, he tries to make out his friend's face in the shaft of light coming through the door. It's a mask of flat skin over the front of his head, churning like the surface of a liquid, beneath which something swims in slow, irregular circles.

THIS IS HAPPENING

In the immediate aftermath of the articles in the *Chicago Tribune* and *The Atlantic* and the resulting television coverage, the whole of Bishop's student body gathered in the Hive to decide whether the school should stay hidden. Headmaster Bishop had strong-armed into all of their heads to advise caution, and the faculty had already made their feelings known. But they all insisted the decision fell to the students, who they knew would do the right thing. There was suspicion that if the will of the students didn't align with the wishes of the teachers, the latter would win out. Democracy suspended, martial law imposed. It was a classic adult move to give the illusion of choice. Still, the students went forward as if it were all in good faith. They milled about, an informal meeting, waiting to be called to order. This was all new to them. They understood democracy as a concept, but no one had given any thought to the dull mechanisms it required.

Carrie was the first to speak up.

"This is happening," she said, "and we should be part of it. The school can be the face of Resonants to the whole world. We can show them this is who we are. We're people learning to be better, to be the best we can."

Ruby Wallace, a fifth-year lithic and, Waylon later told Carrie, undiagnosed agoraphobic, argued against it, saying it would make Bishop unsafe, especially for the younger kids who hadn't mastered their abilities. Ruby came by her fears honestly; she had arrived at Bishop bloodied and bruised. Her left eye pulled slightly downward, a permanent mark of how the outside world had greeted the revelation of her abilities. She imagined mobs at the front doors. Daily bomb threats.

"How do *you* think it's going to go?" she asked Carrie, tears welling in her eyes. Carrie didn't have an answer. All she knew was that everything had to change. She looked at Ruby, whose Hivebody was a collection of flat surfaces like tectonic plates. She felt sad that Ruby had been born too early, that she'd had to suffer through this process. She wanted to tell her the world on the other side of this would be unimaginably different, but she was struck silent by the hurt on Ruby's face, damage Ruby would carry with her into whatever new world emerged.

Others rushed to fill the space. The upperclassmen, who were allowed to leave campus, had been using their abilities regularly in public, although they made a point of never doing so near the academy. Tired of the insular dating scene at Bishop, they hung around city high schools or even Cooper Union and swore the baseliner kids flocked to them. There were some skirmishes, most notably a ten-on-ten brawl outside a school in Brooklyn that had been broken up by the cops. But as Darren Helms pointed out, "It's not like we can't fuck them up." His Hivebody was hulking. Black smoke poured off him like steam off dry ice; he was sublimating, becoming gas. Carrie could see him shrinking and puffing back up to full size in a cycle, like breathing. She worried about this logic, not least because it came from Darren Helms. It assumed a fair fight. If something happened, it wouldn't be fair.

"We're better coming out than being outed," Hayden said. Hayden's Hivebody was unstable, although not as volatile as Darren's. They rotated through aspects of themselves, like turning a gem to admire its facets. Hayden said that was what it felt like to be inside their ability all the time. They'd never bothered putting enough effort into their Hivebody to stabilize it. Carrie and Hayden had this in common. If Carrie wasn't concentrating, her Hivebody was a dotted line around an empty space in the shape of a girl.

Isidra Gonzalez made the point that students and all Resonants of color were most likely to bear the brunt of violence. A dozen boys white-knighted in to say they'd stand by her, and Isidra laughed them off.

"How's the room?" Carrie asked Miquel.

"Light blue," said Miquel, as if that held clear meaning.

What swayed things finally was the underclassmen. Prohibited from leaving campus without chaperones, they'd never used their abilities in public. They didn't take kindly to coddling from their elders, particularly homebodies like Ruby Wallace.

"This is happening," said Viola Wilkerson. Her Hivebody burned blue at the edges and white at the center like the gas flame on a stove. When she said the words, they didn't have the argumentative tone they'd had when Carrie had spoken them. They had a sense of wonder. Carrie had asserted that these things were going to happen whether the assembled students liked it or not. Viola said it was magic to be here in the middle of all of it, with change not inevitable but present, a moment threatening to slip by them into the past.

"This is happening," her classmates agreed. They spoke the words to one another. A pledge.

And the decision was made.

"You should get credit for the motto," Hayden said to Carrie.

"Doesn't matter," Carrie said. All that was left was to pick a day, select a moment, and wait for it to arrive.

When it does, they throng in the lobby. Shen expands to his maximum size, holding them back until the clock hand clicks up to twelve. The doors of Bishop Academy open, and the students spill out onto 57th Street. Carrie holds back a second. She grabs Miquel's wrist.

"Is it real?" she asks.

He smiles and pulls her forward into the street. They've been told all their lives to hide what makes them special. Out in the open for the first time, they fly and glow. They shift fluidly from shape to shape. They puppet elaborate golems made of discarded newspapers and empty coffee cups with their thoughts. They juggle balls of light, launch fireworks from their fingertips, trail streamers of pure energy as they dance. It's a parade, a coming-out party. For Carrie, whose ability is to hide, it's enough to walk alongside her friends as they peacock and strut. She catches the cartoonish mental images Waylon throws at the crowd like Mardi Gras beads. She watches Isidra Gonzalez trace a lemniscate of molten silver, weaving it around her body. Hayden and Jonathan peform acoustic covers of what Hayden calls the queer classics, anthems of coming out, along with some post–civil rights movement say-it-loud songs Bryce suggested. Waves of positive emotion pour off Miquel like heat.

Carrie passes Avi Hirsch and his daughter on the sidewalk. They're tight together until other kids snatch Emmeline away, pulling her into the street to jump, dance. The reporter watches her go. He taps the photographer next to him. "Get a shot of her for me," he says. The photographer trains his camera on the girl's back, clicking as she becomes part of the crowd.

The sidewalk is lined with spectators and the press. Those in the back stretch phones as high as they can to get pictures of the students in the street before they notice the show in the air above. They turn their eyes upward, eclipse watchers, UFO seekers. They search the skies for wonders and are rewarded.

Bryce works the edges of the crowd. His head is a crown of calla lilies. His shoulders blossom lilac and hyacinth. A puffy necklace of peony blooms under his chin. On the curb, a little girl, maybe three years old, jumps up and down, struggling to reach one of the flowers on the top of Bryce's head. Her mother holds her back, whispers in her ear. The girl stops leaping, her face sad and slack. Bryce kneels down in the gutter. He bows to let the girl pluck a lily from his scalp. Behind him, Shane Goss suspends a perfect globe of light in the air in front of him.

A knot of people gather to watch as he shapes it. Four thin veins descend from the globe. A bulb develops at one end and becomes a neck, a head. Details come into focus, take shape, and there is a horse the size of a small dog crafted entirely of light. *They always do a horse,* Carrie thinks, remembering boys in the common room showing off horses made of light, made of metal, to try to impress girls. Like zoetrope images, something about the mechanics of the horse's movement makes them a showcase for a new medium. The horse gallops in place, legs pedaling, the muscles at its shoulders rippling. Shane's face twists in concentration. The legs move faster and faster until they're blurred with speed, and a young boy watching begins to clap, enthusiasm bursting uncontrollably from him. Shane beams at him. Carrie can't help watching them, intruding on a moment that should be only theirs. She has the sense that all of today's moments are shared. They belong equally to everyone here, Resonant and baseliner, spectator and spectacle. It's the last time she'll ever have this feeling. An echo will come back to her, but never with the surety she has right now.

Someone jostles her, breaks her attention. When she turns, she's face to face with a boy she doesn't recognize. He's sweating even though he doesn't have a coat and it's freezing out. He pushes by her and ducks into a walkway. Carrie turns back to find Shane and his assembled audience. Carrie sees the red dot before Shane does, zipping around his face like a mosquito looking for a place to settle. Shane's eye twitches as the dot skitters across it. He swats at it, then turns toward the source of the light. His happiness at finally being able to share his ability radiates from him as the bullet turns his head into a red mist and the horse disperses into nothing.

Carrie screams as another bullet goes wild and hits the asphalt, spraying macadam at the kids on the curb and the startled student revelers. A third catches Doug Shaw in the meat of his thigh. Carrie reaches out and grabs Emmeline, who happens to be the nearest kid. Carrie folds Emmeline in her arms and forces them both down into invisibility. It's the first time Carrie's made someone else invisible with her, and a bright spark of pride fizzles in a cool pond of panic. Emmeline struggles against her grip, and Carrie hears the kid's father calling out for her, but she holds Emmeline tight. Nolan Emerson, Shane's roommate since first year, rushes to the body, shaking Shane as if he can wake him, but Shane is clearly dead. A memory comes to Carrie of their field trip to the Museum of Natural History, Shane making a translucent penguin dance across the tundrascape of the Inuit diorama. She starts to laugh, the nervous tittering of a much younger girl. It's only the hitching breath of Emmeline's body against her, small and fragile like a bird's, that steadies Carrie and returns her to the horror of the moment.

The crowds bolt, running for cross-streets. The students and faculty are paralyzed, caught in a kill zone. A fourth shot shatters the window of a bank. Sarah, calm in the middle of the chaos, closes her eyes. When she opens them again, she points to the top of a building at the northwest corner of 57th and Lexington.

"There," she shouts.

Michaela Michelinie, who teaches first-years and who Carrie thinks of as a kindly grandma, jumps into the air.

Five fliers follow, falling into formation like fighter jets. They rush toward the rooftop. Shots worry their approach, a slow, cruel drumbeat. One bullet passes close enough to Carrie and Emmeline that Carrie feels the hem of her shirt flutter. Another hits Pamela Briggs, ten feet away from them, in the gut. She staggers into the arms of Leticia Hartman. The air ripples with a ring of heavy gravity that Leticia puts up around them for protection. Carrie wishes she was within that circle instead of here, invisible but exposed.

Marian Scholl, a third-year flier, reaches the shooter first because she doesn't waver and dodge. She, too, is a bullet. She snatches him up like a hawk catching a mouse. The rifle falls onto the rooftop. Marian swoops back toward the crowd and drops him. As he plummets, Eli Herrington snatches him from the air. The fliers continue like this, catching and dropping like a malicious trapeze act, and each time Carrie hopes the shooter will fall. She wants to hear the crunch of him against the ground so badly that it's a hunger. Rufina Dahl, who started at the academy the same month as Shane, tosses the shooter onto an open patch of pavement in front of Nolan, who cradles Shane's body. In the still moment, they see the shooter in a heap, a fetal ball that births itself. He's a kid, no older than they.

Nolan comes up off his knees. His right fist is clenched and begins to spark. He approaches the shooter, fist wrapped in a cloud of angry blue flecks of electricity, like wasps around a stirred nest.

"Fucking do it," screams the shooter. He's out of breath from the fall and from sobbing. He holds his face forward to

Nolan, as if waiting for a kiss. "You're just a fucking animal, so fucking do it!"

Nolan's face writhes with pain and rage. *Do it*, Carrie thinks. *Do it and no one will try to hurt us again.* Nolan raises his hand. Carrie hears the buzz his ability makes, the hum and crackle. She smells ozone drifting off him. His whole body courses with current searching for ground, sparks visible around his hand.

Nolan towers over the shooter, a god with unknowable power, a human victim at his whim. Nolan is crying. The tears glint like sapphires. Avi's photographer trains his lens over Carrie's invisible shoulder, over Emmeline's concealed head, catching the moment exactly as the two of them see it. Every breath is held.

Nolan lowers his hand. The charge in him dissipates, spreading out into the asphalt with a crackle like cellophane crushed inside a fist. He stands at the center of a web of scorch marks as police rush in from the sidelines and tackle the shooter. When he's upended, Carrie sees that the knees of his pants have been burned away, the skin beneath angry red. As the other cops drag the shooter away, one goes to pat Nolan on the arm but stops, worried that Nolan is carrying current.

Carrie leans down next to Emmeline. "You okay?" she asks.

"I'm okay. Go take care of him." Carrie steps away from the girl and puts her arm around Nolan. She cloaks them both, this newfound ability second nature now. She leads him back toward the academy.

"He just fucking killed him," Nolan says. "Why is this happening?"

"I don't know," Carrie says as Shen shepherds them back inside.

The next day, the image is all over the papers and the Internet. When people see it, they imagine themselves as the shooter. On their knees. They hear the crackle of sparks next to their ears and know this punishment is just. It's due for what they've done or would have done given the chance. Out of fear or jealousy. To protect their children. To deny there are people like Carrie and Nolan in the world. Dozens of newspapers and websites run an article by Avi Hirsch. They all run the picture with the same headline, one word in type huge enough to bear its meaning:

MERCY.

FOUR

ANNUS MIRABILIS

We shall have everything we want and there'll be
no more dying.
—FRANK O'HARA, *"Ode to Joy"*

THE ANGEL OF MONTGOMERY

Avi's apartment in New York is on the cheap side because it's small and inconvenient to everywhere. Gowanus is one of those neighborhoods people end up in because it's more affordable than where they want to be. They tell their friends in more desirable neighborhoods how great Gowanus is. Everyone here is ten years younger than Avi. Most have jobs that don't require them to be anywhere specific. The neighborhood is studded with coffee shops where young people work diligently at whatever young people work diligently at. Avi gets his coffee to go and comes back to his studio apartment, where he can control the noise except the clanking of pipes in the morning and the boys next door who have no jobs except loudly fucking midafternoon.

He hasn't furnished the apartment. He occupies a triangle within it, vertices at the couch, fridge, and desk. Gowanus is convenient to Ikea. Avi's cabbed back and forth a couple of times to purchase the desk and chair, some kitchen stuff. A bed for Emmeline sits unassembled, a trio of long, flat boxes open like coffins in the small, bare area that's meant to be hers. Anything more would make this feel permanent, which it isn't.

There's a picture on his desk in a simple frame from the Public Day parade almost a year ago: Emmeline joining the crowd, skipping away from him.

Avi straightens his tie, smooths his lapels. If Kay were here, she'd tell him not to wear a suit. *Everyone in a courtroom is used to wearing suits,* she'd say. *They know how to do it. You look like you dressed out of your dad's closet.* Being around young people has taught Avi that he's no longer able to pull off youthful insouciance as an aesthetic. His days of walking into newspaper offices in ripped jeans and faded, pit-stained tee shirts are behind him.

He picks up his cane. It's a requirement lately. He's been falling asleep with the prosthetic on. Proper care and maintenance are necessary, he reminds himself every morning he wakes up with his leg throbbing. He suffers through days and ends up collapsed on the couch, too exhausted or drunk to take the fucking thing off.

A door appears on the bare wall. Avi grabs the two coffees from the desk and tugs the door open. Kimani's holding the knob on the other side, and Avi surprises her, almost pulling her out of the room and into his apartment. She catches herself on the door frame, regains her balance. He wonders what would happen to her if she stepped out. Would she disappear in a puff of smoke or burn up like a vampire in daylight? Or would she become a grainy black-and-white image of herself, Dorothy Gale leaving her Technicolor Oz for a drab Kansas?

"In a rush?" Kimani asks.

"I brought you coffee," he says, holding out the cup. A tongue of steam seeps through the lid.

"Four-dollar coffee to save yourself a three-dollar subway fare," she says, taking the cup.

"It's not the cost," he says. "It's the time. The F is a crawl."

"Yeah, *your* time's precious," she says, almost inaudible. She's on the edge of tired where she's making an effort to hide it: her hair is in a tower of curls, but her clothes are rumpled.

"I didn't mean—"

"It's cool," she says. "I'm just ragged. Bishop's got me running around."

"Anything interesting?"

She hesitates, then shakes her head. "New students," she says. "Thank you for the coffee." Avi shrugs it off. "What time do you need to be there?"

"Not till this afternoon," he says. "I was going to go by the academy first. Take Emmeline to lunch."

"That sounds nice," Kimani says. She shuts the door behind him. Avi doesn't understand how the decor changes in here, and he can't bring himself to ask Kimani about it. It's furnished better than his apartment. Kimani is the kindest of them, but her kindness is a way to avoid talking about herself. Everyone else has explained their abilities at length, but Kimani's seem like magic. She sits in a wicker papasan chair, takes the lid off her coffee, and inhales deeply before venturing a sip. "Nice suit," she says. "Remind me why I'm taking you to Montana."

"There's a woman on trial there," he says. "One of you. *Harper's* is going to pick up the story."

"That's great, Avi," Kimani says. "It's great for us. I hope it has been for you."

"Pays the bills," he says. "I'm doing what I can to help."

"You're helping," she says, but there's a weariness in her voice. He can't tell if it's exhaustion or if she's gotten tired of telling him how important he is, how special.

The elevator delivers a load of students into the lobby. Upperclassmen leave during lunch and free periods. The stores and fast-food spots along Lexington fill up with Resonant kids trying to look cool. They pack the Magnolia Bakery in Bloomingdale's on Third, floating cupcakes across the room over the heads of the patrons. They binge on Skittles and gummies at Dylan's Candy Bar, making their insides transparent so their friends can see the rainbow-colored boluses as they slide down their throats. Avi's interviewed some of the local business owners. They're split on the issue. Some think the kids are good for business. They bring in gawkers, tourists who spend money. Others have been thinking of ways to ban the kids but can't come up with language that doesn't sound racist. "I don't let people bring guns into my shop," the manager of a nearby Chipotle told Avi. "But I have to let in these kids who could blow my place up by thinking about it?"

After the teenage flood comes Emmeline. She spots Avi and continues toward him without increasing her pace. When she was little and he'd pick her up from school, Avi would watch the other kids sprint into their parents' arms while Emmeline moseyed, confident that Avi would be there when she got to him. When she does, she throws her arms around his waist.

"Hi, Dad," she says. "Nice suit."

"Hey, Leener," says Avi. "You hungry?" Avi feels her nod against his rib cage. He releases her and puts out a hand for her to hold, noticing her quick glance around the lobby before she takes it. "I was thinking that Indian place over on 53rd."

"That sounds great," she says. "I have to sign out." She walks over to the desk and talks to Shen, who looks over at Avi, nods, and hands Emmeline a clipboard. When she returns, she takes Avi's hand, more confident this time. They've barely started down Lexington when a man rushes at them, brandishing a microphone. He's breathless from chasing down every other student who's come out the doors.

"Excuse me, miss, excuse me, miss," he says. "I'm with the Kindred Network. I have a couple of questions."

"Leave us alone," Avi says, walking past him. The man follows along.

"You're the guy from television," he says, pointing and snapping his fingers as if he's had a brilliant idea. "The Rezzie lover. Miss, miss, are you his daughter? Have you psychically controlled this man to get him to support your radical cause?"

Avi tries to speed up, but he's slow on his cane and there's only so fast Emmeline can walk. The man dogs them, poking Avi in the back with the microphone. There's a flicker, a glitch in Avi's vision, and they're ten feet ahead of where they'd been. Avi looks at Emmeline, who looks as surprised as he is. Maybe this is her ability, some kind of superspeed, and she's discovering it only now. *How amazing it would be if we could find out together*, Avi thinks. When she was a baby and he had nothing to fill his time but staring at her, he imagined a lifetime of shared victories. Standing ovations for bravura theater performances and whooping cheers at game-winning goals. The taut thrill of opening college admissions responses and finding acceptance letters within. This one hadn't been imaginable to him then, but it seems right that when her ability made itself known, they should share it. He is about to ask her if this is it when despite the jump forward, the man catches up with them and puts a hand on Emmeline's shoulder.

"Miss, what do you say to people who no longer feel safe in Manhattan due to the presence of your kind?"

Avi stops, takes his cane in both hands, and gives the man a small but solid shove. "You need to leave us alone," he says.

"Just walking down the street," says the man. He holds out his hands defensively. "We could grab lunch and talk." He points the microphone at Emmeline. "It talks, right?"

Avi pushes past him, dragging Emmeline by the hand and heading back for Bishop. Shen waits for them outside the door.

"You," he says to the reporter. "I told you a hundred feet back."

"That's around the block," says the man. "By then I can't tell which are the normal kids and which are the freaks."

"Step back to a hundred feet or I'll throw you back," Shen says.

"Why don't you let me inside?" says the man. "Let me grill a couple of—"

Shen leans back on his heels and grows. Watching it happen is like seeing a camera zoom in on an object; Shen expands in all directions at the same time until he looms over the reporter, blocking the width of the sidewalk and shielding Avi and Emmeline.

"Next time I see you is the last time you get seen," he says. His voice is wheezy now, like that of an emphysema patient. It would be funny if he weren't huge and terrifying. The reporter puts his microphone in his bag and walks away, slowly at first but speeding up as soon as dignity allows.

Shen returns to normal size. "Come on back in," he says. "He'll be waiting around the corner to pounce at you."

"We can eat in the cafeteria," Emmeline says.

"Sounds great, Leener," says Avi. He wants to grab Emmeline and make a run for it, away from the academy, away from the reporters and this city and everyone else with their ridiculous abilities. Instead he follows her into the elevator, their hands at their sides, almost touching.

After sharing burgers with Emmeline in the noisy scrum of the cafeteria, Avi calls Kimani to pick him up. He texts to let Kay know they're coming, but she looks shocked when Avi opens the door through the wall of the conference room in the Lewis and Clark County courthouse. In the hallway, people press against the windows to see what's happened, watching Avi as if he's a strange visitor arriving from another planet. If he's being honest with himself, part of the reason he travels with Kimani is to make an entrance. It's a watered-down version of the thrill *they* must get now, being seen, the methadone equivalent of the full rush. They owe him this, at least.

"This shit doesn't help," Kay says, packing papers into her bag. "I'm trying to play down the weird factor, and you've got to teleport in." She nods at Kimani through the doorway. She's practicing as Kay Washington, having reverted to her maiden name in professional situations. Avi wonders if that's how she thinks of herself, the name she refers to herself by when she's alone with her thoughts.

"I came from the school," he says. "I had lunch with Emmeline."

Kay winces. "I'm going to miss our lunch this week," she says.

"Kimani could take you," Avi says, but when he turns around, the door is already gone.

"I'll make it up to her," Kay says. She clicks the clasp of her bag shut. "You look goofy in that suit."

"Emmeline said I looked nice," he says, although he can't remember her actually saying it.

"Emmeline is nine. So is this for the book or just another article?"

"Both," Avi says. Kay nods. He told her about the book deal right away, on a reflex. He can't imagine a time she's not the first person he shares good news with. She said it was fine as long as she and Emmeline weren't in it. "You look nice."

Kay ignores him. "You can't walk in with me; it's bad optics. She's in custody, which already starts us out looking bad. I'm going to try to intercept the bailiffs and get them to let me walk her in."

"You going to win this?" he asks.

"I have no idea anymore," she says. Her hand goes to her forehead, and Avi thinks he's supposed to cross the room and hold her but doesn't. "Last month I had a deportation case. It felt like coming home. A woman who was teleporting over the Mexican border to work. Still lived in Juarez. Her argument was that she never actually *crossed* the border. Just showed up on the other side. Next week, I'm contesting an eviction notice on a single mom whose kid can all of a sudden talk to cats. This is the first case I've had with a white client."

"Change of pace," says Avi. Kay gives him a look he's well familiar with. It's the one that tells him he's said something powerfully stupid.

"Everyone else I've represented was someone who was already hated," Kay says. "If they weren't coming after them for this, it'd be for something else. If they have time and energy to come after nice white ladies? It means they've learned to hate these people just for what they are, without some value-added hatred. It's become worth hating all on its own."

There is something angelic about Janet Goulding, whose real name is Janine Coupland. The papers back home call her the Angel of Montgomery. Avi wonders if Janet's ability seeps out of her like radiation. If by being around her, people are healed. He hopes this comes across to the jury. That like him, they can't help but feel better around Janet. He hopes this makes a difference.

"I'm saying this for the last time," Kay tells her. "I think this is a bad idea." With Kay's permission, Avi is seated right behind them, privy to their conversation.

"I know, sweetheart," Janet says. When she says it, it comes across as two distinct words. *Sweet. Heart.*

"I think it's better if you don't mention the dice," Kay says. "If you can avoid mentioning them."

"I'm going to answer his questions," Janet says. "I'm going to tell the truth."

"Of course tell the truth," says Kay. "But you can decide what parts of it. They will hang you on the dice."

The prosecutor calls Janet to the stand. He calls her Janine because that's her given name, the one she's being tried under, if not the one she prefers. It's who she was when she lived here, in Helena, Montana. Kay tried to get the case moved to Montgomery, where Janet is literally worshipped. There are altars to her in the hospital parking lot. Before she was arrested and extradited to Montana, people made pilgrimages to Montgomery to see her. They brought their children before her, their elderly mothers and their dying fathers, all of them like offerings. She sent them away well and alive, and they thanked her. They called her saint, and they called her angel.

Here in Montana, Janet is on trial for manslaughter.

"Can you please state your name and profession," says the prosecutor. He's burly, the way Avi imagines they breed them in Montana. He looks as if he'd be more comfortable in flannel and Carhartt than the off-the-rack suit he's in. He's a good guy from what Avi can tell. On the phone, he told Avi he'd rather not be doing this. It could have been an *I'd rather be fishing* type of line. Avi took it as sincere regret that it was his job to try to put Janet in jail.

"Dr. Janine Coupland," says Janet. "I'm a surgeon at Montgomery General in Alabama. Before that, I was employed as a surgeon at St. Peter's here in Helena."

"When did you leave St. Peter's?"

"Three years ago," she says.

"And you changed your name at that time."

"Yes, I changed my name to Janet Goulding," Janet says.

"Why did you leave Helena and change your name?"

"People had discovered my ability."

"You are a Resonant. Is that correct?"

"Yes."

"How long have you been . . . that way?"

"I believe I was born that way. But my ability manifested when I was fourteen."

"And what is your ability?"

Kay stands up. "Objection," she says. "Janet, you don't have to answer that."

Before the judge can speak, Janet turns to him and says, "No, I'm comfortable answering the question." She looks back at the prosecutor warmly, as if he's paid her a compliment. "I'm a healer."

"Can you explain what that means?"

"The body wants to be well," Janet says. "It wants to be whole and functioning. Sometimes things get in the way of that. Cancer. Viruses. Bullets. My ability lets me help a person's body get back to the state it wants. I can guide it. Speed it along."

"Can you give an example?"

"Do you have a knife?" The prosecutor pauses, flummoxed. "I lived in Helena for years," Janet says. "Every man I knew carried a pocket knife."

"Your honor," Kay says, "I'd like a moment to speak with my client."

"It's fine, sweetheart," Janet says. *Sweet. Heart.* She looks at the prosecutor. "You can trust me."

He pulls out his key chain, which has a Swiss Army knife the size of a nail clipper attached. He passes it to Janet.

"Give me your hand," she says, flicking the blade open. The prosecutor holds out his hand, and she takes it as if reading his palm. With a deliberate motion, she traces a line across it with the tip of the knife. The jury gasps. The prosecutor doesn't flinch. Janet sets the knife down on the rail. A thin line of blood wells up along the cut. She places her hand over his and closes her eyes. Then she lifts her hand and wipes away the blood with her thumb. There is no cut, only an expanse of calloused skin. The prosecutor holds his healed hand up for the jury to see.

The case should be dismissed right now, Avi thinks. *Miracles are admissible.*

"Thank you," the prosecutor says, stammering. He turns away from her, rubbing his palm with his thumb. "Now, Doctor, is it true that in your last year of practice you haven't lost a single patient?"

"That's true," says Janet. She wipes the blood on the hem of her shirt.

"But you've lost patients before?"

"Yes."

"Have you gotten better at using this ability?"

"I have," she says. "But that's not what's made the difference."

This is what Kay wanted to avoid. There was a simple line of defense, which was for Janet to say that back then she couldn't work her ability as well, and as a result some people died. Same as they would have if she'd been an ordinary doctor. Ordinary doctors lose patients all the time and don't get arrested for it. The important thing is to make Janet seem less special. The knife trick didn't help.

"What *has* made the difference?" the prosecutor asks.

"Early on, I worried about getting caught," Janet says. "A doctor with a perfect record attracts attention. My colleagues already talked about me like I was supernatural. If everyone who came to me lived, every single patient, they'd know something was different about me."

"Something is different about you."

"Yes," says Janet. "As I said, I'm a Resonant. I can say that now. I couldn't then."

"You were hiding your ability," says the prosecutor.

"Not hiding," Janet says. "If I was hiding it, I wouldn't have healed anyone. Or I would have, but only with my training as a doctor. That's a kind of ability as well, I think."

"Not the same kind of ability," says the prosecutor.

Tell him it is, Avi thinks. *Tell him it's exactly the same as being a good doctor. Some people can figure a tip in their head, some people can fucking juggle. You can knit bones back together with your brain. It's all the same thing. Tell him.*

"No," Janet says. "I suppose it isn't."

"So there were patients you healed with your ability and patients you didn't."

"Yes."

"How did you decide?"

"Who I healed and who I didn't?"

263

"Yes."

"I rolled dice."

"Dice," he says. He revels in the word, feels it roll around in his mouth. It tastes like chance, like gambling. He knows it'll sound that way to the jury. He's not the schlub Avi assumed he was. Kay keeps her face still, but she must see the way the jury looks at Janet. A minute ago she was a miracle worker, Montgomery's Angel. Now she's a capricious god, rolling dice to decide the fate of mortals like them.

"A sixty-six percent success rate beyond whatever I could do normally as a surgeon seemed safe," Janet says. "Low enough not to attract attention. I carried a die in my pocket. Before I went into surgery, I'd excuse myself and roll. As long as it didn't come up three or four, I'd use my ability to heal the patient. Even if it meant bringing them back from the brink of death."

"And if the dice came up three or four?"

"I'd do everything within my power as a doctor," Janet says.

"Except you wouldn't," the prosecutor says. "Because your power as a doctor was different from other doctors. You had this extra ability. Choosing not to use it, wouldn't that be like operating with your eyes closed or with your nondominant hand? Just to see if you could?"

"I didn't do it for a challenge," Janet says, angry, offended for the first time. *A little late now,* Avi thinks.

"No, you did it to keep your secret," says the prosecutor. "Doctor, do you remember Donald Morena?"

Janet looks down at her hands. "Yes."

"What do you remember about him?"

"On the evening of May 13, Donald Morena came into the St. Peter's emergency room with a gunshot wound to the head." She points to a spot above her left eye. "The bullet had not exited the skull and had become lodged within the occipital lobe." She pats the back of her head. "I operated to remove the bullet, but Mr. Morena died during the surgery."

"Did you roll the dice for Donald Morena?" the prosecutor asks.

"I did."

"What number did Donald Morena get?"

"A four."

"And that's why Donald Morena died."

"He died because someone shot him in the head," Janet says.

"But you could have saved him," says the prosecutor.

"Yes."

"Why did you stop rolling the dice?" the prosecutor asks.

"They shot that boy in the street," Janet says. "At the school in New York. That boy was brave enough to be who he was in public, and that other boy shot him. And I was letting people die to keep my secret."

"People like Donald Morena," says the prosecutor.

"Do you want their names?" Janet asks. "I can name every one. I can tell you if they came up a three or a four. Should I tell you what I called my system?" The prosecutor looks at her blankly. Janet turns to the jury. One of them, juror number four, nods. "I called it the coefficient of failure. Except that's not how I thought of it. I thought of it as the coefficient of death. I swore I would remember the names of every person who died on that table so that I could keep going. Let one die to save two more. But the ones who live never pile up. I don't remember their names or their numbers. They send Christmas cards, and I throw them away without opening them. They invite me to dinners and weddings and baptisms. They friend me on Facebook. And I remember the ones who died."

Avi watches the jury. He watches Kay school her face, trying not to show how the scaffolding that holds her case up is coming apart. He looks at Janet, who insisted on a trial. She needed to crucify herself to feel whole. She needed to let herself be punished for all her dead. After the prosecution is done, Kay will parade Janet's miracles through the court. She will bury the jury in a pile of living bodies, people who would be dead if not for Janet Goulding and Janine Coupland.

It may keep Janet out of jail. It won't heal her.

LEFTOVERS

Fahima has work to finish. It's difficult to take a functioning device and make it smaller. The right idea came to her last night. Alyssa picked up an extra shift, and so Fahima got to spend the whole night in the lab. Sometimes absence is the best gift a loved one can give.

The problem is focus over distance. The inhibitor's countersignal dissipates quickly as it moves away from the source. It's easier to imagine an inhibitor knife than an inhibitor gun. What would be ideal would be an implant nestled against the parahippocampal gyrus. But that would require Patrick to apprehend Owen Curry and perform quick, clean brain surgery. The thought is not without its appeal. What she comes up with is bulky, the size of a leaf blower. But it can be aimed and should be effective up to fifty yards.

She tries Patrick's phone, but there's no answer. Grudgingly, she sits down and goes to look for him in the Hive.

Without meaning to, she manifests next to the shattered abscess where Emmeline was held. The Hive isn't spatial; there is no "there" there. Still, she lands on the same spot. On the ground, there are shards of something obsidian, pieces of the cage Emmeline was in. Cautious, remembering what happened last time, Fahima picks one up. She's braced for another terrible memory, some emotional wound ripped open. Instead, a hundred images flash on the dark surface, people and places she doesn't know. The flicker of images speeds up, blurring. The shard vibrates in her hand. Fahima drops it as if it's hot. She looks at it lying on the ground: it's still. She steps back, pushes herself away from this place to someplace neutral. Someplace that's not full of questions she can't answer.

She's never been any good at searching for people in the Hive. Sarah's tried to teach her, but it's like shouting while simultaneously bouncing around the room. She calls out to Patrick through the Hive, focusing all her attention on an image of him, a concept of her friend. The landscape around her condenses, like zooming out on a smartphone screen, and there is Patrick, standing as if he's been waiting for her all day.

"Sorry I missed your call," he says. "I was caught up."

"I've got your gun," Fahima says.

"Great. Now all I need is someone to shoot it at." He sounds as tired as she feels. No one's gotten much rest. Bishop's handling interview requests and taking meetings with senators in DC. Kimani's picking up new students at an alarming rate, along with busing Bishop and Patrick around. Sarah's running the day-to-day of the school, dealing with the influx of new students. She's excellent at it, a born administrator. Much to Sarah's horror.

"Where are you?" Fahima asks.

"I got distracted," he says. "I found a little terrorist cell outside of Denver."

"Us or them?"

"Us. Four or five kids putting Kill All Damps bullshit on the Internet. I spoke with them. Convinced them of the error of their ways."

"You didn't *take them off the board*?" Fahima affects her best imitation of Bishop, his slightly nasal Brooklyn Brahmin tone. Patrick does a great impression of him. Less accurate but funnier.

"I made myself big and scary," Patrick says. He looks too bored to be either. "It usually works."

"And when it doesn't?"

"I buy them off," he says. "I enlist them in our cause using the persuasive power of my bank account."

"You are a credit to capitalism," Fahima says.

"There are lots of these little knots out there," Patrick says. "I have to wonder what's going on with Bishop. Usually he's on top of these things."

"He's busy here," says Fahima.

"He's missing something big. I'm not sure these groups are unconnected. Someone's recruited them. That's who I should be looking for. Not Owen Curry. I'm playing Whac-A-Mole out here."

It's strange that she misses him. They've spent half their lives as friends who don't particularly get along, a thing you can be when the pool of potential friends is limited. Patrick and Sarah were late bloomers, and Fahima spent her first years as a Resonant in Lakeview. When they arrived, within a month of each other, the three of them were set apart from the rest of the first-years by age. What brought them together was a shared teenage contempt for the Bishop Academy. In the first years, they were the only ones who deemed themselves too cool for school. Fahima because it didn't give her the answers she demanded. Patrick and Sarah because the sanctuary it provided wasn't new to them or even necessary. They'd never run from a farm town lynch mob or seen horror dawning on the faces of their parents. While the others existed in a constant state of pep rally, Fahima, Patrick, and Sarah stood apart, smirking.

Teenage Fahima, bitter at the time that had been taken from her and experimenting with personalities and sexual identities in a rush to catch up, loved Sarah in a way that made attraction seem tiny and hated Patrick less than she hated everyone else. She watched them with the envy only children have for sibling bonds, the deep desire to insert herself into it. Patrick was the first person Fahima came out to, after a clumsy and halfhearted pass on his part. His easy acceptance of who she was earned a trust that preceded real affection, served as the ground it could grow in.

Despite their teenage sneering, they all found their way back to Bishop as adults. Sarah said that it was meant to be and that they'd found the best place for themselves. Behind her back, Patrick whispered to Fahima that the three of them were too fucked up to hack it in the real world, which felt closer to the truth. It's Patrick, not Sarah, with whom Fahima can be unsparingly honest. Worn out by the need to be upbeat about the way things have gone this year, she's pained by the lack of his candor in her life.

"When can you come home and pick this thing up?" she says.

"No rush, I guess," says Patrick. "What took you so long?"

Fahima laughs. "My mind wandered in the opposite direction," she says. She thinks about a sketch she made the night before. A kind of a bomb. A burst transmitter that wouldn't inhibit Resonance but jump-start it.

"Trail's cold here. I'll have Kimani come pick me up," Patrick says. "Maybe the four of us can have a drink before I head back out."

"Make it back tonight and we can watch Bishop on *Late Night*," she says.

"He doing his *we are just like you, we only want to be loved* routine?"

"Beats the *there are dark forces rising against you, and we lost track of an angry white boy who could swallow Boston in one gulp* routine," says Fahima.

"It's a bad idea. He's painting a target on us."

"He's painting it on himself," she says. "He's making himself a target so he'll know where they're aiming."

Patrick sighs. "I'll be back tonight to get the gun."

"If you find Owen Curry, will you use it?" Fahima asks. "Bring him back to his cozy little cell?"

"No," says Patrick. His voice is casual, easy. "I'm going to kill him."

With a showman's flourish, Fahima opens the minifridge in the lab. Emmeline stares into it. An EEG helmet totters on her head like a colander, her dark curls peeking out from under its edge.

"You need more food," Emmeline says.

Fahima doesn't remember when their sessions became playful or developed a rapport that borders on shtick. They hadn't started out that way. Emmeline was skittish and shy her first month at Bishop. Fahima took on special sessions only with students whose abilities presented threats to themselves or others. Carrie Norris, who Fahima worried might dissipate into nothing. Roberta Draper, whose natural body temperature hovered near zero Kelvin and who couldn't share a room with another student, let alone be touched. Fahima had nightmares about Roberta's first kiss as a replay of the flagpole scene from *A Christmas Story*. And Emmeline, who can do things in the Hive that Bishop says are impossible but has only hinted at a fully manifested ability so far.

"I don't need more food," Fahima says. "I already ate. Before you came in, there was leftover lo mein in this refrigerator, and I took it out and ate it."

Emmeline nods. "You didn't even heat it up, did you?"

"Do you know that, or are you guessing?" Fahima asks.

"I'm guessing because you are gross," Emmeline says, grinning at her.

"Which you know," says Fahima. She likes running these sessions as farcical versions of her sessions with Bishop years ago. *Give me facts. Tell me what you know. Empiricism empiricism.* That Fahima believes in the importance of these things doesn't diminish the comedy.

"I ate a pint of cold lo mein," she says. "And I am not ashamed to admit it. That's not the point. The point is, the lo mein *was* in the fridge."

272

"Okay," says Emmeline.

"An hour ago," Fahima says.

"Before you ate it."

"Yes."

"Got it," Emmeline says.

Fahima pauses. What comes next is risky. Abilities can be daunting, especially when they come early. When Fahima first got a sense of what she was becoming, her mind ran screaming. She has to tread carefully if she doesn't want to risk breaking Emmeline. But if Emmeline can't accept and take control of her ability, there's a risk she'll break everything else.

"I want you to get the lo mein," Fahima says.

"I don't understand."

Fahima shuts the fridge and hops up onto the counter next to Emmeline. "This is what I think," she says. "If I had lo mein in the fridge right now, uneaten, and some other kid came in, I could tell them the lo mein is in the fridge and they could go get it."

"So could I," says Emmeline.

"They could walk across the room and open the fridge and get the lo mein."

"Okay," Emmeline says.

"And I think that I can say to you, 'The lo mein *was* in the fridge an hour ago,' and you can go get it, exactly the same way."

Emmeline looks at Fahima. Fahima sees that spark of fear, the exact thing she was worried about. It's unavoidable, but she needs to keep it small.

"You think I can time travel?" Emmeline says.

"I think you have," Fahima says. "Or *will have*. The grammar around stuff like this is a mess. But yes, I think you can time travel. Remember what you told me about what you saw in the park? The tower?"

"My mom and dad saw it, too," says Emmeline.

"Exactly," Fahima says. "If you were the only one who saw it, I'd be working with the theory that you're precognitive. But I think your parents saw it because they went with you. For a second."

"To the future?"

"This is what I think," Fahima says.

Emmeline scoots away from her. She looks at her shoes. "I can't," she says.

"Maybe you can," says Fahima.

"I've tried."

Fahima nods, adding this information to the mental file she keeps on Emmeline. They're friends, but Emmeline is also a subject. If Fahima is right, the girl presents a risk not only to herself or the people around her but to the structure of the world.

"You tried to go back," she says.

"Yes," says Emmeline.

"Way back?"

"Yes."

"You tried to fix your mom and dad," says Fahima. "And it didn't work." Emmeline doesn't answer. Fahima jumps up, goes to a dry erase board, and grabs a marker.

"Two possibilities," she says, holding up two fingers. "Time—" She draws a line with arrows pointing in either direction. "—assuming it's linear and simple, which is, in this case, an unsafe assumption, the unwed mother of a massive fuckup." Emmeline giggles. Fahima draws a stick figure toward the right end of the line. "One," she says. "You were trying to go too far." She draws a huge arc from the stick figure to the left end of the line. "You're new to this, and you tried to jump back a week or a month when maybe you could only go back a couple minutes." She erases the arc. "Or two," she says, drawing another arc, this one landing in the middle of the line. She circles where the arc and the line intersect. "You were trying to change something so big, changing it would change you." Fahima creates another line, branching off from the intersection, headed down. A new timeline. A separate reality. "It would make it so you were never in the place you left from." She erases all the initial lines from the point of intersection to the end. She erases the stick figure Emmeline. The arc hangs above the empty space. "It's a paradox."

"Pair of—"

"We're going to try something closer, temporally," Fahima says. "And insignificant. The lo mein makes no difference to you. You'll be here regardless of what happens to the lo mein."

"You like saying 'lo mein,' " says Emmeline.

"I do like saying 'lo mein,' " Fahima says. "Are you ready?"

"I can't time travel," Emmeline says.

"Humor me. Go steal my lo mein."

Emmeline scrunches up like she's wishing for something with all her might. Fahima watches her face, her concentration. Something on the screen catches Fahima's eye. A flare-up: the parahippocampal gyrus, burning bright for a blip. She looks back at Emmeline, who's holding a Tupperware container and grinning.

"Here," she says, handing it to Fahima. Fahima looks at the Tupperware, then at the empty takeout container in the trash can, chopsticks jutting out of its mouth.

"This isn't my lo mein."

"It's your lunch from tomorrow," Emmeline says. She bends down to look through the clear plastic bottom of the container. "I think it's a sandwich."

"How did you get it?"

"Sometimes I'm already there," Emmeline says. "I'm here now, and I'm there then. Like the way in the Hive you can be in two places or all the places?"

"Most of us can't do that," Fahima says.

"I can," says Emmeline. "I think I could do anything I want in there." Emmeline shrugs. The impossible is no big deal.

The casualness of the gesture scares the shit out of Fahima.

Fahima performs isha'a while Alyssa sits at the kitchen counter sipping a beer. The night prayer is the only one Alyssa watches her do. Fahima's considered asking her to stop. Being watched changes the nature of the prayer. It cancels it out, forces Fahima's mind outward instead of in, and she never makes dua while Alyssa is watching, as if there's a small piece of her faith she needs to keep secret. But it's Alyssa's one bit of white girl fascination with the mystical other. When Fahima was growing up, the Polish ladies asked her mother to show them how to wrap a hijab, buffeted her with questions about stonings in the square or some bullshit, and her mother suffered through it with grace. You make allowances to keep people in your life.

She finishes her rakats the same time Alyssa finishes her beer. Alyssa goes to the fridge for another. Fahima catches a glimpse of a Tupperware bowl full of chicken salad.

"Something's on your mind," Alyssa says. "You aren't as fluid as you usually are."

"Are you critiquing my rakats, infidel?" says Fahima.

"How's it going with Emmeline?" Alyssa asks.

"Scary," Fahima says. Alyssa comes over and leans against her. "What do you think would happen if I ate a sandwich from the future?"

"What kind of sandwich?" she asks.

"Chicken salad."

"I made some chicken salad this afternoon," says Alyssa.

"I know," Fahima says. "Tomorrow, you'll make me a sandwich. Except that sandwich is already in my fridge at work. Emmeline has served me a paradoxical sandwich, and I'm not sure what to do with it."

"You think she can time travel," Alyssa says.

Fahima can't resist. She grabs a Sharpie and the Bed Bath & Beyond ad that came in the mail yesterday. She uncaps the marker. The acrid scent is like brain fuel. "You and I move along two axes," she says, drawing a cross. "Forward to back, left to right. We can jump or go up and down stairs and elevators." She draws a third line through the center of the cross. "So three." She looks up at Alyssa. "I think Emmeline can move along a fourth."

"Time," Alyssa says.

Fahima opens the fridge. The bowl of chicken salad, the stuff of potential future sandwiches, sits on the middle shelf. She shuts the door. "This sandwich is fucking me up."

"Are you worried about the sandwich?"

"I'm thinking about what it means to be able to move in three directions across a two-dimensional plane," Fahima says.

"I can see where that would be concerning," Alyssa says, mocking her.

"No, you don't," says Fahima. She picks up the Bed Bath & Beyond ad. "The way I drew this is a drawing," she says. "Like when you draw a hexagon with some lines in the middle and say it's a cube but it's a representation of a cube in two dimensions."

"Does this end with origami?" Alyssa asks.

"It ends with this," says Fahima. She takes the Sharpie and stabs a hole through the ad. "That's what it looks like to move in three dimensions across a two-dimensional plane."

"And if Emmeline can move in four directions through a three-dimensional plane—"

"Three-dimensional space," says Fahima.

"You think this nine-year-old is poking holes in space?" Alyssa asks.

"I think she's poking holes in time. I mean, think about the sandwich."

Alyssa smiles at her. "I am taking this beer to bed," she says. "You should join me when you're done worrying about a tween Swiss-cheesing the space-time continuum."

She kisses Fahima on the neck and goes to their bedroom, throwing a come-hither look over her shoulder as she goes.

Fahima misses it, contemplating the Bed Bath & Beyond ad skewered on a Sharpie. By the time she comes back from her wandering thoughts and goes to bed, Alyssa is already asleep, her body propped alluringly on a pillow, tee shirt pulled and stretched to expose one shoulder, head lolled onto the other. Fahima kisses the bare shoulder as she turns out the light and goes to sleep.

A SORT OF HOMECOMING

Carrie can't miss the note in her mother's voice when she calls to say she's coming home. She plays that *Oh* over and over in her head for weeks; each time she hears something different. Surprise. Challenge. Fear. Missing from that list: joy at the prodigal's impending return.

"Was it a question or an exclamation?" Miquel asks. "Like 'oh, wow!' or 'oh, you *think* so'?"

"Both at once," Carrie says.

"It's messing you up," he says. "You're upset that you're upset. It's a knot."

Miquel's working on his empathic ability, seeing emotions in shapes rather than colors. It's more nuanced, the difference between seeing pressure fronts on a weather map and standing in the middle of a thunderstorm. The analogy worries Carrie. He doesn't talk about it, but Miquel is exposed by his ability. He gets inexplicably sad when they watch Marx Brothers movies in the common room with Hayden and Jonathan, and he knows it's someone else's sadness. Or he flies off the handle at Waylon for leaving clothes on the floor, a sin they're both guilty of, then apologizes, looking out in the hall to divine who his anger came from. Carrie feels like a failure because she can't provide whatever calm he needs. She can't be the eye of his storm.

"I'll go with you," he says.

"No," says Carrie. "My family is terrible."

"It's them or a shit ton of Jung," he says. Miquel's family lives in the Bronx, but his mother kicked him out when his abilities started, shouting *brujo* at him as she chased him down the street. He said it meant something between wizard and witch doctor, and nothing good. He hasn't spoken to them in years.

"I'd take the Jung," Carrie says. She worries about the emotions he'd be exposed to if she dragged him back to Deerfield with her for protection. She's also embarrassed by her bland suburban roots. It's impossible to explain to him what it means to come from a nowhere place, to invent yourself out of nothing. Hayden knows what it's like; they've done a better job than Carrie building a version of themself that bears none of the dull marks of where they come from or who they used to be. Hayden and Carrie don't talk about these things. One of the rules of reinvention is that you never speak about the person you've been out of fear you'll summon that person like a ghost.

Just past noon on Thanksgiving, Carrie sits in the back of a cab in front of her parents' house, listening to a wistful Springsteen song about getting out of your shitty hometown. She wishes she had taken Miquel up on his offer. The driveway is full, and Carrie identifies each car. The dark blue Suburban belongs to her aunt Chloe and uncle Jim, with their three little kids. The Mini Cooper is Susie, her divorced aunt from Chicago. The late-model compact with the Domino's Pizza light perched on top must be her brother Brian's, although the idea that he's old enough to drive makes her squirm. The family station wagon, spots of rust around the wheel wells and the edges of the hood. It reminds Carrie of cramped legs and the smell of fast food. Family vacations driving someplace none of them wanted to be. Counting cows with Brian until their tally hit four digits while her mother picked CDs no one loved or hated and her dad stared fixedly out at the road like a trucker indifferent to his cargo.

Carrie lets her fingers trail along the station wagon's bubbling blue paint, its flaking faux-wood paneling. It's proper in this situation for her to ring the bell, request entry into what she thinks of as home. She feels the urge to disappear as she pushes the doorbell but wills herself to stay visible. She's relieved when Brian answers, although he doesn't look all that happy to see her.

"Hey," he says. Adolescence has him over a barrel. His face is spotted with acne, and his body is assembled from mismatched parts. He's growing like Jekyll becoming Hyde: in fits and starts. They stand at the door, unsure if they're supposed to hug. "You have bags?" Carrie pats her army messenger bag. Brian nods and lets her in. Strains of Christmas music come from the living room. Her father spends Thanksgiving morning lugging holiday records out of the attic while her mother preps the turkey. "Mom and Uncle Jim are already drunk," Brian says. "Aunt Susie's on her way there. And the kids are fucking awful."

"They were always fucking awful," says Carrie.

"They got worse," he says. She's grateful Brian is taking her into his confidence this way. It reestablishes a sibling bond.

As proof of their awfulness, one of the cousins comes barreling out of the dining room and into the hall, blasting between Carrie and Brian with no regard for either. Carrie expects someone chasing behind him, but no one comes.

"Is that my daughter?" her mother calls from the dining room. She emerges, glass of red wine sloshing in her hand, a flush rising in her cheeks. She holds her arms out wide. "My little baby's all grown," she coos. Carrie allows herself to be embraced, enfolded. Through the salon-sculpted curls of her mother's hair, naturally thick and straight as Carrie's own, she sees the rest of her family watching this show. She hears that one syllable on the phone. *Oh. Oh? Oh.*

Oh: is that what you think you're doing?

Oh: you're still alive.

Oh: what will they say about my daughter the freak?

Uncle Jim, a ruddy-faced account manager for a meat company in Chicago who smells like cigarettes and salt, pushes past her father, standing in the kitchen doorway.

"Jesus Christ, you're a foot taller," Jim says. "Skinny as a bone. Don't they feed you at that place?"

"They feed us fine, Uncle Jim," she says, her face pressed into the armpit of his sweater.

"Matt, go get your daughter a beer," says Jim. Her father turns toward the kitchen to comply.

"She's in high school, Jim," says her mother. Her father stops dead, a robot with a command glitch.

"We drank like fish in high school," Jim says, wiping his gin-blossomed nose.

"We don't know what effects alcohol has on special people like our Carrie," says Aunt Susie. She's Carrie's favorite. Brian's, too. She has the two best qualities you could ask for in an aunt: a tendency to give cash rather than gifts and a willingness to have them stay at her apartment in Chicago a couple of weekends a year when they were kids. She took them to museums and Indian restaurants and Cubs' games. Things Deerfield couldn't offer.

"I saw a special on *NightTalk* the other day," she continues. "They were talking to that man from your school, Carrie."

"Headmaster Bishop," Carrie says.

"It's not fucking Hogwarts," Brian mutters quietly enough only Carrie hears.

"They were saying how they don't know what the differences are in physiology between people like Carrie and people like us," says Susie.

"I can drink beer," Carrie says. "I won't explode or anything."

"See that, Suze?" Jim says, poking his baby sister in the ribs. "They're not any different from normal people. Matt, where you at with that beer?" Carrie's father vanishes into the kitchen. "Kids," Jim bellows. "Come see your cousin before she disappears."

During pie, a discussion about crime rates in Chicago boils over into something ugly, one of those arguments that aren't about what they're about. Carrie's discovering she has a secondary ability to become subtext. Every racial dog whistle Uncle Jim throws at Aunt Susie points at the new *other* he's been forced to accept, one more foreign or threatening than the black kids he's okay railing about as long as he calls them "urban youth." He mentions something he heard on the radio, and Carrie knows what radio show he's talking about. She's been listening to Jefferson Hargrave's *Monster Report* since Public Day. They found dozens of episodes archived on the shooter's laptop. She wants to know where their hatred comes from, but as she listens to her uncle, she understands the disconnect. He can hate what she is while loving who she is. The issue is impersonal for him in a way it can never be for her.

Carrie's mother is a guitar string tuned taut. She takes her wine in massive gulps. Carrie's father hasn't spoken to Carrie since she arrived. As Uncle Jim gets ruddy-faced, edging closer to saying what he really thinks, her father leans over to Brian.

"You and your sister go play with your cousins in the other room," he says. He doesn't look at Carrie, but she's grateful for his intervention. With a sigh of teenage inconvenience, Brian leads the three small kids out of the dining room. Carrie tags behind. In the living room, Brian clicks on the television.

"You guys like video games?"

The kids erupt in a clamor of yeses.

Brian turns on his Xbox. The sharp white letters of the logo burn in the black of the screen. "Keep the sound low," he says. "If I hear you fighting, I come turn it off."

He turns to Carrie, makes an okay sign, and presses it to his pursed lips, the universal sign for *do you want to smoke up?* Carrie follows him upstairs to the room that used to be hers. Brian has marked his territory. High school textbooks wrapped in brown paper covers, *Red Emma* comics, and discarded socks litter the dark green rug Carrie picked out to make her room feel like Fangorn Forest. Her bookshelf is gone, and there's hardly a patch of wall that isn't covered by posters of bands Carrie can't stand. She notes the *Dark Side of the Moon* poster, the same one Miquel used to have. They must issue it to boys when they buy their first dime bag.

Brian cracks the window and sits down on the floor next to it. Carrie sits across from him, cross-legged on a mound of tee shirts. The air through the window bites at her wrists. He pulls a cigar box out of a desk drawer. Inside is a Ziploc bag full of gray pot, a glassie and lighter, and the obligatory homemade blow tube: a toilet paper roll with a dryer sheet rubber-banded over one end.

"It's ditchweed," he says, packing the glassie. "This guy that works in the kitchen at the D grows it. He's a shithead." Carrie winces to hear him call Domino's Pizza "the D," one of those nicknames each generation of Deerfielders claims to have invented. "You must smoke better stuff in New York." He hands her the gear first.

"I get good stuff off a friend of mine," Carrie says.

"There's a carb on the side," Brian says, trying to take the pipe back to show her. She yanks it away and glares at him. She presses her thumb over the tiny hole of the carb and circles the flame around the little pile of weed. It burns too fast when she inhales, tinder dry, and she coughs like a rookie. "Here," Brian says, handing her the blow tube and taking the pipe. Carrie blows pale smoke into the toilet paper roll and out the window, ostensibly scrubbed of its telltale smell.

"Christ," she says. "That's awful. Are you sure he didn't sell you pencil shavings?"

Brian shrugs and lights the pipe. It's the kind of shrug you see from people when you ask why they're living in their hometown; equal parts don't know and don't care. *If I hadn't left, would I have noticed this passivity of his growing?* she wonders. *Would I have been able to stop it?*

"They never talk about you," Brian says. "Mom and Dad. I think before you called they forgot you existed."

"I talked to them in January," she says. "When the news came out."

"Yeah," says Brian. "I saw the pictures on the Internet." His hand drifts to a pile under the desk, then pulls back. Sticking out of the stack, Carrie sees the corner of the *Atlantic* issue that ran the photos of the parade. The one of Nolan towering over the shooter. Carrie saw it from the same angle, crouching with Emmeline just under the photographer's lens. Every time she sees the photo, there's an echo of what she was feeling, terrified and protective. Like an echo, it gets weaker with each iteration. Someday she'll be able to look at the photo without feeling anything at all.

"So are you going to show me?" he says, watching the smoke drift toward the power lines outside. "Your superpower or whatever?"

"We don't say *superpower*," Carrie explains. "We say ability."

"Here on Planet Earth we say *superpower*," he says. "Let's see it."

Carrie nods and slips down into invisibility. The visible world shimmers when she's not part of it, as if she's looking at everything through frosted glass. Brian stares gape-jawed at the spot where she is, the vacant space in his vision. She smiles, enjoying the voyeuristic thrill of watching his expression without being seen. She reaches across and plucks the glassie from his hand. This part requires concentration: objects close to her when she's invisible disappear as well. Otherwise there'd be an empty set of clothes walking around whenever Carrie sank down. Focusing on the points of contact between her fingers and the glassie, she keeps it outside her field, so it floats in the air. She does the same with the lighter. Suspended in nothing, the lighter flicks twice, catches, and traces little orange circles on the pot. Carrie inhales deeply, and a second later, a plume of smoke emerges out of nowhere. Then she rises up, visible again, offering the pipe and lighter back.

"That's fucked up," he says.

Carrie shrugs, because yes, it is fucked up. It's also her life.

"So how did it happen?" Brian asks. "Did you like get hit by lightning or something?"

"I think we're born like this," she says.

"Then how come you and not me?" says Brian. He laughs after he says it, but he stares at her, waiting intently for an answer she doesn't have. She wishes that she could gift it to him, that Resonance was a virus she could pass or a door she could open and invite him through. But there isn't a way, and without it, they're on opposite sides of that door. She can show him the world where she lives now, but he can never visit, much less live there.

After the rest of the family's gone, her mother shows her to the guest room as if Carrie doesn't know the house anymore. Her mother kisses her on the forehead and retreats to her own room. Carrie can hear her parents through the wall. Not every word but enough. She doesn't disagree with them. It would have been easier if she'd never come back.

Carrie goes into the Hive. Not because she wants to be there but because she doesn't want to be here. She paces among itinerant ghosts. The Hive feels crowded, and Carrie wonders how many Resonants there are in the world. Once, in Ability Theory, Fahima said the numbers were increasing, but she never said what the numbers were. Carrie has trouble thinking of Resonants outside Bishop, working regular jobs or whatever. She wonders about the ones who don't end up at Bishop or at the school out west. There have to be lots who say no, who stay out in the wilderness on their own. To the extent that Carrie feels like part of a community or a race, the feeling comes from Bishop rather than from a connection to something larger. Who would she be if she didn't have that? If she'd stayed in Deerfield? Who will she be when her time at Bishop is up?

"So how bad was it?" Miquel asks, stepping out of nothing to be there in front of her.

"How did you find me?" Carrie asks. *Did I call you without meaning to?* she wonders. Thoughts are dangerous here. They have a way of not staying in your head where they belong.

"Just lucky," says Miquel. He gives her a hug, and although there are no bodies to press together, it carries a physical kind of relief. "Were china plates thrown? Wineglasses shattered?"

"We're Midwesterners," she says. "We don't throw plates. We quietly seethe."

"Sounds nice," he says. Carrie imagines Miquel's mother, cursing him down the street.

"How's Bishop with no one there?"

"Dead," he says. "I walked around the neighborhood. All of Manhattan's deserted. Now I know what it'll be like after the end of the world."

"Did you break into Dylan's Candy Bar and gorge yourself?" she says.

"I walked to Central Park," he says. "Fed the geese."

"That's a very old man thing to do."

"There was an old couple on the next bench," he says. "The geese liked them better than me, I think. They were woven together. The couple, not the geese. I couldn't read either of them alone. It was kind of beautiful."

"That'll be us," she says, then wishes she could take the words back, that the physics of the Hive would let her pluck them out of the air and stuff them in her pocket. "When we're old and nobody else wants us," she adds. "Feeding the geese after the end of the world."

"I can imagine worse things," says Miquel. He smiles at her in a way she wills herself not to think about. The underlying problem with Miquel as a friend is that he's an empath. He reads the feelings of other people like flyers on a corkboard. And Carrie's right in front of him most hours of the day, wanting him like a neon sign in the desert, and somehow he doesn't see it. Or he does and has to pretend he doesn't to keep her close but safe, to keep their friendship protected from the way she feels. She doesn't know which it is or which would be worse.

THE CONFESSION IN POWDER BASIN

Everyone agrees that something's missing. The book feels like a collection of articles, and the evolving nature of the situation makes that a dicey sale.

"We need one story in there that's timeless," Avi's agent says. "Something where the moment expands, the particular becomes general."

Avi has spent the last five months looking for that story. He was chasing it at Janine Coupland's manslaughter trial in Montana. He'd been to a warehouse in Laredo where Immigration and Customs Enforcement held a dozen Resonant women who fled Guatemala to avoid being burned as witches. He road-tripped through the South with a con man who swore he could induce Resonance in baseliners, charging hundreds for what amounted to a three-hour adrenaline rush. Nothing seemed to work; all the stories became additions to the incoherent pile the book had become.

The night before Thanksgiving, Avi gets a call from Patrick Davenport. It's beyond unexpected; Avi doesn't even have Patrick's number in his phone.

"You remember the town I told you about in Wyoming?"

Patrick says without bothering to say hello. "The family that died?"

"Guthridge," Avi says. "Mother and three kids."

"*Four* kids," Patrick says. "One of the killers was arrested last night. I have a contact in the local police department that can get you in to see him, but it's got to be tomorrow."

Avi says no. He's invited to Thanksgiving dinner at Kay's new place in New York at Emmeline's request and over Kay's protest. Kay made sure he knew it wasn't the beginning of anything. It was a concession to their daughter, not a gesture. Unsure whether that made it more important or less, Avi accepted. Even if it isn't a beginning, missing it would be an end.

Patrick continues to feed him details of the case, and there's no getting around it. This is what the book needs.

When they get off the phone, he calls Kimani. Her voice drips with annoyance.

"Haven't you got family or something?" she says.

"Patrick called me," Avi says. "I need you to pick me up tomorrow and take me to Powder Basin, Wyoming. Then back to New York so I can have dinner with—"

"Avi, I've got to go," Kimani says. "Tomorrow is— Thanksgiving is not a good day for me."

She hangs up. Equal parts angry and chastised, Avi goes online and books an overpriced ticket to Wyoming.

Avi struggles against the flow of humans at Denver International Airport. The rush of Thanksgiving morning goes in every possible direction at once, and Avi is buffeted, caroming off bodies, clutching his cane and messenger bag.

He runs calculations in his head. The flight to Cheyenne gets him in around noon. From there, it's four hours to Gillette. Patrick's contact at the police station comes off shift at six, and by tomorrow Scott Lipscombe will be moved to Campbell County Detention Center, cut off from anyone but his lawyer. The window's closing.

At the gate, he calls Emmeline.

"Hey, Dad," she says. "I had my hand up a turkey's butt."

"Well, that's big news," he says. "How did the turkey feel?"

"Cold and slimy," says Emmeline. She crunches on a piece of celery. "Where are you? It's loud."

"I'm at an airport," he says. There's a pause on the line.

"Which one?"

"Denver," he says. Another pause.

"You're not coming," Emmeline says. There's a rustle, a sound like wind. He hears Kay asking Emmeline to check on the turkey, and then she's on the line.

"You're not coming?" says Kay.

"There's something I need to follow up," he says.

"It couldn't be tomorrow?"

"It couldn't," Avi says. "You have to know—"

"Just don't," Kay says. "She's going to be destroyed. She's been talking about this for weeks."

"I'll be done by six. Shit, that's Mountain Time or something. I'm done at eight o'clock. I can call Kimani and see if she can—"

"We eat at four," she says. "We always eat at four." He's broken by the factuality of this, how it calls on all the Thanksgivings of their marriage and deploys them against him. The early dinner had been a tradition from his family, something he imposed on theirs. By eight o'clock, it should be he and Kay alone on the couch, Emmeline sacked away upstairs in a food coma, the two of them moved on to whatever bottles of wine were collecting dust in the pantry. Even if Kimani could get him back to New York the minute he was done, it would be too late for Thanksgiving, a long-standing afternoon event in whatever remained of the Hirsch family.

"Is it worth it?" Kay asks.

They're calling his flight.

"I think this might be the piece that ties the book together," he says.

"Not just this," says Kay. "The whole thing. Everything you've been chasing. I could be okay with it if I thought you were getting what you need."

"I'll have Kimani bring me right there the minute I'm done," he says. "It'll be before eight even. Save me some pie or something."

"I'll see you, Avi," she says. Avi gets in line for boarding, the blind idiot rush of the story convincing him he's solved everything.

Avi drives by the police station in Gillette three times before he finds it. It's past five, the window closing. Avi imagines his contact's replacement looking ruefully at his watch, hauling himself out of his chair over the jeers of family members watching the Broncos on television. He can see him refastening his belt, saying something about time and a half. He can feel his approach.

The receptionist doesn't answer the first two times Avi rings the service bell. Three more minutes click away. When she shows, she glares at him, making him aware that he's an inconvenience. He can see the television on in the break room, a skeleton crew grouped around its glow.

"I'm here to see Officer Brennan," Avi says.

The receptionist shrugs and heads back toward the break room. "Andy," she says. "This one's yours."

Officer Brennan is a hulk, a build that announces linebacker, with two rows of perfectly aligned fluoridated teeth. When he shakes Avi's hand, he closes his eyes and his grip goes limp. For a fraction of a second, Avi thinks the man is going to faint. Then he opens his eyes and looks at Avi warily.

"You're not one of us," he says quietly.

"No," Avi says. "I'm a friend." Brennan looks unsure, but he leads Avi down the hall, back to the holding cells.

"He turned himself in," he explains. "Right away. Basically, he shot the kid, then he called us. He was waiting in the living room when we got there."

"Where was the wife?"

"I don't want to tell tales out of school," says Brennan, "but word is Nora's got a pill habit. Not like she's the only one. Lot of folks down in the Basin are having trouble since. But still. She didn't even wake up from the gun. Her sister's been with her. They're keeping her pretty far out of it." He taps his forearm below the elbow with two fingers, then mimes a shot being administered.

"Listen," he says. "I can't give you much time. Boss is in at six, and I need you out of here by then. But no one around here's going to ask him what needs to be asked, and I figure maybe you will." He opens the door to the holding cells. Avi thinks about the room where Owen Curry is held and how it's a cleaner, shinier version of this room. There's the low smell of sealed concrete with damp already underneath the sealant, rotting out the walls and floors from the inside. The institutional mix of urine and disinfectant plays up the worst parts of both. The hum of bright white fluorescent lights reminds Avi of the green lights in Owen's cell, the flimsy leash they keep on their monster.

Brennan brings a folding chair and sets it in front of the middle cell. Inside, a skinny man collects himself between sobbing fits. His eyes are red, the skin around them puffy, and his breath hitches against his control like an unruly animal. He looks at Avi, immediately pleading for absolution Avi is unwilling and unable to give.

"Scott," he says, opting for familiarity. "My name's Avi. I'm a reporter. I'm here to talk to you about what happened."

Scott Lipscombe looks at Officer Brennan like he's been betrayed. Brennan shrugs and leaves the room, locking the door quietly behind him.

"I think it could help you to have someone to tell your story," says Avi. "These things, they're tried in the press. I have some clout. I write for national outlets. And I think your story is going to speak to people's fears. I think people will hear you if you talk."

"Don't want to talk," says Scott.

"No, I understand that," Avi says. "It's fresh still. But talking can also be a way through it. Have you spoken with a lawyer?" Scott Lipscombe shakes his head. "That's good. Believe it or not, that's good. A story takes shape when you say it out loud. It crystallizes. The way you tell it becomes the way you remember it. And talking to a lawyer, it forces things into a certain shape. That's important, too. It'll be important later. But for now, what's good, what's best for you, is just to speak about it. Just tell me what happened to your son, Scott."

"I shot him," he says, starting to blubber. "That's why I'm here, right? I shot my son dead in his sleep."

"Can you tell me why you'd do that, Scott?"

"He was one of them," says Scott Lipscombe. "Like the . . . uh. Like the Guthridge boy. Like Sam."

The urge to chase this is almost overwhelming, but Avi knows better. He lets it lie for now. "How did you know?" he asks. "How did you know your son was one of them?"

"He wasn't ever anything like us," Scott Lipscombe says. "Like Nora or me. He plays piano and guitar and all. He makes these songs on his computer that I can't barely call them songs. We don't even have a history of anything like him in either of our families. Anyone else, their kid's a stranger to them, they talk about some old aunt who ran off to New York or Grandpa Whoever that never was quite right. Nora and I, neither of us have any of that. He's out of nowhere. I think the music stuff, I think that's his ability. Like he can speak in music or something."

Scott Lipscombe's talking about the dead boy in the present tense, avoiding his name. He's strung between poles of recognition and denial. The full weight of what he's done isn't on him yet. It'll fall tonight or the next night in a cell like this. It'll hit him alone and break the already broken pieces of him, smashing him to sand. Even if Avi got an interview tomorrow, there wouldn't be enough of Scott Lipscombe left to talk to. He presses gently.

"So what if he was?" he says. "Why did it mean you had to kill him?"

"He *was*," says Scott Lipscombe. "I'm sure of that. Not as sure as we—" He catches himself. "I couldn't let it stand. I couldn't let him be one of them after what we did."

"What is it you did, Scott?" Avi asks.

Scott Lipscombe looks at the ground. "I'm not saying."

The door opens behind Avi. Officer Brennan trails behind an older man, the boss he mentioned. Avi checks his watch. He was supposed to have more time.

"That's enough of that," says the sheriff.

"Scott, you see where you are here," Avi says, standing and approaching the bars. "You know what you did, and you know you're going to be punished. But it doesn't mean anything if you're not clean, Scott. If you go down carrying something, you're going to sink. You're going to sink into yourself forever."

"You know," says Scott Lipscombe.

"I said enough," the sheriff says, laying a meaty paw on Avi's shoulder. Avi exchanges a quick look with Officer Brennan. *Whatever it is you can do*, he tries to say, *whatever your fucking ability, I need one more minute.* Brennan's face is a stony blank.

"I know, Scott," says Avi. "But I need to hear you say it."

"I don't want to say."

"It'll feel good to say it, Scott," Avi says. "It'll change you to say it out loud. To have it said and heard."

The sheriff is gripping Avi, pulling him off the bars.

"We killed them," Scott Lipscombe says. The room stops; the sheriff's grip goes slack. "We killed Sam Guthridge and his momma and his little sisters. I stabbed little Paige Guthridge, and the light poured out of her. Me and Danny Randall and Joe Sabine, and Alvin McLaughlin, and . . ."

Scott Lipscombe begins a list of names, and Officer Brennan fumbles his notebook out of his back pocket, catching them as they come, as if he doesn't already know them. The sheriff holds Avi loosely, glaring at him as a litany of murderers washes over them, broken up by Scott Lipscombe's sobs.

He calls Kimani from the rental car, sitting in the parking lot of the police station. It's started to snow, occasional flakes like glitches in his visual field. The line rings and rings until Avi's convinced that voice mail should pick up. He's formulating what he'll say if it does, what phrasing he can use to impart a sense of emergency, when Kimani answers.

"I need you to get me to New York," he says. "I'm in Wyoming, and I need to get back."

"I'm off the clock," she says. Her voice is flat. "Try Delta."

"I'm missing dinner with my daughter, Kimani," he says. "I need your help."

"I'm not a cab, Avi," she says.

"I'm here for *you*," Avi says, losing his temper. "I came all the way out here on Patrick's say-so, and I got a confession out of one of the Powder Basin killers. He gave up all their names. Twenty men who killed those kids and their mom. I did that. Me. Now I need you to get me back home to my daughter for Thanksgiving." He waits, out of breath. There's a click, and the line goes dead. Avi throws the phone at the passenger door and bangs his palms on the steering wheel as snowflakes melt into the windshield.

ENCLAVE

Alyssa eases the car around the first hairpin turn of Oceanside Way, a branch off Highway 1 just north of Ogunquit, Maine. A Leonard Cohen album blasts on the stereo, loud swirls of synthesizers and backing vocals, a wall of sound graffitied with Cohen's baritone.

Despite the cold, the windows are down. Alyssa wants to smell the ocean.

"This is ridiculous," Fahima says, gesturing at the massive empty houses that line the street. "Who lives like this?"

"I always wanted a beach house," Alyssa says. "Imagine: in the fifties, everyone had beach houses. They all went up the shore in the summer."

"A golden age for white people," Fahima says. "A chicken in every pot, a servant in every kitchen."

"You think the Davenports have servants?" Alyssa asks.

Fahima shakes her head. "I asked Sarah," she says. "Servants get Thanksgiving off. Their mother teleports everything in piping hot from Dovetail down in the city. Walks out the door onto 77th, then pop, here on the beach."

"Have we eaten there?" asks Alyssa.

Fahima laughs. "It'd cost us a month's rent."

The house where Patrick and Sarah grew up is set into a natural levee so that the first floor opens out on the shore side and the upper three look out onto the ocean. A salt breeze smacks Fahima and Alyssa as they round the corner of the house. Standing in the doorway to greet them, Mrs. Davenport looks like a senator's wife from a seventies political thriller, down to the string of gob-stopper pearls around her neck. She smiles, and Fahima feels a ping in her brain. Mrs. Davenport reaches through the Hive to check Fahima's bona fides. Her smile goes flat as she tries the same thing with Alyssa but finds nothing. A momentary lapse in decorum, but she recovers quickly.

"You're Paddy and Sarah's friend from school," she says, as if Fahima is in gym class with her son. "And this is your partner?"

"Alyssa," says Fahima. Alyssa holds out her hand. Mrs. Davenport is unsure what to do with it, like she might kiss Alyssa's knuckles. She takes it, and Alyssa gives her a firm, businesslike handshake.

"Your generation is so *progressive* about these things. I think it's wonderful. And this," she says, pinching the trim of Fahima's hijab, rubbing it like a cloth merchant in the souk, "is beautiful."

"This is going to be *aw-ful*," Alyssa sings into Fahima's ear as they follow Mrs. Davenport inside.

Sarah rescues them before they reach the living room, a glass of wine in her hand. She pauses when she sees Alyssa, looking momentarily confused, but then Cortex trots up behind her, brushing her leg, and her memory returns. She hugs both of them: long, genuine embraces that give Mrs. Davenport time to make an exit.

Fahima speaks into her ear, teeth gritted. "You never mentioned your mother was such a—"

"Total bigot," says Sarah. "Was it the Muslim thing, the lesbian thing, or the interdating thing? You guys are a three-fer. I forgot how terrible everyone I grew up around is." She hugs them both again. "I am so glad you're here."

Here turns out not to be the small family dinner Fahima expected but a gathering of a dozen wealthy, aging white Resonants. Fahima has trouble telling the guests apart, so she gives them little nicknames. Old Teddy Roosevelt. Captain Walrus Stache and his wife, Weird Neck Thing. Steel Hair. Oceanside Way is an enclave, a testament to what you can do with money. Everyone on this three-block stretch of beachfront is a Resonant and also rich. Oceanside's residents think about the world in abstract terms because they don't have to live in it. They've built their own world, a bubble of comfort where concerns about civil rights and the responsibility that comes with Resonance are topics for light conversation and not much more. Fahima met a few Muslims like this when she was a student at MIT. There was always an alum made good, some slick 'am looking to adopt a promising Muslim student as his mentee. They invited her to the Back Bay brownstones and showed off their wives, silk-clad 'ammes who thought of themselves like any other American wives and didn't understand what everyone else was so worried about.

Seeing Sarah in this element recalls certain things about

her that Fahima sometimes forgets. That she is funny, that she is rebellious in the bored way of people who've had to deal with mildly terrible things all their lives. When her mother starts to make a statement about breeding, Sarah heads her off. When Old Teddy Roosevelt informs Fahima that a Muslim Resonant is exactly what normal people are afraid of, Sarah counters, "What they should be afraid of is aging alcoholic telepaths with money and no ethics." She keeps her eyes on her father as she says it, and no one in the room fails to notice. They go silent for what feels like a full minute before Mrs. Davenport chimes in with another "I think it's wonderful." The specific object of her wonder remains undefined.

Patrick is quiet and withdrawn. His father, trim, fit, and so tan that his ultrawhite teeth seem to glow, keeps pouring him whiskey, slapping him on the shoulder, and encouraging him to loosen up, but Patrick keeps to the corners. Abandoning Alyssa to the inquiries of Mrs. Davenport, Fahima goes to check on him.

"How goes the hunt?" she asks.

"You see Owen Curry's head mounted on the wall?" he says. "I'm chasing smoke. I'm starting to miss teaching is how bad it's gotten."

"At least your parents seem horrible," Fahima says.

"My dad is why there are all those stories about sons killing their fathers."

Fahima stands on tiptoe and puts her arm awkwardly around Patrick's shoulders.

"You're not a total asshole, Patrick." He laughs and reaches across his chest to pat her hand.

The food is amazing, although it seems as if it's never been touched by human hands. Fahima imagines machines shaping mashed potatoes into a symmetrical sea of whitecaps, laying the green beans in crosshatched layers, and placing golden pats of butter at the vertices. Being the only sober one at the table, she has the pleasure of watching the conversation slide and slur its way into politics.

"It's such a lot of fuss," says Steel Hair. She looks the same age as Mrs. Davenport but has opted for an aesthetic more June Cleaver than Lynda Carter: powder blue gingham with white collar and cuffs. As she gets drunk, she starts to twinkle, little sparkles of light dancing around her eyes and under her chin. When she notices it, she concentrates and it goes away, but she notices it less and less with each glass of wine. "Why do they need to flaunt themselves that way? I've always been happy enough knowing what I am. I don't need the whole world to know."

"It was always built into the philosophy of *that school*," says Mr. Davenport. "You can't tell children they're special and then ask them to hide. Bishop primed an entire generation for this . . . coming-out party for twenty years."

"That's exactly it," says Steel Hair. "A coming out. So flamboyant."

"It's the culture he came from," Old Teddy Roosevelt says. "Chelsea and Fire Island. Those men all throwing it in your face."

"Do you have a problem with the fact Kevin Bishop is gay?" Sarah asks.

"No, not that," says Steel Hair.

"No, never that," Patrick mutters into his glass, smirking.

"It's just the culture around it," Steel Hair continues. "It's so loud. We were never that loud when we were that age."

"And we did all right for ourselves, didn't we?" says Davenport. He laughs, a braying sound. In the sixties, Davenport used his ability to persuade all the homeowners on Oceanside Way to sell at a fraction of market prices, then sold the houses off to Resonants, pocketing a fair profit on each deal. To hear Sarah and Patrick tell it, most of his money came from psychically bilking people out of real estate. It's part of what the people at the table object to about how "loud" the younger generation is. The publicity risks drawing attention to Resonants who've quietly used their abilities for personal gain. What happens to a man like Davenport when the world finds out how he's made his money?

The moment plates are empty, Mrs. Davenport and the other wives begin to clear them to the kitchen. Mr. Davenport and the other men rise solemnly, as if drinking whiskey and smoking cigars in the solarium facing the ocean is a duty they must regrettably dispatch. Fahima hands off her plate to Weird Neck Thing, who huffs with affront. "Let's do this, then," she says. The men look at her, but only Patrick is smiling.

"Yes," says Sarah, standing. "Let us discuss matters of the world. And sports."

"Also the relative attractiveness of ladies," says Fahima. "I am here for that."

"No, you're not," Alyssa says. She kisses Fahima on the cheek. "I'm going to take a little postprandial nap."

"It's the tryptophan in the turkey," explains Captain Walrus Stache. "It's a natural—"

"Yeah, I'm a doctor and that's a myth," says Alyssa, balling up her napkin and tossing it on the table before she exits. The wives watch as Sarah and Fahima join the men. Fahima isn't sure if they look offended or impressed.

"So how is Kevin Bishop?" Davenport asks once the air is thick with the shoe leather smell of cigars.

"Busy," says Fahima.

"The whole thing's ridiculous," Davenport says. "Announcing ourselves to the world like we're aliens who just landed. There's power in the shadows." He pokes his cigar at Patrick's chest.

"Bishop used to understand that," Captain Walrus Stache says.

"Raymond Glover understood that," says Old Teddy Roosevelt. "Bishop was so holier than thou. Convinced we owed the world something."

"Who's Raymond Glover?" Fahima asks.

"One of the first," says Old Teddy Roosevelt. "A true visionary. He was our Casteneda."

"Glover was the one who taught us who we were," says Davenport. "He'd gather big groups of us in the mountains or the desert. We'd consider the *meaning* of what we could do, not just the implications."

"You've never told us about that," Sarah says.

"I had a life before I had children, duckling," says Davenport. He waggles his eyebrows suggestively. It's pretty gross. "Raymond Glover's retreats weren't the kind of thing you tell your kids about. Glover left us a few years before you were born."

"I like to imagine him in some castle in Europe, writing a great treatise that no one will ever have the pleasure of reading," says Captain Walrus Stache.

Old Teddy Roosevelt nods sagely. "Figuring it all out," he says. "Really delving in. Cracking the case." He makes a gesture like breaking a stick in his hands, forgetting he's holding a glass of whiskey, which he spills on his pants.

"Glover enlightened the adults while Bishop suffered the little children," Davenport continues. "I brokered the deal for that building. Prime piece of real estate. Not that Kevin Bishop ever said thank you. There were other options, but the Bishop Academy was still the standard. Relentless class mixing. But he did teach them how to live within the agreement. To keep themselves quiet without going completely insane." Davenport sips his drink. "He thinks of himself as our Martin Luther King, but at best he's our Booker T. Washington. That school's no better than vocational training. But my Sarah's practically running the place now. She'll whip it into shape." He throws his arm around Sarah, who shrinks in his inebriated embrace.

"I'm on it," she says.

"The thing is," says Davenport, "you can't be all things to all people. Bishop doesn't get that. He wants to be the face of our people, and police the bad eggs, and run the academy like he's Merlin to Arthur or Aristotle to Alexander. You can't do them all and do them well. Assess your human resources and put them to work for you. Like Patrick here," he says, slapping his son on the shoulder. "He's not going to set the world on fire, but he's a natural bloodhound. No shame in doing a small job well."

Patrick pours himself a healthy refill of whiskey. Sarah rolls her eyes and holds her glass out. The two of them can have entire conversations in facial expression and gesture, a secret sibling language they share. Patrick's arm stretches across the room, the bottle coming dangerously close to knocking the cherry off his father's cigar.

"It's the bedroom window," says Sarah, pointing.

"It's the bathroom," Patrick says, adjusting the vector of her arm to a different window. His other arm is coiled around the half-empty decanter of whiskey they liberated from his father's study.

"Are you sure?" she asks.

Patrick rolls his eyes. He hands the decanter off to Fahima, who caps it. His torso stretches up to the window on the second floor, and he pours up into it, liquid flowing back into a pitcher. Fahima watches closely, a thought occurring to her for the first time.

"We used to break in here all the time as kids," Sarah says, grabbing for the decanter. "Patrick found it first, then he started bringing me. This was after he first resonated. Before I did."

"Are you sure there's no one here?" Fahima asks.

"Only the hard-cores are here in November. Bishop is strictly summer people," Sarah says in a spot-on impersonation of her mother.

Patrick opens the sliding back door of the house to let

them in. Sarah steps through the door as if she's done it a million times before, which she probably has. Cortex hesitates for a second, then follows. Patrick stands, holding the door. Fahima pokes him in the ribs.

"Patrick," she says, "do you breathe?"

He laughs, and Fahima leans close to try and hear an inhalation. No luck.

"I'm serious," she says. "Do. You. Breathe?"

"Of course I do," says Patrick.

"Maybe you don't even notice you don't," Fahima says. "But what you just did—" She swoops her hand upward toward the window. "—I don't think you have lungs."

"That doesn't make any—"

She pokes at him again. "A mass of undifferentiated cells," she says. "All of them ready to carry out any necessary function. Even . . ." Fahima gasps a little. "Patrick, does your whole body resonate?"

Patrick blows a boozy breath in her face. "From my lungs to yours," he says.

An undifferentiated mass of cells *could* create a cavity, a lunglike space, and inhale into it for show. She imagines Patrick as a huge parahippocampal gyrus wrapped around a breath.

"Come on," Patrick says, smiling at her with teeth that have to be made of enamel and nerve showing between lips that must be skin rather than some cell pretending to be skin while acting as brain and muscle all at once. Fahima puts the idea out of her mind. She walks into the living room as Patrick turns on the collection of table lamps made out of kerosene lanterns. The room is full of kitschy maritime memorabilia. A half-scale ship's wheel on the wall. A stuffed seagull staring dumbly from the shelf.

"It's so quaint," says Fahima. "I can't imagine Bishop buying any of this stuff."

"He didn't," Sarah says. "He bought it as a package. Knickknacks and all."

Fahima looks at an astrolabe mounted on the wall, unable to think of its name. She tries to hear it, but none of these devices are real enough to speak to her. They're replicas of machines.

"Patrick broke in here first," Sarah says. "I think he used to hide in here and jerk off."

"I jerked off at home like a normal kid. I came here to try my ability out."

"Everybody on the street was waiting for us to resonate," Sarah says. "I made Patrick promise we'd tell each other before we told our family. They were patrolling the Hive waiting for us to pop up. Patrick resonated first, and he found a corner of the Hive where no one could see him."

"The onyx room," Patrick says. "That's what we called it."

"How did you find it?" asks Fahima.

"Lucky," Patrick says.

"His imaginary friend told him about it," Sarah says, elbowing him in the ribs. "What did you call him?"

"Raygun," says Patrick. "I had an imaginary friend who talked to me in my head, and I called him Raygun."

"That's some creepy *The Shining* shit," Fahima says. She holds up her index finger. "Patrick isn't here, Missus Davenport," she croaks.

"*I* didn't end up in a mental institution," Patrick snaps back.

"Fair point."

"Patrick and I used to meet in the onyx room to talk," Sarah says. "Then we'd come in here to try out our abilities. Patrick let me puppet him around."

"Hot," says Fahima.

"We kept it secret for months," Sarah says.

"Until the thing with the dog," says Patrick.

"It wasn't the dog's fault," Sarah says, rubbing Cortex behind the ear. When she was a kid, a dog had come off the leash and attacked her. New to her abilities, Sarah panicked and jumped her whole consciousness into the dog to get him to stop. She immediately pulled back, but a sliver of her mind remained in the dog. The owner apologized and took the dog home, but something in him pined for Sarah, that shard of her calling out to the rest. Sarah, for her part, became deeply absent-minded, forgetting names, entering rooms unable to remember what she'd come in looking for. One day, the dog showed up at Sarah's doorstep, tongue lolling out cheerfully, thrilled to be back by her side. Sarah didn't name him, but he came with her to Bishop. The initial fracture had left scars, and at some point in their third year at Bishop, Sarah began to lose memories, like an audiotape played so many times that it demagnetizes. Bishop came up with the idea to use the dog like an external hard drive. Sarah backed up her memories into the dog's mind, trailing her hand back toward him to access them as she needed to. Patrick, sixteen and constantly smirking, had named the dog Cortex.

"What ever happened to Raygun?" Sarah asks.

"Nothing happened to him," Patrick says. "I made him up."

CONEY ISLAND BABY

It's a tradition that no one acknowledges has happened before. Every generation has to discover rebellion for itself. Otherwise what's the point? One night, ideally the coldest night of the year, the final-years sneak out after hours and go to Coney Island. As if it's suddenly occurred to them to do so, not because it's been done before. They sneak out in small groups, each one with a separate plan.

"You sure you got this?" Bryce asks Waylon in the elevator.

"I got this," he says, annoyed. Despite their long-term business arrangement, Waylon's always been peevish around Bryce. Waylon claims that it's because Bryce flaunts his appearance: he's a head taller than anyone else at Bishop and has skin like the bark of an oak tree that scrapes and grates when he moves. Carrie suspects that it's because Bryce is openly gay, a hot item in Bishop's queer community, whereas Waylon has barely managed to scrounge up a date in years here.

"We can just walk right past him," Carrie says. "I can do that."

"Let him have his moment to shine," Miquel says. All of

them are bundled against the cold except Bryce. He wears one of the beautiful silk shirts someone at the Commune custom tailors for him. Its deep green sets off the paper white of his skin. In the lobby, Waylon raps his knuckles on Shen's desk to get the doorman's attention.

"You kids headed out?" Shen says.

"We're going for pizza," Waylon says.

"Cheap slices or fancy?" Shen asks.

Waylon reaches awkwardly over the desk and lays a hand on Shen's massive shoulder. He has to stand on tiptoe to do it.

"We're going to go out in this weather for a cheap slice?" Waylon says.

"So you're going to Rubirosa on Mulberry," says Shen.

"We're going to Lil' Frankies on First," Waylon says, hand resting on Shen's shoulder.

"No," says Shen, "you're going to Rubirosa on Mulberry, and then you're coming back and saying *thank you, Shen, for saving me from my own ignorance.* Take the 6 down to Spring, you come right up next to it," says Shen.

Waylon pulls his hand back, scratches his chin. Then, with another awkward stretch, he touches Shen on the shoulder one more time. "We'll try it," he says. "You want us to bring you back a slice?"

Shen hardly ever leaves the desk. He survives on food brought to him by students and teachers who venture out into the city. He is a connoisseur of the leftovers of Manhattan and Brooklyn. So it's a shock when he says, "I'm good."

Each of them signs the sheet, and after specific menu recommendations, Shen sends them on their way.

On the sidewalk, set back the legally required fifty feet, there's a throng of the most dedicated worshippers, who are out here daily, no matter the weather. They call themselves "harmonics" or "latents" or "aspirants," and they're convinced they have the potential to be Resonants. They call out to students and faculty exiting Bishop to touch them. A touch, they know, they *believe*, will jump-start something within them. Carrie recognizes one of them, a girl with bright purple hair and vine tattoos that creep out of the collar of her Carhartt and up her neck. Carrie first saw her at one of Hayden's shows, but she's a regular with the sidewalk set. Maybe it's her persistence that puts Carrie off, or the fact that the girl's need feels familiar, not unlike Carrie's own. She wants to tell the girl, *It doesn't fix you.* She wants to say the need doesn't go away, it only changes shape.

The girl spots Carrie. She tries to hold eye contact, pleading silently. Carrie tugs at Miquel's coat sleeve.

"Let's go this way," she says, taking the long route to the liquor store. When she looks over her shoulder, the girl is huddled back in with the others, clapping her mittened hands together for warmth.

"Did you see that?" Waylon says once they're out in the street. "I made Shen refuse food. I am a mind control master. I'm a fucking Jedi."

"What's with all the touching?" Bryce asks.

"It forms a connection," Waylon says, taking on the air of an expert. "Hypnotists do it all the time on TV."

"You're learning mind control from TV hypnotists?" Carrie asks.

"What I did was the psychic equivalent of a posthypnotic suggestion," says Waylon. "In two hours, for reasons he cannot even fathom, Shen will sign us back in. Then, under cover of darkness, Carrie will sneak us through the lobby."

"You sure this will work?" Miquel asks.

"The man said no to fancy Nolita pizza!" says Waylon. "He is completely in my thrall."

"It's amazing that with this ability to put the whammy on someone you're still a virgin," says Carrie.

"I am not a virgin," Waylon says.

Miquel mouths *Yes, he is.* Carrie and Bryce stifle laughs.

Alcohol is easy to acquire. Thirty-four final-years, thirty-four methods for getting booze, ranging from felonious to unethical. Waylon's deep-seeded a clerk at the bodega on 59th with the idea that he's thirty-two, and she never ID's him anymore. He and Miquel and Bryce chip in on four magnums of red wine, waving Carrie's money away.

Carrie puts her earbuds in but doesn't put any music on. It's a lesser form of invisibility, a way to eavesdrop in plain sight. Bryce hangs off one of the subway straps on the Q train. A young black kid, sitting in his mother's lap, stares at him, jaw open. Not in fear but in wonder. His mother notices and pulls him tighter, but the boy squirms loose. On shaky legs, he approaches Bryce.

"Mister," he says. Bryce looks down at him. The boy stammers.

"Dennis," chides his mother, pulling at the back of the boy's jacket.

Bryce holds his hand out to the kid, palm down. "Go

ahead, kid." The boy rubs the back of Bryce's hand. His eyes, impossibly, get even wider.

"You're so cool," says the boy. His mother yanks him back into her embrace, whispering harsh words in his ear.

"You're so cool," Waylon says, rolling his eyes.

"A grown man asked to touch me, I'd knock him out," Bryce says.

Waylon smiles at him with a tenderness Carrie finds surprising. "No, you wouldn't," he says. Bryce looks down, embarrassed.

At the Beverley Road stop, Hayden Cohen steps on to the train and holds out their arms, Christlike, waiting for applause.

"Holy shit, I thought you had a show," says Carrie.

"I had an opening gig," Hayden says, giving Carrie a hug. "Played a short set and left Jonathan to pack up the gear. I wouldn't miss this."

"How did you find us?" Carrie asks.

"I can always find you," Hayden says. Miquel laughts into his fist.

"You knew?" Carrie says.

"We wanted it to be a surprise," Miquel says.

"We're all thrilled you could grace us with your presence," says Waylon. "Did you bring booze?"

"I brought drugs, child, because we are adults now," Hayden says.

Hayden tucks in between Carrie and Miquel for warmth.

"How was the show?" Bryce asks.

"Boring as fuck," says Hayden. "We're the flavor of the fucking month. I want them to be afraid of me, but they're

318

not. We've got labels calling, can you believe it? They want to put our songs in Gap ads and shit. I wanted it to be dangerous for a while. It's over before we had the chance to be scary."

At its last stop, the Q spits them into a tile-lined tunnel, a cavern in ceramic. All the shops are shuttered for the night, the last remaining people loading onto the inbound train, abandoning this place, ceding it to Carrie and the final-years. They walk down the tunnel, out into the freezing night.

Carrie has no idea what they're supposed to do now that they're here, and neither does anyone else. But they've done it, all of them. Even though Eli Herrington is still pissed at Nolan Emerson for stealing his essay topic in ethics class two years back and Michele Summers started sleeping with Vince Cole before he and Rufina Dahl had technically broken it off. Even though Ruby Wallace has literally not left academy grounds since the day she started there, skipping every field trip, avoiding classes that ventured off site, even watching the Public Day parade from her dorm window, they're all here, on a beach in the middle of February. Drunk. Together.

Crowded in the shadow of the Ferris wheel, Carrie is halfway through her big bottle of red, and the pills Hayden gave her shift in her stomach like a cat searching for a perfect napping spot. Miquel makes them all *feel* warm, an effect he warns them won't ward off hypothermia. Carrie uses it as an excuse to cuddle in under his arm as a source of actual heat.

"I'm glad Hayden made it," Miquel says. "It would have been wrong without them here. Incomplete."

"You thinking of how things might have been?" Carrie asks.

Miquel laughs. "We kissed one time!"

"You made out," says Carrie.

"Hayden's too glamorous for me," Miquel says.

"I'm not glamorous?" Carrie turns to see his face. He's got a big shit-eating grin. His face softens, and he stoops to speak into her ear.

"It's tough to be around Hayden," he says. "They hurt a lot. I don't think it even registers as hurting anymore, but it's there. Spikes."

"What's being around me like?" Carrie asks.

"Like a heartbeat," Miquel says. He gives her a squeeze, bringing her back into the moment.

"Light it up!" Hayden yells at Nolan. He's been standing at the base of the Ferris wheel for what feels like an hour, passing test sparks between his hands.

"It's a hundred years old," he calls back. "I don't want to kill it."

"By the time you're done, I'll be a hundred years old," Bryce yells.

"And *I'll* want to kill *you*," Waylon adds. This cracks the two of them up, and Bryce throws an arm around Waylon. To Carrie's surprise, Waylon doesn't move away but pulls in closer to Bryce. She can't help thinking of Bryce in tree-related terms. His branch around Waylon, Waylon leaning against Bryce's trunk.

"You've got this," Miquel shouts. Carrie gets colder as Miquel pushes confidence toward Nolan. He can push only one thing at a time. He holds Carrie closer to compensate.

"All right," Nolan shouts. "On three."

"Fucking do it!" Ruby screams. She never drinks, but someone fixed her something that tastes like Tang. Everyone laughs about this new uninhibited Ruby. Not cruelly. Happy that finally, in these last few days together, Ruby is one of them. Their laughter becomes applause, becomes a chant of *fucking do it fucking do it.*

"One two three!" Nolan shouts. He slams his hands onto the mechanism like a mad Amadeus at the piano and holds them there.

"Nothing's happening!" Ruby shouts.

The Ferris wheel blazes to life, and the final-years lose their collective shit. The fliers hit the air, dancing through the spinning, shifting light. Lynnette Helms blasts a Beyoncé song into their heads. Carrie wants to tell her it's perfect. Before she can, Lynette is somewhere else, dancing. The final-years couple off, group into tiny cliques. In the choices they make, the people they join up with, they reify their whole history at Bishop. Friendships that will survive their departure must be cemented here, and this is the last available burial ground for grudges. Anything they don't leave behind now will be carried. Anything they don't carry will be forgotten.

Waylon grinds against Bryce's trunk. Bryce grabs the sides of Waylon's head and kisses him, and Waylon kisses him back desperately. *This had to happen tonight*, Carrie thinks. *They were about to miss each other. These things come so close to not happening.* She watches the two of them and smiles. None of the other final-years, even Miquel, sees. They are absorbed in themselves. They are caught up in the lights and the air and the end of everything they know looming over them. They're caught up in freedom and terror.

"This is amazing!" Miquel shouts. There's no way to tell if he's drunk or high on everyone else's euphoria or genuinely ecstatic. Carrie needs to know which it is. Miquel and Waylon and Hayden have made plans to move to Chicago after graduation. Hayden says there's a neighborhood in Wicker Park filling up with Resonant kids their age. Hayden says it's like St. Mark's Place in the seventies, which Carrie knows is intended to lure her along, although no one's invited her. She's waiting to hear about jobs in Boston and here in New York. She didn't apply anwhere in Chicago. It felt too close to home. But if Miquel asks, she'll follow.

Miquel grips her by the shoulders of her heavy coat. His wide grin is lit in rainbow colors by the Ferris wheel behind her. "It's like a Lou Reed song," he says.

Carrie played Lou Reed for Miquel when they were sixteen to cure him of Pink Floyd and the Dead and all the other lazy things he listened to stoned. She started him out in the deep end of the pool with "Heroin," Reed wheezing and sputtering, guitars screeching over his vocals.

"Hear that?" she'd said. "That's dissonance. Can't you feel it in your teeth?"

Miquel smiled. His teeth were perfect. He wanted more, wanted every song Reed had recorded. Carrie gave them to him, and now he's offering them back to her as something changed, new.

"Which song?" she asks, yelling over the music Lynette is playing in their heads.

"What?"

"Which Lou Reed song is it like?" Before Miquel can answer, blue and red lights cycle across the boardwalk. Cops, attracted by the Ferris wheel lights. The final-years scatter. They run for the streets and take to the air. Miquel is ready to bolt, but she holds him.

"Stay still," she says. She pulls him in tight, pushes them both down, invisible. A cop sprints by, close enough to touch them. Two more, three.

"I can see you," Miquel says. His arms are around her waist, hers around his shoulders. Carrie lifts her face to his, her lips to his.

Down the beach, the other final-years laugh. They fly and shoot fireworks into the dark from their fingertips.

FIVE

LAST YEAR'S MAN

The trilling wire in the blood
Sings below inveterate scars
Appeasing long forgotten wars.
—T. S. ELIOT, *"Four Quartets"*

OWEN CURRY
AND THE FULL BIZARRE

The cook raps a greasy knuckle on the flyer Owen Curry has been staring at for five minutes. "You been?" he asks.

Owen is startled. He jostles his coffee, his fifth cup. It spills on the picture, a still from an old movie. Freaks! the flyer declares. Welled on the surface, the drops look like pale blood. They soak into the paper dull tan.

"Not yet," Owen says. The cook is sweaty, unshaven. He smells like hamburger and that body odor cattle have. Bread soaked in soured milk. Owen feels nauseous being around so many of them. *Couldn't I—*

No, says the friend in his head.

Owen crams cold pancake into his mouth and looks at the cook as he chews. "You?"

The cook holds up three fingers, then leans in so close Owen gets a whiff of his stale breath. "Seriously fucked up," he whispers. "They got this girl with tentacle arms. Normal except for that, but her arms are tentacles with suckers and everything. Imagine you saw her on the street. You'd check out her ass, because it's like an easy eight. Maybe whistle or say something. And then, bang, tentacles."

"That's fucked up," says Owen. He knows this is how guys talk to one another. Girls' asses rated like movies, thumbs up or down. His manager at the Planet gave three letter grades to every girl who worked at the mall, one for tits, one for ass, and one for face.

"Worst thing is I can't stop thinking about her," says the cook, wiping his hands on a dirty towel tucked in his belt. "I get these nightmares of those tentacles touching me, but it's like I've got to know what they feel like. If they're warm or cold." His eyes go out of focus. *Someone's fucked with his mind*, Owen thinks. *Someone like me has laid their mark on him.* He wonders how long and how badly this hapless cow will be haunted. "Anyway," the cook says, "you got to go. Bring a sick bag in case you get queasy. But you got to go."

Owen looks at the flyer. He points to the address, some county road. "How far is it?" he asks.

"Twenty-minute drive."

"I don't have a car," Owen says.

The cook stares at him. "How'd you get here without a car?"

"I'm on a sort of walking tour," says Owen. "Like a pilgrimage."

"Like Moses."

"Yeah," says Owen. "Like Moses."

"Me and Jake are going to drive out there after work," says the cook, cocking his thumb at the dishwasher in the back. "It'd be tight, but we could take you out."

"That'd be fucking great," says Owen. Twenty minutes crammed in a pickup, the doubled stink of two cows' obsolescence thick in the air. *When I'm done,* he thinks, *I could come back here and—*

No, Owen, says his friend. *You are my justice, my scalpel. Soon you'll feed on cities. But for now you have to stay secret.*

Owen's been secret almost a year. Not a single cow fed to the null. No one hurt. Hiding in one hotel room after another, gorging on takeout, and isn't he a little thick in the middle lately? Hasn't his face, once a flinty collection of sharp angles, softened until it's cherubic? He used to have the face of a predator instead of a sheep. Owen's spent three days frequenting the diner in Damascus, Ohio, population 578. Waiting for a sign. Getting soft. The best look for a predator is blood in the teeth.

Annoyed, bored, defiant, Owen Curry reaches into the part of his belly where the null resides, ready to let it out, let it have this cook with his stained apron and milky bread smell, and Jake in the dish room, and the cop at the other end of the counter, and the old ladies stuffing envelopes in the corner booth. He's about to open himself, like the cracking of a terrible egg, when pain stabs his head, a sword made of heat piercing his brain.

Not. Yet.

"You okay, guy?" the cook asks. Owen is white-knuckling the counter. He lets it go, rubs the spot between his eyebrows.

"I'm good," he says. "I've been getting these headaches."

"It's all that coffee," says the cook. He delicately removes Owen's mug, his arm coming close enough that Owen could lurch forward and bite it. "I'm cutting you off."

o

Damascus isn't big enough to have outskirts. If it did, this would be beyond them, into the interstitial wastes between Damascus and the next one-stoplight nowhere. In school, Owen learned that the universe is empty space spotted with dense bits of matter. America is like that, too. The cattle cluster and huddle in cities. Coagulate in small towns. The bulk of the landscape is fallow. *Maybe that's the solution*, he thinks. *We'll take everything they built. They can have the wastes.*

The cook, Paul, is drunk by the time he picks Owen up from the motel. Jake the dishwasher is drunker. The truck careens along dirt roads. Headlights flirt with ditches and dead trees. Jake offers Owen a beer, and he accepts it, although it's warm. Jake and Paul have each finished off two before Owen drinks his first.

"We're lapping you, O," says Paul.

"And we had a head start," Jake adds. They decide Owen has to shotgun a beer, which he can't do in a moving truck. They pull over and step into the glare of the headlights. Paul demonstrates, holding the can of beer up so the headlights glint off the aluminum. He takes his Swiss Army knife and punctures the base of the can. He puts his lips to the hole and cracks the top of the can, swallowing frantically.

"You're up," he says to Owen, wiping foam from his chin. Owen takes a can and the knife. He lifts the can like Hamlet with that skull, then stabs it. He turns the knife to leave a dime-sized hole, like a bullet through a forehead. The liquid is suspended, held back with no air to displace it. He covers the hole with his mouth and pops the top, spraying lukewarm beer down his throat. He manages to glug it all down, but when it's done, he's coughing and hacking, tears in his eyes. Blood pounds in his ears. Jake and Paul laugh. It's been a joke on him. Everything from the meeting in the diner to this moment, ridiculing him in the woods.

He reaches for the null in his guts, and the pain floods his head again. He's determined to push through it. His friend can turn his brain into jelly. Owen doesn't care.

Jake slaps him on the back. "That's not bad, O," he says. "Got it down and kept it down. Better than Paul did his first time."

"Launched my lunch," Paul says. "Come on, let's get going."

They come to a convoy of three trailer trucks and an RV drawn into a semicircle around a muddied stretch of dirt, stray patches of dead grass slicked down like a bad comb-over. There are a handful of cars and pickups parked along the road, maybe twenty customers milling around. Smoking cigarettes, lining up at the backs of the trailers. As Owen and his new friends approach, a young man with pale, delicate features and a powder blue suit spattered around the legs with mud comes up to them holding a cash box.

"Twenty for the strange, forty for the weird, fifty for the full bizarre," he says. "That's the suggested donation. You're welcome to give more." He puts his hand on Paul's bare forearm as he says this, and Owen watches Paul pull out five crisp twenties. The boy gives Paul three tickets and thanks him. Jake sees this, too, and shakes his head as he gives the boy twenty bucks. "Only the strange?" says the boy, reaching for him. Jake twitches away.

"I'm good with the strange," Jake says, taking his ticket.

Owen hands him twenty dollars. As he does, the boy brushes Owen's index finger. Owen takes another twenty out of his wallet and hands it over.

"Thank you," the boy says, smiling and backing away.

"She's usually in the bizarre trailer," Paul says. "I'm starting out there—"

"And staying till they kick you out," Jake says.

"—but if you guys want to start at the first one."

"We'll give you two some alone time," Jake says.

"It's not like that," says Paul.

"Is so," Jake says. "Come on." He tugs Owen by the arm. They head for the trailer on the left. The strange. There's a wooden set of stairs with a railing on one side that leads up into the back of the trailer. A ticket collector sits on the middle step, engrossed in the glow of his phone.

"Beyond lies the strange," he says flatly. He gestures to the shabby piece of industrial carpet draped from the trailer's roof, weighted with cinder blocks. "Tickets please."

Owen and Jake give him their tickets. He stands with visible effort and pulls back a corner of the carpet. Enough so Jake, who's done this before, can lift it to let them in.

The trailer is dim lit with black lights. Their buzz puts Owen's teeth on edge, reminding him of his cell, the green lights that pushed down on him, that felt like someone shoved bees in his mouth and duct taped it shut. The black lights pick up garish fluorescent signs hanging above a row of standing shower stalls. Each is fronted with two-way glass, mirror side out. THE SKINLESS GIRL! screams the first sign in hot pink horror movie lettering. Paint drips from the dot of the exclamation point. THE LIVING SPECK! THE BONEYARD! THE WOLF-FACED GIRL! At the end, a larger cell, a double wide, with red curtains hung over it. THE ANGEL OF SILENCE, the sign proclaims. The words are rendered with care. Each letter has rounded little feet. Owen steps toward it immediately, but Jake holds him back.

"Save her for last," he says. "She's something." He presses a doorbell button on the first cell. An overhead light comes on. It's too strong for the room, making Owen blink. In the cell, there's a girl whose skin is transparent, a thin slick of clear snot over her muscles and blood vessels. She holds up one hand to shield her lidless eyes from the light. With the other she covers as much of her body as she can. She retreats to the back corner.

"Does the light hurt her?" Owen asks. Jake shrugs. The possibility has never occurred to him. The null twitches in Owen's gut. Jake points to the next sign, THE LIVING SPECK. Under it, there's a card table with a two-eye microscope like the ones they used in chemistry class.

"That one's boring," Jake says. "She's little, but she's also fat. So what the fuck?"

Jake steps up to the booth that contains THE BONEYARD. Owen walks past him to the end of the trailer. THE ANGEL OF SILENCE. He presses the button, and buttery yellow light pours into the cell. Robed in white, there's a girl, her dirty blond hair done up like a woman in a gladiator movie, a mountain of spiraling braids. Her head hangs, and she eyes Owen like a puppy that's been kicked. Her arms are wings, gray and wide, folded across her chest protectively. Owen can see the layers of feathers on them: soft down that extends from her shoulders and biceps, a tufty band below that, and then the long ones, like fingers splayed wide. It hurts to see her cramped into such a small space. Owen wants her wings spread. He wants her in the air. He puts his hand on the glass.

"She doesn't talk," Jake says. The words are barely out of his mouth when Owen's mind is caught on a hook, dragged out of his body into a vast, shimmering room.

"What the fuck?" he screams with a mouth that is not his mouth. The Angel stands in front of him, wings tight around her body. "Where the fuck are we?"

"The Hive," says the Angel. "You've been here before, right? I mean, you're one of us."

"This isn't what it looks like," Owen says. He walks a small circle around her, watching as people appear and fade out in the shimmering room. "It's so big. Where's the black bone room?"

The Angel looks at him, confused.

"Why are you here?" he asks her. "Why are you in a cage?"

"It was my boyfriend. Bobby," she says. "We started out with the circus idea. We lived in the Commune, and we were seeing Resonants on late-night shows, doing stupid pet tricks for laughs. Like circus animals, Bobby said. He was born in the Commune, but he didn't have to stay. He looked normal. Not like the rest of us. It was his idea to go on the road like a freak show. It was going to be subversive. Confront people with who we were. It was going to be some fucking art project. Bobby was the manager. Because he's the pretty one. The one who looks normal." Owen struggles to keep up with this barrage of new terms. The Hive. The Commune. *We have our own language*, he thinks. There's a pang of betrayal, too. If they have their own language, why hasn't his friend taught it to him? Why is he learning it only now? "Bobby can make you do things, want things, by touching you," the Angel says. "That's how he got me to even date him. He's such a skeev."

Owen thinks of the brush of a finger on his, the urge to fork over more money for no reason. The boy in the powder blue suit. Bobby.

"He made me *want* to get into the cage," she says, crying. "It looked so beautiful. He held me by my wing and said, *Wendy, step in, I built it for you.* Then he closed it behind me. I was the first. He brought us in here one by one: me, then poor little Gail, then Andre. We were all so happy when he put us in here."

Owen is half drunk on how beautiful she is, on how beautiful this place is. The Hive, she called it. It feels the same as the black bone room. But this place is different. There's air to breathe, space to move. The black bone room is like this place in the way they vibrate, the way they're gauzy to look at. But it feels like confinement. This shimmering room must belong to everyone like Owen. For all he's thought about the cattle, for all he's thought about enemies, he's never thought about people like him except the friend in his head and the ones who kept him in the cell. The one he loves most and the ones he hates. He's never imagined having real friends with abilities. Angels and skinless boys.

"I'll get you out," he tells her. "No one should be in a cell."

"You can't," she says. "He touched you, didn't he? He can make you do whatever. He'll put you in a cage with us."

"I'll get you out," he says again. He feels a hand on his real, actual shoulder, reminding him that he has a body, and the shimmering room is gone. There's the Angel behind the glass, the twin reflections of himself and Jake hanging like ghosts over her face.

"You got a crush there, O?" Jake says. "You went all spacy for a minute."

"Freaked out," says Owen.

"I don't know what your bankroll looks like," Jake says, leaning in close, "but there are arrangements you can make if you can pay for it." The Angel turns away. Owen wonders if she can hear them. "Paul talked to that boy out front about it. For his tentacle girl. If he wasn't dropping a hundred bucks at the door every time, he could afford to fuck her out back or wherever. They let you do all kinds of shit."

"Like what?" Owen asks.

"Eddie who tends bar at the Eight of Swords paid three hundred to beat on bony there with a bat," says Jake. He jerks his thumb at one of the other cells, where the lights are fading on a boy with gray nubs of bone protruding from his joints. Owen can see ossified ridges at the boy's shoulders and hips. "I threw in fifty, and they let me watch."

"You paid to watch your friend beat him," Owen says. Not a question, a reckoning with the fact. Jake gives him an idiot nod.

You see now, Owen, says the friend in his head. *Why I brought you here. What you're meant to do.*

Owen turns his back on the Angel and faces Jake full on. The null roils in his gut, hungry for this one. But the pain stabs in his head. He's gotten it wrong.

"What's going on with you, man?" Jake asks. "You look like shit."

From behind Jake, there's a little sound. Owen's never heard it before, but he knows what it is. Bone tapping on glass. Owen peers over Jake's shoulder. He stretches the null out, shapes it so it's broad and flat. He feeds the null the glass that holds the bone boy back. It doesn't fill the null, doesn't sate that hunger at Owen's core. But he smiles as the boy approaches Jake from behind, raising an elbow that ends in a jutting gray blade. It plunges into Jake where the shoulder meets the neck, and Jake the dishwasher dies with a disappointing burble of blood in his throat. Owen opens the other cages, leaving the Angel for last. As she steps out, her wings spread to half their span.

"Stay," Owen says. "Wait."

"Where's your friend?" asks the ticket collector as Owen comes down the stairs. Owen glances back over his shoulder.

"Still staring at that tiny girl?" Owen says.

"Every guy comes here's got some twist," says the ticket collector. "Busy nights I go in once an hour to squeegee jizz off the glass." He sizes Owen up. "What's your kink, kid?"

Owen makes a show of shyness, examines his shoes. "That Angel is something."

"She sure is, Vanilla," says the ticket collector, bored with the predictability of Owen's fetish. "See the office trailer over there?" He points to the RV at the end of the row. "Go ask Bobby, in the suit. He can set you up some time with her. She even talks." He smiles. "If you want to talk."

"Thanks," Owen says. The ticket collector holds out an open palm. Owen stares at it, then realizes what's being asked. He pulls a twenty out of his wallet and folds it into the man's hand. He'll take it off the body later.

"Thank *you*, Vanilla," says the ticket collector.

Owen walks across the muddy field toward the RV. As he crosses, Paul steps out of the trailer on the right, the truly bizarre. "Where's Jake?" he calls.

"In the strange," Owen says. "You should check on him."

Owen speeds his steps. There's not much time. There will be screams soon, and Owen wants a minute alone with Bobby. He has a special place for jailers. He knocks on the door of the RV.

"Come on in," says the boy's sweet voice. Owen couldn't *not* come in. Something in the voice compels him: the spot where Bobby brushed his finger tingles. The Angel said, *He can make you do whatever.* Owen steps into the office.

"Did someone send you?" Bobby asks. He's sitting behind a small pine desk with stacks of bills and coins. "Is there a Resonant police force after me now?"

"Passing through," says Owen.

"Stay right there," Bobby says. Owen obeys. Bobby stands up, comes around the desk. He moves slowly, no reason to hurry. Owen wonders if Paul has found Jake's body yet. "That is some seriously bad luck on my part. The megabucks lottery of shitty luck."

"Let them go," Owen says.

"No, Moses, I don't think I'm going to let your people go," says Bobby. "I think I am going to keep them in their cages until people are no longer paying to see them." He reaches behind his back and pulls a small gun out of his waistband. He puts it on the desk. "I also think you are going to wander about an hour into the woods and then shoot yourself in the face."

The gun glitters. It will feel perfect in his hand. The cool of it pressed against his forehead. The relief as the bullet pushes through his brain and his body falls back into a pillow-soft layer of dead leaves. Bobby smiles approvingly. Owen wishes he could tell the Angel what he's going to do. *Sorry*, he'd say. *I would free you, but first I need to—*

Owen, says the friend in his head. *You're stronger than him.*

All I want is the gun, Owen thinks.

Get rid of the gun, says his friend. Owen looks at it. The sculpted metal. A perfect play of cylinder and line. Bobby's hand rests next to it, fingers on the handle gently, lovingly. Owen wants to touch it. Hold it.

He reaches out with the null. He forms it into a circle that devours the gun, a chunk of the desk underneath it, and two of Bobby's fingers up to the first knuckles. Bobby draws his hand up in front of his face, staring at the lack, at the smooth edges where the fingers end. He screams. An animal sound. Outside there are more screams. Bobby slams his mutilated hand on the desk, and Owen can sense Bobby's ability welling up, aimed at him.

"Fucking di—"

Owen is inside his head, rooting, looking for that glowing

339

little bit where Bobby's ability lives. He finds it in the middle of Bobby's brain and feeds it to the null. It's inelegant surgery. A baseball-size sphere of brain comes along with it, and the null growls appreciatively as blood spurts from Bobby's nose and wells in his eyes like tears. Bobby pitches forward onto the desk, twitching.

Owen steps out of the RV. People run wildly around the patch of dead grass, their paths chaotic like those of flies. The Angel swoops overhead, tracing a figure eight against the night sky. The ticket collector is facedown in the mud, deep gashes on his back. Paul sprints to Owen, shirt torn open. His torso and the left side of his face are covered in perfectly circular red welts. Sucker marks.

"We gotta get out of here," he screams.

Owen holds his shoulders as if he's trying to calm him down. "Wait," he says.

Can I? he asks his friend.

All of these are yours, his friend says.

Owen smiles, a wolf again at last.

EXAMINATION

Fahima and Patrick have a text chain of names for it. *Kevin Bishop's Victory Lap. The Peace and Unity Tour. Electric Kool-Aid Resonance Test.* Fahima stopped following Bishop's slate of lectures and media appearances because she has her own life to worry about and there aren't enough hours in the day. Alyssa insists they go to his talk at Columbia, the first in a semester-long series on posthumanism. Along with colloquiums on issues of consent for sex robots and the potential barriers to diplomatic relations between humans and extraterrestrials with non-logic-based linguistics is Kevin Bishop, speaking on the shadow history of Resonants hiding in plain sight through the twentieth and early twenty-first centuries. The lecture title is "The Nobody People."

Alyssa works nearby, so she meets Fahima at the lecture hall still wearing her scrubs. They're shuttled backstage, where Bishop is pacing in the wings, doing a series of verbal warm-ups Sarah taught him that contort his face into funny shapes.

"Nervous, Bishop?" says Fahima.

He smiles. "This is my alma mater," he says. "I was one of Enrico Fermi's first graduate students. I don't want to let the old man down."

"Name-dropper," says Fahima. "Some day I'm going to get you so drunk, you'll tell me your whole life story."

Bishop smiles his frustrating, enigmatic smile, then turns his attention to Alyssa. "Doctor Pratt," he says, extending his hand. "It's so very good to meet you."

"Alyssa, please," she says.

"Then you should call me Kevin."

"You should call him Bishop," Fahima says. One of the organizers comes by and whispers something in Bishop's ear. "Kevin doesn't carry any weight."

"We all do the best with what we're given," Bishop says.

"I'm looking forward to hearing you speak," says Alyssa. "I feel like I don't know how to think about all this."

"None of us do," Bishop says. "That's a good thing. Our thinking should be constantly evolving. Always learning. Always—" He shakes his head as if a gnat has buzzed into his ear. "I'm sorry," he says. He grabs Alyssa's shoulder, leaning on her for support. A thin trickle of pink fluid dribbles from his left nostril.

"Mr. Bishop?" Alyssa says. She's gone instantly into her doctor voice. Bishop's eyes are distant for a second before coming back into focus.

"I'm sorry," he says again, wiping the spot under his nose. "I've been having these headaches."

On stage, someone is introducing him, using the kind of hyperbolic language deployed at academic lectures.

342

Visionary. Revolutionary. No one man has had the impact. Only this time they're accurate.

"How long?" Alyssa asks.

"Hmm?"

"How long have you been having headaches?"

"They're occasional."

"I think you just had a seizure."

His hand on her shoulder gives her a patronizing pat. "You're young. You don't know how common little spells like that become at my age."

"I'm a doctor," Alyssa says. "I know a seizure when it's in front of me. We need to get you to a hospital."

Fahima feels the quiver in her mind that occurs whenever Bishop uses his ability. He's so powerful, his ability has to be held in check. When even a little of it vents into the world, it rattles any mind nearby.

"We'll go after the lecture," Alyssa says. Her voice is flat and mechanical.

"Very good," Bishop says. Fahima glares at him, sends the thought as loudly and clearly as she can: *Don't ever do that to her again.* But the audience is cheering, the students still flush with the enthusiasm of a new school year beginning. Bishop steps out into the lights, waving energetically.

Alyssa goes over it with Fahima first. There are things in the results Alyssa can't make sense of, things specific to Resonant biology. Fahima sends for a few items to be couriered over from her lab to fill in details. But they are all beside the point. The main issue is clear. There's nothing special, nothing magical about it.

Fahima hands him their report, and he pages through it while she hooks up the contacts on the EEG helmet, a colander studded with nodes and strung with wires.

"Did you know?" she asks.

"I knew something was wrong," Bishop says, flipping through the report.

"You've been fighting it," says Fahima. "A war inside yourself that you're not winning and you're not losing. Détente."

"For the moment," he says, tapping a pen on one of the pages. Fahima nods and points to the monitor screen.

"Look at this," she says. "You know what that little glowworm is?"

"My Resonance," Bishop says. He has an annoying habit of saying *Resonance* as if it's a holy word.

"Your parahippocampal gyrus," Fahima says. "It's glowing because it's active. Your ability is actively engaged."

"Always," says Bishop.

"Fighting the cancer," she says. "Maintaining détente. Let me show you something else." She types in a command, and the screen splits, the image twinned almost. "This is your EEG scan six months ago. Last time you let me give you a physical. Look at your little glowworm back then."

"Bigger," he says. He leans in to confirm. "I'm burning out."

"You are engaging your ability constantly," Fahima says. "I've never seen anyone do that. The toll it must be taking."

"I'm not tired, Fahima," he says. The pen seesaws back and forth in his hand, quicker and quicker, slapping at the paper.

"Kevin, do you sleep?" The familiarity of his first name

sounds strange to her. But if she can't be informal telling him he's dying, when can she?

"In my way," he says.

She puts her hand over his, stilling it. "You're burning out." He looks up at her. She forgets sometimes how old he is, because he doesn't wear all of his years on his face. But they're in his eyes, years of hiding and fighting. Horrible actions taken for the right reasons. A ledger of his dead.

"How fast?" he asks.

She looks at the screen as if the answer is written there, but it's only an excuse not to meet his eyes. "I'd be estimating," she says.

"Estimate."

Fahima sighs. She closes her eyes, tugs at the edge of her hijab. "You've lost a quarter of the mass of your gyrus in the last six months."

"So eighteen more months."

"Assuming a constant rate of decay."

"More likely?" he asks.

"No way of knowing," she lies. "Maybe weak cells burn off faster. Maybe it'll speed up."

"You'd say a year."

There it is, the truth she's been tap-dancing around. "A year, yes," she says.

"And then what happens?"

She takes the capped marker, traces an imaginary circle around the glowing spot on the screen. "This region is classically associated with memory encoding," she says. "You'll be unable to form new memories."

"But I keep my old ones?"

"You won't be able to access them," Fahima says. "It won't be dissimilar to Sarah's condition, but you won't have a mechanism like Cortex to compensate. We're talking endgame stuff, though. Severe late-stage atrophy."

"What about the early stages?"

"You'll start missing social cues," Fahima says. "You won't be able to detect sarcasm."

"That might make our conversations difficult," he says, grinning.

"Asymmetrical atrophy of the parahippocampal gyrus is associated with schizophrenia, and stop fucking around about this, Bishop," she snaps.

"I'm listening," he says calmly.

"You'll be dead."

"Yes," Bishop says.

"When you lose enough mass in the gyrus," Fahima says, returning her attention to the screen, "and we don't know how much that is, you'll lose your ability. You won't be able to wage this constant cellular war on your cancer, and it will advance. Rapidly. And you will be dead."

"Within a year," says Bishop.

"Yes," Fahima says.

They stare at each other in silence.

"You know what my mother used to tell me?" Fahima asks.

"What's that?"

"She said it was important to find something only you could do," she says. "You and no one else. And then do it."

"I've had a school to run," he says.

"Anyone could run this school," Fahima says. "Sarah's been basically running it since Public Day."

"What about you?"

"I barely want to teach here."

"Sarah can run the academy," says Bishop. She can't tell if he's trying to convince her or himself that this is true. "A year?" he asks.

"Maybe less," says Fahima.

He nods grimly, but the EEG helmet makes him look silly, a bobblehead doll.

"Then I have things to do."

ON THE AIR

When Avi was on embeds, Kay would hold the phone so Emmeline could see her dad on the other side of the planet. Like most kids who grew up this way, at ten years old Emmeline has a knack for framing her shot: her phone is propped up against something stable, negative space on either side of her. Avi holds his too close. The thumbnail in the corner is all nostrils and white teeth.

"They have your book in the library," she says. "They have lots."

"I donated my author copies," he says.

"Then nobody will buy them and you won't make any money," Emmeline says.

"I'll be okay." Emmeline's eyes dart back and forth, watching other kids, communicating like bees as they pass. Her eyebrows send silent hellos. She taps her watchless wrist to indicate *later*. She twitches her head at the screen to say *sorry, I have to finish this thing*.

"I should let you go," says Avi.

"No, it's okay," she says. "I have a couple minutes before class."

"I've got to do this taping," he says. "It's going to take them a while to make me pretty."

"You're a TV star!" she says, throwing her arms in the air the way she did when she was little. "I'm going to stay up and watch. Some of the older kids said they'll have it on in the common room."

"You don't have to stay up," he says. "You know what I look like."

"But you're going to be *pretty*," she says, then giggles. Out of frame, a kid says something to her, drawing her full attention. "Dad, I've got to go. Love you, okay?"

"Love you," he says. Her image freezes, disappears. Avi pockets his phone and steps out of the green room into the *NightTalk* studio, where cameras, teleprompters, and lighting fixtures are being readied. Lakshmi goes over script notes with one of the show's writers. She's an NPR darling graduated to network. He's interviewed with her a half dozen times, all for radio. She reminds him of Kay, the way she carries herself like she's walking against a strong wind.

"Where's the beast?" Avi asks, scanning the set.

"He brings his own makeup team," Lakshmi says. "He says our people make him look 'unmasculine.' Which, by the way, is not a word."

"Bringing your own makeup team is supermasculine," Avi says.

"You know how it is with these guys," says Lakshmi "If you want to know what turns them on, look at what they're most afraid of. Look at what they claim to hate."

"Why have him on the show?"

Lakshmi shrugs as if they both know the answer. "You talk to your kid?"

"I talked *at* her," Avi says. "She's busy with friends."

"I was a boarding school kid at that age," says Lakshmi. "Other kids are your whole world for the first couple years. It passes. She'll come back. It's good she has friends."

Avi nods as the makeup people beset him. This is what they wanted for Emmeline, the thing she never had at her school in Chicago. They assumed it was the mixed-race thing, but now Avi thinks the kids there intuited something different about Emmeline. They pushed her to the margins. He loves watching her relax into her new world at the academy even if it means she's moving away from him. Some days he wants to call Kay up and talk about it. Some days he brings up her name in his contacts before thinking better of it.

A door bangs open, and Jefferson Hargrave enters, yelling at a hapless lackey. He travels with an entourage, this lone wolf, this voice of the common man. He's a bloated sack of wind whose rise to media prominence has run parallel to Avi's. Or, better put, they've been entwined. Parallelism implies that their paths have never intersected, which is sadly not true.

Lakshmi comes up behind Avi, puts both hands on his shoulders. "You smell brimstone?" she whispers.

The taping hasn't started, and Avi is perspiring under the lights. Someone dabs his forehead with a cloth. New droplets form. Jefferson Hargrave sits across from him, sweating like Nixon. The stage manager calls for quiet and counts them in. Lakshmi throws Avi one last eye roll before she dons a mask of professional neutrality.

"Good evening and welcome to *NightTalk*. I'm your host, Lakshmi Rameswaram," she says. Her voice carries the sweet tonal quality of her NPR past. *A Resonance*, Avi thinks. It's hard to make that word nonspecific in his vocabulary. A word he hardly ever used creeps into his speech all the time, like trying not to think of a polar bear. *Resonance. Ability.* The words are weighted. They're scared out of their common meaning, permanently capitalized.

"With me tonight are two leading experts on Resonants. Avi Hirsch, author of *The Coming Race: Resonants and Their Place in the World*. Avi, nice to see you again."

"It's great to be here, Lakshmi," Avi says.

"And also with us, host of *The Monster Report* on the Kindred Network, Jefferson Hargrave. Jefferson, thank you for joining us."

"Thank you, my dear," he says in the smarmy southwestern accent he adopted after he graduated Yale Business and moved out to the desert to live deliberately, or whatever half-ass Thoreau quote he took as his mantra. "I'm proud to be here to defend the rights of normal humans to live free of fears of violence and predation by these creatures who, for the moment, walk freely on our streets."

"Jesus, Jefferson, are we not even going to get to the questions before you start?" says Avi.

"Mr. Hirsch, I think the company you keep has impaired your ability to keep a civil tongue," says Jefferson.

"You want to talk civility?" Avi says, "Last week you

called for Resonants to be forcibly sterilized."

"I don't see any way around it," Jefferson says. "We already have an indeterminate number of dangerous individuals—"

"You can't label all of them as dangerous."

"I certainly can," Jefferson says. "Just the other day I read a report about a veritable massacre out in Damascus, Ohio. Three dozen God-fearing Americans brutally—"

"How many Resonants were killed in hate crimes last year?" Avi asks.

"I object to the term *hate crime.*"

"They hung a kid from a lamppost in Pittsburgh last night," Avi says. "In Wyoming, Samuel Guthridge and his mother and two little sisters and little brother were lynched by the very people Sam had saved from—"

"There's no evidence—"

"There's a confession!"

"From a man on trial for killing his own son."

"They killed little kids," Avi shouts. "They killed them because they thought *maybe* the kids were Resonants. Maybe. By definition, it's a hate crime."

"The police ruled it an electrical fire," Hargrave says. "And you're being hysterical. Now what I'm talking about, these people in Damascus were torn up. Pieces missing like they were attacked by animals. A man with a hole on the inside of his head. Wounds cut as smooth as glass." The phrase triggers a thought Avi doesn't have time to fully form. "Do they mean less because they don't have wings or scales? Because they're not special?"

"Resonants have never claimed to be special. They—"

"They don't have to claim it," says Hargrave. "They brag about their inhumanity and then cry when they get hurt."

"The Guthridges didn't cry, they bled," Avi says.

"What color?"

The question shocks both of them into silence for a beat.

"Mr. Hargrave," says Lakshmi. He waves her off.

"I've never seen one of them bleed," he says to Avi. "I'm curious what color it was."

"Mr. Hargrave," says Lakshmi, "I'm wondering how you respond to accusations—"

"I *am* happy to hear they can bleed." He leans back in his chair. He looks like a sated tick, bloated and ruddy-faced.

"About accusations that your program incites racial violence against—"

"See, there you go with race, dear," Hargrave says, turning back to her, all smiles and gentility. "I love black *people.* I love brown *people. People.* The introduction of these individuals into our midst has done wonders healing the divide between the actual races."

"In referring to Resonants as a race," she says, "I'm respecting their stated self-definition as such."

"That's very respectful of you," Hargrave says. "It doesn't mean I have to follow suit."

"So how do you respond—"

"I give people facts," Hargrave says. "Mr. Hirsch prefers fluffy profile pieces. This one can slice you in half with her brain, but she loves puppies. That one can put the psychic whammy on your wife and daughter, but hey, he's a Cubs fan, so he must be a swell guy."

"I want the public to understand," Avi says, "that these are people who—"

"See, right there is where you and I diverge," says Hargrave.

"Where's that?"

"You think of them as people," he says. "A gun has no rights. A bomb does not get to vote. You want us to treat these weapons, these threats, like human beings. I am not willing to do that."

"Mr. Hargrave," Lakshmi says, "if we can't start from the basic premise—"

"I sympathize," Hargrave says. "I can't imagine what it must do to a man to find out that what he thought was his daughter is a *thing*."

Avi is up and out of his chair before he's aware of it. He lands hard on his prosthetic leg at a bad angle and starts to fall. His fist glances weakly off Hargrave's chin on the way down. Production assistants rush to help Avi up. Hargrave feigns shock for the cameras but looks down and throws Avi a wink as Lakshmi signals to cut to a commercial.

"I touch a nerve?" he says. All that western smarm is gone, icy Boston Brahmin in its place.

"Get him off my set," Lakshmi shouts.

"I'm going to want a copy of that tape," says Hargrave. He points at the nearest camera operator and snaps his fingers, as if she's going to hand over a VHS cassette. "Personally, I can't see filing assault charges for something so minor." He rubs his chin. "But I'm not the one who makes those kinds of decisions. Good luck with the book, Avi. Come on the show sometime and we'll talk about it."

GLITCH

They're supposed to meet some of Alyssa's work friends for dinner. Not people Fahima likes much, but she agreed to it. She's making an effort to be normal. To meet Alyssa in her otherwise normal life. Fahima's packing up to go when Sarah's scream blazes through the Hive.

In the time the elevator takes to get from the lab to the ninth floor, Fahima comes up with ways she could make it faster. *A regenerative drive to capture the friction heat from braking and channel it back into the grid. A maglev system, like trains in Japan.* Two fluorescent bulbs in the hallway are dying. They're sorry they won't be able to go on much longer. They've worked so hard. They want Fahima to know, and she wants to listen. But she has to hurry. In the room at the end of the hall, Emmeline is sobbing.

The residents of the ninth, second-years, most of them a little older than Emmeline, line the hall. They whisper among themselves. Some cry. Sarah hugs herself in the doorway as Cortex cowers behind her legs.

"I tried to go in. Help her," she says. "When I touched her." Sarah holds her hand up and stares at it. "It got stuck. It was going to pull the rest of me in. I couldn't help her. I tried."

Fahima steps past her into the room. Emmeline is curled up against the wall. She can hardly get enough breath to keep up her sobs. Emmeline's roommate, Viola, stands near the desk. Emmeline likes Viola a lot. She's told Fahima how kind Viola is. Viola picks up a glass of milk from the desk, holds it up, and examines it. Then the glass is back on the desk. Viola holds it up, examines it. It's back on the desk. It's like listening to a record skip or watching a computer program glitch. A piece of reality, hiccupping.

"Em, close your eyes," says Fahima, squatting down so she's face-to-face with Emmeline. "I need you to calm down. Deep breaths, Em. Deep. Breathe."

Emmeline's breathing slows, each inhale hitching at its apex. Eyes closed, she exhales into Fahima's face. Her breath is sugary sweet.

"Can you tell me what happened?"

"Viola knocked over the glass," Emmeline says. "It broke, and it spilled everywhere. I fixed it. I put it back on the desk. Viola was looking at it. She got stuck."

"Can you stop it, Em?"

"It's a loop," Emmeline says. "I can see it in my head, but I can't straighten it out." She opens her eyes wide. "I can see it in my head. It's me. I'm doing this."

"You are, Em," Fahima says. "But it's not your fault. Stay with me, okay?" She puts out her hand, and Emmeline grips it. Fahima leans toward the doorway so she can see Sarah. "I need you to go to my lab. There's a device sitting on the big table. The one that has blueprints all over it. Not the one that has the bag of chips on it. It's a bracelet. It's metal. I need you to get it for me."

Sarah runs down the hall.

"Viola's going to be mad at me," Emmeline says. "She won't want to be my friend anymore."

"I'll be your friend," says Fahima.

Emmeline cracks a smile, although she has trouble holding it. "But you're old."

"I have unlimited access to snacks," Fahima says. She thinks of Sarah in the slow elevator. *A shaft of variable gravity.*

"I wanted to fix the glass," says Emmeline. "I did. I fixed it. It was nearby and insignificant. Like the sandwich."

An Einstein-Rosen bridge with off-ramps like a highway, one at each floor.

Sarah returns with the bracelet. It hangs open like the mouth of a hungry bird.

"Can you close the door?" Sarah obliges, leaving Fahima and Emmeline alone with Viola, stuck in her loop.

"Em," says Fahima. "This is something I've been working on. I've been calling it the Shackle." She started working on it for the people Patrick was hunting down. The idea of putting it on Emmeline makes her sick. "It dampens abilities. It shuts them off."

"Will it hurt?" Emmeline asks.

"It might," says Fahima. "I tried it on myself, and it didn't. But my ability isn't like yours."

"Will it help Viola?"

"I think so," says Fahima.

"Okay," Emmeline says. Fahima takes her hand, examining her skinny wrists.

"I have to put it around your bicep," she says. "Can you roll your sleeve all the way up?"

Emmeline hesitates, then obeys, pushing her long sleeve up until her whole arm is exposed. Her forearm is a swirl of shiny keloid tissue, a map of the ocean in flesh. Fahima stares long enough that Emmeline notices. She places the Shackle around Emmeline's arm. It's still too big. It slides down and rests at the crook of her elbow. She clicks it into place and secures the clasp.

"I'm going to turn it on, okay?" says Fahima. Emmeline nods. Fahima slides a panel open and flips a switch inside. Emmeline's body tenses, and Viola drops the glass of milk. It shatters, spraying its contents across the tile floor. Viola looks down, flustered.

"I dropped it again," she says to Emmeline, sounding full of regret. "After you saved it for me."

"It's not your fault," Fahima says, rolling Emmeline's sleeve down over the Shackle, over her scars. She reaches out, taking Viola by the arm and pulling her away from the desk. She feels a strange resistance as she does it, as if the air is thicker. As if time is moving more slowly within the affected space. "It's not anybody's fault."

"Hi, Professor Deeb," says Viola. She sounds like she's waking from a dream. "I thought you and Emmeline had special class on Wednesdays."

"I got my days wrong," says Fahima.

Viola nods. "My dad's a scientist, and he forgets things all the time," she says. "I'm going to go find a mop."

"I'll get one," Emmeline says, looking at the door. All their classmates are in the hall, waiting to see what happened. The moment Viola steps out, she'll know what Emmeline did.

"I'll show you where they are," Fahima says. She opens the door and ushers Emmeline out. She puts her finger to her lips, shushing Sarah, then shoos the kids to their rooms. None listen. Sarah makes the same motion, and they flutter off like sparrows.

Fahima kneels down by Emmeline outside the door. "How does it feel?"

"It hurts my teeth," Emmeline says.

"It's temporary," says Fahima. "We'll figure out something better soon, I promise."

"Is Viola going to be okay?" Emmeline says.

Fahima doesn't answer. She thinks of a trick Sarah pulled once at a beach party at Sarah's parents' house when they were kids. Steven Huff was being a drunken asshole to Fahima. Tugging at her hijab. Asking if the Koran said it was okay to eat pussy. Sarah tapped him on the forehead and implanted a loop command in his brain. Every time he opened a beer, he'd drop it on the ground and sprint into the freezing cold water. Then he'd trudge out of the surf, unaware that he was soaked, and go find another beer. As soon as he opened it, he'd drop it in the sand and sprint back into the ocean. It was fun to watch until Steven started to turn blue. April Carroll, a fourth-year thermic who wasn't all that skilled with her abilities, had to warm him up. She left scorch marks on his biceps and thighs, bright red handprints. There was enough culpability involved that no one reported it to Bishop. Sarah felt awful, and Fahima loved her for it.

What Fahima had seen upstairs wasn't Viola performing a loop task. Time around her was looping. Thinking about it in terms of Steven Huff and the ocean, it would be as if Steven ran in only once but his running in happened over and over again. From the outside, it looked repeated, but Steven would experience it once. There would be no hypothermia, no blue flush to his lips. When he exited the loop, he'd be aware only of one idiot rush into the surf, like Viola thinking she'd dropped the glass and nothing more.

So the question isn't whether Viola would be okay. Nothing happened to Viola. The question is whether the world around Viola has been harmed. If it has, is it a wound that will heal?

THE FIVE OF CUPS

Avi waits in the Five of Cups on Fifth for an hour. Long enough to know what's coming. The decision to meet back at the same bar where they got drunk after the taping was ridiculous, trying to make a meet-cute out of a one-night stand. This is what he's supposed to be good at, making narrative out of wreckage. The problem isn't the time it's taken to get a response from Lakshmi. Since the *NightTalk* footage leaked, a half dozen interviews and appearances have been canceled. The book's been out a week, and there's complete media silence surrounding it. At least it feels that way. Avi's on his third drink when the text comes.

"I'm sorry," it says. "I should have shown up in person. But the optics are bad. The network isn't happy."

He puts the phone back in his pocket without bothering to text her back. He looks at the television behind the bar, and there she is, interviewing Kevin Bishop. He understands it was taped earlier, but there's a visceral response as if she texted him from that seat a second before starting the interview. They've caked Bishop in makeup, filling the age lines of his face, making him flat and bland. *Harmless*, Avi thinks. Maybe that's the idea.

"Can you turn the sound on?" he asks the bartender.

She reaches for the remote, but another patron stops her. He's wearing a navy Brooks Brothers suit, tie loosened. He's surrounded by guys dressed exactly the same. It reminds Avi of one of the Bishop students he met who could create perfect duplicates of himself. "Leave it off," he says. "No one needs to hear anything that freak has to say."

"I do," Avi says. "Turn the sound on, please."

"I know you," says the suit.

"You don't," Avi says, looking down.

"Leave him be, Gerald," says the bartender.

"I saw him on TV. He's an expert. I want to talk to an expert about this shit."

"I'm finishing my drink," Avi says. He downs the rest of his whiskey and leaves a twenty on the bar. He fumbles for his cane, knocking it over.

"Let me help you out," says Gerald, bending down to pick up the cane. He holds it out to Avi, then pulls it back when Avi reaches for it.

"You know what? Let me show you to the door," he says. He takes Avi by the arm and drags him across the bar. Everyone watches, and no one says anything. Gerald gives him a shove on the sidewalk, hands him the cane, and turns to go back inside. *The best way to handle this is to keep quiet and limp away*, Avi thinks. But there's so much anger he carries around with him every day. Here is a moment when it's justified. Here is a worthy and appropriate target. What else is anger for if not to use?

"I know what you're afraid of," Avi says. Gerald steps toward him again. "You're afraid of being replaced. You're afraid of not being special."

"Fuck off," says Gerald.

"You should be afraid," Avi says. "You're not special. You. Me. We're dead ends. We're not special like them. We're—"

He's about to say *Damps* when Gerald's fist crunches into his right eye. He feels something burst, a sharp stab wrapped in a dull thud as he goes down, landing in the crust of a snowbank. His cane clatters on the sidewalk. Gerald picks it up, holds it in the air over his head. Avi wants it to fall. He wants to be hit again and again until he crumbles into pieces on the sidewalk. Gerald pauses, and Avi knows it won't happen. He swings, striking Avi hard in the fleshy part of his left side: below the ribs, above the pelvis. Bruises, no breaks. Gerald spits at him but misses. It plunks on the sidewalk. He turns and goes back into the bar.

"Hey, mister," says one of the kids smoking out front. "You okay?" He's been standing there the whole time, making no effort to stop this.

"I'm fine," Avi says. He picks up his cane and leverages himself back up to his feet.

"You want me to call the police?" the kid asks.

"Are they going to unpunch me?" Avi's vision swims. It returns blurry and lopsided. He closes his right eye, and everything is clear. He closes his left, and the world is a smear of color and light.

One tree trunk arm wraps around Avi's waist, keeping

him from making another run at the elevator, holding him a few inches off the ground. With a finger the size of a beer can, Shen presses the intercom button. After a few seconds, Sarah's voice comes through, crackly with static.

"What is it, Shen?"

"Sorry to wake you. We've got a problem in the lobby."

"I'll be right down," Sarah says. The intercom clicks off.

"Why'd you have to call her?" asks Avi.

"Ms. Davenport's acting headmaster," he says. "Headmistress. You're her problem."

The elevator dings, and the doors slide open. Sarah is in sweats, her hair up in a topknot. Cortex runs out ahead of her and attempts to nuzzle one of Avi's dangling legs, but Shen lifts Avi away and the dog retreats. Shen gives Avi a squeeze to remind him who's in control of the situation, then sets him down.

"I need to see her," Avi says, straightening his clothes.

"What happened?" Sarah asks.

"I got beat up," Avi says. "I was standing up for you people, and I got the shit kicked out of me. Now I want to see my daughter."

"We don't need you to defend us, Avi," says Sarah.

"You did," he says. "You asked me to."

"We never asked you to."

"Let me see Emmeline," he says. "Let me upstairs to see her."

"You don't want her to see you like this, Avi," Sarah says. "Go home."

"I don't have a home," he shouts. "You people took that.

You took my wife, and now you're taking my daughter. What does that leave me with? What do I get for all this? For everything I did?"

Sarah puts her hand on his cheek, below the bruise on his eye. He feels her push into his mind. Her presence makes him aware of his mind as a space, a geography. It's hot and confused, the pain from his eye spreading out, filling his thoughts. Her mind expands into his, projecting cool, calm. Like turning the burner down on a gas stove: the flame in Avi's mind contracts but doesn't disappear.

"Go home, Avi," she says. Hearing the words, the idea takes seed in his mind, an imperative.

Go home.

There's something about the bomb Avi never told Kay. Louis knows because he was there. He doesn't understand it the way Avi does and probably blames himself. But it wasn't his fault. It was Avi's.

Mosul was quiet when Avi landed the embed with Echo Company. No one thought the fighting was over, but it had moved elsewhere. The day after he arrived, a routine patrol in one of the eastern neighborhoods was taken out. The whole sector fell, and forces started expanding west, block by block, to the center of the city.

Louis told Avi it was a minor flare-up. He kept shunting Avi off on side projects. A week of inspecting every well in Tel Skuf, thirty klicks north of the city, or overseeing a training camp for Turkoman soldiers in Erbil, which had been secure for two years. Avi was used to being embedded with companies that had low combat priority, but he wasn't some rookie stringer at his first dance. Everyone in Echo knew they were being called up the next morning. Over cards and beers, they performed the mix of swagger and reverent fear Avi had seen a dozen times. "Gonna see some fireworks," Garcia said, clapping Avi on the back. After lights out, Avi heard Garcia mumbling prayers in his bunk, his voice cracking like a teenage boy's.

In the morning, the men suited up. Avi went to the quartermaster to get himself a vest, but no one had requisitioned one for him.

"No chance," Louis said. "You're going north with Bravo to keep eyes on a med base."

"Bullshit," Avi said, standing as if at attention. "I'm part of Echo, and I'm staying with the guys."

"Let him come along," Garcia said. "He's one of us." Too tired to bother with something so minor, Louis scribbled a requisition note and passed it off to Avi.

"You're in the JLTV with Hex Squad," he said. "Watch your ass."

Hex Squad headed into the city from the northwest. Recon said there was a weak spot; forces had gone slack at their initial incursion point, and a small group could get right up in there. No one considered that the eastern edges had been held for days. Enough time to seed the ground with IEDs. Avi remembers Garcia sitting across from him, singing "Call Me Maybe," a summer hit Stateside two years before enjoying an afterlife in Iraq that month, when the JLTV lifted into the air. This model of Joint Light Tactical

Vehicle was armored up the ass, as the men in Hex Squad bragged, but there was only so much armor you could slap on a glorified jeep before it was a tank, and tanks were no good on the roads out here. The desert was dotted with tanks from Gulf War One, where they'd gotten mired in sand and been abandoned. The JLTV was impervious to mortar fire, but a directed explosion to the back of the drivetrain that was near and severe enough to puncture the gas tank could blow through the undercarriage. Which, in this case, it did. Garcia went up like flash paper. Avi's leg, extended casually into the center aisle of the vehicle, looked like a wooden match burned down to the holder's fingertips: a blackened shinbone with the flesh seared away.

Of all the ways he cursed himself later, there was one that he kept secret. He never shared it with Kay, or the shrink, or Louis. *You fucking child*, he thought to himself. *So afraid of being left out. Had to rush off to die with everyone else.*

Avi gets to LaGuardia early so he can drink. Even in New York, it's tough to find a beer at six in the morning. He has two whiskeys on the plane and another at a bar in O'Hare on his way out. There are so many choices; the airport is a city in miniature. He picks one called Good Judgment, because the name stings and because it feels more like a movie set for a bar than an actual place. It's somewhere to lose track of time, not just minutes and hours but years.

By the time the cab drops him in front of the house on Jarvis Avenue, it's late afternoon. He should be picking Emmeline up from school. He imagines a world where she is jumping into the back seat, telling him about math classes and science projects. It hasn't snowed in Chicago, but the lawn is dead. The car in the driveway is tiny, fuel-efficient. It could fit inside their old van. Avi thinks of the pieces of his life that way now. Old van. Old house. Old wife. Old daughter.

Avi trudges across the slick dead grass to the front door. He fumbles with his keys, then decides to knock. The man who answers could be a younger version of himself. Taller, paler, less broken. They've only talked on the phone. Avi can't remember his name. Professor of something at Loyola. Married. No kids.

"Can I help you?" the man asks.

Avi's eye is blackened; the cornea swims with blood. The clothes he's been wearing for thirty-six hours have been tossed into a New York City snowbank and slept in.

"I'm sorry," he says. *I should have that tattooed on my forehead*, he thinks. "This is my house."

"I think you've got the wr—" The man looks more closely. He sees Avi under the blood and bruises and stubble. "Mr. Hirsch, I'm sorry. Come on in. If you could take your shoes—"

Avi starts up the stairs, tracking water and mud. "I'm sorry to crash in," he says. "I promised my daughter I'd pick up some of her things while I'm in town."

"No, of course," says the man who lives in Avi's old house. He eyes Avi's tracks on the floor. "We've been using her room as a guest room. We moved her things up to the attic for storage. Do you need a hand getting up there?"

"No," Avi says. "I'm good. Thanks."

"Since you're here," says the man, standing at the base of

368

the stairs, looking up at Avi. "I admire the work you've been doing. It's amazing. But this house is listed as your address? Online? And someone has made it public." He glances at the door. "We've been getting threats."

"Threats?"

"Taped to the door," he says. "Left on the stoop. It's nothing. Jan freaks out. I keep telling her, *It's nothing. People like this are cowards.* But if you could change that? Online? There're a couple spots. There are websites you can go to—"

"I'll take care of it," Avi says. "You shouldn't have to be afraid."

"Yeah," says the man. "Anyway, if you need a hand."

"I'm good," Avi says. "Maybe coming back down. I'll yell for you . . ."

"John," says the man. "John and Jan. Can't get more forgettable than that."

"Thanks, John," says Avi. "I'll yell."

The upstairs hallway is lined with vacation photos. John and Jan at the Acropolis. John and Jan at Aztec ruins. Each photo is of two beautiful people with their faces pressed together in front of something they were supposed to see, a place they were supposed to visit. A checklist that made up a life. Avi thinks about the places he's been, alone. Basra. Kabul. Aleppo. Kigali. Laundry list of horrors. There are no photos of him from any of them. He was there to be an eye looking out.

He yanks the pull string, and the ladder comes down, raining dust. Except for a handful of boxes, the attic is as he left it. A time capsule. All of his things, all of Emmeline's. A few boxes of Kay's the movers missed that she'd never sent for.

Emmeline didn't want any of her things either, and Avi didn't need any of his. He wonders why they're keeping any of it.

On the desk is the journal he took from the motel room in Roseland. Owen Curry, on the run and pouring hate onto the page. He feels sympathy for the boy. Not for the monster who blew up the food court and the church, who wiped out the life of that little girl. For the boy immediately afterward. On the run and broken.

He starts up the old computer, going to the shared drive he stores pieces on. There's the book in all its various drafts. Avi opens a document file titled "NULL." He reads it, giving it the kind of once-over he does before sending a piece out. It's perfect, the prose tight, the gaze of it unflinching. He's memorized the first line: *On December 4, a young Resonant named Owen Curry opened up a hole in the world and fed nineteen people into it.* In a ritual he's repeated any number of drunken nights, he creates an e-mail to Carol at the *Trib*. He attaches "NULL" to it. The text of the e-mail is simply, *here.* The cursor hovers over the send button for a second, two, before he deletes the e-mail.

Avi looks at the wall under the porthole. The place Kimani's door used to appear. He feels Sarah's hand on the side of his face, his skin tender to the touch, the bruise starting to take on form and color beneath the skin. *She could have made me forget,* he thinks. *She was already in my head. She could have erased it all. It would have been better.*

Avi takes out his phone. The screen cracked during the fight. He hasn't been paying much attention to anything the last couple of days. He hasn't been taking care of himself or the things that belong to him. He scrolls through his contacts and dials.

"Look who finally came home," Louis says. "I saw you on the news last week. Where the fuck did you learn to punch?"

"Why haven't you arrested me?" asks Avi.

"It's been too long," Louis says. "We've moved on to bigger things. There's a war on; didn't you hear?"

"Is that how Homeland sees it?"

"More or less," Louis says. "We all read your book. Your new friends sound real nice. I notice you left out our mutual acquaintance."

Avi touches the wood paneling of the western wall. There was a door there once that led to a room that led to a whole world, but it's gone, as if it never existed.

"You want to find Owen Curry?"

ARRIVAL

Fahima will never admit the amount of time and money she spent on the look of it. A certain bulk is necessary to house the mechanism, but she wanted it to be something a ten-year-old would want to wear. Not knowing much about the aesthetics of ten-year-olds, this meant thinking in terms of what she might have wanted to wear at that age. She wasn't the kind of girl who pined after jewelry, but she remembered an armband Aunt Majeda wore: a broad piece of engraved silver studded with ovals of blood-red carnelian. The engravings looked like calligraphic Arabic but were much older Turkmeni symbols that stood for mountains and rams. She'd found an image online, not the same piece but something similar. She found a jeweler in the Diamond District on West 47th who could get carnelian cheap and had someone who could do the metalwork. While she waited on that, she worked on making the mechanism smaller. She ran into the same problem she'd had when she made the gun for Patrick: the best design, the ideal form of the thing, was minuscule. But it would have to be tucked in alongside the parahippocampal gyrus, emitting a small countersignal directly at the origin point of a person's Resonance. It was an elegant and permanent solution. Emmeline would have to settle for a device the size of a watchband that fit perfectly into a beautiful housing. Still, Fahima can't help thinking of it as the Shackle.

Emmeline undoes the clasp on the older model, and it clunks to the counter. The sound makes Emmeline jump. She must have expected the world to end as soon as she took it off. They both pause. Fahima hadn't ruled out the possibility that they were venting a container whose contents were under pressure. Emmeline's ability might be like soda in a shaken can. No one had been exposed to inhibitors long-term except Owen Curry, and he hadn't stuck around for a physical. There was no way to predict what ending that exposure would look like. But the Shackle lies on the counter, two leering grins connected at a hinge, and nothing happens.

"No quantum singularity," says Fahima. "No rip in space-time."

"You thought there might be?" Emmeline asks.

"There was a chance," she says.

"But you took it off anyway?"

"It was ugly," says Fahima. She holds up the new one. It's half the size and a quarter of the weight.

"It's pretty," Emmeline says. Fahima isn't sure if she's being honest or trying to make her feel good about her efforts. Emmeline's warmed in her time here, but there's a persistent strangeness to her affect, the sense that she's here and somewhere else at once. Fahima attaches the bracelet around Emmeline's right wrist, which she's measured already.

Emmeline holds it up, admires it, then rolls the sleeve of her sweater down over it. Fahima rolls the sleeve back up to expose it, and Emmeline pulls her hand away. She's very self-conscious about her burn scars even though Fahima has seen them. Fahima reaches out and takes Emmeline by the wrist. She lifts one of the pieces of carnelian to reveal the switch.

"I forgot," says Emmeline.

"Don't forget," Fahima says. She turns the inhibitor on, trying not to notice Emmeline's wince. *It only hurts at the start*, she tells herself. Emmeline said the second model wasn't as uncomfortable as the first and didn't bother her teeth the same way. This one should be better. Whether it's actual discomfort or the memory of discomfort, the wince is there.

"It's got a kinetic charging mechanism," Fahima says. "It gets power from you moving it. But you need to check it before you go to bed."

"Where do I check it?" Emmeline asks. Fahima lifts another carnelian, showing a small digital clock. She clicks the jewel back into place. "How do I know which one is which?"

Fahima points to the word carved into the carnelian. Three Arabic letters: nuun, miim, nuun. Nuuns like bowls with diamonds floating over them. Miim a sailboat, traversing the space between them.

"Zaman," says Fahima. "It means 'time.' "

Emmeline runs her fingers over the engraving, accepting the bracelet as part of her skin, a new scar.

Emmeline is helping Fahima reduce the overall entropy level of the lab when Fahima's phone buzzes on one of the desks. SARAH, the screen reads.

"What's up, boss lady?" Fahima asks.

"I need you up in the lobby right now," Sarah says, then hangs up.

Fahima starts to tell Emmeline to wait for her here, but she knows the girl better than that. Emmeline drops the trash bag she's holding, and the two of them run toward the elevator. They look like a gender-switched Batman and Robin from the old TV show, headed up an elevator instead of down a fire pole.

When the elevator reaches the lobby, the door is eclipsed by Shen's extended back, a broad expanse of dark suit coat. Fahima has always wondered how Shen's clothes expand and contract with him, even considering the possibility that they aren't clothes but a part of Shen himself.

"Go back downstairs," he says.

"Sarah called me up," says Fahima.

Shen looks over his shoulder. "Sorry, Miz Deeb," he says, stepping aside. Sarah stands in the middle of the lobby, staring down three government agents. Fahima can recognize feds by their cheap almost-matching suits. *This was only a matter of time,* she thinks.

"You FBI?" Fahima asks as she crosses the lobby.

"Homeland Security," says the man in the middle. He's older than the men flanking him, sliding softly into the warm pool of middle age. Growing pudgy and hasn't shaved in a week. The other two are cookie-cutter white boys, crisp pleats in ill-fitting pants, fresh haircuts.

"You guys used to wear blue shirts," Fahima says.

The older government man smiles nostalgically. "We

haven't worn those in ten years," he says. "Only TSA wears the blues now."

"I'm thinking farther back than that," Fahima says. The men who took her uncle wore blue, like cartoon cops. These men were dressed more like the FBI agents who took her father. Maybe those departmental distinctions didn't matter anymore.

"I called our lawyer," says Sarah. As if summoned, a woman strides into the lobby, heels clacking on the tiles.

"Mom!" Emmeline shouts. She runs across the lobby toward her mother, and Fahima feels a tiny umbilical tug. She can't tell if she's pining for Emmeline or missing the feeling of having a mother to run to. She sees one of the Homeland agents' hands twitch toward his gun. Another takes a step as if to restrain Emmeline, but the older one holds him back. Emmeline grabs her mother tightly around the waist, and her mother returns the hug, if not as enthusiastically.

"Hey, Leen," Kay says. "It's great to see you. I need to take care of this thing, okay?"

Emmeline releases her mother, who takes one step and regains her composure. By the second step, she is no longer the mom with the kid wrapped around her knees. She is a shark with a whiff of blood in her nostrils.

"Louis," she says to the older agent as she marches toward him, "you'd better have the most impeccable warrant or you can hop a plane right back to Chicago."

"Hello, Kay," he says. "It's nice to see you. We have evidence this school is harboring a known terror suspect." He regards Kay coolly.

"I didn't hear the word *warrant* in there," Kay says.

"An anonymous informant told me Owen Curry was being held at this school," he says. "He's wanted in connection with two bombings. The church back home, Kay." Kay flinches, and Fahima wonders how much Avi's told her about Owen Curry. Then she wonders how much Avi's been told about Owen Curry, and in that moment she knows the identity of the anonymous informant.

"Why would you think he's here?" Sarah says, trying to step in.

"I was told. By someone I trust." He never breaks eye contact with Kay, and Fahima's suspicion is confirmed. Sarah looks at Fahima. She knows, too. She told Fahima about the incident with Avi in the lobby earlier in the week, trying to force his way in. That's what Avi's been doing since he met them. Sarah's just the first one to literally shut the door on him.

"You're not getting anywhere without a warrant," Kay says, crossing her arms. "So you can pack up your goon squad and go find a judge that'll take an anonymous informant as sufficient cause."

"Fine, Kay. We were hoping the folks here would be willing to cooperate, is all." He turns away from them to the loose knots of students hanging out in the lobby. "Owen Curry is responsible for the deaths of twenty-one people," he announces. "He is a bad, scary man, and we have reason to believe your teachers are hiding him here at this school. We're going to come back tomorrow. And every day after that until we find him. Maybe you want to check the closets? Under the desks? Maybe you want to think to yourself, do we have a secret set of jail cells in the basement where we're illegally holding a wanted man in custody? And if you realize the answer is yes, give us a call. Or tap me on the shoulder, because I'm going to be right here."

"Go fuck yourself," Fahima says.

"That's not helping," Kay says.

"Feels good, though." She's lived with the sense that the government was watching her since they day they took her uncle. None of this feels new, just bigger. A change in degree rather than kind.

The agents file out, giving everyone in the lobby menacing looks over their shoulders as they do. Once they're gone, Kay gives Sarah her business card.

"When they come back," she says, "and that is *when*, call me directly. I won't be here as fast as I got here today, but I'll be here."

Emmeline tugs at her sleeve. "Can you stay a little bit?"

Her mother looks around as if she needs another emergency, a reason to escape. Fahima can tell that Kay isn't comfortable with all this. What her daughter is now, the world she's stepped into. But what tethers mother and daughter is the same in both worlds, the old and the new.

"Of course, Leenie," she says. "I can stay as long as you need me."

Emmeline smiles and wraps her arm around her mother's legs, a full circle. Behind her mother's knees, Emmeline flicks the Shackle with her fingers so it makes quick orbits of her wrist.

THE EXCOMMUNICATION

Avi and Bishop agree to meet at the Magician. This time, Bishop is waiting for him. It reinforces the same power dynamic as the first time. Bishop is making it clear he has no time for this shit. Arriving from the shitty hotel he's been staying at out in Cicero, Avi limps across the room to Bishop like a penitent, a child who must explain to his mother about the broken lamp.

"Order something," he says as Avi sits down. It sounds like a dare. He spins the olives in his glass on their skewer. He doesn't take his eyes off them.

"I'm good," says Avi.

"You're not," Bishop says, sipping his half-finished martini. "You want a drink so bad, your eyeballs itch. I can feel it from here. We'll both feel better if you have a drink."

Avi came here to apologize and seek absolution, but something in Bishop's tone curdles his guilt into anger.

"Are you trying to say something?" he asks.

"I'm saying get a drink," says Bishop. "Or don't. You make your own decisions, Avi."

"You sure?"

"I understand you're upset, but I can't figure out why." He holds his hand up for the bartender. "This gentleman will have a whiskey."

"What's your poison?" the bartender asks Avi.

Avi stares at Bishop. "You tell me," he says.

"He'll have your cheapest shit," Bishop says, looking up from his drink for the first time. He twirls the olives again. "The better to flagellate himself." The bartender gives Bishop a weird look, then pours Avi a double from the rotgut well liquor.

"You put my academy at risk."

"I didn't mean to do that," Avi says.

Bishop shrugs. "It was a predictable outcome," he says. He's right. Avi has tried to convince himself that he's done the right thing, that he was correcting a mistake he made at the motel in Roseland by not calling in Louis as soon as he located Owen Curry. But that wasn't it at all. He'd been spiteful and drunk and wanted to see someone get hurt. The academy was a stand-in for Bishop himself.

"Did they find him?" Avi says.

"Owen Curry isn't at the academy," Bishop says, looking away.

Avi is confused. "Did you move him?" he asks. "Did you kill him?"

"Someone let him out," Bishop says. "Patrick's been searching for him a year now with no luck. Personally, I hope he wandered in front of a truck. But it seems unlikely we'd be that lucky."

A rush of fear and anger floods him, so overwhelming

that it nearly drowns out a small thrill, a dark hope. *It'll be me*, Avi thinks. *I'll find him.*

"Why didn't you tell me?"

"Because I don't trust you."

"Why didn't you trust me?"

"Because you're not one of us," Bishop says. "You're playing a game. You're having an exciting adventure. I am not. And I cannot trust those who are."

Avi slams his hand on the bar. "It's not a game to me," he says too loudly. The bartender looks over at him, a caution. Avi lowers his voice. "I'm *practically* one of you. My daughter—"

"We should talk about Emmeline," Bishop says. Avi searches his face. They are clearing up final things now. Avi may not be a psychic, but he sees what's coming.

"You can't cut me off from her," he says.

"I could," Bishop says. "I could make you forget you have a daughter." Avi thinks about Sarah's hand on his face, how much he wished she'd make him forget everything. When he imagined it, what he saw was not forgetting but the careful excision of everything about Resonants and the Bishop Academy from his life. What would be left behind would include his marriage, intact, and his daughter, no longer a stranger to him. "But that would be cruel," Bishop continues. "I'm making concerted efforts not to be cruel anymore."

"So what, then?"

"I don't want you in the building ever again," Bishop says. "If you want to talk to Emmeline, you call her. If you want to see her, you set up a time and a place through me. If she needs to travel, she can call Kimani and ask."

"I can call Kimani—"

"I don't want you to call any of my staff," Bishop says. His anger spills over the edges of his words; Avi can feel it in his head. A tiny flame Bishop quickly shakes out.

"You can't—"

"Fahima and I are the only ones who know it was you," Bishop says. He's collected now, calm. He's scarier this way. "Sarah suspects, and I'm sure Patrick will put it together. Patrick never liked you." He plucks the last olive out of his drink and regards it. Avi wonders if Bishop chose martinis as his drink of choice to give himself stage business in conversations like this. Ways to look casual while destroying someone outright.

"Emmeline was there in the lobby when your friends from Homeland showed up," Bishop says. "Did you know that? Do you realize how lucky we are they came in with their guns holstered? The situation between us and them is a powder keg, and you flicked matches at it."

The full weight of what he put at risk hits Avi, along with something he's failed to realize fully. He can't threaten Bishop, threaten them, without endangering Emmeline. Her fate and well-being are tied to the rest of them more than they're tethered to him. He never should have stopped fighting for them, not for a second. It meant he stopped fighting for her.

"I'm sorry," Avi says.

"I have fuck-all time for your sorries," says Bishop. "I know you're unhappy, but I'd like to gently remind you that you were unhappy when we found you. At some point, it might be worth admitting the problem is you." He produces a bill from his wallet and lays it on the bar. Avi expects some sort of good-bye. A handshake or at least a nod of acknowledgment. Bishop walks out without another word.

BARGAIN

Once there was a girl who whistled and brought the wolves down. When the wolves came for her father, the girl tried to offer herself up in exchange. She would have fed her body to the wolves to keep his flesh from their mouths. But wolves are choosy. When they have a scent, they stay on it. Their heads won't be turned by another. Even if the girl confessed she was the one who whistled for them, if she squeezed the words around the press of her mother's hand, the wolves would have passed her by. You have to distract wolves before the smell is in their nostrils. You have to be their first, best option for blood.

This is her reasoning when she asks Kimani to door her into Louis Hoffman's house.

The living room is dark, lit by a television's glow off to the side of where Fahima is standing. Louis is lying on the couch under a blanket. A small head peeks out from under its edge, a boy, sleeping. Louis doesn't register her at first. He's nodding off. When he sees her, his hand jumps to his hip, reaching for a gun that thankfully isn't there.

"It's okay, Agent Hoffman," Fahima says, holding up her hands. "I'm here to talk."

"You don't have a phone?" he says, a hissing whisper. Things explode on the television. Fahima cranes her neck to see what's on. It's one of those prestige movies about World War II, shot with handheld cameras near the actor's ankles, sprays of mud and blood spattering the lens. Louis mutes it.

"I have an offer to make," she says. She holds up a thumb drive.

"Unless you have Owen Curry trapped in there, I'm not making any deals."

"How would you detain him?" Fahima asks. "This is someone who can create black holes. How are you planning to keep him in custody?"

"Maybe we'll put a bullet in his head," Louis says.

"You refused to conduct a warrantless search of the school," she says. "You showed up at our door without kicking it down. I don't see you summarily executing a suspect. So how will you hold him?"

"No one knows," he says. "There are fifty-three Resonants in police custody across the country as of close of business today. I get a report on my desk just before I come home. Any one of them could walk out of their cells tonight. Phase through the walls or blow the doors off or mind-wipe the guards."

Fahima holds up the thumb drive again. "This is how you keep them," she says. "These are schematics for a modified arbitrary waveform generator and a low red light source. A high schooler could build it with parts from RadioShack. Set the waveform generator to the specs in the documents, and it inhibits abilities within a five-foot radius of the source. More if you build it in a sound-reflective space. I'm a fan of ceramics, myself. You'll need one generator per cell, definitely. The red light will up melatonin levels, which keeps your guests dopey. Melatonin seems to interfere with abilities. My thinking is that we were set up that way so no one's ability goes off when they're dreaming. I'm not a hundred percent on that. Anyway, it works."

"And you're going to give me this?"

"I'm going to tell you Avi Hirsch was wrong," she says. "We don't have Owen Curry. We have people looking for him, and they will work with you. If they find him before you do, they'll hand him over."

"They won't kill him?"

"Not my department," Fahima says.

"How long have they been looking for him?" Louis says. "Since he blew up a mall and a church or since we came knocking?"

"Not my department," Fahima says. "You know the guy in the Bond movies with the gadgets?"

"Q," says Louis.

Fahima nods. "That's me," she says. "I sit in my lab and invent cool gadgets. Other people chase the bad guys."

"So what do you want?"

"You leave the academy alone," she says. "You don't come into my school with guns ever again." She thinks of the agent's hand moving toward his weapon as Emmeline ran across the lobby to her mother. "We watch our own.

If one goes bad, we'll hand them over. But you get off our front lawn and you stay off."

"And if we don't?"

"I designed this," Fahima says. "You think I didn't build a back door?"

"I have guys that can shut it."

"You don't."

"How long?" he asks.

Fahima looks at the drive. Her father used to talk about the war between Muslims and the West. Not in terms of jihad or any of that bullshit but in the adopted terms of American politicians. Maybe there were places it could be called a war, places where combatants met on a field of battle and the outcome was determined by luck and skill and strength of arms. In America it wasn't like that. The government had all the weapons: it had the prisons and the courts; it had oubliettes to put you in and boats home to put you on. Bishop talked about the possibility of war, saying that some day they might have no choice but to fight. "If it happens," he said, "the biggest weapon they'll have is numbers."

Now they'll have this, too: an off switch. Fahima can work out the numbers thing, work it so that even an off switch won't matter. She just needs time. She can't do it with a boot on her neck. She doesn't know Louis Hoffman, but she knows men like him. She's seen men like him drag her father away from the dinner table and disappear him out of a world where the law could keep him safe. And her father and uncle were on the lucky side. For every disappeared man Fahima heard about growing up, there was another gunned down, bleeding out on his prayer mat in front of his family. That agent could have pulled his weapon, shot Emmeline, and kept firing. Fahima has a mental list of every student in the lobby that day. Eleven of them. She knows how close they came to being lost. These are not men governed by laws. They may not even draw a distinction between the law and themselves. But they can be reasoned with, tricked and appeased, and sated.

"Forever," says Fahima. "I give you this, and you stay away forever."

Louis nods. They both know they're not talking about forever. Sooner or later, someone will give a nod and someone, maybe Louis, maybe a man just like him, will knock down the doors. "I build it and test it, and if it works, I pull my guys out of your lobby and never send them back."

"You pull your guys tomorrow," Fahima says. "You build it and test it, and if it doesn't work, I will come to your place and smack the stupid out of whoever couldn't read the specs."

"And I tell Miss Davenport my source reconsidered and I apologize for any inconvenience," he says.

"That's obvious?"

"We're talking in my living room in the middle of the night," Louis says. Despite herself, Fahima sighs in relief. She's been thinking about when she'll have to tell Sarah, or Bishop for that matter. Kimani knows, but Kimani's kept worse secrets. If everything goes as planned, this will be a funny story they'll share after everyone is safe.

"One more thing," says Louis.

"No more things. This is the deal." She has drawn an

exact line, how far she's willing to compromise herself.

"I get that," Louis says. "This is a favor." He pauses, stares intently at the war movie for a few seconds. Fahima can see tears building in his eyes. "My kid. He's amazing at math. Like *do I send him to a special school where he learns nothing but math?* That kind of good."

"That's wonderful for you," Fahima says. She's not sure if it is.

"His mother couldn't balance a checkbook," Louis says. "And every time one of my guys puts in an overtime request, I've got to pull out a calculator to figure time and a half. This with him, it's out of nowhere. Which makes me wonder. Can that be an ability? Being good at math?"

"You want to know if he's one of us," Fahima says.

"It shouldn't matter," says Louis, looking down at the boy.

"It *doesn't* matter," she says. "He's your kid."

"If I knew, I'd know how to talk to him," Louis says. "I could deal with him better if I knew."

"Knowing won't make it any easier to talk with him," Fahima says.

"I need to know," says Louis. "I'll keep your secret. But I need to know about him."

Fahima walks across the room. Behind her on the screen, the survivors smoke. They set up camp. She can tell which ones are going to die because she doesn't know the names of those actors. Fahima sits on the coffee table and faces the kid. She goes into the Hive to find him. This young, he'd be faint at best, a ghost of a bird. A coherent bit of breeze. But there's nothing there. The kid is a normal prodigy, an average genius.

"He's not," she says, coming back into the room. "His gifts or whatever, they're his own."

Louis lets out a sigh. Fahima thinks about the flip side of what she's said. If the kid's talents are his own, who do Fahima's belong to?

"I'll call my guys off," Louis says. "And this should go without saying, but if you show up in my house again, I'll shoot you dead."

"Same goes for you, boss," says Fahima. As she stands to go, she does a little pistol motion with her fingers, shooting from the hip. She opens the door, letting light from Kimani's room fall onto the boy's face. He stirs but doesn't wake. As Fahima closes the door, she hears the sound go up on the television, a new battle starting.

SIX

THE NEXT MOVEMENT

We build ourselves into a
configuration.
We tremble as we do this.
Even after we have built, we
tremble.
—JULIANA SPAHR,
"Fuck You-Aloha-I Love You"

GATHERING

"How do I look?" Fahima asks, twirling to model a new purple dress and a hijab so expensive that when she clicked the buy button, Fahima could practically hear her mother sucking her teeth. "I'm going for 'sexy terrorist.'"

Kimani sips on the beer Fahima brought for her. "Mission accomplished."

"I don't even know why I'm going," Fahima says.

"Bishop's growing into his celebrity status," says Kimani. "He's got his driver. Now his personal assistant-slash-arm candy."

"Is that an actual thing straight people say?" Fahima asks.

"I saw it in a movie," says Kimani.

"You realize it's a trap," Fahima says. She tries to make sense of her distorted reflection in the silver sculpture on Kimani's end table. "We're going to show up at Senator Smith's house, and the FBI will be there waiting for us."

"It's Senator Lowery," says Kimani. "And it'll be Homeland Security." She pauses the movie. "Also, it's not a trap. I've met Jim Lowery. I brought him to the school a half dozen times. He's concerned about the state of things, same as we are. He wants to help."

"Or he says he wants to help and it's a fucking trap."

"He's been working to set this up for months," Kimani says.

"He's playing the long game."

"Stop being paranoid," Bishop says as he steps through the door. He's dressed in a gray flannel suit that fit him perfectly once. Now he looks like he's slowly shrinking inside it. "James is a good man and sympathetic. He's the highest-ranking ally we have right now. So be nice."

"If you want nice, bring Sarah," Fahima says.

"I'm bringing you," Bishop says, attempting to end the discussion.

"Senator Lowery is allergic to dogs," Kimani says.

Fahima glares at Bishop. "I am going to invent tiny itchy bugs and let them loose in your bed," she says. "Microlice. Nanoscabies."

"Fahima, please," says Bishop. "There are things at stake here. No more mention of roboscabies."

"Roboscabies *is* better," Kimani says.

"I don't like either of you," Fahima says, hiding her smile. None of them get to joke anymore. She has to hold on to moments like this to remember what the fuck they're even fighting for. For stupid jokes and the right to pay too much for a pretty hijab. To feel like a person and not a point of contention, all day, her whole life.

Kimani opens the door into Senator James Lowery's foyer. It's one of those high-ceilinged rooms you find in DC brownstones so deep that they can afford to waste vertical space. Senator Lowery, a handsome young black man, rushes in from the next room in a flurry of handshakes and greetings.

"I'm so glad we put this together," he says. "So glad. I've been on Capitol Hill two years now, and you know what I miss? Dialogue. People talking to people. Did you know the Democrats and the Republicans have separate commissaries? That, to me, is Armageddon. That's the point where you say *no, it's broken. It's busted.* When you can't break bread and engage in civil discourse, it's all over."

He takes a deep breath, about to start another conversational sprint, when the doorbell rings. "Our other guest," he says. "Right on time. Not as punctual as you but not bad for traveling by conventional means."

"Other guest?" Bishop asks. But Lowery has already opened the door. The other guest is stocky, a guy who used to be fat and may end up fat again but has committed to the advice of some stern taskmaster of a trainer. He offers Lowery a bottle of red wine with a nondescript label that means it's either very expensive or very cheap.

"Senator, I can't thank you enough for inviting me into your remarkable home," he says. The voice is familiar, silky and practiced, an accent that pivots from down home to genteel on a dime.

"Kevin Bishop, Fahima Deeb," says Lowery, "I'd like you to meet Jefferson Hargrave."

"It's a fucking trap," Fahima mutters.

Fahima's no psychic, but she can see through the senator's thinking. It's a standard ally line of thought: *Have the homophobe and the queer sit down for a cup of coffee together!*

Get the Klansman and the Black Lives Matter activist to go out for a beer! Heal the world one conversation at a time. It ignores a major inequality. The queer person doesn't walk into the coffee shop wishing the homophobe would die. The Black Lives Matter activist may hate the beliefs, the actions of the Klansman, but she doesn't threaten his right to exist as an individual. *Come on*, the ally says to the oppressed person. *Show him you're human. Convince him you deserve to live and we can make everything better*. The ally assumes these are viewpoints, meeting on equal ground. No. One person is right, one is wrong. One person wants to be, one wishes the other was dead.

"Isn't this great?" Senator Lowery says despite the situation's obvious not-greatness. A servant of some kind pours wine, and each time she says *no, thank you*, Fahima dies a little inside. "I think conversation is so important. It's a lost art."

Fahima eyes her butter knife, determining that it's insufficient to cut Hargrave's throat.

"I'm sorry we couldn't sit down at a proper restaurant like normal people," says Lowery. Hargrave snorts. "The rumor mill in this town. If I was seen with either of you, the *Post*'d have a field day. And both? Hoo boy."

He doesn't bother to mention Fahima. She isn't present any more than the guy pouring the wine or the woman making dinner in the kitchen. Kimani's right: Bishop is building up an entourage, a crew of invisibles to float behind him, indicating status, strength. Fahima is less than a pawn; she's a prop.

"I've been trying to arrange a sitdown with Kevin for ages," Hargrave says. The sound of Bishop's first name in the man's mouth makes Fahima reach for her butter knife. "I've invited him on the show a dozen times with no response."

"You threaten and terrorize my people," Bishop says. He sounds calm, as if he's talking about Hargrave's prize hydrangeas. "I'm not going to sit down and chat with you about it on air."

Hargrave laughs. "I have never *terrorized* anyone in my life." He puts air quotes around the word with his thick sausage fingers. "You'll be surprised to hear it, but my employers at the Kindred Network keep me on a fairly tight leash. FCC regulations and such."

"Stochastic terrorism," Bishop says. "Someone in a position of power or authority dehumanizes another, casts them as a danger in such a way that an impressionable member of their audience decides violence against that other is both necessary and acceptable."

"Fancy word," Hargrave says. He's the kind of guy who got the shit kicked out of him at private school, then decided elites were scum. "How could I de*humanize* you? You're *not* human. You never get tired of telling us." He sets his glass down. "I've heard our government has a device that can—"He makes a gesture like polishing a mirror that takes in Fahima's entire body. "—shut all this down."

Fahima flinches. She can feel Bishop's eyes on her. "We have no such technology," Lowery says, trying to reassure Fahima and Bishop. Bishop asks her the question in her head, but Fahima shuts him out.

"My employers may have . . . better sources of information than a junior senator," Hargrave says. "But let me ask you,

Miz Deeb. Have you ever tried not being a Resonant?"

Fahima drops her fork. "What the actual—"

"Now I'm being kind," Hargrave says. "I could have insinuated that you have a disease and it would be foolish not to accept an available cure. But I'm using your words here. I'm talking in terms of ability. I'm an excellent singer, did you know? Almost went to Juilliard on a music scholarship." He pronounces the school's name to make his contempt for it clear. He sounds like a farmer calling in pigs. *Jooooo-lliard.* "But I don't go around singing all the time. I don't. Simple as that. So instead of floating in the sky, complaining you're being de*humanized*, have you considered keeping yourselves to yourselves? Maybe if you don't bother us humans, we won't bother you."

"I don't think anyone's asking that," Lowery says. "We want all Americans to be their best, true selves. Jeff, if you want to sing, there's a piano in the next room. I've been known to tickle a little ivory myself." Lowery twiddles his fingers in the air and laughs. No one joins him. "This nation is built on the talents of its citizens," he continues. "That's all these abilities are. Talents. Gifts. Like your singing voice, Jeff." He crams some greens into his mouth, trying to affect informality. He points his fork at Hargrave. "I think you hit it on the head with that one." Hargrave huffs, happy to be affirmed even if his point's been missed.

"I can see that when it comes to philosophy," Lowery continues, "we're going to be . . ." He bumps his fists together. He nods as if this has deep meaning. "But I think there must be some common ground on a policy front. That's where I live, at the level of policy. Let a man believe what he wants to believe. It's the law that matters. And on that level, I think I have something."

He pauses, waiting for them all to lean in. Despite herself, Fahima does, ready to be told a secret.

"Registration," Lowery says.

"You've got to be fucking kidding," Fahima says.

"Miss Deeb, I feel where you're coming from," he says. He looks pained, gesturing at her with his thumb like he might press her nose playfully. "The movement to register Muslims in this country came at the end of a decade of profiling and Islamophobia."

"You realize that shit's not over?" she asks.

"A registry of Resonants could be created not out of public *fear* but for the public *good*. To demonstrate trust between our—" He fumbles for a word. Fahima can't pick the right one either. *Peoples? Nations?* "—between you and the federal government," says Lowery. "Kevin, I was thinking the other day about those kids you sent out to the great Pacific garbage patch."

"Senator Lowery," Bishop says, "this idea is not within the realm of things we've discussed."

"Hear me out, Kevin," Lowery says.

"We were talking about protections," Bishop says. "About civil rights."

"Let the man talk, Kevin," says Hargrave. He's grinning like the cat who ate the cream.

"Those kids," Lowery says, shaking his head. "It was a miracle. A major environmental disaster. Insurmountable.

The low-end estimate is it's a patch of trash as big as the state of Texas. They cleaned it up in a day. One day. I speak on behalf of a grateful nation, a grateful world, and say that deserves recompense. But these kids, they're not government employees. Government employees go through vetting. They have files. They're in a database that indexes their talents. When a job opens up and someone in the database is suitable for it, well, we've got that information right there."

"You want us conscripted?" says Bishop. "Our service for our freedom?"

"Conscription is a very negative way of looking at this," Lowery says.

"Well, I think it's a fine idea, James," says Hargrave. "An excellent first step."

"First step to putting us in camps," Fahima says. "To mass deportation."

"No one's talking about camps, young lady," Hargrave says. Fahima isn't sure if she'd rather have him call her by her first name or *young lady*. "Regarding deportation, I do think the U.S. government should consider that this country overwhelmingly bears this burden. Why is this not a problem in France or Germany? Why should we be the only nation saddled with it?"

"We were born here," Fahima says.

"Not all of you," Hargrave says. "That school you run brings them in from all over the world."

"See, I think that's an opportunity," says Lowery, turning to Fahima to make his case. "We're the country that stands to reap the benefits of you."

"And if we don't want to be reaped?"

"Like you said, James," Hargrave says. "We disagree on philosophical points. But as to policy, I think it'd make people sleep easier. This won't surprise you, but a lot of my listeners are also gun enthusiasts."

"Like the boy who opened fire on my students," Bishop says.

Hargrave waves the accusation away. "When you say registration, they clutch their pearls. Same as Kevin and the young lady are doing. *The gummint gonna come seize ma guns!* But it doesn't mean that at all." The mocking tone he adopts and drops drives a fearful point home to Fahima. He doesn't believe in shit. He'd throw them all on the fire to show he could do it. He's playing genocide like a video game. Hargrave points two fingers at Bishop's head, an imaginary pistol. "A registered gun still shoots."

"We're not fucking weapons," Fahima says. Hargrave cocks an eyebrow, skeptical.

Lowery looks at her sadly. "I don't know how to put this to you, Miss Deeb," he says, "but some of you are."

"Fahima, we should go," says Bishop.

"You have to give up something, Kevin," Lowery says as Bishop stands to leave. Bishop turns on him.

"Three of my students erased a man-made ecological disaster. Three," he says. "We could power cities. We could stop earthquakes, save countless lives. But it won't count unless we do it with collars around our necks and you holding the leash. You won't have my support on this. I won't take this to my people."

"What do you think your support counts for, Kevin?" Lowery asks. He's angry. He expected love would save the day or some shit. "Are you going to vote me out? Are you going to run against me? I've got to say, you don't look like you've got the stamina for a political race." Fahima winces. It's the first time she's heard anyone call Bishop out on the obvious decline of his health. "Resonants are barely a demographic blip," Lowery continues. "I'd earn more votes calling for concentration camps. And someone will, Kevin. Some freshman congressman right now is out there crunching the numbers on an internment bill. Registration buys time."

It's the first thing he's said that makes any sense. Everything now is about time. A collection of countdown clocks and fuses.

"I think we should go," Bishop says. "Mr. Hargrave, I hope you have a pleasant evening."

"I hope you get ball cancer," says Fahima. "In your balls." She manages a sharp pivot away from the table on her heel.

Lowery grabs her by the arm on the way out. "Please, take some rolls," he says, holding out a bread basket. It's an awkward gesture. It makes no sense until words appear in Fahima's head the way they do when Sarah communicates with her ability.

You have to convince him.

The words are shoved out of her head, plowed away like snow. Fahima glares at Bishop, who holds the front door open. She gives one last look at Lowery, then leaves.

"Where are we going?" she asks as she follows him

down K Street. The night air is humid but cool, dense with oncoming spring rain.

"I didn't want to wait for our ride," he says. He sniffs, then wipes his nose with his sleeve, leaving a pale pink streak on the cuff of his white shirt.

"Was he right?" Bishop says. "Does the government have inhibitors?"

"He's a talk show host," Fahima says. "What the fuck would he know about it?"

"That's not an answer."

"Then go into my head," Fahima shouts. "Like you did in there. Scan my fucking brains and check."

Bishop stops dead. They have an agreement that's stood for years, and he's broken it. "I saw him going in," he says. "I wanted to be sure—" A fresh gout of pink pours out his nose, and he grabs on to a lamppost to steady himself. He doubles over, lets it drip down. The stuff evaporates when it hits the sidewalk.

"Hold on," says Fahima. "I'll call Kimani. We'll get you home."

Bishop crouches. He wipes his hands on his suit coat, staining it.

"I don't know what to do," he says. He looks at Fahima like a child with a broken toy. "I don't want a war, and I don't know that they'll leave us other choices. There are so few of us. They'll round us up and put us somewhere they can forget about us. We're not something they have to reckon with."

We could be, Fahima thinks. Something Lowery said.

Barely a demographic blip. Fahima remembers a talk at Columbia last year about disability rights. The speaker was in a wheelchair after a car accident. She waited as undergrads removed the podium and lowered the mic stand to accommodate her. Then she gave the audience a sly grin.

"The issue of rights as related to disability is different from those related to race," she said. "Those of you born white will never be black. You might have black friends or be concerned about racial issues in terms of abstract societal good. You will never wake up black. Never be at risk within that struggle. You may, however, wake up one morning to discover, with all the shock of Gregor Samsa, that you are disabled. And that day, the words you have said dismissing the disabled as a protected class or a people worthy of study? Those words will taste like ashes in your mouth."

It will never be enough to help them or to be their friends, Fahima thinks. *They'll be afraid of us until they become like us.*

OWEN CURRY AND
THE HELTER-SKELTER

After Owen liberates the circus, some of those he freed stay with him. Andre the skeleton and Maryanne with the tentacles. Little Gail. Wendy the Angel stays one night at a motel two hours' drive from the circus. They steal Jake's truck, and Owen has enough money to rent rooms for them all. He's drifting off when Wendy knocks on his door. He understands it's repayment. It's only going to be this one time. She tells him so. She gives him her body but not her heart. Owen's surprised that he's not more upset when she leaves in the morning. He understands she doesn't love him, and she understands he does love her. He'll have the memory of that night, her wings folding around him, hiding them from the world. He can think about it while he touches himself and imagine it's her again. It's complicated, and it hurts.

He and the group keep west after Damascus. They meet up with others, people his friend sends to them. Darren, who can do a couple of useless things with televisions and reminds Owen of his manager at the Planet. There's Oliver, who looks like a gorilla fucked a wolf and put pants on the baby. And the girls, Tabitha and Marita. Owen assumes they're lesbians, but they're not. At least Marita isn't. She comes to him in the black bone room some nights. She likes to visit him right after she's fucked Darren or sometimes Oliver. She promises that what they have in the black bone room is special. She does things to him there she can't do in real life. She burns him all up until there's nothing left, except he's still there. He's seen the red handprints on Darren. Scorched bits of fur on Oliver. "Little flames," she says. "Not like you and me." If her needs are anything like Owen's, it's dangerous to let her use him as a canvas. It's only a matter of time before she burns him all up for real. Some guys might get off on that danger. Not Owen. He gets off a different way.

They spend a year this way, running missions. Tabitha calls them *ops*. Marita and Oliver broke her out of a military prison. The winter was long, all of them cramped in the van, in cheap motels. Now it's summer, and they can sleep under the stars. They have room to breathe again.

They're at a rest stop diner outside of Topeka. Yesterday they burned down a medical research facility where people were working on a cure for Resonance. After the building burned, they went to the lead scientist's house and Owen fed him into the null. The stuff and the idea, all gone. Oliver and Andre and Maryanne stay in the van they stole near Jefferson City. It's not fair, but they're too scary-looking to be seen. Soon there'll be no one to tell them shit like that. Owen thinks about Wendy. When she left weeks ago, heading north back to the Commune while the rest of them went west, she was wearing a massive trench coat, her wings cramped inside. It shouldn't have to be that way.

On the television behind the counter, a reporter stands in front of a church. There is a massive cross lit by ground lights, Wendy nailed to it by her wings. The camera crews don't get too close. There are shadows and that digital blurring television does, but you can tell she's naked. Owen can see her face, the bruises and the cuts. She's strobed in blue and red police lights. Two men from the coroner's office reach up toward her. It looks like they're asking her to come down, but they're pointing at the spikes that hold her up.

"Oh, fuck," says Gail. Her voice is a whisper in the front pocket of Owen's shirt. "Oh, Wendy, no."

They cut to the man who runs the school in New York, the one where they kept Owen in the basement.

"This is a hate crime," he says. "Pure and simple. The police here fail to appreciate the gravity of this incident. People need to understand this is an attempt to terrorize and intimidate us. This girl was killed because of what she was."

Owen will show him such a hate crime. He'll make him understand what the words mean. But the friend in Owen's head says no. *The school is not to be touched.*

After the man from the school, they show the other man, the fat one. JEFFERSON HARGRAVE, TALK SHOW HOST, the words underneath him read.

"This was an act of species self-defense," he says. "You all want to hug it out with these *things* and pretend they're not dangerous. But they are. I feel terrible for the parents of this pigeon girl or whatever she was. But I also applaud the individuals who saw a clear and present threat to their community and decided to act."

That one, says the friend in Owen's head. *Him.*

Owen looks around the table. These are the best friends he's ever had. Even Darren, whom he doesn't like. They've formed a bond. Like those guys who go to war and meet up fifty years later. Forged in fire. Marita catches him staring at her. Darren's hand is in the back pocket of her jeans. The look she gives him is mean, twisted up. It reminds him how Amanda Smoot looked at him. Even though he just ate two cheeseburgers, something rumbles in his gut. Marita sees the change in his face, and hers softens. She's never kind to him, even when they're fucking. But she's afraid of him, which is the right way to be.

"You get a message, O?" she asks. They all have the same sliver in their heads that Owen does. But Owen's connection is deeper. Owen is a kind of chosen one.

He points at the fat man on the screen. "He's next."

Jefferson Hargrave gets bigger and bigger in Owen's mind. Owen sees the fat man driving the spikes into Wendy's wings, jowly face grinning as he does it. In the two days it takes them to drive to Arizona, Owen sits in the back of the van and practices his ability. He takes an apple and nulls shapes out of the inside of it, where he can't even see. He cuts it open with a pocket knife to check his work. That's what he's going to do to Jefferson Hargrave. Take pieces of his insides. Cut him open to check the work.

Maryanne and Gail wait in the van. Ostensibly Maryanne is the getaway driver, but she's just squeamish. "She needs to get bloody or get gone," Marita said to Owen last night in the black bone room, Owen's Hivebody blackened, smoldering. Owen doesn't disagree, but he also doesn't want to leave Maryanne alone. She's family.

"Look at this fucking house," Darren says. "Can we keep it, you think?"

"We can stay a couple days afterward," Tabitha says. This is her plan. Her op. "My intel says he holes up here alone for two weeks. In his book he calls it *recentering time*."

"You read this asshole's book?" Darren says.

They stole a copy from a library in Boulder, along with a couple of books on the Manson family. Tabitha's studied photos of Roman Polanski's house from the night of the killings. The bullet holes in the ceiling, the writing in blood on the walls. Owen wanted to tell her that there wouldn't be as much blood this time, that she shouldn't get her hopes up. Tabitha barely spoke until yesterday, when it was time to lay out her plan, sequestering herself in the back seat of the van with pictures of a fifty-year-old murder scene.

Marita sneaks up behind him as he looks up at the big house. She slips her hand down the front of Owen's pants and wraps her fingers around his cock. They burn a little. Owen isn't used to the feel of her actual skin.

"Excited yet, O?" she whispers in his ear.

"I'm concentrating," Owen says, removing her hand. She looks insulted.

"And now we walk in," Tabitha says, leading them up the long driveway. Each dark window of the house holds its own reflection of the sun setting behind them over the desert: four red fireballs dealt out like tarot cards on a table.

"You sure he's alone?" Oliver asks. There are three cars in the drive.

"Doesn't matter," says Tabitha. "We kill whoever we find."

Any of them could take out the lock except maybe Darren. Owen's way is the quietest. The doorknob, the whole mechanism of it, along with a piece of the door frame, gone. Darren pushes the front door open with a finger, and they step into an entryway with stairs leading up to the second floor. The house rumbles with music: plodding bass and a dipshit carnival keyboard line.

"I fucking love this song," a man shouts from upstairs. His voice is a rich baritone, booming through the house over the music on the stereo. "Three Dog Night. This has gotta be before your time, right? You kids. You perfect little girls." A woman squeaks and giggles.

"Not alone," Andre says. His skeleton fingers scrape along the drywall.

"Honey, where's the coke?" yells a girl's voice.

"Kitchen," shouts another.

Hargrave passes the top of the stairs, towel wrapped around his waist, bottle of whiskey in his hand. He does that dance the guys Owen's mom used to date did, where he shimmies his shoulders, elbows bent, like he's trying to squeeze his ass backward into a tight space. The ceiling light explodes behind him as Tabitha lobs a globe of energy into it. Hargrave dives to the ground.

"Shooter!" he shrieks. "Shooter!" The whiskey bottle rolls down the stairs one step at a time, *plunk plunk plunk.*

It leaves a trail and turns Hargrave's attention to the entryway. He's lying at the top of the stairs, towel undone, ass hanging out, hands covering his head. He looks at Owen. "What the fuck?" he says.

Oliver is the first up the stairs, taking them in two bounds and sweeping Jefferson up in one hand. He pins the naked fat man against the wall. "How many in the house?" he growls.

"Three girls," Jefferson says. "Me and three girls."

The answer is no longer necessary. The girls, in bikinis and silk robes, are standing in the doorway to the kitchen, gawking at Oliver in horror.

"Hello, ladies," Darren says, doffing an imaginary hat. "I wouldn't move if I were you." The blender on the counter blows up, spraying strawberry daiquiri and shattered glass onto one of the girls. Andre moves behind her, wrapping a bony arm around her shoulder and wiping daiquiri off her breast with his finger. Marita grabs the bottle of whiskey, takes a swig, and lights the trail of spilled booze on fire. Darren ogles the girls as Oliver eases Jefferson back to the ground. Owen looks at Jefferson the way a sculptor looks at a fresh block of marble. He assesses what needs to be cut away to reveal the beauty beneath.

Marita passes the bottle to Darren, who takes a long pull off it and holds it out to Hargrave.

"Take a hit, fat man?" he says. "Everyone's entitled to a last drink."

Owen doesn't like the way Darren is taking point on this op. He does this every time, and every time afterward Tabitha chews his ass about it. Owen's never said anything because he wants to let Darren think he's special. They all have a piece of Owen's friend in their heads, and for a while that made him jealous. But his friend *knew* about the jealousy. He felt it. *Remember you're special to me*, he told Owen. *There are many terrors, but you are my Great Destroyer.*

Hargrave refuses, and Darren shoves the bottle at him. He takes Hargrave by the back of the neck and pours whiskey into him. Hargrave sobs. He's so scared, he pisses right on Darren's leg.

"Holy shit," Marita says, pointing and laughing as the thin stream of piss soaks Darren's jeans. Oliver and even Tabitha break out laughing.

"What the fuck?" Darren screams. He pulls out the pistol he carries in the back of his pants because his ability is basically useless and shoots Hargrave in the forehead. Hargrave slumps against the wall. Owen's visions of long and painful torture pop like balloons. He waited so long for this. He went with them on every bullshit errand they had to run. He cleaned up after their messes and their murder scenes like a fucking maid to get here, to get in this room with the man who killed Wendy. Might as well have driven the fucking spikes into her wings, and now he's dead without suffering for one second.

Owen forms the null into a flat plane, a plate of nothing that slices Darren in half, diagonally, from his left bicep to above his right hip. Darren's face goes from anger, to shock, to nothing. His left arm, cut free, drops to the ground, and the upper part of his torso sloughs off the rest. It hits the floor and tumbles down the stairs. Darren's legs fold, and what's left of him sits down, almost gracefully, at Tabitha's feet. All the girls are screaming except Marita, who laughs. But her laughter doesn't sound that different from a scream.

There's a pain in Owen's head like a bright white light. He is sure he's about to die, and he mumbles, "I'm sorry, I'm sorry, I'm sorry," clutching his skull as if he can hold it together with his hands.

Owen, says his friend. *My impetuous boy.* The white light fades, and its ebbing is a mercy.

It's the most powerful love Owen has ever felt.

THE INVESTIGATION

The house smells like copper and spoiled meat. A breath of hot bad air comes out the front door when Avi opens it and shoves him back onto his heel. Inside, a plastic sheet is laid over the doormat, covering a lump the size of a dog. Fingers peek out from under the edge.

"Watch it," Louis shouts from the top of the stairs. "Don't step in that fucker's guts and contaminate my crime scene."

Avi steps over the lump under the sheet, wobbling on his cane as he does. The stairs are spattered with blood. It's all Avi can do to ascend without stepping in it. At the top of the stairs, he puts his cane into a pool of blood that hasn't dried and leaves a trail of bull's-eye stamps behind him as he crosses the kitchen.

"They took Hargrave's body out a half hour ago," Louis says. "If you're looking to get kicks in, you're out of luck." He holds out a jar of VapoRub. Avi dips his first two fingers in and slathers it under his nose. It doesn't cut the smell or cover it, but it distracts. Anything helps. "You knew the guy, right? Didn't you try to take a swing at him once on *The Tonight Show* or something? Shit, Avi, are you a suspect here?" Louis

414

laughs, big and overloud. He laughs for the same reason they're wearing VapoRub. It distracts. Anything helps.

"You see these guys?" Louis asks, leaning in to Avi and speaking quietly. "They'll all quit in a week, I guarantee it. You can tell right away."

"It doesn't look that gruesome," Avi says.

"The hot tub on the patio," Louis says. "It's a fucking cup o' soup."

Avi looks over Louis's shoulder to the sliding doors. Every few minutes, they spit out another green-faced agent rushing to a nearby trash can to puke.

"How many?" Avi asks.

"Hargrave and three girls," Louis says. "Plus the unlucky fucker in the front hall. We're guessing he's a delivery boy or something. Except there's no car."

"His name is Darren Helms." In the entryway, Patrick Davenport lays the sheet back over the remains. "He was one of our students."

"That is surprisingly helpful," Louis says, writing the name down on his notepad. "Are you positive?"

"You only forget the nice ones," Patrick says. "The true assholes stay with you." Avi remembers Darren Helms from the first day he was at Bishop, the scene in Sarah's class. *Asshole* is about the right word. Patrick extends one of his legs across the entire set of stairs, then pulls the rest of his body up after him. It's a dizzying effect. Patrick used to be shy about using his ability in front of baseliners. Clearly that's no longer an issue.

"Avi, this is Patrick Davenport," says Louis. "He's a liaison from the Resonant community who's been helping us with the investigation."

"We know each other," Patrick says, not bothering to shake Avi's hand.

"Of course you do," Louis says.

"So this was Owen Curry?" Patrick asks.

Louis scratches at his eyebrow. "Your friend in the front hall I am almost sure was Curry," he says. "Clean slice down the middle. Hargrave caught a bullet, but the body got good and fucked with afterward. Again, it looks like Curry. But the precision here . . ."

"He's getting better," Patrick says.

"Some would say worse," Louis says.

Patrick gives Louis an annoyed look. Patrick's expressions have a cartoonish element to them, as if he overshoots the mark and his face distorts further than it ought to. "He's getting more adept," he says. "We've seen that at other crime scenes. He's more precise. Controlled."

Avi turns to them. "There've been others?"

"Nothing like this," Louis says. "Murders with internal organs missing and no cuts. Disappearances where we've found indentations and gaps in the room that don't make sense."

"I haven't heard anything about this," says Avi.

"I took you off speed dial," Louis says before returning his attention to Patrick. "We think he's hooked up with other people."

"Agent Hoffman has been kind enough to keep Owen Curry's involvement away from the press," Patrick explains.

He clearly relishes the fact that Avi's in the dark and needs Patrick to bring him up to speed.

"Why hush it up?" Avi asks.

"Things are bad enough without me giving people a boogeyman," Louis says.

"And yet you invited the press in on this one," says Patrick, glaring at Avi.

"I thought you all were friends," Louis says. Avi wants to argue that he's not just "the press," but his press credentials swing on a lanyard in front of his chest, a scarlet letter. "Hargrave has—had a cult behind him. We're tracking at least three separate groups who treat him like a prophet. Two of them look a lot like militia. And they're funded."

"By whom?" Avi asks.

"If we knew, they wouldn't be funded anymore," Louis says. "There's going to be fallout here. Given who the victim was, his followers are going to know it was you."

"It wasn't *me*," says Patrick.

"You *people*," Louis says. "Press is going to be unavoidable. The Kindred Network will be tributes for a day, then howling for blood."

"They won't wait a day," Patrick says.

"I figured you'd want to go with a friendly face," Louis says.

"Might as well go with the devil we know," says Patrick.

"What can you tell me about the kid in the hallway?" Louis asks.

"I wouldn't have predicted he'd be involved in something like this, but I'm not surprised," Patrick says.

"You think he was one of the attackers?" says Avi.

"I don't think Jefferson Hargrave invited him to the orgy," Patrick says. "We try to raise these kids on nonviolence, but you've heard the kind of things Hargrave says about us."

"Said," Avi corrects. He's trying to insinuate himself into the conversation, but it isn't his place. He feels like a kid listening to adults argue, and he remembers the first time he met any of them. Sarah reprimanding Patrick to let the grown-ups talk. Patrick looks more mature than he did that day. He seems assured where once he came off as arrogant. Avi's sliding down the opposite slope of age, into decrepitude. Rather than a kid shushed by parents, he's the elderly father, ignored as his children decide whether to send him to a home.

"You don't get to talk that way without consequences," Patrick says. "A kid like Darren, who hurt people for kicks, figures out a way to do one bit of good in his life, putting his shitty personality to use. Some of us get to be peaceful protesters because others are willing to do this."

"Come take a look at the patio before you decide this is one bit of good," says Louis. Patrick shrugs and heads toward the sliding glass door. "You coming?" Louis asks Avi.

Avi has spent much of his career describing the horrors done to bodies by bombs, but something about Owen Curry's ability undoes his strength. The smooth slice taken out of the church haunts him. The thought of seeing the same thing done to a human body is more than he can stand.

"Feed it to the press pool," he tells Louis, starting back down the stairs. "I'm done with this guy."

"But I thought Owen Curry was your baby," Louis says. "Your special little monster."

Avi opens his mouth to argue, but it's true. He feels an ownership over Owen Curry, the hole Avi fell through to land in this world. There was a tinge of pride when Louis told him Owen Curry was the one who killed Hargrave, as if Owen was landing the punch Avi threw at Hargrave years ago. *My monster*, Avi thinks. *My boy.*

CRAZY CLASSIC LIFE

There were clusters even before they were identifiable to the public as such. From beach houses on Oceanside Way to crumbling apartment buildings in East Oakland, Resonants had quietly clumped together to create spaces they could return to at the end of a day in secret and drop the cloaks in which they'd draped themselves. Since Public Day, there had been a debate about whether this was a good thing. Blanket yes or no answers whitewashed differences within the larger community or populace or however one wanted to define Resonants as a group. Some of those enclaves were created for safety, some for comfort. One person's intentional community was another's ghetto. Some groups rose together; others fell.

North Avenue in Chicago's posh Wicker Park neighborhood was a Resonant community built out of affinity and privilege. Since the nineties, it had been quietly populated by hip young Resonants of some financial means who wanted to keep to themselves. When Hayden Cohen used the money from an album advance to open a Resonants-only nightclub and recording studio at the fulcrum of the street, North Avenue became the first Resonant community, other than the Bishop Academy, that everyone knew about. There were news coverage, think pieces, plans for a unity concert in Wicker Park proper languishing in perpetual permit limbo. There was a constant stream of tourists and sightseers, pointing and gawking at the residents of the street like animals on safari. But there was also the feeling of a burgeoning neighborhood, a by-us, for-us sense of solidarity.

Carrie and Miquel, along with a handful of their classmates, found apartments within a four-block span of Hayden's bar. Bryce said it was self-ghettoization, and when he couldn't convince Waylon of this, he rented a one-bedroom in the Ukrainian Village. It meant they weren't all as neatly coupled off as they could be. But it felt like a start.

Hayden named the bar Vibration, and the goal was for it to be CBGB and Studio 54 rolled into one. Chic but legitimate. Posh but punk. At the same time, Hayden's career was taking off. They had a new band and tour dates, and they didn't want to be bothered with the effort necessary to make Vibration big. They hired Waylon to run the place, and he did his best.

Part of that meant drugs. Waylon dealt pot and mushrooms to supplement the receipts and to provide a value-add to Vibration's customers. Hayden never explicitly endorsed or forbade selling drugs through the bar, but whenever they were in town, they took the opportunity to regale Waylon with lists of drugs that ran hot and cold through the discos of midseventies New York, buoying before ultimately drowning the scene. Coke and Quaaludes. Angel Dust and alkyl nitrates. Waylon hooked up with a transmuter named Hong Wu from out in Cicero who'd been fired from Dow Chemical when his employers found out he was a Resonant. Hong produced immaculate synthetic drugs out of base materials. By the end of Vibration's first summer, it was an emporium for designer drugs, abetted by the fact that cops never came down North Avenue. They parked at the corners on Ashland and Western, daring the residents of the street to come out into the regular world. Most didn't. North Avenue was a world in itself, another iteration of the Bishop Academy or the Hive.

Waylon brought Carrie into the operation that spring. She was temping at the time, moving unnoticed through the offices and steno pools of Chicago and the surrounding suburbs. The widening circle of jobs threatened to land her back in Deerfield, an hour's train ride away, so she limited herself to gigs she could bike to. It meant a lot of days off. Miquel was struggling to get an in-home counseling business off the ground, and between the two of them, they were barely making rent. Carrie was open to ideas.

"What does every baseliner want?" Waylon asked her, tenting his fingers and leaning on his elbows. He'd shed the baby fat he'd sported at Bishop. Bryce had him eating better, and he kept himself clean despite the volume of drugs that passed through Vibration. His face was long, thin, permanently dour. He'd waited until Miquel was off playing darts with Jonathan, who was dating Hayden but had left the band the moment before they got big. Waylon must have intuited already that this job offer was best kept secret.

"No idea," Carrie said.

"They want abilities," Waylon said. "They want to be like us for an hour, then shut it off and go back to their shit lives."

It felt true to Carrie. She and Miquel had driven out to Deerfield the night before to have dinner with her family. Her brother wanted his boss off his back. Her mother wanted her daughter to not be a freak. Her father wanted what Carrie had, to be able to move through the world without being seen. They all wished things were different and knew this meant becoming different people. They felt the impossibility of change. Carrie and Miquel, people like them, represented the chance to break through the limits of an ossified self. Her family watched them move through their new lives with a mixture of resentment and jealousy.

Waylon pulled out a small metal tube that looked like the nitrous cartridges she used to steal from the cafeteria at Bishop so they could do whip-its.

"Rez," said Waylon.

"You're not actually calling it that," Carrie said.

"Hong named it," he said. "I wanted to call it TurboBoost."

"Rez is not that bad," said Carrie. She reached across the table, took the cool metal, and closed it in her hand. It stayed cold, drawing heat from her palm until it was painful to hold. "This gives them abilities?"

"Nothing dangerous," Waylon said. "A glimmer of what they could have been, if."

"If?"

"If they'd been like us and not like them," Waylon said.

"You've seen it work?"

"I've felt the warm thermic glow off a homeless Damp in an alleyway," he said, doing his shitty impression of Rutger Hauer from the end of *Blade Runner.* "I've seen a UIC undergrad who thought she was in a psych study float gleefully across a lab."

"You did studies," said Carrie. She put the cartridge back on the table. It left a red shadow of itself on her palm.

"This isn't bathtub crank," Waylon said. "I take drugs very seriously."

"What'd you tell this undergrad after she went Tinkerbell for an hour?"

" 'You've inhaled a shitload of hallucinogenic drugs. Keep your ass hydrated the next three days. Here's a hundred bucks.' "

He didn't mention the early abreactions, test subjects in St. Elizabeth's with flimsy and superfluous limbs that were reabsorbed into the body the morning afterward or patches of dragonlike scales that flaked away to reveal fresh pink skin beneath. He didn't mention that the psych ward at Presence Saint Mary had seen cases in which people claimed to be besieged with voices, only for the symptoms to fade after a few hours. What he did mention was the retail price, the number of buyers already clamoring for it, and the low-double-digit percentage of gross she'd take home. He was recruiting Carrie for distribution, the invisible circuit along which the drug would travel.

The next day, she dressed for her temp job: white button-down blouse and beige pencil skirt. She kissed Miquel good-bye in the little kitchen of their apartment, hopped onto her bike, and rode to the end of North Avenue. She pulled over, called the temp agency, and asked them to take her off the call lists indefinitely. Then she put in her earbuds, clicked "play" on a Clash album, and went to pick up some drugs.

There wasn't a moment she decided not to tell Miquel. She simply never did. She learned to make the job invisible. A collection of conversational blocks and feints did the trick. Paying their rent gave Carrie moral high ground if it ever came to an argument. More important, she loved Miquel. Loving him required her to protect him from the real world.

Every time she runs a pickup to Hong's Auto Repair, she tries not to think of it as a meth lab. It's on Laramie, down the street from a horse-racing track. The block is pawn shops and liquor stores and e-cigarette retailers. Hong's has been there three generations, as Hong likes to remind her.

"My grandfather didn't realize shops in America used first names, like Joe's Body and Glass or Bob's Muffler and Brakes," he said. "He named the shop Hong's Auto Repair after the family name, but everyone started calling him Hong like it was Steve. Same with my dad. Except dad would correct them every time. Next visit? Same thing. I go by Hong because no one's going to bother to call me anything else." Hong was the kind of guy who talked when he was nervous, and he was always nervous. "He'd kill me if he knew what I was doing with the place. He had a horror about drugs on account of certain stereotypes regarding Chinese people and opium or whatever. But he's dead five years and I'm keeping the doors open, so suck on that, Dad."

There's no one in the front office when Carrie arrives. She shouts for Hong, and there's a clang of metal before he steps out of the back, sweaty and grease-streaked.

"I forgot you were coming," he says. "Come on back."

The inside of the garage is lined with electrified chicken wire as a makeshift Faraday cage. When Carrie asked him what it was supposed to keep out, he winked knowingly at her.

"Waylon's been trying to contact you through the Hive," Carrie says.

"Yeah, I hear him," says Hong, making a motion like putting on earmuffs. "I don't go in there anymore. You ever see the black coral in there? On the ground?"

"Yeah, of course," Carrie says. It was like Starbucks. She noticed when the first one showed up, but she stopped noticing when they were everywhere. Carrie knew there was a time it hadn't been there, and she could remember how odd it was seeing it the first time, a patch of black flowers in the Bishop kids' Hivelounge. Then it was everywhere, and she stopped noticing it, like a smell she'd gotten so used to that she'd be surprised if someone pointed it out.

"A guy I know, his cousin licked some of it," Hong says. "Drove her totally batshit." Hong makes a wild-eyed face and waves his hands in the air. He always has a guy he knows: a hookup for parts on an import or evidence Resonants are the result of millennium-old alien conspiracies to tamper with human DNA.

"I'll stay away from the black coral," she says.

"Stay out of the Hive altogether," he says.

"You don't answer your phone either," says Carrie.

Hong looks at her like she's said something blitheringly obvious. "Brain cancer," he says. He roots in drawers of papers and work bins of loose auto parts before coming up with a kid's backpack. "I tweaked the psilocybin levels a little," he says. "It might take longer to come on. But it's the stuff."

"Thanks," Carrie says. She hands him an envelope. Hong opens it and counts the bills in front of her.

"This isn't paranoia," he says. "It's best practice." Satisfied, he puts the envelope in a drawer. "You seen any white vans out there?"

"Florists?" Carrie asks.

Hong shakes his head. "Unmarked," he says. "No plates. They snatch people up. People like us. A girl I know, her boyfriend got disappeared. Guys he works with say they saw a white van in the neighborhood."

"Who's driving?" Sometimes it's fun to let Hong spin out his webs.

"Scientists, grabbing test subjects," Hong says. "They're working on a plague that will take us all out. They have labs up in Canada, working with a department in the Canadian government."

Carrie smirks and puts in her earbuds, flooding her head with an early Prince album. "I'll stay away from the white vans," she shouts.

The apartment is rife with the smell of sautéed garlic. Everything Miquel knows how to cook starts with garlic simmering in olive oil. Carrie wishes he'd serve her plates of garlic cloves brown and shiny with oil, nothing else. She hears a sizzle, and the coppery tang of tomatoes joins the smell.

"Pasta?" she asks. She pulls out her earbuds and kisses him on the cheek.

"Pasta," Miquel says.

"You should start the water."

"I know," he says. "I forgot."

"Timing, babe," Carrie says. A fat white bulb floats like an eyeball in the sea of diced tomatoes. She snatches it and pops it in her mouth.

"How was work?" he asks.

Carrie shrugs. "Same old," she says. "You?"

"Remember Doug Shaw?" he says. "Worked in the office at Bishop."

"Downer Doug," says Carrie.

"Downer Doug," Miquel says. "Shit, now I'm worried I'm going to call him that next session."

"He's in Chicago?"

"Lives up the block," says Miquel.

"I guess the moment of North Avenue's cool has passed."

"If our session today was any indication, he'll be paying our grocery bills the next couple months."

"He's a basket case?" Carrie asks.

"I don't like to use that term," Miquel says. "Public Day messed him up bad. He's got some stuff to work through." He hefts a pot of water onto the back burner.

"Salt it," Carrie says. Miquel throws a palmful of salt into the pot.

"I talked with Hayden," Miquel says.

"They stop by?"

"Hive," says Miquel.

"Is that what you do all day?" Carrie asks. "You hang around the Hive talking to your old flames?"

"Hayden was never a flame," says Miquel, lighting the stove. "Anyway, what do *you* do all day?" He makes it sound like a joke, but there's an edge in the question. There are so many holes in the story she's fed him about her employment, such a gap between what an office temp ought to make and the cash she brings home daily. Part of her wants to get caught. *Care enough to come find me*, she thinks. If Miquel has suspicions, he keeps them to himself. "Are we going to their thing tonight?" he asks. "They really want us there."

"It's at Vibration," says Carrie. "It'll be crowded."

"It's cute you worry about me," he says, kissing her on the forehead, his hands resting on her hips. "Go put a record on for us?"

Carrie goes to the living room and stares blankly at the shelves full of her records. Last week, Miquel asked how she could afford so many. Carrie claimed that most of them were her dad's rather than admit the bulk of them were purchased with drug money. She smiles, imagining her dad listening to A Tribe Called Quest, the Pixies. She's in the mood for something slow, but Hayden's thing this evening looms. She finds Patti Smith's *Horses* and hovers the needle over the platter. There is a tiny space, a silence where confession could fit. She wonders how their relationship would change if rather than starting the record, she went into the kitchen and told Miquel how they pay their rent. Every few days, she tells herself she intends to. She's not lying but temporarily withholding, waiting for a moment. But moments are cheap and frequent between them. There are silences like this she could fill, moments she's sure he knows but won't call her on it. If she spoke, a spell could be broken and they would wake. But she's not sure anymore who they'd be once they woke up. She can't remember a version of herself that wasn't made of secrets.

Carrie hears the pasta splash into the boiling water and sets the needle into the groove.

In the middle of the dance floor, two beer bottles orbit each other, six feet in the air. Beneath them, invisible, Carrie dances like a live wire, attached to the ground and flailing with current. Hayden grins at her from across the room. In the air above the crowd, two iridescent horses made of light collide. They shatter into a hundred smaller horses that rain down in a flurry of pink-purple hooves and swishing green tails. Isidra Gonzalez, hot shit on the new Chicago art scene, traces lemniscates of liquid silver in front of her, weaving them through the lights to the beat of some other song playing in her head at double the beats per minute. Jonathan dances with Miquel, the two of them flirting with queerness in a way that makes Bryce throw Carrie a raised eyebrow, which cracks her up. She can't remember what she's taken, and Waylon's comping her drinks, erasing the need to keep count. Jonathan's Paisley silk shirt is unbuttoned to his navel, the glow from his torso cast out on the crowd like a searchlight, searing bright paths across Miquel's chest. There is so much goodness pouring off Miquel, such raw positive emotion, Carrie worries that she might come if he so much as touches her.

Hayden snatches one of Carrie's beers out of midair.

"I fucking love this song," they say.

"Bowie had to be one of us. He had to be," Carrie screams above the music, her voice coming out of nowhere.

"All of them were," says Hayden. "All the magic ones. We'll adopt them as saints. Saint Bowie of Change and Saint Prince of Fucking. Saint Siouxsie and Saint Janet. We'll beatify them."

The way they say the word, *bee-AT-if-I*, makes Carrie crack up. *Not saints*, she thinks. A silver font arcs over the room, a mercury snake. You can see time reflected in it. Futures and pasts, possibles and fails. *Saints have to be dead*, Carrie thinks. *We don't need saints. We need heroes.*

Miquel comes over, kisses her invisible cheek, and dances back into the crowd.

"He's fucking gorgeous," says Hayden, sounding hungry.

"I thought you and Jonathan were together," Carrie says.

"Not exclusively," Hayden says. "You should invite us over. All four of us." Carrie watches Hayden, not sure if they're serious. "Is that weird?" Hayden asks, looking worried. They stop dancing for a beat, pulling back into themselves. It's easy to forget how shy Hayden can be. Carrie thinks of them as huge, a star, but they're also the person who stayed in their dorm room perfecting their Am9 chord while everyone else got drunk at Darren and Lynette's house on Long Island.

"It's not weird," says Carrie.

Hayden sighs with relief and starts dancing again. "I'm rolling, and I just want to fuck everybody," they say. "And I love you. And Miquel is beautiful. Think about it."

Hayden kisses Carrie on the corner of her mouth, where it could be passed off as a missed stab at her cheek or read as a real kiss. The song fades, trailing a beat too long before it crashes into another. Hayden wraps their arms around Carrie's invisible waist, and when their skin touches, it is like being loved and loved and loved. Their bodies fall into rhythm, leading and following at the same time.

In the morning, Hayden wakes first and shakes Jonathan until he mumbles groggily and gets dressed. Miquel, half asleep in a tangle of blankets, offers to make coffee, but Hayden waves him back to sleep like a fairy in a story. They kiss Carrie in that same spot, the corner of her mouth, then stand over her, smiling sadly. Carrie's asleep again before the door closes, all of it a thing in her dream.

When she wakes, she's alone. She wrangles matted curls out of her eyes. She extricates herself from the sheets and surveys the new map of their bed. It's threatening. Too full of chance and risk. The echo of last night's drugs hits her. Euphoria becomes its hollow opposite; desire curdles into aversion. She strips the sheets and crams them into the hamper.

Miquel is in the kitchen in boxers, nursing a steaming cup. Carrie puts her arms around his waist, pressing her face to his bare chest, reasserting her claim on him.

"Hey," he says.

"Hey," says Carrie.

"Was last night okay with you?" he says. "It all moved fast."

"It was good," Carrie says, her eyes on the dish rack. "Did you like it?"

She feels him shrug. "I have trouble keeping track of what I want," he says. Carrie understands him. Miquel can be like the moon, reflecting other people's emotions so brightly that they seem like his own. Desire is an emotion. Wanting is no different from sadness or jealousy.

Maybe Hayden wanted him enough for both of them, she thinks. "I know we're supposed to be hyperevolved and everything," he continues. "But there's that, and then also there's us. So, are you okay?"

"It was good," Carrie says again, a little more emphatic but no more sincere. "Maybe not here?" she adds. "Maybe in our space, in our room, it's just us."

Miquel kisses her on the top of her head and pulls her closer. He smells like sex that isn't theirs, but she tries to put it away. She tries to send a message to him through her skin, although she spent enough years at Bishop pouring *I love you*s into the air between them to know it won't be received.

I'm lying to you. Come find me out. Care enough to see me.

THE WHITE VAN

Avi wakes up alone in the house on Jarvis Avenue, surprised by the hollow silence of it. He can feel where the sounds of his wife and daughter belong in the rooms below him, the cold echo where Kay should be lying in their bed. After his last conversation with Bishop, he refused to renew the lease and moved back in without telling Kay or Emmeline. He wonders what Kay would say if she knew.

Once he gets himself put together, Avi drives down to North Avenue, parking a few blocks over on Greenfield and hoofing from there. It's autumn, and the air is crisp and dry. Avi's favorite weather is what comes between the sweaty end of August and the onset of winter, when sidewalks become slick and unnavigable. There's a coffee shop he likes. He gets there early and sets up by the window to watch the foot traffic. It's like looking out on an alien planet. Young people float and zip along sidewalks. They lean against unused mailboxes and gesture at each other, fingers tracing bright orange lines in the air that fade like a flashbulb afterimage on the eye. The vogue this month is for animated fabric:

jackets whose patterns shift and swirl, print pants whose neon Rubik's cubes rotate and reconfigure. Travis and Diane Weinstein, a couple on the corner at North Hoyne makes them. Diane paints the cloth and brings it to life; Travis stitches it into clothing using the skill of five generations of Eastern European tailors. He's also precognitive over short spans of time. Avi did an interview with them for the *Reader*. He kept answering one question ahead. The constant motion of their tiny shop was seizure-inducing.

What Avi loves most are the older folks. Many don't live on the block or lived there before it became impossibly cool. They grew up hiding their lights. They've kept their secrets so long that they can't bring themselves to strut. Memories of a time when showing off risked bodily harm are too near for them. They watch the kids, sometimes bitterly envious, sometimes smiling at how far things have come. Avi feels allied with them. They're tourists here, too, visitors to this strange planet. They can observe but can't breathe the air.

The boy with the glowing light in his chest brings Avi's coffee. He looks over Avi's shoulder at the computer screen, the cursor blinking on the blank page.

"Writer?" he asks. It's the first time the boy's talked to him other than to take his order.

"Journalist," Avi says.

The boy makes a face of mild disapproval. He taps his breastbone above the glowing hole. "Poet," he says, expressing both pride and burden. Avi feels a tug at the base of his brain. It would be imperceptible if he hadn't learned to expect it. The boy tries to Hivescan him, to figure out if he's a Resonant. Coming up empty, the boy gets bored and returns to the counter.

Avi spends an hour working on a piece for the *Reader* about North Avenue zoning disputes. It's the last one he'll do for them. His editor thinks they shouldn't hire baseline stringers to cover Resonant issues any more than they should hire white stringers to cover community meetings in predominantly black neighborhoods. He'll be back to the *Trib*, where the wheels of cultural change grind slowly. The *Trib* wants blood, and Avi's had his fill. They were livid when they got pipped on the Hargrave murder, but Avi's managed to weasel back into their good books. He prefers working for the *Reader* even if it pays for shit. But the reasons he likes it are forcing him out.

A half beat apart, his laptop dings and his phone buzzes, reminding him of his appointment. He's canceled three times. If he doesn't go today, he'll stop rescheduling. From the coffee shop, he can see the second-floor apartment where he's supposed to be. Three times he's watched the boy peek out to scan the street below, looking for the client who hasn't shown. Avi packs up his laptop and notes. He places his empty mug in the bus bin and crosses the street.

The buzzer for the second-floor apartment reads RADICAL EMPATHY STUDIO and under that NORRIS/GRAY. It squawks when Avi presses it, and the approximation of a voice shouts at him, static and blur.

"Mizzer Hurts?" it says. *"Elbows you win."*

The lock clicks, and Avi lets himself in. The kid holds the door open at the top of the stairs. Avi needs to stop thinking of everyone younger than him as a kid. This one has a face made handsome by the feelings and thoughts that animate it. He must look bland in photos, but in person he radiates attention and kindness.

"I'm glad you finally made it, Mr. Hirsch," he says. "I'm Miquel. Come on in."

They enter a small living room, the walls floor-to-ceiling with shelves of books and records. It reminds Avi of his attic, which he hasn't been up to since the day he told Louis where to find Owen Curry. When he works from home, he sets up at the kitchen table. It's not as if there's anyone to bother him.

"The studio's back here," Miquel says. A curtain partitions the living room from a sitting room where two plush chairs sit facing. Miquel doesn't indicate one or the other. This show of equanimity bothers Avi for some reason. He takes the one facing the curtain, and Miquel takes the one facing the windows, which are slatted with blinds.

"So Mr. Hirsch," he says, pausing afterward.

"Avi," says Avi.

Miquel smiles. "Why are you here?"

Avi cocks an eyebrow. "Aren't you supposed to know?"

"I'd like to hear you tell me," Miquel says.

"Emotional healing, right?" Avi says. "That's what you're selling?"

"Are you wounded?"

Avi's hand falls to his knee, above where his leg was amputated. "Aren't you?" he asks.

"This time is for you," Miquel says. "You can fight if you

want. It's better than not showing up. Either way, you pay for the hour."

"I'm here because I'm wounded," Avi says after a pause.

Miquel leans forward, elbows on his knees. "What I'd like to do, if it's all right with you, is come into your head a little. It's called—"

"Reading," Avi says. "I've been read before."

Miquel nods. "What I do is a little different," he says. "I'm not a psychic. I can't read your thoughts. So don't worry about keeping secrets. I'm an empathic. Which means I'm reading your emotions, if that makes any sense."

"As much sense as anything else."

"Exactly," Miquel says. "It's easier to do if you let me in."

"So come in," says Avi. Miquel nods and closes his eyes.

Something opens up behind Avi's forehead. There is a feeling like warm water sluicing into his skull. His thoughts float on a rising tide, drifting and unconnected. He sees Emmeline's birth, blood and fluid, and then this screaming thing in the world, a raw red semicolon crying out for him and the urge to take the child from the nurse, wrench the baby from her hands even as she offers it to him, kiss the fury of its little face, but he's fumbling with a girl, not Kay, someone before her whose name is lost on the whitecap of a different wave, but her tongue is warm and wet in his mouth and her hand creeps down into his teenage disbelief that anyone will ever touch him, and the JLTV hits a bump, a pothole probably but part of him knows already it isn't as the vehicle lifts into the air and a metal panel slices Garcia in half but Kay is talking about class while he makes dinner, days they ate for survival rather than taste but she says *this is great* and has seconds, even comes home from class starving so she can wolf down whatever he cooks and the wine tastes coppery but everything is better with her and all of them at the big school say the same thing which is *go home, Avi, we did not ever need you and yet you are here go back to somewhere we do not care where but you are not were not were never the hero of this story and that you ever thought you were is making us sad now,* and Emmeline says, *I've got to go, Dad, I'll call you this weekend,* and Kay says nothing because she's a smooth wall with no handholds or grips and everyone else is polite and cold and the warm water feeling spirals down a tube, a path Owen Curry is carving through the inside of Avi's neck, and it drains away and Avi opens his eyes.

"You're okay," Miquel says. His hand is on Avi's knee, steadying. "I mean, you're not. You're kind of a mess. But you're here. You're in the studio. We're on North Avenue, and none of those things you were feeling are happening now."

"They're always happening," Avi says.

"That's true, too," Miquel says. "I'm sorry. I would have warned you, but that's not usually how it goes. Mostly, I read someone and it's passive. Everything in your head was knotted together. I gave a tug, and it all came loose."

"So put it all back," says Avi. "Put things back where they go."

"It doesn't work that way. Believe it or not, you're better off with it all rattling around. Things get lodged into place. We stop being able to see them. We can't take them out and examine them and put them into a better place."

"Then let's start reorganizing," Avi says, tapping his forehead.

"Our time is up for today," Miquel says.

"It's been two minutes."

"I've been in your head for an hour," Miquel says. "For clients it doesn't feel like much time has passed. Sometimes it doesn't feel like *any* time has passed. You were reexperiencing old emotions, moments you knew. This can register as all of them happening at the same time. But I was in there like a funnel, making sure they didn't come at you all at once. It's more than the mind can handle. Even the body isn't equipped for that kind of massive emotional aggregate."

Avi can feel the truth of this. He's bone-tired, the way he might feel hitting his bunk at the end of a long day on an embed.

"So what do I do now?" he asks.

"You come back," says Miquel. "You spend some time in your head. You pick up what's broken. And you come back."

The poet with the glow in his chest is off shift. The sun goes down over the buildings across the street. Avi stares at the half-finished piece for the *Reader*. He's had too much coffee and not enough to eat, which accentuates the feeling of a nest of sparking live wires in his head.

At the center of it, a still eye, sits a moment that feels to Avi like the last time things were right between him and Kay. It's the two of them sitting on the couch, reading comics. It's the one before he asked her to look at the footage from Salem Baptist, before this world and his marriage smashed into each other. Everything after that felt inevitable. That was the last time Avi feels like he could have stopped it all.

He wants to call Kay but instead decides to call Emmeline, to let no excuses from her keep them from talking, seriously talking. Better, he'll fly to New York, catch a red-eye, and surprise her with bagels before class in the morning. He's typing in a search for cheap tickets when something on the street catches his attention. A white van, unmarked, pulls up in front of the apartment across the street. Three men in dark blue suits load out. Avi recognizes the shade, the deep navy Homeland Security agents used to wear, back in their early days. They go to the door of Radical Empathy Studio. One faces the door. The others watch the street. Two let themselves in.

Avi gets up, knocks into his table, and spills coffee precariously near his laptop. He weaves through patrons and stands in the doorway, watching the entryway across the street. An agent comes out, then Miquel, then another agent. The van door slides open. Avi looks around to see if anyone else is seeing this, but no one registers it. The van door slams shut. One of the agents comes around the back and gets into the driver's seat. He pauses as he climbs in, seeing Avi watching him. He moves like he's about to come barreling across the street and throw Avi in the back of the van. Then he closes the door and pulls the van into traffic. Avi starts after the van, but it runs a red and turns down Western, off North Avenue, and back to the real world.

Avi's enough of a known quantity that people answer his questions. They know he's a baseliner, a Damp. Either they've Hivescanned him with no luck or they just know. Maybe there's a way to tell from how he talks, the way he stares as if each one of them is a god writ small. He's known in the neighborhood and known not to be a threat.

It only takes a mention of white vans to set people talking.

The disappearances have been happening for weeks, although many people he talks to won't call them disappearances. Some explain them away. "You build a community and it feels like it'll last forever, and it doesn't," one of the older folks told him. "People leave." But Avi's watched the girl who goes in and out of the apartment across from the coffee shop. He can't bring himself to talk to her, but he can see the shock on her face, even two days later. She's been left behind. With a breakup, part of you sees it coming or can do the postmortem and recognize signs. There's none of that in the girl's face. Miquel Gray didn't leave; he was taken. It follows that the other people who've disappeared were taken as well. Several stories involve white vans.

When nothing else comes together, Avi calls Louis. They haven't talked since Avi passed on the Hargrave story. Afterward, Avi understood it as an olive branch, one Louis needed to poke him in the eye with before making peace. He feels like a line is open between them. The risk is that he's wrong and Louis tells him, once and for all, to fuck off.

"What do you need, Avi?" Louis says when he picks up. His tone is flat, his office voice. It means there are limits on what can be said. People are listening. Avi presses on anyway.

"White vans on North Avenue," he says.

"A baby blue Dodge Dart on South Division," says Louis. "What the fuck are you talking about?"

"There've been disappearances," Avi says. "Going on for weeks. Witnesses keep seeing white vans at the scene."

"Any of these reported?"

"These people don't go to the police."

Louis pauses. "White vans mean nothing to me," he says. "Lake Shore Drive, half the traffic is white vans."

"I saw a kid get taken," Avi says. "The guys that took him looked like old-school Homeland."

"Not everybody in a blue suit works for me."

"Your guys aren't cherry-picking Resonant kids off North Avenue?" Avi asks.

There's the pause again. It's not a complete tell: Louis clears his throat when he's lying. A pause means he isn't sure. A sign of doubt, a crack. "I'd know if we were," he says, trying to sound confident. Doubt creeps back in. "This kid have a name?"

"Miquel Gray," says Avi. "Address is 413 North Avenue. Upstairs apartment."

"I'll see what I can find," says Louis. "But from what you're talking, if someone was going to authorize this, it'd be me."

"And you didn't," Avi says. He phrases it as if it's something he already knows rather than a question.

"I've never been that guy," says Louis. "Even over there, when there were plenty of those guys, that wasn't me."

Setting an empty glass on the coffee table, Avi looks balefully at the stairs, considering whether the comforts of his bed outweigh the discomfort of the trek up. He hasn't gotten over how much easier it is to be single, how much less adult you have to be. The sink is full of dishes, the living room is strewn with laundry, and there's no one to call him out on it.

He's resolved to go up when the doorbell rings. He hoists himself off the couch and considers going up to the attic to get the pistol in his desk drawer. By the time he got up there and back, whoever's at the door would have broken in or gone away. He peers through the peephole. Louis's face is distended by the fish-eye lens.

Avi ushers him into the living room and pours him a whiskey without asking. "I'm not here," Louis says. "You understand that?" By the smell of him, he's already drunk. He takes a seat on the couch and stares into his glass. Avi stands over him.

"Two months ago, I was tasked with a viability study," Louis says. "Coordinating with police to create local-level internment camps. Chicago was top on the list of test sites because Chicago PD got away with something like this before. You know about Homan Square?"

"Interrogation site," Avi says, pulling the story up in his head. "It got busted by Spencer Ackerman at the *Guardian*."

"Look for a U.S. story that follows up with anything that isn't in the *Guardian* piece," says Louis. "They ran a black site prison for a decade, and all they got hit with was an article in the foreign press."

"It got closed down," says Avi.

Louis looks at Avi like he's said you can't get a girl

pregnant if you do it standing up.

"The determination I passed along to my bosses was that it could be done but obviously it shouldn't be done," he says. "You're talking preemptive arrest and detainment of citizens. At some point, you stop and say, *This is America and there are things we don't do.*"

Avi has seen the things America does. He gives Louis back the same look, eyebrow cocked at his naiveté. "Someone's doing it."

"Not in the system," Louis says. "But some of our guys are involved. Entirely off the books. Big funding from someone on the West Coast. I had to get the right guys the right kind of drunk to hear about it. Some of the younger guys think we're already at war."

"What do you think?"

"This is America," says Louis. "There are things we don't do."

"Where's the site?" Avi asks.

"I don't know," Louis says. "One of my guys was about to tell me, but his friend clammed him up. My understanding is this has gone on for months. Our guys, local cops. Working with fringe militia. Hargrave's disciples. I couldn't get a sense of the scope. Maybe it's a dozen assholes reliving the glory days of Homan Square in their off hours. Some tech billionaire bankrolling them for kicks. But Avi, my guys are not unique. Any office, the guys are more or less the same. If they're doing it in Chicago, they'll do it everywhere."

He finishes his whiskey and gets up to leave. His hand

is on the door handle when he stops. "Your kid," he says, turning around. "Go get Emmeline and get her on a plane. In Europe they're not thinking like this. Get your kid out of this country."

BETWEEN THE BARS

The cops are as useless as Carrie expected but kinder. Chicago PD set up a Resonant liaison working out of the station house on California Avenue: Officer Kowalski, a portly Polish man with a walrus mustache. "My nephew's one of youse," he explains to Carrie as he fills out the missing persons report. "Speed. He tried to keep it hidden. Track star his freshman year. One race he took off in a blur, and that was the ball game. School stripped him of every medal. It's not fair what they do to youse for doing your best."

The officer's enlightened views aside, there are no follow-up calls from the police. No one comes to their apartment to look for clues or dust for prints or whatever they do in a situation like this. Cops don't come to North Avenue, not for anything good. Not to help. The residents of North Avenue have an unspoken policy of not calling the cops. There was an incident a year before. Some polo shirt–sporting U of C undergrad swore he'd been mugged by a gang of Resonants on North. It made the news, and Chicago's sizable angry white population descended on the neighborhood. The cops obliged by rolling through, banging on doors and soliciting alibis. It was a week before they figured out the kid hadn't been anywhere near North Avenue. He had paid his friends to rough him up so he could look the victim. Crowds and cops ebbed, but there were never any apologies given. Only the promotion of Officer Kowalski in the California Street station, with his Resonant nephew and accompanying sympathies.

Carrie imagines that kindly old Officer Kowalski will dispatch an investigative team to scour the apartment. Every day she sits in Miquel's studio, jumping at the buzzer to find one of Miquel's clients. She questions each, but none of them knows anything. They offer condolences, leave numbers to call when Miquel shows up. They assure her he will.

When she tells Waylon, he goes into paranoid mode. He hasn't talked with Bryce in three days, and he'd taken that as a sign they were breaking up. Carrie wishes Waylon had had a girlfriend before he came out or that he'd dated one boy before Bryce. All his newly outed anxieties collided with his first real relationship anxieties until he was convinced every argument was the end of the world. But Miquel and Bryce both dropping off the map holds deeper significance, and Waylon promises to put his people on it. He's not the fumbler he was at Bishop. He's becoming someone new, possibly dangerous. He's also told Jonathan that Carrie drinks for free, which she appreciates as much as any other help he might give. The fourth day Miquel's gone, Carrie's in Vibration, taking advantage of her open tab.

"Dead in here," she says to Jonathan as Friday evening turns into Friday night and a weekend-size crowd fails to arrive.

"Hayden's got their big show at the Biograph," he says, pushing a second whiskey across the bar. The light from his chest glints and plays in the ice cubes. Carrie and Miquel had tickets to see Hayden. Carrie couldn't bring herself to go alone. She hasn't talked to Hayden, hasn't told them Miquel's missing. "I don't know why they don't play shows here."

"They'd wreck the joint," Carrie says.

"Might as well. It's their joint," Jonathan says.

Down the bar, a woman in her sixties reads a news magazine. A glass of white wine hovers at her shoulder like an advisory angel. In the corner, a couple the age of Carrie's parents are on a first date. His eyes glow pale blue, and her fingers snake like vines around his wrist and forearm. Carrie sips her drink as their downstairs neighbor, who Miquel refers to as Thought Bubble, enters and comes up to the bar. The word *beer* flashes over his head like a pink neon sign, the letters in clumsy cursive. Thought Bubble is a beatific presence on the block, a holy idiot. Shackled with an ability that renders his thoughts legible, he's taught himself to be simple and honest at all times. He looks down the bar at Carrie. Above his head it reads *you look sad but also I want to have sex with you.* Carrie smiles sadly and shakes her head. Thought Bubble shrugs and returns his attention to his drink. Once again, the word *beer* strobes over his head.

On the television behind the bar, a reporter stands in front of a wall made of couches and planks and all manner of cast-off items. It looks like they've been fused together. There are no captions, but the chyron reads RESONANT STANDOFF IN REVERE, MASS. Carrie tries to pick something up from the reporter's body language but gets nothing. She returns her attention to her drink.

By nine, she's more drunk than she wanted to be. She resolves to go back to the California Avenue station house tomorrow. She won't let herself be charmed by Officer Kowalski's Polish accent, its echo of Chicagos gone. She will be the angry young girl the situation demands. She will cuff herself to a railing and will not be moved until questions are answered. Tomorrow she will be a better detective, a better girlfriend.

Leaning heavily on the bar, her hands supporting her head, Carrie goes into the Hive. She knows Miquel isn't there. She's checked every day. She stands in the shimmering space of the Hive. People flit by her like ghosts. Black roses wreathe her feet. Carrie screams as loudly as she can, *I'm coming for you.* Ghosts stop and regard her before moving along. When she comes back to the bar, all the patrons look at her, sad-eyed, understanding. How much did she communicate? What did she send? She thinks about her scream packed with metadata, carrying an encoded story of the last few days.

A man walks into the bar. It takes Carrie a moment to recognize him. She met him only once, years ago in the hallway at Bishop. But his name's been at the front of her brain the last few days. It was the last name written in Miquel's appointment book before he disappeared. *Avi Hirsch.* No contact number. As he steps to the bar, Jonathan stands up straight, setting his shoulders back to look larger.

"I'm sorry, man," he says. "We're a Resonants-only establishment. I know that sounds harsh, but some of our customers—"

"I need to be here," Avi says. There's a nervous energy coming off him. He looks around the room like he's being chased.

"It's okay, Jon," Carrie says. "I know him."

"That's great, Care Bear," says Jonathan. He has annoying nicknames for everyone in their circle: All the Waylon. Miquel Mouse. Roll in the Hayden. "But I mean, is he your guest?"

"Sure," she says. Jonathan relents. Carrie moves to the stool next to Avi. As she does, she sees the word floating over Thought Bubble's head in crimson: *Damp*.

"You shouldn't be here," Avi says. "You have to leave."

"That's a funny thing for you to say," says Carrie. Avi stops, sits up straight, and looks at her as if he's seeing her for the first time.

"You went to school with my daughter, Emmeline," he says. "I didn't recognize you. You're all grown up."

"You met with my boyfriend the other day," Carrie says. "Miquel Gray. You went to him for—"

"I want to talk to you about it," Avi says. "But it's a bad time right now. How about I stop by and see you tomorrow? We could meet for coffee."

Carrie stares into his eyes. They're rimmed with red, his pupils huge. "Are you high right now?"

"No."

"You're on Rez," she says.

"It's for work," says Avi. "We can talk about it some other time."

"How about we talk about it now?" Carrie says.

"You don't understand," Avi says. "It's important that you not be here right now."

A wineglass shatters. The woman reading her magazine looks dumbly at the shards on the ground. Thought Bubble turns toward the sound, and above his head the word *crash* flashes for a second and fizzles out. Carrie hears a low rumble build into a buzz. It feels like an electric toothbrush scrubbing the inside of her skull. Jonathan gives a pained gasp. He clutches his chest like he's having a heart attack. The light there goes dark.

The next sound is a boot against the heavy wooden back door, the splintering rip as it tears off its hinges.

In the back of the van, under the green lights, Carrie holds Jonathan's head in her lap. His breathing is labored, and his eyes are squeezed shut. Carrie tries not to look at his chest. His shirt dips into the spot where the light had been, a sinkhole. The couple on the date hug each other. He blubbers, and she tries to comfort him. Carrie wonders what will happen to them after this, whether this is the kind of experience that brings a new couple together or destroys them. Avi is calmer than he was in the bar. He's taking everything in, observing.

"You knew," she says.

"I need to see where they take you," Avi says, not looking at her. "I can't confirm anything until I see it."

"Are you a fucking idiot?" Carrie says. "You need to tell them you're a baseliner so they'll let you out and you can get us help."

"I will," Avi says. "I just need to see it."

After a twenty-minute drive, they're loaded out at a warehouse off the 290. Carrie sees the lights of the United Center off to the east, which puts them halfway to Cicero. There are more men dressed like the ones who took them: dark blue suits, carrying devices that look like leaf blowers but emit that horrible buzz that apparently shuts down their abilities. The van was equipped with devices in each corner that did the same thing. They looked like the lighting rigs on the Vibration dance floor. On the sidewalk, there are times Carrie can't hear the buzzing. The leaf blowers must send the sound in a stream. Sometimes she's on the edge of it. She tries to slip down into invisibility, but it doesn't work. It's like picking up a fork with numb fingers. Jonathan is nodding off.

"Help me with him," she whispers to Thought Bubble. He wraps his arm around Jonathan as they're herded into a warehouse under a flood of green lights.

"What the fuck, Maxwell?" says one of the blue suits, standing by a heavy metal door. "I thought this was supposed to be a fucking bumper crop."

"Big grab's the raid on the Biograph, Smithson," says Maxwell, the one who threw Carrie onto the floor of the bar and clipped plastic restraints around her wrists. "That tranny singer's got a show."

"That's gonna burn us for big raids," Smithson says.

"Back to snatch and grabs. We should throw a net over the whole block and drag it."

"We should plow through with ordnance, then go out for beers," says Maxwell. He shoves the couple on the date in front of Smithson like he's a justice of the peace at a shotgun wedding. Smithson looks through them, blank and mechanical.

"When you step through this door," he says, "your abilities will temporarily return. Someone will be standing behind you. If you attempt to use your abilities in any way, he will shoot you in the head. Do you understand?"

"Oh, God," wails the man.

"Say you understand," Smithson shouts.

The woman pulls him closer. Her wrists are zip-tied in front of her. She holds him in the sealed circle of her arms. "We understand," she says. Smithson opens the door and pushes them in, closing it behind them. He turns his attention to Carrie and Avi. "When you step through this door, your abilities will temporarily return," he says. "Someone will be standing behind you. If you attempt to use your abilities in any way, he will shoot you in the head. Do you understand?"

"We understand," Carrie says. Smithson opens the door, and they step through into a small, dark hallway. There are no green lights here, and she can feel her ability, her Resonance, return like a sleeping limb waking. Doug Shaw, Downer Doug, who worked in the office at Bishop, who's been one of Miquel's clients for months, sits on a stool at the end of the hall. His face is bruised, his right eye black. He looks at Carrie as if he's trying to apologize. There's a man standing behind her, gun drawn. Doug pulls her down into the Hive. His Hivebody looks worse than his actual one, skin and bones, black roses climbing his calves like kudzu, rooting him to the ground. He says, "He's inside. He's okay. I'm sorry," before letting her back into the dark hall. He turns his eyes to Avi, then closes them. They shoot open in panic.

"He's not one!" Doug shrieks. "He's not one!"

The armed man is on Avi in a second. He sweeps Avi's cane out with his foot and knocks him to his knees. Avi yelps in pain as he smacks the floor. Green lights click on, flooding the room. The door behind them opens, and Smithson shoves Carrie against the wall, holding her by the base of her neck. Maxwell and two more enter, guns drawn and pointed at Avi's head.

"What the fuck are you doing here?" Maxwell says. "Who the fuck are you?"

"My name is Avi Hirsch," he says. "I'm a reporter. Call Louis Hoffman; he knows me."

"Did I not fucking tell you not to tell Hoffman?" Maxwell yells at Smithson.

"Fucking shoot him," says another in what is unmistakably a Chicago PD uniform.

"Call Louis," Avi says.

"Get him the fuck out of here," Maxwell says. "Drop him in the United Center parking lot with bus fare."

"We're letting him go?"

"I got into this to save human lives," Maxwell says. "I'm not going to shoot him in the head. Blindfold him, drive him out, and drop him somewhere. He doesn't know shit. Get him out."

"I'm sorry," Avi says to Carrie. "I'll get you out. I'll get you help."

"Like fuck you will," Smithson says as he drags Avi back out the front door, leaving his cane in the hallway. Maxwell opens the door behind Downer Doug and leads Carrie inside. *Here's the limit of allies,* she thinks. *This is where helpful people get you.*

She wanders the large open space. The people all look sickly, bathed in green light. *Prisoners,* thinks Carrie. *Not people.* She starts to see people she knows. The black kid who sells mix CDs for five bucks on North and Oakley. Janet, who did a pop-up gallery show in the old barbershop on North and Artesian. Benny the See-Through Drunk, who's a regular and translucent customer at Vibration. Miquel tried to tell Carrie about the value of a neighborhood. Child of the suburbs that she was, Carrie never felt it. Until now, with this network of connections lifted out of context and placed onto a stark backdrop. *Next time anyone asks where I'm from, I'll say North Avenue,* she thinks. She wonders if she'll get a chance.

She finds Miquel sitting next to a cot in a makeshift triage area. He looks haggard, with an irregular splay of dark stubble spotting his cheeks and blue bags under his eyes. He's the most beautiful thing in this ugly, horrible place, and she can see he's cracking under the weight of it. She runs to him, grabs him, thinking she needs to support him and then that she needs him to hold her together. Arms around each other, she waits to feel some kind of strength return, but it doesn't come. There's only a fear that isn't lessened by being shared.

After a few minutes of holding him and being held, Carrie sees who he's sitting vigil by. Bryce lies in the bed. His bark is drying out, curling and peeling away. Carrie thinks about Jonathan clutching his chest cavity under the lights.

"I said we need a doctor, and they told me they'd send a lumberjack," says Miquel. "I think he's dying, but I don't know how to tell."

Carrie puts her hand on Bryce's chest, comforted that it rises and falls. When she pulls it away, a papery piece of bark clings to her palm like a Post-it note. "Have you slept?" she asks Miquel.

He shakes his head. "They keep the lights on. The buzzing makes it hard to sleep. It's strange not to know what people are feeling. Everyone is a mystery."

Miquel leans close to her. He examines her face in the green light, trying to suss out what she's thinking. It's like watching someone listen to a language he doesn't understand. "How are *you*?"

BARRICADE

On the car stereo, Leonard Cohen croons like molasses poured over broken glass. In the back seat, Bishop's breathing rattles, a moth battering its wings in a cigar box. Kimani's off with Patrick, chasing ghosts, so they're traveling the long way. The normal way. Fahima leans against the passenger side and watches Alyssa drive, sunglasses on, unfazed by the Technicolor vividness of spring in Massachusetts. Alyssa grew up normal. She knows how to do shit like this. People don't get how amazing normal is if you grow up without it. Driving lessons and proms and failed attempts at heterosexuality. Fast food and family car trips and Sunday school. Trappings of the dream of white suburban America, the kind of shit you see on television.

Even if Fahima's life hadn't jumped the tracks, she would have grown up other. She'd watch from the intersection of Immigrant and Muslim while blond girls rode by on bikes with streamers that bloomed from the handles, hair billowy in their wakes while Fahima's curls stayed secret under wraps. After years in Lakeview, she skipped the normal world for Bishop, exchanging one asylum for another. She hadn't emerged until she was fully formed. The carapace crust of a twenty-year-old. Striding into her first class at MIT ready to swing at the first person who asked to touch her hijab. Normality was a thing to combat, take down. When Fahima saw Alyssa at a party, picture of an all-American girl, she saw a target. Fahima drew a bead on her, hiding in the corner like a sniper, sipping lukewarm soda out of a plastic cup while Alyssa floated around the room.

Fahima felt powerless in the face of this normality. She felt second place to it, a shadow of the thing itself. In the end, swagger went only so far. Alyssa had to make the first move. Always the driver.

"He should be in a hospital," Alyssa says for the seventeenth time. Her eyes stray off the road to check Bishop in the rearview, and Fahima tenses up.

"How can you look at anything other than where we're going and not drive us right off a cliff?" she says. What she thinks is, *My girl's got superpowers.*

"That is the sound of one lung breathing," Alyssa says. There's a note of pedantry and annoyance in her voice that's been more and more present in their conversations about Bishop. Fahima notices but doesn't have time to fix it. Too busy fixing everything else. "His insides are more cancer than organs. Not the ideal situation for a road trip."

"I'll wake him up, and you can talk him out of this," says Fahima. Alyssa goes on about metastatic spread and renal function, but Fahima thinks about Patrick that night outside Bishop's house in Maine. Her realization that he might be a mass of undifferentiated cells, the possibility that all of them resonated. What if instead of using his ability to fight the cancer, a losing battle, Bishop allied himself with it? It's impossible. But what about them isn't? Could he force the cancer to resonate? And if he could, would it save him?

"Are you even listening?" Alyssa asks.

"Dyspnea. Dysphagia," Fahima says. "Catastrophic hemorrhage." She plucks words she's caught in Alyssa's monologue or read in the literature. Alyssa knows but doesn't bother to call Fahima on it. They hit a pothole, and the glass vials resting in her lap tinkle musically in their steel case. Alyssa glances down at it.

"What is that stuff you're giving him?" she asks. "And please remember, I am a doctor and you are a sexy machine genius who is not a doctor."

"They're sexy genius machines," Fahima says. "Tiny, tiny ones."

"What are your tiny sexy genius machines doing to him?"

"They'll keep him alive," Fahima says.

"How long?"

A week, thinks Fahima. *Tops.*

"As long as he needs them to."

They're out of Connecticut when Bishop pings her from the Hive. Communicating there is easier for him than speaking, at least without a recent dose. The tiny sexy genius machines amplify Bishop's Resonance, but they burn out after a few hours, like lightbulb filaments running too hot.

"I'm going to space out for a minute," Fahima tells Alyssa.

"Where are we on the map?" Alyssa asks.

"We stay on 84 another half hour," says Fahima.

"Go talk to him."

Fahima rests her head against the window and goes into the Hive. Bishop is waiting for her, sitting full lotus in a field peppered with black flowers. In the real world, he couldn't contort his legs this way without screaming pain. His Hivebody is younger, fully fleshed. Seeing him like this highlights how thin he looks, tossed in the back seat like a bag of sticks. His fingers trace the petals of one of the flowers.

"These shouldn't be here," he says. "They're like needles poking through the skin of the world." He looks up at her, face cherubic with subcutaneous fat and an acceptance of oncoming death. "Have these always been here?"

Fahima bends over and tries to pluck one by her feet. It's rooted to the ground. It's so cold her fingertips stick to it and pull away hard. There are tiny circles on her fingers where she touched the thing, angry mouths on index, middle, and thumb.

"I never liked it here," she says. "I only come here to talk to you."

"We worked very hard on it, you know," he says. "Like God separating the land and the water. Poor Raymond and I spent years creating this place between the actual and potential. I used to love it here."

The way he skirts around the edges of his biography grates on Fahima no end. But this isn't the time to dig deeper. That time isn't ever coming.

"We should be in Revere in an hour or two," Fahima says. "Alyssa's a good driver."

"She's nice," says Bishop. "Listening to the two of you reminds me I should have found someone. Then I realize the fact it's an afterthought for me, like *I should have tried the salmon*, is the reason I never did. I had everyone." He taps his forehead. "I never felt the need." When Bishop talks about his abilities in interviews or public speeches, he tells people he's telepathic and telekinetic. One night, after an ill-advised third martini, he told Fahima it would be closer to the truth to say he was omnipathic. "Everyone all the time," he said. Fahima wonders what it's like for him to be without his abilities. It must be like losing one of your five senses and access to the Internet at the same time.

"Do you need another shot?" she asks.

"Not till we get there," Bishop says, flicking the flower with his fingernail. It makes a sound like a crystal goblet.

"You know I don't think this is a good idea," Fahima says. "I'm not sure your being there is going to make any difference."

"I'm sure that it won't," he says. "Not to them. But it will make all the difference in the world to me. Going out on my feet. You get near the end, and everything takes on impossible weight. Mistakes. Miscalculations. As it approaches, the manner of death becomes important. I've known this moment was coming. Not my moment. Ours. I imagined it would be at the academy. I saw them coming to our doorstep. I saw myself standing arms akimbo, all of you behind me. Bold and strong. I saw the people of New York rising up against the forces of oppression, crying out

462

in support of us. Until those forces grew so small, they were pressed down like coal into diamond. They would collapse, burst, and shine. The birth of a new world and me there to midwife it.

"And now we're off to Revere, Massachusetts, the new world already stirring in its crib. The moment is a tricky fucker."

FACTION

The town of Revere changed as much as it was willing to before the residents—which is to say white people who grumbled as the blocks between Furness and Dedham became Koreatown and the neighborhood along Mountain Avenue became Little Tripoli—had enough. When Ji Yeon Kim, whose parents had bought the ranch-style on Dedham last summer, decided to flaunt her special powers, producing bright glowing needles as long as baseball bats from her hands and dancing them across the Revere High cafeteria, the town board met with the sheriff. The Kims weren't invited to the meeting. All present agreed it would be best for the Kims to move on, and the sheriff was sent to relay the message.

Only they didn't move on. Ji Yeon Kim kept coming to school as if nothing had happened, intent on finishing her senior year. Tae Sung and Min Jin Kim both showed up at their jobs and smiled like they weren't the parents of a freak. After a week of this, the sheriff got a couple guys together in their off hours and headed over to Dedham Avenue to restate the town's position.

They didn't make it to the ranch-style on Dedham. Little Korea had barricaded itself off. Two blocks from the Kims' house, Furness Street was obstructed with couches and picnic benches and dinghies that hadn't been seaworthy for summers. The residents of Little Korea, along with those of Little Aleppo and Little Tripoli and others of Revere's ethnic microenclaves, stood by the ramshackle barricade and said no. *They are with us, and you will not take them.*

Soon they were joined by strangers. Strangers who glowed and flew. Out-of-towners with feathers and scales. The future landed in the middle of Revere, Massachusetts.

The resolution was easy to see. When the past and future run up against each other, the past is supposed to back down. If it doesn't, things get bloody. But the past is stubborn and stupid. The town board called the governor for assistance. While a flurry of ACLU lawyers, with Kay Washington in the lead, rushed to the courthouse in Boston, the governor called in the Guard. To de-escalate the situation, he said.

Because nothing de-escalates a situation like sending in tanks.

Alyssa drives around the perimeter of the National Guard cordon, and they get to see what the town's become. No one on the sidewalks. Shops shuttered. Most of the vehicles on the streets are army jeeps or news vans. Trying to run the Kims out of town, the citizens of Revere evicted themselves from their own homes, displaced by national attention and the forces they summoned for protection.

They pull into the parking lot of a motel in Saugus, twenty

miles north of Revere. Fahima gently shakes Bishop awake. "We're here."

His rheumy eyes take in the pastel-painted stucco of the buildings, the cracked gray asphalt of the parking lot.

"Looks as good as anywhere else," he says.

Fahima gives him another shot, then she and Alyssa help him out of the car. Sexy genius machines take a while to kick in. Thankfully, they're only headed to the first floor. Their connection, a teleporter who doesn't look old enough to shave, is playing video games among fast-food wrappers and discarded balls of Kleenex Fahima wills herself not to think about. The shades are drawn, and the room has a thick fug that reminds her of where they found Owen Curry holed up. The boy, in a Sox tee shirt and oversized shorts, gives a nod, then stands bolt upright when he recognizes Bishop. Fahima half expects him to bow.

"No one told me you were coming," the boy says.

"We didn't want to make a fuss," Bishop says. The boy is already making frenzied attempts to tidy the room. Fahima feels Bishop reach out to the boy's mind to calm it, and she's angry with him for expending any of his ability. He has nothing to spare.

"How does this work?" Alyssa asks.

"Take my hand," says the boy. "Clench your stomach like you're about to take a punch. There's a good chance you'll puke."

"Super," Alyssa says.

"You go first," Fahima tells her. It's so she'll be there to catch Bishop when he comes through. Alyssa holds the boy's hand, then blips out, gone. "Okay, old man," says Fahima. "You're next."

Bishop passes Fahima his cane and takes the boy's hand in both of his.

"Were you one of my students?" he asks.

"No, sir," says the boy. "My parents said no. I wanted to."

"There's still time," Bishop says. He smiles at the boy and disappears.

Fahima tucks the cane under her arm, and the boy extends his hand. "You want to tell me what that hand's been up to?" she says. The boy blushes and looks at his bare feet. "Hey," Fahima says, knocking him on the shoulder. "You need anything here?"

"They keep me fed and shit," he says. "It's lonely. All my friends are on the other side, and I've got to stay here."

"They also serve who stand and wait," says Fahima, quoting from something she barely remembers. She grabs the boy's hand, and the motel room blinks out. She's in a living room indistinguishable from the one in the house where she grew up. The acquisitional clutter, the protective accumulation of random objects as ballast, marks the home of an immigrant family desperate to anchor itself to its new country with the weight of *things*. Alyssa supports Bishop, although she looks shaky herself.

"Clenching your stomach does nothing," she says.

"That's why we got the bucket," says a young woman in the doorway to the kitchen. She's tiny, her dark hair cut with a dull razor, wearing a faded *Aladdin Sane* tour shirt long enough to function as a dress. Her arms are sleeved in blue and green ink, and she chews on a toothpick that glows like a purple ember. A trio of teenagers stand in wait behind her, eyeing them warily. They look like a band prepped to shoot their album cover. *This is what the revolution looks like*, Fahima thinks only half ironically.

"You're the ones from the school?" says the razor cut.

Bishop steps forward like he's greeting alien life on behalf of Planet Earth. "I'm Kevin Bishop," he says, taking his cane from Fahima and extending his hand. "From the Bishop Academy. And this is—"

"Ji Yeon Kim. From Dedham Street," she says, ignoring the proffered hand. "I'm the one all the fuss is about."

"It's nice to meet you, Miss Kim," Bishop says. "Are your parents here?"

Ji Yeon throws back her head and laughs in quick, bright barks. The glowing toothpick hangs precariously from her bottom lip. "No, officer, my parents are not here," she says when she recovers. "I sent them to Boston to stay with my aunt and uncle. They're safe." She cocks her head toward the couple to her left. "This is Adnan and Yana, they live on Furness. Hassan just got here. He found us through the Hive."

"Hey," says Hassan.

"I don't know what they told you or what you read," says Ji Yeon, "but we're not looking for Martin Luther King. The time for speeches passed when the tanks pulled up."

"I'm not here to take the lead," Bishop says. "I'm here to help. What do you need?"

Ji Yeon sizes him up, then shrugs. "National Guard gummed up the sewers, and it's been raining the past four days," she says. "Can you dig a drainage ditch?"

Fahima shakes her head at him.

"If you have shovels," says Bishop.

"I'm a doctor," Alyssa says. "Is there anything I can do?"

"Know anything about Resonant biology?" asks Ji Yeon.

"She knows a thing or two," Fahima says, smirking. Alyssa swats her on the arm.

"We've got triage over on Mountain Avenue," Ji Yeon says. "There's a boy came down from the Commune to help out and got some kind of infection. But he's basically a lizard person, and no one knows what to give him."

"I'll take a look," Alyssa says.

"Adnan, you want to take her over there?" Ji Yeon says. The oldest boy in the group steps forward and offers his arm like he's taking Alyssa to the prom. She wiggles her eyebrows at Fahima as they leave.

Fahima could invent them a rain collector that would produce potable water or a way to shunt runoff into the ocean. She could walk around their camp and find a hundred problems to solve. Or she could grab a shovel.

"Come on," she says to Bishop. "Let's get digging."

Fahima never gave much thought to the phrase *in the trenches* until she spent her first day digging one. Hours ankle deep in mud and clay make her think the entire world is nothing but mud and clay. She feels like she'll never be clean again. Mud forms a subdermal layer; dirt that appears on the skin hasn't accumulated from outside but seeped out like sweat.

Bishop is having a ball. The tiny sexy genius machines amplify his Resonance enough that he can hold back the cancer with telekinesis left over to help his frail body hoist a shovel. They're teamed with Hassan, a geopath who sweeps dirt up the embankments with waves of his hand.

"Home I would wander off," Hassan says. "You're from Lebanon?" he asks Fahima.

"Buffalo," Fahima says.

Hassan nods. He taps his chest.

"Morocco," he says. He's bright and chatty. His cheer shines through the layers of mud like a jewel half buried in earth. "Fez is massive, but we lived on the outskirts. You can walk a mile into Moulay Yacoub prefecture and you're in a desert, like a movie. I would shape turrets three stories high. I would conduct whirlwinds of dirt and sand. Hidden and alone, I was a god."

"Did your parents know?" Bishop asks.

"Everyone in the quarter knew," says Hassan. "It made no difference to them. I was the same boy they'd always known."

"If only it was always so simple," Bishop says.

"Americans have not enough things to worry about," he says. "How do they have time to fear something new? How do they have fear to spare?"

When their crew goes on a break, another takes over, a dozen young people, bending and rising in rhythm like worshippers at a mosque. Fahima catches a bit of melody, a pop song from a couple summers ago broadcast into her head, barely audible. She spots Lynette Helms in the group. Lynette looks like she's grown a half foot since she left Bishop, most of which is a matter of standing up straight rather than stooping to avoid being seen. None of these people know her brother. She's flourished outside of his shadow.

Bishop points at a young woman near the barricade. She spits in her hands, silvery goop she molds into balls and uses to plug chinks in the wall.

"She was one of ours, wasn't she?" he asks. He's losing days and months as his ever-burning Resonance scorches the neighboring parts of his brain. As it happens, he becomes younger, more childlike, and physically lighter, as if he's equal parts memory and flesh, both burning away.

"Isidra Gonzalez," Fahima says. "She did the fountain sculpture in the lobby. The fish things or whatever."

Bishop nods and starts over to her. "Miss Gonzalez," he says. Isidra turns around. When she sees Bishop, she stands at attention.

"Headmaster Bishop," she says.

"Kevin is fine," he says. "I was hoping you could help me with something."

"Of course," says Isidra. "Anything." Fahima is glad Bishop won't outlive his students' reverence for him. He'll die a saint.

"You're a shaper, yes? A sculptor?" he asks. "If I gave you a piece of something, a lump, could you turn it into something better? Something beautiful?"

"Beautiful could be tough," she says with a self-deprecating grin, "but I could try."

"That's all I ask," Bishop says. He hunkers down on a patch of dead grass between sidewalk and street. He lays his hands flat on the ground. The tendons in his neck strain. A trickle of pink liquid runs from his nose, a mix of blood and something else, something unique to him. Fahima has an urge to reach out and wipe it away, a sample to analyze. The ground beneath his hands swells up like a bubble forming. A white milky substance seeps upward in thin tendrils that knit together to form a web, then a solid. It's the size of a fire hydrant, the color of ivory with a shimmer that reminds Fahima of the Hive.

Bishop steps back and points at it. "Go ahead."

Isidra puts her hand on the lump and pulls it back, smiling idiotically. "What is that?" she asks. "It feels amazing."

"It is amazing," Bishop says. "But unsightly. Make it look as beautiful as it feels."

Isidra puts her hand back on the lump. She smiles as if a crowd's applauding for her. The lump shifts, becomes fluid again. It draws upward into two points, like horns. The one on the left is slightly longer and thicker, and the asymmetry has an elegance Fahima likes. She wants to scrape off a piece, put it in a jar along with whatever runs out of Bishop's nose, and retreat to her lab.

"How's that?" Isidra asks.

"That's excellent, Ms. Gonzalez," Bishop says. "It's exactly what I wanted."

She puts her hands in her pockets and smiles. She's straining not to touch the thing again.

"What is that stuff?" Fahima asks as she and Bishop walk away.

"That's what the Source looks like when you force it into

the real world. It's a signal booster. It'll make everyone here stronger. Better."

"I didn't know you could do that."

"There's a lot about me you don't know," Bishop says. He lowers his little round glasses and winks at her like he's thirty years younger and not dying. Then he returns to his ditch.

Fahima goes back to the house where they first arrived and finds Ji Yeon filling out requisition orders for more food.

"Hey, can I ask you something that might be insulting?" Fahima says.

"Yeah, shoot," says Ji Yeon without looking up.

"How much of what's happened here was intentional? How much of this did you plan for?"

Ji Yeon looks at her like she's an utter idiot.

"All of it."

She hands off the forms to one of the other kids, who runs them off to wherever they need to go.

"I mean, the National Guard was an unexpected bonus," says Ji Yeon, "but everything else. Look, you're like forty, right?"

"I'm thirty-two," Fahima says.

Ji Yeon waves this away as if the numbers are equivalent. "Who's your Rosa Parks?"

"What?"

"You grew up with the Rosa Parks who was a tired old lady who wanted to sit down, right? Only that wasn't her. Rosa Parks was a trained activist. She made a calculated decision that day."

"And that's you?"

Ji Yeon shrugs as someone hands her another clipboard.

"I don't want to tell you how to run things," Fahima says.

"Yes, you do," says Ji Yeon. "You're dying to. Go on, try."

Fahima is struck silent for a minute. She's used to dealing with teenagers she has structural authority over.

"There are better ways to put Bishop to use," Fahima says. "I know you're struggling to keep the pantry full. If you put him in front of the camera—"

"Then the whole thing is about him," Ji Yeon says. "Everything we've done gets folded into his message."

"It's not a bad message," says Fahima.

"Love thy neighbor and forgive thine enemies?" Ji Yeon says. "My parents brought me up Baptist. I got enough of that bullshit to last me a lifetime."

"There's more to him than that."

"I know the whole thing," says Ji Yeon. "They came to our house and did the sales pitch. He's like the original, right? The first Resonant? Doesn't mean shit to me. All it means is he had half a century or whatever to make a change and he only got us this far."

"How far do you think we should go?" Fahima asks.

"Stars, kid," Ji Yeon says. "We should be in the stars."

After their third day, Fahima walks the streets. Her arms hang off her shoulders like dead weight. The streets are empty, and the streetlights are out. The Guard cut the electricity a week ago. Fahima told Ji Yeon she could build converters so some of the energy users could power the enclave's whole grid, but Ji Yeon said it wasn't a priority. They had clusters of generators at the makeshift hospital and at a couple houses that served as hostels and charging stations. The moon is full and gives great light when the clouds aren't blocking it. Fahima walks the perimeter, along the edge of the barricade. A young man weaves two-by-fours into the structure. The beams are as pliant as cooked pasta in his hands. They corkscrew into holes in the barricade. Through the gaps, Fahima sees the National Guard's klieg lights, the movements of soldiers, the dark metal skin of tanks.

After dark, committees move into living rooms to discuss media strategy, rations, governance. Every front door is open. Fahima can walk in, join any assembly. Each meeting begins by selecting a facilitator. They have no stable heads. No leaders. Alyssa is on the medical committee, which regularly interfaces with the supply acquisition committee. People are pouring in, outpacing supplies, not to mention space. The facilities committee talks about the need to take another block, as if saying it will push the Guard out of Hill Park, giving them the school and the green. Fahima has drawn up plans for solar generators and sewage purification units. The necessary parts go on a list below more immediate needs. Toilet paper and antibiotics. Tampons and soap.

Yesterday Alyssa asked Fahima flat out what the endgame was here. Fahima didn't have an answer to give her. There's a value to being here for the sake of being here. It's intuitive, something she can't put a name to, and the fact that Alyssa doesn't feel it highlights the space between them, the differential in how much skin each has in the game. Alyssa wants to know what they're fighting for. Fahima is coming to understand that fighting is a continued condition of her existence. There may not be an endgame, only another battle and another after that.

Walking down Essex, Fahima hears a familiar voice from one of the powwows and follows it in. Patrick sits cross-legged at the end of a coffee table. Teenagers group around him, dressed in black. She's seen most of them before, but the only one she recognizes by name is Ji Yeon, directly to his right, looking like a lieutenant to Patrick's general. Patrick glances up from the map of Revere spread out on the table.

"Have a seat," he says. "We're discussing tactics."

On the map, they've labeled crisis points in the wall. One of the boys, a flier, plots out locations of troop amassments. Ji Yeon has a list of resources, including weapons and those in the camp who are effectively weapons. It's a short list.

"What's your assessment?" Patrick asks her.

"We can continue to hold them off, but we can't attack."

Patrick nods. "What are our options from here?"

Ji Yeon pauses to think. "A full offensive is useless," she says. "Some of us could make covert runs across the barricade. Low-level sabotage. Targeted assassinations."

Patrick shakes his head. "First soldier turns up dead, they'll roll tanks over the whole camp. I like the idea of supply missions, though."

"We need more fighters," says Ji Yeon.

"Only if we want a fight," Patrick says. "It's better to have people and not need them than to need them and not have them. Can we ask public relations to send word through the Hive? A recruitment drive focused on people with offensive capability?" He looks at Fahima. "There are some students we could call in." Despite herself, Fahima nods.

The conversation peters out from there. Fahima can't tell if they're playing war games or seriously preparing to fight. Once he's had a last side conversation with Ji Yeon, Patrick and Fahima walk out together.

"What do you think of special ops?" he asks. "They call themselves the Black Rose Faction after the flowers in the Hive."

"That sounds very Nazi Germany," says Fahima.

"You have to give it to the Nazis on aesthetics," Patrick says. "They're the blueprint for a century of evil names and uniforms."

"Your kids don't have uniforms yet?"

He chuckles. "They're not my kids. They organized themselves before I got here. Bishop called me in as an adviser. It's all a little above my pay grade. I'm a gym teacher, not a general."

"You seemed like you were holding your own," says Fahima.

"I'll slow them down," Patrick says. "Maybe keep them from getting killed. For a while."

"At some point do we let it happen?" she asks. "If the kids want to fight?"

Patrick shakes his head. "Bishop worked his whole life to keep them safe. I'd like to at least stave off a war until he's gone."

"He told you?"

"He gave me a sense," Patrick says.

"We're talking in terms of days," Fahima says. "I worry about what comes afterward. If we rise up, what does that make us?"

"Dead, most likely," says Patrick.

"Even if we win," Fahima says. "Do we put *them* in camps? Deport them? Don't we end up becoming what we fought?"

"Nothing says we have to," Patrick says. They're coming up on the intersection where Bishop and Isidra made the sculpture. Patrick's brow furrows, and he rubs at his temples.

"You okay?" Fahima asks.

"I've been getting headaches," he says.

"You look like shit," says Fahima. "Been on the road too long."

So have I, she thinks, but it's not entirely true. She has Alyssa here with her. Even if they're not sleeping in their own bed, there's a strength in carrying her home with her, a touchstone, a turtle's shell.

Patrick looks at the sculpture, an abstracted tuning fork in ivory.

"That's an odd thing," he says.

"You should touch it," says Fahima. "It's like having an orgasm and a great idea at the same time."

"That doesn't sound nearly as appealing as you think it does," he says. He recoils from it almost fussily.

Fahima shrugs. "Your loss." She raps her knuckles on the sculpture, and it rings quietly like a struck gong. She lays her palm against it. Her mind floods with ideas that pass too quickly to register. A parade of impossible inventions. Medical scanner, universal translator, Dyson sphere. Along with the ideas there's a feeling. The sense of being warm and protected, threaded through with the knowledge that it's soon to be taken away.

Fahima, Alyssa, and Bishop are housed on the near side of Cambridge Street with the Rhees, who have two kids away at college. Alyssa and Fahima share one room, and Bishop is in the other. Alyssa left a note saying she'd be at the triage unit till late. The Rhees are already asleep. Fahima hears the buzz saw of Tae Min Rhee's snoring as soon as she closes the front door. She goes to the basement to check on Bishop. His room belongs to the Rhees' daughter, who moved out at seventeen. The decor is an effort to abandon girlishness. Riot grrrl posters on pale pink walls, Sharpie drawings of flying V guitars, princess dolls bursting from behind the closet door. Bishop is propped up in a canopy bed under sheets the color of cotton candy. He's reading *Tripmaster Monkey*, plucked off a shelf where it sat with *The Second Sex*, *Rubyfruit Jungle*, and a full set of Pippi Longstocking books.

"How are you?" Fahima asks.

Bishop takes off his glasses and sets them on the nightstand. "I am in an incredible amount of pain," he says. "It feels earned. It's mine and no one else's."

Fahima ducks under the canopy and sits at the foot of the bed. "Patrick's here. I saw him a while ago."

Bishop nods. "We talked this morning."

"He has very different ideas about what's going on here," says Fahima.

"Good," Bishop says. "Maybe we've all had enough of my ideas for a while. It's nice feeling obsolete. No longer needed."

She pats his knee under the thick down comforter. "You're needed."

"Do you see what they've done here?" Bishop asks. "What these kids have built?"

"A hill to die on?"

"Maybe," he says. "There'd be a power in that, too. You shouldn't underestimate the metaphorical weight of dead children."

"Is that our strategy now?"

"I don't know what our strategy is," Bishop says. "Or if we have one. There're so few of us. If there's a war, we lose. We have no strength to bargain, so we lose the peace as well. Maybe what's best is to gather on a hill and fight for the sake of fighting."

Fahima laughs because she's been thinking the same thing. "You sound like a Greek myth."

"You sound old before your time," Bishop says. "Get some rest, Fahima. The rain's coming tomorrow."

The sun never shows, and rain batters the windows. Alyssa snuck into bed in the middle of the night, and Fahima lets her sleep. If they hurry, they can carve out the last stretch of ditch before the camp floods. Fahima checks the case of needles. Three left. Enough to get them through today. Tonight she'll insist that Bishop let them take him to a hospital. Or a hospice. Tomorrow these kids will continue on their own.

She knocks on his door, but no one answers. He must have woken up and taken something for the pain. Alyssa brought a grab bag of purloined narcotics. Oxycodone and Percocet. Vicodin and codeine. If Bishop dipped in, there's no chance of waking him. She tries the door, which turns out to be unlocked, and lets herself in.

She knows he's gone as soon as she enters the room. It's the way the air sits. Bishop's eyes stare blankly at the stucco ceiling. Fahima kneels down next to the bed, numb. She puts her hand on Bishop's cold forehead. She reaches back into her memory to find the dua for closing the eyes of the dead, words she learned from her mother before the concept of death held any meaning. Meaning came later, saturating the words and giving them weight, substance that outlasted the end of Fahima's faith. The ritual of words is a home, too, a place of returning.

"O Allah, forgive Kevin Bishop," she says. "And elevate his station among those who are guided, and be a successor to whom he has left behind, and forgive us and him, O Lord of the Worlds. Enlarge for him his grave and shed light upon him in it."

She slides her hand down, forcing his eyelids shut. They pull upward against her fingers as if there's more he wants to see.

FALL

Fahima assumes that the standoff is over when they open the barricade to let Kevin Bishop's body out. Magnetics and dendrics and lithics peel back each element they built into the wall, unweaving it. Isidra Gonzalez raises her hand and extracts threads of silvery liquid from the barricade. They float around her like streamers. The curtain draws back to reveal an audience of Guardsmen and news vans.

Patrick carries the body out. Fahima lifted it out of the deathbed herself. It's as light as balsa wood. Patrick's arms coil around it like a winding sheet, a cocoon of flesh from which Bishop might be reborn. In the ambulance, at the urging of paramedics, his arms unwind and give the body over.

"I'll go with him," Patrick says. Fahima has already converted the body to an object in her mind. Patrick sees Bishop in the skin and bones.

"You should stay," says Fahima. She looks around at the Guardsmen. They're unsure whether to move in, flood through the gap. "They'll need you."

"Make sure they don't," Patrick says. "I'll be back as soon as I can."

The ambulance eases between tactical vehicles and transports, bearing the body away. Fahima looks back across the hundred yards between her and the barricade. She expects hands forcing her down, the bite of zip cuffs on her wrists, but the moment holds. Slowly, alone, she crosses the mud and tire tracks until she's within the border the enclave has set for itself. Behind her, the barricade knits back together like the edges of a healing wound. A crowd is gathered. Fahima sees Ji Yeon and Hassan and Lynette. They're looking at her for answers. It's hard, even when you're young and rebellious, not to want a leader. It's hard to ward off the urge to be led.

"I'm going to take a shower," Fahima says, "then I'm going back to work."

Ji Yeon looks at her, then turns away. "You heard her," she shouts. It's not an order, but they take it as a directive, eager to be set back into motion.

On her way back, Fahima passes the statue. It's mottled with cavities like a rotting tooth, as if it's receding back to wherever Bishop pulled it from. When Fahima touches it, she feels nothing.

The Guard comes through the next morning, before dawn.

When the barricade goes down at the corner of Cambridge and Dedham, it's under the blade of a bulldozer rather than the tread of tanks. The press has been alerted. In the footage, the collapse looks like the sun rising minutes too early. The bulldozers plow through, flanked by sunlight. The tanks are out of the frame.

The Rhees' house is near the incursion. Shouting wakes Fahima but not Alyssa. Alyssa sleeps like the dead. It's her ability. Fahima dresses quickly in a tee shirt and sweats, wrapping her hijab clumsily into a knot under her chin. She bursts out the front door into a torrent of people rushing down Dedham, toward the break.

Behind the bulldozers come troops decked out for combat. They split into two groups. Half move down Cambridge, the other half down Dedham. Most carry rifles, but the frontline troops carry weapons that look like leaf blowers. It takes a moment for Fahima to recognize the bastardized versions of her design. She doesn't understand until she watches a Guardsman train the bulky thing on one of the camp's fliers and fire. She hears the familiar hum of the inhibitor, and he drops toward the sidewalk, flailing his arms and legs.

Standing in someone's front yard, Fahima turns her back to the bulldozers and soldiers. She waves her hands in the air. "Get back," she screams at the Resonants who rush forward to stop the incursion. She sees a boy trying to patch the barricade, pulling branches across from one ripped edge to the other like stitches. A Guardsman hits him with the inhibitor. The boy stares at his hands, confused. He flicks them at the wall ineffectually, as if he's trying to do a magic trick. A bullet pierces his chest, and he drops to the ground.

The shot turns shouts into screams. People scatter down side streets. Ji Yeon leads a group down Dedham toward the soldiers. Hassan creates a wave of dirt and debris in front of them. They want so badly to look like the small band of rebels who defeat a massive army, but they're children.

Fahima's head fills with a deafening noise, the sound of a thousand trumpets blaring inside her skull. Everyone hears it. Soldiers grip their ears, failing to understand that the sound is being fed directly into their brains. Ji Yeon's fighters, prepared for this but not immune, launch themselves at a knot of soldiers. They fight to disarm and disable, not to kill. Ji Yeon throws spears of light at the Guardsmen, aiming for pain points, shoulders, and legs. Guns are tossed away from their owners, brains already addled with the imaginary blare of trumpets are shut down, their owners crumpling like puppets with cut strings. *Even when they kill us, we don't become them*, Fahima thinks. *Even now, we are not the worst we could be.*

One of the soldiers looks around for the source of the sound. He spots Lynette Helms perched calmly on the eaves of a ranch house, not a hint of pain on her face. He levels his rifle and shoots her in the head. She slumps and spills onto the lawn. Dazed, relieved, units move in on Ji Yeon's group from all angles.

Fahima takes a deep breath. She braces herself against the ivory sculpture with one hand and drops into the Hive. Her body wavers, the beginning of a faint, even as her Hivebody manifests in midair, falling toward the ground, its opalescent surface honeycombed with black.

"Kimani!" she screams. "We need you right now!"

She comes up, returning to her body too late to stop it from toppling. When she picks herself up off the asphalt, she sees the door in the middle of Dedham, standing on its own. The door opens inward. The sight of Kimani's room in the middle of the open air, war raging around the door frame, makes Fahima feel nauseous.

"Come on!" Kimani shouts. Her face is pained. Fahima's never seen her make a door that isn't on a wall. Fahima rushes inside.

"There!" Fahima says, pointing at Ji Yeon and her fighters, who are engaged with soldiers in the intersection. "Go there."

Kimani slams the door shut and opens it again in the middle of the throng. Bullets strike the asphalt around them, shatter windows in the houses nearby. Fahima grabs the nearest person, who happens to be Ji Yeon. The girl struggles, protests, tries to get back into the fray. Fahima tosses her back into the room. She spots Isidra, not one of the fighters but nearby, holding a round shield of flowing silver stuff. Fahima pulls her in as well. She reaches out a third time, grabbing Hassan by the wrist. He looks at her, encircled in a cloud of dust, eyes tearful and panicked. Before she can get him through the door, his body is riddled with bullets. Fahima pulls at dead weight. She drops his hand and pushes the door shut.

"Let me go!" screams Ji Yeon, lying in a heap on the floor. "You can't keep me in here while they're dying."

"I just saved your ass," Fahima says.

"Fuck you!" says Ji Yeon. "We have to fight them. They're going to keep killing us unless we fight them." She grabs the silver sculpture off an end table and throws it hard. It hits the wall and shatters into a thousand tiny droplets of silver, like ball bearings. They pool together, a half dozen puddles of mercury. Isidra gapes at the ruin of her work.

"There aren't enough of us to fight them," Fahima says. "You were going to die, and it wouldn't mean anything. It wouldn't change anything."

"You don't know that," says Ji Yeon.

Isidra sits on the floor, dazed but uninjured. Kimani is out of breath. "We'll go house to house," she says. "We'll get everyone out we can."

"Get Alyssa," Fahima says. "She's in the basement of 224 Cambridge Street."

"Your Damp girlfriend's on her own," says Ji Yeon. She pulls herself up. "Start at the triage unit on Furness," she orders Kimani, "then hostels on Essex and Mount—"

"We start with Alyssa," Fahima tells her, voice tight. She turns to Kimani. "I'm the one who called you, and I say we get Alyssa first."

Fahima looks at Ji Yeon, daring her to argue. Kimani opens the door into the basement room of the Rhees' house, where Alyssa sleeps through the start of a war.

SEVEN

NEW SKIN FOR OLD CEREMONY

The gull inquired into his dream which was,
"I must not fall".
The spangled sea below wants me to fall.
It is hard as diamonds;
it wants to destroy us all."
—Elizabeth Bishop,
"The Unbeliever"

WAKE

The service is an afterthought, a public screening of grief. They hold it at a megachurch in Cobble Hill. Former students, a contingent from the Commune, Resonants who never attended the Bishop Academy, who'd stayed out in the cold. They pack into the church. The service is Resonants only. Sarah thought this was exclusionary, but Patrick pointed out that it was practical. All those seats and there isn't enough room. Shen works the door, Hivescanning mourners on their way in. Police block off Smith Street as a sea of allies and enemies stand in front of the church with candles and placards, tiki torches, and American flags. Since Revere, Fahima has developed a radar sense for violence. It's not pinging as she and Alyssa wind their way through the crowd. *They'll let us put him in the ground,* she thinks. *They'll at least give us that, if nothing more.*

They stop at the doors. Shen gives Alyssa a pained expression, and Fahima nods. She kisses Alyssa on the cheek. "This is where I leave you," she says. Alyssa looks shocked. Fahima told her this was coming, but she must not have believed it. There's a case to be made for her inclusion: Bishop owed his last days to Alyssa as much as to anyone. Fahima hadn't bothered to make the argument.

This is for us, she thinks. *And I love you, but you're not one of us.*

Seeing Fahima's resolve, Alyssa turns to go. "I'll see you at home," she says. She looks so hurt, Fahima nearly calls her back, but the motion of the crowd urges Fahima inside. *There are more moments like this to come,* Fahima thinks. *From here out, there will be fewer places we can go together.* It won't be that different from before, when Fahima kept herself secret from Alyssa. But to get past that, to stay together through it, Fahima had to promise that things would never go back to that way.

Sarah and Patrick saved Fahima a seat. Craning her neck to the back of the nave, she sees Kimani, door perched in the wall above the balcony. She looks down on them the way you hope God would, a sad smile on her face, a beer in her hand.

Fahima doesn't know the woman who performs the service but falls immediately in love with her. Everyone in the church does. Janine Coupland gives off a warmth that registers deeper than the skin. Sarah found her from a story Avi had written for *Harper's* about her murder trial and acquittal, one of Kay Washington's biggest legal victories since Bishop brought her on board. Janine Coupland's a healer. Most of the healers Fahima has encountered have a cold practicality about their ability. Abby Burgess, the school nurse at Bishop, can weave sundered skin back together but has all the bedside manner of a dead trout. Janine Coupland exudes healing. Fahima's lucky to be in the front row, soaking up more of it than the rest of the congregants, even if it's less than she needs.

Janine Coupland begins with apologies. She's not a preacher or even much of a public speaker. There's not much to the words she says beyond platitudes. It's her presence that does the work, leaving an impression on all that they've shared something important, a moment that changed them. It's a failing on Fahima's part that she's too smart, too critical to be part of it. Alyssa once remarked on Fahima's inability to turn her brain off long enough to watch a movie. "You don't have to be so smart all the time," she said, grinning playfully.

"Thing is, I do," Fahima said. It's difficult to explain how tightly you cling to your intellect when it's all you are.

"Is there anyone who'd like to say a few words about Kevin Bishop?" asks Janine Coupland. Sarah, Patrick, and Fahima exchange looks. One of them should speak. A former student, older than any of them, comes to the dais and waxes on about her time at Bishop, saying plenty about the school and very little about the man. The next couple of speakers run the same course, talking about what Kevin Bishop built without addressing who he was. Fahima wonders what she could add.

The thing she knows most clearly about Bishop is how little she knew him. He kept his past a secret. He said it was important that it stay that way. "We can't focus on who we've been or where we've come from," he said. "We need to think of where we are and where we're going." Bishop's past was tangled up with the beginnings of Resonance, the Hive, and the way their community had taken shape, but he drew a veil over that part of their story. Days when she was feeling charitable, Fahima thought it was about Bishop's idea that mystery and unknowability had intrinsic value, the seeds of faith. Fahima grew up around people who valued faith for its own sake. Faith could keep you good. It could hold you together and hold you up when a more empirical mind might fall apart. She was evidence of that. The years in the mental institution were the price she paid for her lack of belief. She suspected that there were parts of Bishop's story that would poison the well they all drew from. His secrecy may have been spiritual and benign, or it may have been adopted to protect himself from judgment.

By the time Fahima decides there's nothing she can say about someone as complex as Kevin Bishop, the service is over, the congregants dismissed.

"That was nice," says Sarah. Cortex huffs in agreement. Even Patrick nods. He's hardly spoken since Bishop died. Fahima tries to think of moments when he and Bishop seemed close. Maybe they'd been in touch while Patrick was away, hunting. Maybe Bishop was there for him on the road. She likes to imagine Patrick and Bishop as a buddy movie. *One's on the hunt for a cold-blooded killer. The other is a disembodied voice in his head.* She stifles a laugh that feels sacrilegious for being not just in church but at a funeral.

On the way out, Senator Lowery finds Fahima and falls into step behind her.

"I'm sorry for your loss," he says quietly.

"You could have gotten in," says Fahima. "Maybe thrown

on a clever disguise? Groucho mustache and glasses?"

"Are you who I talk to now?" he asks. "I need to know."

"What are you talking about?"

"With Kevin gone, someone needs to be the public face," he says. "Is it you?"

There's real worry in him, a sense that things have become unstable. It's worse for him because he thought things were stable to begin with. At the awful dinner Lowery hosted, Jefferson Hargrave suggested Resonants would be better off if they hid what they were. Lowery has done just that, and it's working for him. He belongs out here on the street with the allies and well-wishers.

Fahima stops and turns to him. She clasps his hand in both of hers and shakes it. "Thank you for your thoughts and prayers," she says. "I'm sure we'll be in touch."

"Come on," Sarah says, pulling her away. "Kimani's picking us up."

"You go on ahead," says Fahima. "I've got some things back at the lab I need to finish."

"Not today," Sarah says.

"It's for him," says Fahima.

"He's not going to take a point off for late work anymore," Sarah says. Fahima smiles, kisses Sarah on the cheek, and heads to the F train.

Fahima changes into jeans and a work shirt. She hangs her black dress and nice hijab off the corner of her whiteboard, covering the notes she's least comfortable with. *Emmeline. A pulse.* In the center of the board, she's drawn a timeline that starts with the Trinity test and extends through today, into the future. A registration act by the end of the year. Internment camps soon afterward, if not concurrent with legislation. From there, two paths. One leads to submission. The other leads to war.

Fahima thinks about ways to change the course of a stream. Drop a rock in its path or pour in a ton more water so the stream overflows its banks. From there it could go anywhere. It could reconfigure itself as something new.

She doesn't notice the pop when the door reappears. She doesn't even notice the door is there until it opens and organ music floods out. It's Prince's opening monologue from "Let's Go Crazy," his sexy preacher bit.

"Fahima, we're not taking no for an answer! Get in here and drink with us," Patrick yells. "Quick, before Kimani starts singing!"

Fahima glances at her timelines. She's already decided on a course of action. She decided when she drew up plans for the device instead of letting the idea slip away, forgotten like a dream. *You'll have to answer for this*, she thinks. *Whether the results are good or bad, you don't do something like this with impunity.* She turns away from the whiteboard and goes through the door. Kimani's room hasn't been cleaned or tidied since Revere. The sculpture Ji Yeon smashed is on the floor, a swarm of ball bearings beneath a shallow dent in the wall. She tries to catch Kimani's eye, but Kimani is fixing a drink, whispering lyrics to herself as she does.

"I don't know how you drink these things," Sarah says. She scratches under Cortex's chin with one hand and holds up a half-finished martini in the other. "It tastes like pine needles steeped in paint thinner."

"It's an acquired taste," Fahima says, accepting a drink.

"When *you* die," Patrick says, "we'll drink white wine spritzers in *your* memory."

"Don't talk like that," Sarah says, sounding genuinely hurt. "I've never had a white wine spritzer in my life."

"How far along are you all?" asks Fahima.

"One round and this much," Sarah says, indicating the empty top inch of her glass. "These things have a lot of booze in them."

"Patrick was telling us about his travels," Kimani says.

"The great white hunter," Sarah says.

"I wasn't telling them anything," he says. "They were badgering me. We've been through all this. It's not something I want to talk about."

"So don't talk about it," says Fahima.

"He's been gone for *years*," Sarah says.

"I'm coming back next term," Patrick says.

"You caught all the bad guys?" Fahima asks.

"It's time to come back," he says. "The job is too big for one person. It's not just Owen Curry. There are groups. Cells. I couldn't tell if they were connected or reporting to someone higher up. But I kept finding these little knots of Resonants waiting to blow shit up. It was like Whac-A-Mole. Every time I smacked one down, another popped up."

"Would you say you were stretched too thin?" Sarah asks, stifling a laugh.

"Sarah," says Patrick.

"Would you say you overextended yourself?"

"You're drunk," Patrick says.

"Yes," Sarah says.

"I had a strange conversation on the way out," Fahima says. "Have you met Senator Lowery?"

"Our wolf in sheep's clothing," Patrick says. Cortex growls, low and lupine.

"He asked me which of us is the new face of Resonants," she says.

"What does that even mean?" Kimani asks.

"It sounds like a *Cosmo* article," says Patrick.

"He wanted to know who becomes Bishop now," Fahima says. "It's not as ridiculous a question as it sounds."

"Then you do it," Patrick says.

"Let's put the queer Muslim lady out front," says Fahima. "That'll chill people right the fuck out."

"Sarah's the pretty one," Kimani says. "Everybody loves a pretty white lady."

"I don't—" says Sarah, flushing bright red. "I can't—the academy."

Patrick nods. "Sarah was born to run that school," he says. "Maybe no one should take Bishop's place."

"I was about to say it should be you," Fahima says.

"He did the things he had to," Patrick says. "It doesn't mean they should continue. Let it die with him."

"What are you talking about?" Fahima asks.

Patrick smirks his most Patrick of smirks. "The scientific mind of Fahima Deeb," he says. "Did it ever bother you that in seventy-five years, Owen Curry is the first of us to go really and truly off the rails? Didn't that strike you as statistically aberrant?"

"We all know what Kevin did," Kimani says. "I was there. I helped. The people he took off the board were—"

"I'm not talking about that," Patrick says. "I don't have a problem with that. You think I'm out there converting people back to the fucking flock? I'm continuing his work. That's not what I'm talking about. We *all* followed him. Not just those of us who knew him. Every fucking Resonant on the planet listened to what he told us and kept ourselves secret. He said sleep and dream, and we closed our eyes. Did that never strike any of you as odd?"

"Maybe we listened because he was right," Fahima says. Doubt creeps in. What Patrick is talking about is obedience across a wide spectrum. Why didn't she see it before? It was glaring at her out of the data.

"What do all of us have in common?" Patrick asks. "What binds us all together?"

"The Hive," says Fahima.

"And who built the Hive?"

The question hangs in the air, unanswered. After a second, Fahima carries the argument forward. "He talked about it like a lens," she says. "It's not just a place or a conduit energy passes through. It bends the energy as it passes. Light through a lens."

"He built it to keep us complacent," Patrick says. "I don't even fault him for it. It's a fucking brilliant idea. But he built the Hive in such a way as to keep us docile. So what happens now that he's gone?"

"Black flowers," Fahima says.

"This is some bullshit," Kimani says. "This isn't what we're here for." She starts fixing another drink.

"They showed up when he got sick," Fahima says. "When his control started slipping."

"That's enough," Kimani says, slamming the shaker down on the table. "That man is in the ground five minutes and you're going to start this shit? That is enough. The things he did, he did for us. They weren't all good, and he'd've been the first to tell you. Where we go from here, that is up to us. But you will not sit here in judgment on him. Not today."

"You're right," Patrick says. His hand stretches across the room and finds Kimani's shoulder. "Not today."

Sarah, relieved the conflict has been diffused, nods in agreement. Kimani bites her lower lip and goes back to making drinks. Patrick and Fahima exchange a look that says they're not done, not by a length.

Sarah passes out on the couch, and Cortex curls up next to her. Patrick drinks himself into a state of tenderness and kisses Sarah on the temple before hugging Fahima and Kimani and having Kimani drop him off at Bishop's house on Oceanside Way. Patrick's been clearing out some of Bishop's things. He says it's helping him deal with the loss. She wants to go with him, but the point is for him to be alone.

"One more?" asks Kimani, eyes already swimming. The needle on the record player scratches against the label, giving the room a soft pulse.

"Yeah, but I'm driving," Fahima says. She steps past Kimani to fix the drinks. She does this exactingly, with the care Kimani lacked. Care that Fahima learned from Bishop. Kimani's a beer drinker. To her a decent martini tastes the same as an excellent one. Fahima knows you can taste the attention to detail when it's done right. Anything worth doing and all that. As she swishes dry vermouth in the base of the glasses, she watches Kimani move around the room, the sound of Prince in her head. She knows this space the way Fahima knew the house she grew up in, which stairs creaked and what it sounded like as it eased itself to sleep. Kimani knows this space because it's part of her.

"Kimani," Fahima says. "Where are we?"

"Here at the end of all things," Kimani says dreamily.

"Kimani," Fahima repeats. "Where are we?"

"In the Hive," she says. "All of this. The Hive."

"But in our actual bodies," Fahima says.

Kimani nods. "A piece of physical space, embedded in transspatial Hivespace. That's what Kevin used to say. He helped me build the room. Expand it out. I was in a tiny, dark space when he found me." Fahima hands her the drink, and Kimani sips it. "That's good," she says. "That's better than mine."

"When you see the world," says Fahima. "The real world. Is it—"

"Like looking at a map," Kimani says. "I put the door where it needs to be and open it."

"All of everything," says Fahima. "Like a map."

"Hivespace is everywhere at once," Kimani says.

"Wherever I want to be, I'm already there."

Fahima thinks about something Emmeline Hirsch said to her. *Sometimes I'm already there.* But Emmeline was talking about time.

"You remember Emmeline?" Fahima asks. Kimani looks at Fahima like she's an idiot.

"Emmy's in here all the time. Good kid."

"Is it like that for her, too?" Fahima asks. "Like a map she's looking down on?"

Kimani shakes her head. "From what she can tell me, it's more like a cube," she says. "I'm at a point in Hivespace, which is everywhere, right? But Emmeline is everywhere in Hivespace. Which is maybe everywhen? She's me squared."

"That's some scary shit," Fahima says.

"Fucking right," Kimani says. She perches on the arm of the couch behind Sarah's head.

"Was it true what Patrick said?"

"What are we all trying to do but tip the tables toward the good?" Kimani says, an edge of anger in her voice. "That's all he did was tip the table a little."

"Is that *all* he did?" Fahima asks.

Kimani takes a gulp of her drink and coughs. When she recovers, she says, "Too many of us would be a bad thing. The energy we add to the system could burn it out. That's what he used to say."

"The system," Fahima repeats. "The system is the world, the actual world. The Hive keeps the numbers down. Limits the number of Resonants." Even Patrick hadn't suspected that. Things in her head shift. The device she was designing comes apart, and its pieces reassemble themselves differently. Better. The final piece is obvious, but Fahima turns her attention away from it. She'll have to consider it soon, but not now.

"He built it strong. Good," Kimani says. "I see those flowers, and I worry. But it won't break unless somebody breaks it."

"Maybe someone should," says Fahima.

"You take a listen to your own advice," Kimani says. "Allow the possibility that we followed him because he was right."

"No one's right about everything," Fahima says. She plucks an olive from her drink, places it between her front teeth, and neatly slices it in half, just as Bishop used to do.

THIS IS HOW WE
WALK ON THE MOON

Sunlight pours in the high, narrow eastern windows of Hall H, and Carrie Norris lies awake. Miquel's body wraps around hers like kudzu through chain link. One of her earbuds is still in. The other dangles over the edge of the bed like a rock climber detached from a cliff face. The battery on her iPod has been dead for months, but she still finds it a comfort to put the earbuds in before she goes to sleep.

She's not the only one up. She can hear the shift in breathing. She's attuned to it. After four months in the camp at Topaz Lake, somewhere in western Nevada, Carrie inhabits Hall H like a body teeming with other bodies. The slow sleep breaths of the room and the measured, snotty lung rattles of kids sharing the same December cold is dominant, layered over the buzz of inhibitors that glow a constant green. Another rhythm rises out of it: the hasty inhale-exhale pattern of others like Carrie, who wake into a panic, rediscovering where they are. The horror of their circumstances greets them fresh each morning, grips something in their chests, and squeezes.

There are 643 Resonants in the facility at Topaz Lake. The number shifts in either direction, but it hovers in the mid-600s. Many were already in some form of custody. Small-town jails, immigration detention centers. People whose disappearance could be effected with a lost piece of paperwork. Those people keep coming, with stories of getting picked up by local police for minor violations and ending up here. Then there are those who were grabbed off the streets, out of their homes. That seems to have stopped. Or at least paused.

Thirty-one people live in the cots and bunks of Hall H, a tarpaper shack the length and width of a school bus. Miquel is the odd extra: unmarried. Warden Pitt denied their request to cohabitate, but none of Hall H's residents complain about Miquel. He's loved more than Carrie. Not just here but throughout the camp. He tells Carrie it's because he works in the schoolhouse with the dozen kids among Topaz's population. People are indebted to those who tend to children, but it's not just that. People love that Miquel listens and that he remembers. Carrie's access to the camp's black markets provides Miquel endless chances to show up with little favors for people. *I remember you said you like marmalade,* he says to Edith Fowler in Hall F, a widow who used to be able to read minds like newspaper headlines but now can only smile sweetly and say *Bless you* in a way that carries weight, a blessing that will be passed up the chain. The camp's affection rarely passes to Carrie, the procurer of these gifts. She's liked to the extent that she makes Miquel happy. It's enough.

"Hey, baby," he whispers through a fog of half sleep. Others in the bunks murmur. The hall wakes like a large hibernating mammal, slow and lumbering. Feet slap the floor, and Miquel pulls her close as the front door lets in a bitter blast of high desert winter air. No one told Carrie the desert got this cold. No one tells you the truth about anything. Miquel takes a lock of her hair and curls it around two of his fingers.

"You sure?" he asks.

Carrie nods, scratches an itch behind her ear. "It grows back," she says. Miquel hmmmphs and extracts himself from her, pushing his body up and over hers to land on the floor like a gymnast. At the apex of this maneuver, he plants a kiss on her cheek.

"I'll go get the things," he says, and takes off into the cold without a jacket. A Hall H mother has to stop him and remind him. No sense of self-preservation. No understanding of the borders between himself and the world. *Remember, you love these things about him,* she thinks. The thought undoes itself like a magician's trick knot, appearing solid only to resolve into nothing.

Carrie heads to the women's bathroom. The women of Hall H outnumber the men and are for the most part mothers. All the halls are coed, but the distribution seems designed to discourage procreation, if not fucking altogether. Hall B houses the camp's young single women, but the only men there are ancient to the point of sexual irrelevance. Hall H has a couple of young bucks but insulates them with women·grieving for their children who are on the outside.

Considering this as a plan assumes that their jailors think of them as human, with desires and motivations. There's little evidence to support that.

The ablutions of the mothers strike Carrie as theatrical. Black market requests for brand-name mascara and blush are frequent. The markup on these products subsidizes the costs of smuggled antidepressants and antibiotics. In the mirror next to Carrie, a woman in her thirties applies concealer to a fading black eye. Carrie can't remember her name, only that she "dates" Mister Benavidez, one of the guards. In the fall, her arms and legs bloomed with bruises. Territory markings. The shiner was a bold announcement of Mister Benavidez's claim on her and his ability to hit her with impunity. There are no consequences for the guards here, although it took them a few months to realize it. The woman offers the jar to Carrie.

"It's dehydration that does it," she says. "I'm grateful not to freeze, but the heaters suck the moisture right out of you." Carrie waves off the concealer, although she's aware of the dark circles under her own eyes. Because they are mothers, the women in Hall H treat Carrie like a daughter, with gentle corrections and cluckings. They size her up with loving disappointment Carrie recognizes too well. Carrie does the minimum preparation for the day, the maintenance a body needs not to become decrepit or offensive, and leaves the mothers to their self-care.

Bundled in an army surplus parka, Carrie meets Miquel outside. The inhibitors are weaker out here. Sometimes she feels the tingle of her ability returning, a song she almost remembers. Miquel opens his jacket like someone selling counterfeit watches in Washington Square Park. A cord dangles out of the inside pocket. He waggles his eyebrows at her lasciviously.

"You have time?" she asks.

"The kids'll be gluing cotton balls to cardboard all morning. Each shepherd needs a sheep." He nods to one of the guards, who leans on an elaborate rifle, a gun out of a video game. Carrie digs her fingernails into a spot high up on her scalp.

The disposition of the laundry in its off hours depends on who's guarding it. Most nights and early mornings, it's a rendezvous spot for guards and female prisoners, consenting or not. One night, sneaking out of Hall H for a smoke, Carrie watched Mister Herschel drag a girl in there, a blonde in her late teens who works with Carrie in the commissary. Mister O'Keefe held the door open, then winked at Carrie as he shut it. "Don't worry, Plain Jane," he said. "We only want the pretty ones." It should have been Carrie's moment to rise up. Instead, she stubbed out her cigarette and retreated to her bunk. She shoved her earbuds in as if they could shut the world out and held on to Miquel as tightly as she could.

The guard outside this morning, Mister Bailey, is sweet on both of them. He's older and avuncular and regularly ribs Miquel about *marrying that girl.* Miquel smiles warmly at him. "I really appreciate this, Mister Bailey."

"I'd appreciate if you'd call me John," says Mister Bailey. All the guards are *Mister* except for Warden Pitt. A lot of them are ex-military and ex–law enforcement, along with some hobbyists, gun nuts, and weekend warriors. They're paid by someone, but no one's working at Topaz Lake purely for the paycheck. The individual guards' attitudes range from genocidal to paternal, and they go by *Mister* as an indicator of status, if not specific rank. Carrie and Miquel have discussed this. Never call them by their first names, never delude yourself that they're your friends. John might tip his cap at you in the morning, but it could be Mister Bailey's gun butt smacking you in the temple by afternoon.

"Mister Huerta mentioned you smoke a pipe," Miquel says.

Mister Bailey nods sheepishly. "Everyone's entitled to one vice."

Miquel deftly slips him a pouch of high-end pipe tobacco, which Mister Bailey pockets without looking at it. He opens the door for them. "Don't worry," he says. "I'll make sure you're alone."

"No peeking at the keyhole," Miquel says, throwing him a wink. Carrie gives a razor-thin smile as they close the door.

"We could actually just have sex," Miquel says. Carrie takes in the room. First laundry shift starts at eight. Thirty women will file in, stoking boilers and washing the clothes of Topaz Lake's 643 residents. In the winter, the cinder block walls of the building sweat. Droplets of water reverberate off the tiles.

"You take me to the nicest places," she says.

"We don't have to do this," says Miquel. "It's only two of the kids. I checked you last night, and you don't have any."

"I've been itching since you told me." They don't

mention the word because it sends her into paroxysms. Carrie examined Miquel's scalp for nits as he slept, then woke up in the middle of the night scratching at her own frantically enough to draw blood. This is the prophylactic measure she's chosen. Miquel finds an outlet and plugs in the borrowed hair clippers, flipping the switch to make them buzz like an engine revving in the small tile-covered room. The clippers are shiny, metallic, weaponized. These are military-grade, not the kind you'd pick up in a Rite Aid. Most of the guards at Topaz rock the high-and-tight, a quarter inch of bristle protecting their pates from the wind. Whoever runs Topaz recruited the straightest of the straight. Softies like Mister Bailey slide in under the radar, along with sympathizers like Mister Guzman on the western fence. Miquel could coax Windex tears out of a robot's eye, but most of these boys are John Wayne wannabes who look at their captives like cattle and keep kind thoughts at bay with discipline and routine.

"You sure?" Miquel asks one more time. The clippers hover at the nape of Carrie's neck. She can feel the chittering of their metal teeth.

"Fucking do it," she says.

Hayden's out back of the commissary, smoke rising from their cigarette, steam squeaking out through the lid of the hot lunch cart. Wednesdays, Hayden and Carrie run lunches out to the work crews. Today, they're headed to southeast quad, where Bryce and a half dozen others try to crack the frozen soil to dig graves for three prisoners who made a break for it last week. Carrie didn't recognize their names, although she'd know them on sight. Official word is they fell. Misadventure is the most common cause of death here. *Gravity's high around Topaz,* Mister Benavidez likes to say. The bodies have been in storage waiting for a thaw, but Mister Howerton, who oversees the outdoor work crews, thinks grave digging's hilarious. Especially in the cold, when the effort's futile. He'll be out there with a parka and a hip flask, chuckling to himself as he watches prisoners struggle to bury their own.

"Are you waiting for me to tell you how butch you look?" Hayden asks. Suddenly self-conscious, they adjust their ill-fitted platinum wig. After a few days under inhibitor lights, Hayden started to physically revert to their deadgender, all the beautiful changes they'd written on their body coming undone. Their hair was the last thing to go, long blond tresses shriveling like unwatered vines. Hayden petitioned Warden Pitt for hormone therapy, but the warden had as much sympathy for Hayden's gender identity as he did for their Resonance. Bigotries travel in packs that way. Hayden does their best with makeup and procured wigs but bears the pain of losing their ability more heavily than anyone at Topaz. They've lost access to theirself. Carrie's only cut off from a parlor trick.

"Fuck you," Carrie says, rubbing her freshly shorn head. She hadn't appreciated the insulating power of her hair. With her scalp exposed, the cold digs right into her brain. Hayden hands her a cigarette and lights it for her. She blows a column of smoke at Hayden.

"Or punk. Is that better?" Hayden asks. "You look very punk."

"I will settle for 'you look like you are not covered in bugs,'" Carrie says.

"Children are disgusting," Hayden says. "It's unfair to the rest of us to be locked up in here with children."

"It's better than snatching the parents and leaving the kids out there on their own," Carrie says, although she's unsure. She used to get pissed off with people who held freedom as a sacred abstract, but now it's something she can hold in her hand. Or, more to the point, can't. It's easier here to weigh freedom against other things. Is it better to be a free orphan or a loved but imprisoned child?

"I've got something for you," Carrie says. She hands Hayden a mesh bag she found in the laundry, the kind her mother used to wash pantyhose in. Hayden cocks an eyebrow at her, loosens the drawstring, and peers inside.

"Tell me you didn't just give me a bag of your hair, single white female." Carrie tries to grab it back, but Hayden yanks it away. "All creepy crawly with bugs, I bet," Hayden says. "Merry Christmas to me."

"I thought there might be someone who could—"

"Glue it to my fucking head?"

Carrie looks at the ground. Miquel tried to talk her out of it, but she felt like she needed to do something for Hayden to close the gap of loss between them. "I don't know," she says as they start toward the southeast quad. "People make wigs. Someone might know how to use it to make you one."

Hayden throws their arms around Carrie, pulling her so

close that she can feel the hitch in their breath as they stand together for a second.

"You're sweet," Hayden says. "Also a fucking idiot." They let Carrie go, and they are once again composed, although Carrie can see red rimming their eyes.

"So are you not coming to the pageant tonight?" she asks. "It's a good alibi."

"I've got my alibi lined up," Hayden says. They've been spending time with Guzman, one of the less terrible guards, who works the eastern fence. He's promised Hayden he can get them Rez, that he's working on it. Topaz gives it out to any Resonant whose ability has a physical manifestation that causes pain or death when shut down. Taken in small, constant doses, Rez sustains physical manifestations of ability without allowing the user back into the Hive. Without it, Bryce and Jonathan would be dead. Hayden argued to Warden Pitt that without their ability, they would revert to their deadgender, to no avail. Guzman is trying to help. Hayden's not fucking him but swears he's in love and he'll come through.

"Watch him show up with a ring," says Carrie.

"Fuck off."

"Christmas eve? The snow falling on the barbed wire and gun turrets?" says Carrie. "That's some romantic shit right there. I'd marry him."

"Are we even allowed to get married?" Hayden asks. "Have they made it illegal yet?"

"Probably," Carrie says. "It's not like we get any news in here."

There's a one-page weekly newsletter Bryce circulates,

but it's only camp goings-on. Tonight's pageant. Movie night in the commissary. "Accidental" deaths. Topaz Lake is an Internet dead zone, and they're cut off from the Hive. No one knows anything about the outside.

"You tell Miquel what's happening?" Hayden asks.

"Of course," says Carrie, looking away. One thing hasn't changed since they were snatched off North Avenue: Carrie doesn't talk to Miquel about work.

"You think we're going to pull this off?"

"Of course," Carrie says.

She misses being able to disappear when she lies.

The pageant is the biggest social event since Topaz started. Everyone is here, or close enough to everyone that anyone who isn't can say he or she was and be believed. The kids arrive early and are handed over to Miquel's care. Carrie's mix of pride and worry about Miquel isn't unlike what the parents must feel. It's a point of concern that sometimes she thinks of him as delicate. She's coming to understand it as a symptom of caring. Fear is a by-product, a terror at the object of caring's potential loss or destruction. It demonstrates not so much that Miquel could break but that Carrie could, shattered by the loss of him.

Bryce finds Carrie in the lobby of the community center, staring at the door that Miquel and the kids disappear through. "It's a great turnout," he says. "He must be excited."

"Nervous," Carrie says.

"Him or you?"

"Both."

"It's nice to see everybody here," he says.

"It means they're starting to accept," says Carrie. "They're making it into real life."

"Some of us have been here a year," Bryce says. "You can't fight all the time."

"*I* can," Carrie says.

Bryce smiles at her. "That's my girl." This is the way they take care of each other. Each guards the other against complacency, against sleep. They keep the other's anger stoked.

Carrie spots Hayden on the other side of the crowd. For all the noise they make about hating children, Hayden served as a musical director for the pageant, even writing a couple of nondenominational winter-themed songs. They're thanked in the program and everything. They wouldn't have missed this. All this is becoming normal; people are finding ways to live like this. They make sense of the nonsensical because a year is made up of days and the days are made of hours and small units of time have to be endured and survived. Carrie's worry, one she and Bryce share, is that the goals will become subsumed in the day-to-day. Once they realize they can find joy within misery, they'll forget the misery is there.

The lights go down, and the stage lights come up. A flurry of children crosses the stage, dressed as snowflakes. They sing one of Hayden's songs, a bouncing number about blizzards. Carrie catches the look on Hayden's face as they sing. They're in wonder.

A heavyset teenage girl Carrie knows from the commissary steps to the center of the stage. She looks around nervously at the crowd. Silence hangs around her, bright as the spotlight. Miquel rushes out and pretends to adjust the microphone stand. He puts a hand on the girl's shoulder and whispers something to her, then darts off the stage. The girl takes a deep breath. She looks at Hayden in the crowd, who gives the girl a thumbs-up and then quickly tucks her hand away. The girl nods at the accompanist, who starts in, laying down thick, slow chords. It's a departure for Hayden, whose songs are usually kinetic and shifting, but it works immediately. Carrie feels the weight of the song before the lyrics begin. The girl sways behind the mic stand, her eyes closed. The room is fading away, leaving her by herself with the song. Her voice is strong and big, the kind that fills a room. Carrie wishes she'd step away from the mic. She doesn't need it.

The lyrics are strange and playful, a riddle game. A list of contradictions and possibilities. The song builds toward an answer, lifts into a major key, but before it can resolve, the lights sputter and die, leaving the room dark. The inhibitor lights in this section stay on, their pale green glow coming through the high windows. Carrie starts the count in her head, knowing that Bryce and Hayden are doing the same thing. She wishes that this didn't have to happen right now, that the girl could have finished her song first. Sometimes minutes need to be sacrificed for the sake of years.

After a pause, the accompanist continues, tentative. In the dark, he watches the singer to see if she's shaken, if she'll continue. He sustains the chord that brings in the chorus, and the singer comes in, a half beat behind. Without amplification or light, the song continues, the singer invisible. The song is the only thing, and each person in the room is alone with it. The singer is giving them the resolution they want, but Carrie's mind is somewhere else. Her count climbs, approaching a full minute. It's more than they hoped for. At eighty seconds, the lights flicker back to life. The singer's voice becomes shockingly loud, and she draws away from the mic. It's beautiful, but the momentary spell cast in the dark is broken.

"Was that enough time?" Bryce whispers under the applause.

"We'll see," Carrie says.

The back doors of the hall burst open, and guards come pouring in, rifles drawn. Some of the guards think the people here should be liquidated. They're keeping tigers in cages, pretending they're tame. The kids on stage flinch as weapons are pointed at them, aware of themselves as targets. At the piano, the accompanist starts playing "Simply Having a Wonderful Christmastime," bouncing B-flat chords. Mister Benavidez kicks him in the side, knocking him off the piano bench. Shouting profanity and threats, they force people to the ground, shove them to the exits. They separate parents from children, break couples apart. Carrie doesn't bother to look for Miquel in the scrum. They've been through this before. Later, they'll reassemble. They'll be okay, if a little more broken. She has to believe this. For now at least, she needs it.

Carrie lies in bed with Miquel long enough to doze off herself, skimming the surface of sleep like a bird. She wakes quickly, worried she's missed her opportunity. Mister Wentworth, the guard on this sector on Thursday nights, passes Hall H at 11:20, then again at 11:50. In between, when he's at the apogee of his orbit, there's an open path to the laundry. This assumes that patrols aren't doubled tonight. Carrie untwines herself from Miquel and hurries out into the cold without a jacket.

Hayden's waiting inside the laundry, scowling at their cigarette. The lights in the room are always on, and Carrie can see every hair she and Miquel missed sweeping up this morning, clinging to the wet tiles.

"They got Rafa," says Hayden. "Guzman says they beat him up pretty bad."

"Fuck," Carrie says, taking the cigarette. *We'll get him out*, she thinks. *We're going to get them all out*. "Did Siu send the message?"

"He thinks so," Hayden says. "He told people, but he can't be sure it was anyone who could do anything for us." They picked Siu because he claimed he was a ninja when it came to Hivecraft. They needed to get the location and conditions of the camp out to somebody in the very limited time the inhibitor lights on the northeast quad went down, after Rafa disabled the generators. It got complicated because none of them knew where they were. Siu said he'd be able to locate himself from inside the Hive. *Triangulate*, he said. It rang of bullshit, but it was what they had. A month of planning to send out one broadcast that may not have been received. It cost them Rafa. It alerted the guards to a crack in security that now would be shut. If it didn't work, they'd have to come up with something else. In the year they've been here, they haven't come up with anything else.

"We wait," says Carrie. She wants to be the kind of princess who rescues herself, but she's done all she can. She's leaped out into the dark, hoping there will be arms to catch her.

THE LAST VISIT

Avi watches as Shen pushes through the crowd of protesters in front of Bishop, Emmeline and Viola trailing in his wake. Avi can't see them, but he knows they're there. The protesters are here every day, sometimes a handful, sometimes a mob. Emmeline says the handful are the most dangerous. People dedicated enough to show up every day are the most likely to run at you, get in your face. Bishop students never leave the building alone. *We travel in packs, for safety*, Emmeline told him.

Once Shen's through the crowd, Emmeline and Viola emerge from behind him. Emmeline's wearing a new winter coat, slim and dark. Kay must have bought it for her. It makes him miss the puffy purple coat that made her look like some sort of confection. Emmeline spots Avi but keeps a steady pace. She wants to blend back into the city once she's through, to distance herself from Bishop so she won't be accosted. When they get near him, he falls into step along with them, waiting for Emmeline to signal that it's okay to hug her. It happens as they turn the corner onto 59th and find a doorway they can step into. Emmeline squeezes him tight.

"You're never in New York anymore," she says.

"It's hard getting around these days," Avi says. He hasn't talked with Emmeline about his break with the Bishop Academy, how it means he can no longer call up Kimani and appear in New York in an instant. Why he's never the one to escort her out of the building, protect her from the crowds.

"Last week there were lots of them," she says. "Miss Zavala came out front with us and pushed the crowd apart, like the Red Sea." She laughs nervously, because she's leaving out the part where one of the protesters threw a brick into the gap the teacher created and hit Vernon Lister, a second-year telekinetic, in the head. The cut took nine stitches at Mount Sinai. Avi had seen the police report. The cops dispersed the crowd but didn't make any arrests. There was a bigger crowd the next day.

He never told Emmeline about the detention site, and his e-mails and phone calls to the Bishop staff went unanswered. Louis Hoffman cut him off after that late-night visit. The site was wiped clean by the time he got back there. No sign anyone had been in the warehouse in months. The *Trib* said they wouldn't run with what he had, and the *Reader* said they'd put someone "from the community" on it. To the best of his knowledge, they hadn't. It's been over a year, and nothing about it has seen print.

The only person who listened to him was Kay, when he called on Christmas to share Louis's advice that they get Emmeline out of the country.

"Do you think those people at that school can keep her safe?" she asked. She said things like *those people* and *that school* even as she spent her days arguing their personhood in court. Avi thought about the kid who got shot right in front of the academy on Public Day. He knew there was little Bishop or his staff could do to protect Emmeline. But *they* could, he and Kay. Her in the courts and him in the press, working together even though they were apart.

"Yes," he said.

They had the same conversation after Kevin Bishop died. Avi was in Revere, covering the barricade standoff from the outside. Kay was in Boston, trying to get the National Guard pulled back by judge's order. They met up in a bar in Logan Airport after the barricade had been bulldozed, the motions denied, and the stories filed. They both looked like shit and felt defeated. There was an intimacy in letting themselves be seen like that, a veneer of resolve and hope that they cast off only in front of each other. It was like their marriage, the safety in being naked without fear of judgment.

"Should we go?" she asked, staring blankly into her second glass of wine. "Should we just fucking go?" The powerful thing was that if he said yes, they'd leave together. The three of them could be a family again, elsewhere. All Avi had to do was give up.

"We can't," he said. He put his hand on hers, and she let it stay. It occurred to him that he should stand up, step around the table, and hold her. Then they called boarding for her flight to Cheyenne. She dropped twenty dollars on the table and was gone.

"You want to have lunch with us?" Emmeline asks Viola.

"I'm going to MoMA," Viola says. "Now that I'm out,

might as well do something normal." Fourteen to Emmeline's twelve, Viola is striding awkwardly into adolescence. She's rail-skinny and newly tall, unaccustomed to the body she finds herself in, and her freckled cheeks are flurried with acne. None of this has diminished her bright demeanor, the positivity that radiates off her. "I'll text you when I'm heading back. We can walk back in together." She hugs Emmeline, a show of solidarity, and splices herself into pedestrian traffic.

"What're you in the mood for, Leener?" Avi asks as they walk.

Emmeline shrugs. "Let's go far away," she says. "So far that I can't see the academy anymore."

"You having a tough time?"

"It feels like it's my whole world," she says.

They take the 6 downtown. "There's a burger place Mom likes," says Emmeline. Kay's in Wyoming, advising the prosecution in Gillette for the trial of the men who killed the Guthridge family. She and Avi spoke about it on the phone for an hour the other day. They've been talking more lately, a fact he tries to avoid giving too much weight to.

"I wish we could get the venue moved to somewhere more civilized," Kay said. "I'm the only black person in this town."

"It's not like it's a race issue," said Avi.

"It's got to play like one," Kay said. "Half the cases I win are by analogy to race. Once the jury is looking at what these people are, it's a lost cause."

"What *are* they?" Avi asked. Kay didn't answer, and for a second Avi expected her to hang up. She's still having trouble with all this. She manages to keep her feelings hidden from Emmeline, which he's grateful for. Through practice, careful wording, Kay never makes their daughter feel like an alien.

The restaurant is crowded and noisy, tile walls and floors reflecting the conversations of every lunchgoer back into the room, remixing them into a din. It's the kind of place Kay tended to hate, preferring dark and quiet on the rare occasions they went out. Coming here is part of her "dealing" with Emmeline. Quiet moments carry the potential for revelation. Best to avoid them, hide in noise and crowds. Avi once asked Kay if she knew what Emmeline's ability was. His tone was ambiguous, leaving open the possibility that he already knew.

"It's never come up," Kay said, and changed the subject.

When the waiter comes, Emmeline knows exactly what she wants: the bacon cheddar burger, medium, no mayo, no onions, and a ginger ale. Put on the spot, Avi orders the same and a beer. He immediately regrets the latter, but he's relieved when it arrives.

"Their fries are really good," Emmeline says, shouting to be heard. Avi nods and sips his beer. He examines Emmeline's face for signs that she's turning into a teenager, but it's not as easy as it was with her roommate. He thinks of her so often that her appearance is fluid, keeping up with who she is right now. Viola moves through time in jumps, changing drastically between their encounters. Emmeline always looks like Emmeline to him. Someday it won't be true. He'll look at her and be unconvinced she ever was his little girl. He'll look at her, and there will be something about her he doesn't recognize. It hasn't happened yet, but he can feel the day coming.

"How are things at school?" he says. "You learning anything?"

Emmeline shrugs. "Usual stuff," she says. "History and math."

"That's it?" asks Avi. "What about stuff with your ability?"

He's come to understand that she's not going to tell him what it is she can do. She must know. Every other kid her age at Bishop seems to know exactly what his or her ability is. His hope is that if he talks about it as if he already knows, she'll let something drop. Kay won't talk with her about it, and Avi thinks he can give Emmeline the safe space to open up.

Emmeline toys with the bracelet on her right wrist. She's worn it every time Avi's seen her for the last year or so. It's strange-looking, African design maybe. He assumes it was a gift from Kay, although Kay's never been much for jewelry. Catching him watching, Emmeline puts her hands under the table.

"That stuff, too," she says. "Mostly it's regular high school stuff. I like my art class."

Avi's not interested in her art classes. His reporter brain overrides his dad brain, needling him to ask Emmeline for details about her ability and how she's training to use it. He has questions he wants answered about the Hive and how the school has changed since Bishop died. He wants to know if she's heard about anybody going missing. But she's looking at him with her pale blue eyes, not an interview subject but his daughter who used to spend hours on the floor of her room drawing, who asked for paints and colored pencils at the ages most girls ask for expensive dolls.

"You should show me some of what you're working on," he says.

"I've got a lot of it hanging in my room," Emmeline says. "You should come up and see." Avi's face must give away the impossibility of this, and with Emmeline there's always the question of what she knows even when she can't possibly know it. "I can send you some pictures. I could even mail you a couple. Are you living back in the old house?"

Avi forgets that Emmeline doesn't know where he lives. Why would she? Sometimes he feels like he doesn't know. He's not sure when he'll be back there next. The neighbors are on permanent alert to pick up the mail, and there's someone paid to make sure the lawn doesn't grow to feral heights.

"Pictures would be good," he says. The waiter arrives with two towering burgers. Emmeline, eyes saucer-wide, grabs hers with both hands and chomps in, showing none of the caution or reserve of a teenager, only the voracity of a perfectly normal kid.

WORKING FOR THE CLAMPDOWN

Warden Pitt's office is an old trailer that reminds Carrie of the head counselor's office at the summer camp she and her brother Brian had been forced to attend when they were kids. It has the same faux-wood paneling that makes it look like a ski lodge crossed with a travel agency. It smells like years of stale cigarettes. Warden Pitt personalized the space by using framed posters with the name of a virtue in bold white below an image that embodies it. A marathoner throwing his body across the finish, the word PERSEVERANCE stamped below it. A bear nuzzling a kitten. Emblazoned underneath: TOLERANCE.

"You understand this is a formality, Miss Norris. We're putting the whole thing to rest." He's pudgy and sweaty, squeezed into a secondhand military uniform decorated with a spatter pattern of buttons and pins you'd expect from a chain restaurant waiter. He likes to give the impression that he's where the buck stops. Carrie's figured out enough about Topaz Lake to know Pitt's a regional manager in general's clothing. He signs paychecks and requisition forms. He moves someone else's money around. She's surprised he's involved in the investigation of the power outage the night of the Christmas pageant. Usually something like this is handed off to men with more stomach for cruelty. The fact that he's questioning her means she's safe. The real investigators moved through anyone they thought was involved in the days immediately afterward. What he's said is true: this is a formality.

"I'm taking this incident as an opportunity to speak to some of our residents about what it is we're doing here," he says. "To clear up any ambiguity of mission."

"You call yourself 'warden,'" Carrie says. "That's pretty unambiguous."

Pitt shakes his head the way a teacher might at an ignorant child. "The word actually means something closer to 'guardian,'" he says. "I'm here to watch over you all. I see to it you're fed and clothed. Like a father, really."

Carrie imagines jumping across the table, sinking her fingers into the roll of fat above his collar, and squeezing until his eyes bug out.

"Of course," she says.

"What we're doing here is an experiment," he says, clicking into the practiced part of his speech. "An intentional community, if you're familiar with that phrase. The people I work for believe that you people will ultimately be happier separate from the rest of us. The general public is happier with you separated from them. They feel safer. I think in time, you'll come to feel safer as well, among your own kind. At some point, we were sold the idea that integration is an inherently American ideal. But what is that based on?

Where's the evidence? If you think about any group of people, they will naturally tend toward their own. That's how you get your Chinatowns and your Koreatowns. Your Harlems and your Comptons. I think of Topaz Lake as a prototype. Resonant Town, version one point oh. Do you follow me, Miss Norris?"

"Chinatown doesn't have armed guards at the gate," she says.

His jaw tenses. "No, but there were structures that pushed people together." He forces his palms against each other like he's compressing a cartoonishly large sandwich. "Laws, economic conditions. Now, because of the *idea* that we should all be one big melting pot, such things no longer exist. The people I work for have been forced to be more proactive. Thinking outside the box."

"You have literally boxed us in," Carrie says.

"But have we hurt you?" he says, cloyingly sweet. "Haven't you found here a wholeness that eluded you on the outside? A sense of true community?"

Carrie glares at him. She thinks about Public Day, before the shooting. The sense she had that everyone was in it together for a second, before it was shattered. She thinks of the night on the beach at Coney Island and the feeling of unity. She could never separate that night from that first kiss, but it seemed as if the kiss could have happened only that night, she and Miquel part of something bigger than themselves. Something large enough to draw them together. There were more people like them at Topaz Lake, but it didn't feel bigger than that night on the beach.

"The thing you fail to understand is that these incidents make it harder for us to keep you safe," he says, seeming truly hurt. "This morning, I got a report that a young man named—" He rifles through papers on his desk. "—Siu Zhang was repairing the inhibitor tower on the northwest fence when his harness broke and he fell to his death." Warden Pitt overpronounces the name, saying it as *See You*. He looks at Carrie with mild inquisitiveness as her friend's death registers. Siu, who sent the signal. Siu who volunteered, even though, like Miquel, he'd made his peace with life in the camp, found a girl he wouldn't have met on the outside, a grad student from Wisconsin. Siu, who preferred Robert Fripp to Mick Ronson but played guitar like Ronson because he didn't want to embarrass himself, who convinced Carrie that *Easter* was a better Patti Smith album than *Horses*, who put honey in his coffee and hot sauce on everything else.

"An accident, of course," says Warden Pitt. If he has a gift, it's his convincing belief in obvious lies. In the months Carrie's been at Topaz Lake, Warden Pitt's announced a dozen *tragic accidents*, always tagged with *of course*. "Think how unnecessary that is. Obviously my thoughts and prayers are with his friends and loved ones. There's also the fact that death is off brand for what we're doing here. It makes *us* look bad. Makes our experiment look like a failure."

All Carrie can think is that this won't be over until she kills Warden Pitt. Nothing else matters, not freedom, not Miquel. She will dream of his death the way she dreamed of meeting rock stars when she was a kid.

"I brought you in to offer you something," he continues. "A show of good faith. You have a boyfriend, yes? Miquel Gray?" Carrie gives the faintest nod. "We generally don't approve of premarital cohabitation. We're not prudes by any means. But many people in our organization come from religious backgrounds, and they get a bit squeamish when it comes to this kind of thing. I've been looking at your work record and at Mister Gray's work with the children. I've issued a special dispensation for the two of you. Mister Gray will be allowed to move into Hall H with you. One of the other residents has agreed to move into Mister Gray's spot in Hall D, so everything is neat and tidy. He can pack his things today. Isn't that nice?"

Pitt grins at Carrie, but there's a nervous edge to his smile. He's decided she's a person on the fringe of insurgent groups within the camp, and he's trying to buy her off with something she's already secured for herself with the help of other prisoners and the sympathies of the occasional humane guard. What is it he hopes to get in return? Compliance? Carrie envisions the message Siu sent out into the Hive, moving like a great boomerang, gathering up help, a force of arms, and dragging it back here to land on Pitt's desk. It's been over a month, but maybe it's taking that long to organize a proper response, summon an army to come tear down the fences around Topaz Lake. An answer to his hypocritical rhetoric. A reckoning for all the good he imagines he's done.

OWEN CURRY AND THE
JUDGEMENT OF POWER BASIN

Owen resents how cheap the phrase *trial of the century* has become. Google it and you get a hundred results. Ones from way back were trials related to major issues. The Scopes monkeys. Dreaded Scott. They decided the path of the country. But the phrase devolved into low-rent celebrity murder trials: roid-raged jocks past their expiration date, washed-up record producers, B-list television actors. By the time reporters affix the Powder Basin trial with *of the century* status, it doesn't mean shit, except that the lowest tier of cable networks runs constant coverage. But this one meant something. Twenty-one men accused of lynching a family of Resonants, torching their home with the bodies inside. A crime that took years to come to light, covered up by the police and the town since it happened.

Go there, the friend in his head says. *On your own. Go there and see to it justice is done.*

Owen looks around the table at what's left of his team. They respect him more since he killed Darren. Or they're more scared of him. It doesn't matter. Either effect suits him.

"I have to go on a side trip," he says. "A couple days. I'll find you when I'm done. There's something he needs me to do."

If Darren were alive, he would have said something stupid, ruined the solemnity of the moment. And it is solemn. Because Owen's not sure he's coming back.

In the parking lot, they say their good-byes. Little Gail hops off Tabitha's hand onto Owen's shoulder, crosses it, and gives him a kiss on the cheek like butterfly wings. Marita yanks him into the black bone room for a split second. *Don't forget me, lover,* she says, her skin like the coil of an oven burner against his. She pulls his head back by his hair and presses her face into his, not a kiss but an assault. She burns through his Hivebody, hot knife through butter, then lets him up again, breathless.

It takes two days to hitchhike to Gillette, where the trial is being held. There's a room waiting for him at the Arrowhead Motel in a strip mall outside of town. In the room, there's an envelope full of cash. His friend has physically been here, making preparations for him. Owen searches the room for traces: depressions in the carpet or wrinkles in the sheets. There's nothing except the envelope.

The morning after he arrives, Owen tries to get into the courtroom for the trial, but there's a queue. Family members and reporters get priority. Beyond that, there's a lottery system for seats. Owen loses out the first two days but gets in on the third, when the lawyers present closing arguments. The air-conditioning in the courtroom is dead, and a collection of large, loud fans blow air hot as breath around the room. The lawyer for the prosecution is a black lady who looks like she has eaten exactly her full helping of shit from these people and wants no more. It takes a moment, but Owen realizes he recognizes her. She was sitting down the pew from him in the church, the one he didn't feed to the null. He can't be positive, but he feels sure of it. There's something right about it, her being there at the beginning of his becoming, when he held back, and here now, when he is about to fully bloom. Owen likes her even though she has no vibration. This happens now and then, even to him. Affection for the cattle. Farmers must get it, too, but at the end of the day, they're in the business of meat.

Kay Washington steps into the open space in front of the jury, sets her feet, and begins.

"A hundred fifteen years ago, outside Atlanta, Georgia, a black farmhand named Sam Hose was dragged out of his jail cell. He'd struck his employer, a white man, and gone on the run. It took the police ten days to find him, and in that time the papers whipped people into a frenzy, accusing Hose of rape, infanticide. When he was caught, excursion trains brought two thousand people to see him strung up, stripped, cut up, skinned alive, and burned. Souvenir hunters scrambled through the ashes and fought over his organs and his bones.

"Sixty years ago, in Money, Mississippi, three men dragged fourteen-year-old Emmett Till out of his grandparents' house. A white woman in town said the boy had whistled at her. Turns out she was lying, but it didn't matter. They beat on him and mutilated him before shooting him in the head and throwing his body in the river.

"Four years ago, in Powder Basin, Wyoming, twenty-one men gathered together in order to lynch Lucy Guthridge and her children, Sam, Paige, Jeb, and Melody. We owe it to the Guthridges to call this what it is, to use a hateful word we hoped we'd put to rest. You can call these men defendants, or assailants, or murderers. But when you talk about them as a group, you owe it to their victims to name them as the horrific assembly they were: a lynch mob.

"Sam was sixteen. Jeb was thirteen. Melody, eleven. Paige, ten. We know from the sworn testimony of Scott Lipscombe, one of the members of the lynch mob, that Sam and Paige were shot before they died. We know that all of the Guthridges were stabbed and bludgeoned. Spit on and kicked. We can't be sure who was alive when the lynch mob barred the doors and set the Guthridge house on fire, standing on the lawn to watch as it burned to nothing. We can't be sure how each of the children died. Only that they died. They were lynched for being different. With their deaths at the hands of these men, Lucy and Sam and Paige and Jeb and Melody Guthridge enter the ledger of names this country must never forget. Emmett Till. Sam Hose.

"Many men and women who died in a frenzy of racial violence never received justice. We were not far enough along in our moral development to condemn their killers. I like to think we are now. Finding *this* lynch mob guilty for the lives they've taken, holding them to account, will not settle our debts with the past. But we owe it to the

Guthridges, and Emmett Till, and Sam Hose to find these killers guilty. We owe it to ourselves to say we have gotten better. We recoil in proper horror from what these men have done, and we cast them out of our society, which will no longer stand for this kind of blind violence. It falls to you to speak for the dead and for the living. To administer justice needed, if too late in coming. If men and women before you had been brave enough to do so, the Guthridge family would be alive. If you are brave enough, the next Guthridge family, the next Emmett Till or Sam Hose, won't have to die at the craven hands of a lynch mob."

She goes back to her seat, and the defense attorney rises. He begins with a small chuckle to himself. He looks like every upperclassman who used to beat the shit out of Owen in high school.

"My colleague Miss Washington," he says, "who's come to us all the way from New York to lend her expertise to the prosecution, is a lovely speech maker. It's easy to get a jury riled up by invoking the injustices of the past. If these men were part of the loathsome tradition she cites, I would step across the aisle and join her in condemning them. Lynching is a horrific crime with no place in this country, in this century. It's a relic of a past we'd do well to put far behind us.

"The trouble is, Miss Washington has scant evidence that these men are guilty of the crime she claims they've committed. Or that there was a crime at all. The prosecution's case rests on the testimony of a man on trial for the murder of his own son. In a fit of paranoia, he kills his son while the boy sleeps rather than allow the possibility his son might be a Resonant. The next day, broken by shame and guilt, his mind in fragments, he concocts the story of a crime whose horror outshines the one he's confessed to. He makes a movie in his head and casts it with these men, the only friends he has. He groups them in with him, makes them culpable. *You see,* he says, *I'm not the only one who thinks the only way to deal with these new beings is to kill them. Everyone I know is as guilty as me.*

"Miss Washington would like you to take him at his word.

"Not the word of the police chief who investigated the deaths of the Guthridge family and declared it an accident. Or the medical examiner who autopsied the family and found nothing to indicate foul play. Or the community members who, one after another, have lined up to speak to the character of these men. And not the men themselves, who Miss Washington has already decided are monsters of the lowest order.

"She would like you to listen to Scott Lipscombe. A child killer. She would like you to weigh his word heavier than that of the entire town of Powder Basin, to see unbridled hatred where there is only an accident, a crime where there is only tragedy. She would like you to believe Scott Lipscombe beyond any reasonable doubt and label these men monsters.

"A fire destroyed the lives of the Guthridge family. Do not compound that tragedy by destroying the lives of these innocent men."

The jury retires to deliberate. A wing of the Arrowhead's third floor is reserved for them. Owen sees bailiffs taking trays full of fast food up to their sequester. The next day, his name doesn't come up and he can't get into the courtroom, where the audience waits to see if the jury returns a verdict. He goes back to his motel, then across the parking lot to a bar called the Chariot Lounge, where he finds a seat by the window. He nurses a Sprite, writes in his notebook, and watches the front of the motel. At four o'clock, two vans pick up the jury and take them to the courtroom.

Owen walks up to the bartender, who's been watching him warily, and orders a vodka soda. He worries the bartender will ask for ID, but it's dead and the man shoves him his drink, a browning wedge of lime perched on its rim. Owen finishes it and another. As he orders a third, the prosecution lawyer, Miss Washington, comes into the bar, looking defeated. He watches her order a glass of white wine, which the bartender pours from a single-serve plastic bottle. She reaches into her purse and pulls out a book, one of those little paperbacks. Something science fiction-y. Cautiously, aware of the sound of his footsteps in the empty bar, he crosses to her, sits down on the stool beside her.

"Is it over?" he asks. She looks at him, startled. "The trial. I've been watching it. On television, mostly."

She nods. "Not guilty on all counts," she says. "The jury didn't believe there was a crime."

"They didn't believe a crime happened, or they didn't believe killing a Resonant is criminal?"

"No idea," says Miss Washington. "I'm sure someone will interview one of them. Maybe we'll get a hint of what they talked about in deliberation. But something like this,

I can't help thinking they couldn't hold these men guilty without holding themselves guilty, too."

"I don't understand," Owen says.

"Everyone in that town fucking knew what happened," she says bitterly. "The cops and the ME and the wives and kids. They all knew, and they all shut up about it. We should've had every single one of them on trial. Not just the rednecks who held the knives and the bats."

Owen Curry nods. He thinks of what his friend told him about delivering justice. He thinks about Miss Washington's speech to the jury. Before he can take the next step, the doors of the bar swing open, and the defendants parade in. Owen knows them by name. He's been studying the case. The first one through the door is Danny Randall, who, according to Scott Lipscombe's testimony, organized the whole thing. "Troy, I want to buy these innocent men some beers," he crows.

The men file in behind him, itching in suits they're not used to wearing. They collectively let up a whoop, as if they came from a softball game rather than a murder trial. Danny Randall takes up a spot on the other side of Miss Washington, close enough to cast her in his shadow. "Troy, let's make it six pitchers of Bud and keep it simple." As the bartender turns away, Danny Randall notices who he's standing next to.

"Well, shit," he says. "I did not imagine you'd be staying in town very long. Troy, get another glass of wine for the little lady."

"I'm good," says Miss Washington.

"It's on me," Danny says. "Part of how we do things out

here in Wyoming. No hard feelings, is what I mean."

Troy the bartender pours Miss Washington a glass, and it sits in front of her untouched. The bar is loud with the sounds of victory. Owen spins on his bar stool, scanning the room. He looks at Miss Washington and thinks about the Bible story his mother used to tell him in which God asks to see one good man in a city before he decides to destroy it. Owen can't remember how it ends. Something about salt. He leans over to Miss Washington, whispers in her ear.

"For what it's worth," he says, "I think you're a good person. And what you said yesterday meant something to me. I'll tell people what you said. I wrote it all down." He taps his notebook.

"Thank you?" says Miss Washington. She looks confused, nervous.

"I'm here to do what you couldn't," Owen says. "I looked you up, and I see you've been trying to fight for people like me. But we have to fight our own battles. That's me. I'm the one who fights. I wish you didn't have to be here. I'm sorry. It doesn't change anything, but I am."

Owen reaches into the place inside him where the null is. When he brings it into the world, it's usually like lifting an egg, bringing a treasure up from the sea. This time, it's the sea he's bringing up. Owen Curry opens himself wide, and an ocean of beautiful nothing pours out, swallowing Miss Washington and Danny Randall and the other killers, and Troy the bartender, and the whole Chariot Lounge, and the towns of Gillette and Powder Basin and everyone in them, guilty or innocent, just and unjust alike.

THE DIAMOND SEA

The crater that was once Powder Basin is wide enough across that Avi can hardly see the agents working the opposite edge of the rim. The smooth, shallow bowl is striated with lines of white that catch the afternoon sun. There was heat here, pressure. The veins of coal that kept the people of Powder Basin employed and fed for three generations were crushed into diamonds in an eye blink on the ground where they died.

Louis Hoffman's SUV pulls up behind him. He watched it make its way around the circumference toward him. All the Homeland agents drive essentially the same car, but Avi knew this one was Louis's and that it was headed for him.

"There's an argument to be made that this is on you," Louis says, slamming the car door. He walks up to the very edge, digs his toe under a clump of dirt fused to glass on one side, and kicks it. It skitters down the curve with a sound like metal scraping teeth. "Assuming we're looking at what we're looking at. If you and I had been together on this years ago—"

"Kay was here," Avi says.

"What?"

"Kay," says Avi. "She was working with the prosecution. She'd been here for weeks."

"I went over the list of the missing and didn't see her."

"She was practicing under her maiden name," Avi says. "Kay Washington. It wasn't legally changed yet, but that's what she was going by professionally."

"Jesus. Kay." Louis stands with his back to the crater. His wife ran off when their kid was small. Before Avi lost his leg, Louis used to bring his kid over to play with Emmeline, but the two never got along. Kay spent time with the boy, helping him with his math homework at the kitchen counter while Avi and Louis drank beer and Emmeline drew countless pictures at the table. Avi knew she and Louis had kept in touch, not close but as close as Louis got to anyone.

"Anyway," Avi says, "what were you saying?"

"I didn't mean—"

"No, you're right, Louis. This is on me."

"Are you so desperate to feel important that you'd take the deaths of thirty thousand people on your conscience?" someone asks from behind them. Avi turns to see Patrick climbing out of a rental car. He puts on a pair of sunglasses before he approaches the glare of the crater.

"My wife was here," Avi tells Patrick. "Emmeline's mother."

The stridency leaves Patrick's face, as if he's been replaced by another person, one with a functioning set of emotions. "Avi, I'm sorry," he says. He puts a hand tentatively on Avi's shoulder, and when Avi doesn't swat it away, he rests it there.

"I haven't told Emmeline," Avi says. "I came here first. I should have gone to Emmeline. Tomorrow's Wednesday. They have lunch together on Wednesdays." It occurs to Avi that Emmeline already knows. Kay must have missed weeks' worth of their lunches together. She told Emmeline where she was. If the news is out there already, if Emmeline has heard what's happened here, she knows. Leaving all that aside, Emmeline has her own way of knowing things. She has since she was little, so pronouncedly so that Avi remains convinced it's her ability. Since the beginning of all this, he's had a question and an answer. He's waited for someone, Emmeline, Fahima, any of them, to confirm that the two are a pair. Now he assumes that they are, that they always have been. Emmeline's ability is knowing, even knowing something before it happens. Maybe she never told him because she's known what would happen to Kay. Maybe she knows how Avi dies, too.

"Are you sure you want to be here?" Louis asks.

Avi shakes his head to clear it. Light glinting off the diamond veins burns on his eyelids. "I'm fine," he says. "It's fine."

Patrick and Louis decide to continue as if Avi isn't there. Avi returns his attention to the crater. He tries to imagine the spot above which Kay was standing when it happened. All points along the curve slide into one another. He pictures her floating over the center, the zero point. She's reading her book, having a drink. He likes to think that she didn't know what was happening. That she was there one second, gone the next.

"It's amazing," says Patrick, lowering his glasses.

"You sound impressed," Louis says.

"I can be impressed and horrified," says Patrick. "You think people who saw the atomic blasts weren't impressed?"

"Scary analogy," Louis says.

"Owen Curry is become death," Avi mumbles. "Devourer of worlds."

"Oppenheimer said that because he'd created the bomb," Patrick says. "You didn't create Owen Curry."

Avi's not sure this is true. He sees himself in the manager's office of the Roseland Rest, about to call Louis and Homeland down on Owen Curry. Would they have gotten there before Patrick and Kimani and the others grabbed him? Would they have shot him down the way he deserved rather than throw him in a cell and forget to keep eyes on him? Owen Curry was a monster then. Now he was close to being a god. Avi had provided the time Owen Curry needed to blossom into a true horror.

"I can hold off press conferences another day," Louis says. "There were people taking shots of the site before we got here. Photos are out there. People are going to assume one of you did this."

Patrick nods. "There's already been an incident near Bishop. One of the second-years was chased down an alley. They threw stones at her. I suppose the classics never go out of style."

"Is she okay?" Avi asks.

"She's a lithic," Patrick says. Avi and Louis look at him, confused. "She controls rocks. She sent the stones flying back at them. If it'd been beer bottles or bullets, it would've been a different story."

"I can have the New York office—" Louis begins, but Patrick cuts him off.

"We'll take care of it," he says.

"Working with Homeland could be seen as a sign of cooperation," Avi offers. "Or it could get you disappeared. Anything ever come of that, Louis?"

Louis glares at him. "No comment," he says.

"Working with Homeland would be a gesture of appeasement," Patrick says. "A sign that our people need protection." He sweeps his hand out toward the place Powder Basin used to be. "Which of our people need protection, Agent Hoffman?" There's a dictatorial grandeur in the gesture that makes Louis shuffle his feet nervously. *Look on our works, ye mighty,* it says.

"I've got to get back to it," Louis says. He puts his hands on Avi's shoulders awkwardly, the prelude to a potential hug. "About Kay—"

"Thanks, Louis," Avi says.

"I'll call you," Louis says, getting back into his SUV.

"Yeah." Louis drives away, leaving clouds of pale dust in his wake. Avi and Patrick stand side by side at the edge, looking at the crater in respectful silence.

"You should call your daughter," Patrick says without turning to him.

"I should tell her in person," Avi says.

Patrick lowers his sunglasses and looks at Avi over the rims. "You're not allowed at Bishop."

"Don't you think they'd make an exception?"

"I wouldn't let any one of you people through the door," Patrick says.

Avi sniffs, pinches dust out of his nose. "I'll have her meet me somewhere else," he says. "The bakery on Lexington."

"You want her leaving the school?"

"Well, what the fuck am I supposed to do?" he snaps.

"I actually don't care what you do, Avi," Patrick says. "I never have. But I'd ask yourself if you're helping Emmeline by staying in her life. Or if you're blundering around, doing more harm than good because you can't imagine the world as anything but a story with you as the main character."

There's no anger in Patrick's voice as he says it, only calm disdain.

"I can't leave her," Avi says.

"Because it would hurt her or because it would hurt you?" Patrick asks. Avi doesn't answer. "It seems impossible to cut yourself off from the people you love. But there are times it's necessary. It can be done. I'm not sure it can be fixed after you've done what you need to do. After you've gotten yourself right. Once it's done, it's done." He kneels down. His arm extends an extra yard so he can lay his hand flat on the surface of the crater. "There are days I don't think about my friends at all," he continues. "I think about what's necessary. I wake up, and I move forward like a car someone else is driving. I get to the end of the day, and I don't even know what I've done, but I know I'm one day farther along. They don't even feel like bad days anymore." He looks up at Avi and smiles, a grin that's too wide and pulls the corners of his mouth out like someone's tugging at them with hooks.

"I almost asked if you were staying in town," he says, staring at the space where the town used to be.

"I'm in Moorcroft," says Avi. "Twenty miles east. They have a Best Western."

"Sounds nice," Patrick says.

Avi shrugs. "It has a bar. You?"

"I've seen what I need to see," Patrick says. "I'm headed back."

"To Bishop?"

"Maine," says Patrick. "Bishop left me his house up there. I'm supposed to be resting. I've been having headaches."

"Now you're back on the hunt?"

"My time 'on the hunt' hasn't done sweet fuck-all," Patrick says. "So no. I'm going to go do what damage control I can here, and then I am going to stare out at the ocean and wait for war."

"It won't come to that," Avi says.

"No, of course not," says Patrick. "Everything will be just fine."

The bar at the Best Western in Moorcroft consists of four bar stools. Avi walks in and sees Louis sitting at one of them. He could take the one on the far end, but it would be a useless bit of aggression. He sits down next to Louis and orders them each a shot of whiskey. Louis downs his without saying anything, and Avi orders himself a beer.

"Your friend's a piece of work," Louis says after a while. "Real fucking charmer."

"He never liked me," Avi says. "From day one."

"And you're such a lovable guy," Louis says.

"You're never going to find Owen Curry, are you?"

"I've missed my best chances," Louis says. "My guess is no. On the plus side, I am expensing my drinks to Homeland, so I am on my way to getting very drunk."

"You stopped taking my calls."

"Don't act like a jilted prom date," Louis says. "I gave you what I could."

"I have missing persons reports," says Avi. "Hundreds, all across the Midwest. I have names on the guys who picked me up, Louis. They match people on the payroll of the same corporation that funds the Kindred Network. There are land deals—"

"So what?" says Louis, turning toward Avi, angry. "You see what I saw today and you want to tell me those guys wouldn't be justified? One of them killed your wife, Avi. Isn't that enough?" Avi wants to argue with him, but he's had enough. It's not that he wants them put into camps, but there are days he wishes he could forget that the Bishop Academy and Owen Curry and all the rest of it existed. A flush of shame blooms on Avi's face at the thought as Louis relents. "I'm sorry. Long bad day." He signals the bartender for another round. "You want to see something strange?"

Louis pulls out both of his phones. He has one for work and one for personal use. The personal one is newer, nicer.

He puts the work phone back in his pocket and pulls up an image on the other. It's a large sample jar full of clear liquid. Louis hits "play," and a small piece of matter, the size of one knuckle of a finger, wriggles and twitches in the liquid like a worm on a hook. It distends until it is a thin needle the whole length of the jar, then shrivels back up, a dark kidney bean in suspension.

"They found it when they were doing the autopsy on the kid from the Hargrave murder," says Louis. "Darren Helms. It was in his fucking brain. The kid had been dead for hours, but this little guy was wiggling around in there, nestled up against his—" Louis snaps his fingers, looking for a word. "—para hippo."

"Parahippocampal gyrus," says Avi. He presses "play" on the short video again.

"It's still alive in a fucking jar in a fucking lab," Louis says. "The tech guys say it's giving off a signal like they do."

"Like who do?" Avi asks.

Louis looks around the empty bar, then leans in very close. "The freaks, Avi. The Resonants. It's doing their whole resonating thing in the jar, just humming the fuck along like we didn't cut it out of a dead kid's brain." The video ends, and Louis pockets his phone. "If you know one of them that's got superbrainworm powers, let me know. I'd like to bring them in for questioning."

An ugly thought forms in Avi's mind, too large and terrible to share with Louis, to even speak yet. He tells himself it's ridiculous as he orders another drink. The liquor won't wash it away, and in the middle of the night he's thinking it. It's becoming more solid, crystalizing from wild theory into probable fact.

When Avi lands in Portland, Maine, he has eight messages and countless texts from Emmeline. He eyes the departures board. There's a flight to New York leaving in forty minutes and another late tonight, six hours from now. *I'll go and talk to him and make it back in time*, he thinks. *I can be at the school before midnight. I'll go to her room and wake her. I'll take her out of there, and we can be together.*

He rents a car and drives south and toward the coast. Out of the city, on Highway 1, he speeds by a gun dealer at seventy miles an hour. He takes a hard U-turn and goes back. For an extra hundred bucks, waiting periods and background checks are forgotten, and Avi walks out with a .38 revolver, the same gun he has at home. *What good is it going to do you? What are bullets to a man made out of rubber?* But there's a comfort in having it, seeing it on the passenger seat next to him.

The address is easy to find. Kevin Bishop is listed in the phone book. 2246 Oceanside Way. He thinks about this enclave of Resonants hiding in plain sight, shielded by their money. What would Kevin Bishop have been if he wasn't rich? What would the world have looked like if Kevin Bishop hadn't possessed the resources to hide them all?

Avi listens to talk radio the whole drive. On a Kindred Network station, a new Jefferson Hargrave, one lacking the original's veneer of civility, is calling for open war. He's calling for extermination squads. He's calling for an attack on the Bishop Academy, "a nest of them right in the middle of Manhattan. Burn it down. Burn them out."

Avi parks in front of the little bungalow. He fumbles bullets into the gun, four of them, before his shaking hands make the exercise ridiculous. He shoves another fistful into his pocket, tucks the gun into the back of his belt. He shuts the car door quietly and goes up the walk. Communities like this, you don't need to lock the front door. Oceanside Way is a bubble of another time, when people felt safe around each other. Avi lets himself in.

The living room is decorated with beach kitsch. A miniature ship's wheel. A stuffed gull. There are pictures of Kevin Bishop when he was younger. With faculty and students at what looks like a softball game. With Fahima and Sarah at a bar, wearing a paper party hat. Avi picks one up. It's a faded sepia shot of two men in dark suits and fedoras in front of a massive scaffold in the desert that is topped with a huge metal globe. The wire-rimmed glasses identify the man on the left as Bishop, in his midtwenties. The other man Avi doesn't recognize. He's shorter with dark hair and the square jaw of a silent film star. Written in the lower corner it says, KEVIN, RAYMOND & THE GADGET. ON THE HILL. JULY 1945.

Avi sets down the picture and looks around. He can hear music from down one of the halls. Something soft and folky. He draws the gun and follows it. He tries to be as quiet as he can, but his prosthetic clunks on the hardwood like a peg leg on a ship's deck. He stops in front of a closed door, the source of the music. Avi focuses his attention on placing the song. A bit of lyric floats toward him. James Taylor's buttery voice, assuring the listeners they've got a friend. *The soundtrack is wrong*, Avi thinks. *It should be something ominous and terrible. Black metal. A wavering minor chord.* The disconnect between song and situation makes whatever's behind the door more threatening, a cuddly thing with insides of razors and teeth. He rests his hand on the doorknob and turns it slowly.

The room looks like a dorm room at an expensive private school but divided by a sheet of heavy glass. A keypad lock and an intercom are set into the glass. The room is bathed in green light. One large window looks out onto the ocean. Owen Curry reclines on the bed, scratching words in a notebook, uninterested in the scenery. Avi approaches the glass. He taps it with the barrel of the gun, a sound like teeth dropping into a metal bowl. Owen looks up.

Avi presses the button on the intercom. "Nice to see you again, Owen."

Owen glances over. "I remember you. You're the reporter. You came and saw me when I was in that cage."

"Looks like you're still in a cage," Avi says.

"I'm healing," Owen says. "Getting ready for big things. Even bigger."

"Can you get out?"

Owen shakes his head. "Lock's right there."

"Then it's a cage." A hateful look passes over the boy's face. It's replaced by that same smug grin. "You killed my wife," Avi says.

"Could have. I killed lots of people." He swings his legs

over the edge of the bed and points at the keypad. "Seven seven three four. Come on in. I'll send you to see your wife. It might take you a while to find her." He pats his belly. "It's crowded in here. But you'll have plenty of time. You'll have forever."

Avi pauses. *She's alive,* he thinks. *Kay is somewhere inside this monster. If I let him take me, I can get her out. I can save her.*

Owen grins sickly. There's no limbo inside him. Powder Basin is dead. The girl and the pastor from Salem Baptist are dead. The people in the mall food court. Kay's dead.

Owen Curry killed her.

Avi types in *seven seven three four*.

The hum stops. The green light goes out.

Owen's grin widens, showing teeth. "Shit," he says. "That's not the door code. That's the code that shuts off the inhibitor. Sorry about that."

The glass disappears in a perfect circle. Owen lunges for the opening, eyes wild, arms extended like he's going to grab Avi and shove him into whatever void is at Owen's center. Avi levels the gun in his left hand, steadying himself with his cane. His right arm goes numb up to the shoulder and his balance slips, but he recovers and fires three shots. The recoil knocks him onto the floor. The first two hit Owen in the chest, and the third hits the center of his forehead, snapping his head back. Wet chunks spatter across the bed and the window. Owen's body drops back, hitting the bed and slumping to the floor. The echo of the shots rings in Avi's ears. Pools of blood spread on the plush carpet under the body.

It's the body of a boy, not a monster.

I thought I'd feel something, Avi thinks. *I thought I'd feel fixed.*

He notices calmly that his right arm is gone, cleanly bitten away at the shoulder. The bottom six inches of the shaft of his cane sits on the floor. There's no blood. Avi feels the smooth surface of the wound with the back of his hand. It's tender to the touch, like the socket of a pulled tooth.

He hears the door open and shut back down the hall. "I brought you some books from my parents' house," calls a voice Avi can't immediately place. "I'm meeting Senator Lowery, then going to New York. I'll be back in a day or so. It's important you don't go out. You've done an amazing thing, but you need to rest."

Patrick Davenport stands in the doorway, holding a small stack of paperbacks. Mysteries and sci-fi novels, the kind Kay used to read. Avi levels the gun and fires the last bullet. It tears through Patrick's shirt and sinks harmlessly into the flesh of his chest. Patrick drops the books and watches as Avi continues to pull the trigger, the hammer clicking into empty chambers.

"What have you done, Avi?" says Patrick. He's smiling, but there's no warmth in it. He doesn't look like the man Avi knows but someone else, someone crueler. He steps toward Avi slowly. "Don't you know what he was? What he was capable of? He was going to win the war to come. That little town full of bigots? Your wife? Those were a warm-up. A snack." Avi can't tell if Patrick's wincing or grinning, but his teeth are bared. "You killed him like it was nothing."

"You made him do it," Avi says.

Patrick stops, calmed. He puts his hand on Avi's cheek almost tenderly. It feels wrong. Something twitches and writhes under the surface of the skin. "How did you know?"

"They found a piece of you in Darren Helms's brain," says Avi.

"Ah," Patrick says.

"Why did you—"

"Shut up," Patrick says, squeezing Avi's cheeks until his eyes tear up. "You know I can't control Damps like you." One of Patrick's fingers stretches along Avi's face, behind his earlobe, into the edge of his hairline. "It's frustrating. When I put a piece of myself in someone with no Resonance, a useless Damp like you, it does the strangest thing. It goes to the same spot it would in one of us. But instead of nestling in and letting me speak to them, it roves around, knocking things over. Looking for the magic bit of them that just isn't there. We're talking about the midbrain here, so the things it's destroying are memories. Isn't that funny?"

It slides into Avi's ear, thick and viscous like a glob of spit. It blossoms inside his head, splitting into a dozen, a hundred tendrils. By the time Avi understands that they're tearing his memories to shreds, it's too late. He tries to hold on to one thought, a single moment. Standing with Kay in Central Park, Emmeline spinning at the center of a flock of geese. But the moment breaks. He sees the image, but it doesn't mean anything to him. *Who is that woman, that girl?* Pieces slide away, and there's only him, lying on the floor of a strange room. A man he doesn't know towers over him. The man kicks him in the shoulder where his arm should be, and he screams in pain.

"Now I have to change my shirt," the man says. With his finger, he plays with a hole in the shoulder of his dress shirt. He leans down, his face close to Avi's. There's something in his breath, a smell like something is dying inside him. Avi struggles not to throw up. There are things moving in his head like a school of terrible fish.

"You haven't stopped me. You haven't saved anyone," says the man. "Everyone, even you, is going to forget you ever were."

The man walks out. Avi listens to him going down another hallway. He can hear the man humming to himself. He listens as a door opens, closes. A car starts, pulls away.

He brings himself up to sitting. There's something he knows. Not a memory but a structure. A container you put things in. A way to start. *Whowhatwhenwherewhy.* He begins with the most basic.

"Who?" he mutters to himself. No answer comes. The structure falls apart. He starts to sob because he knows something has been lost and because there is no way back. You can't get anywhere from nowhere.

He's sitting on something. He shifts his weight and digs it out with his remaining hand. It's a gun. It smells of spark and burn. He turns it over, admires it. He's aware of a weight in his pocket. He sets the gun down and reaches in, pulling out the bullets and looking at them as if they're birdseed, nickels, something benign. He loads them into the gun, holding it between his knees to compensate for his missing arm. It's an action his body knows, inscribed farther down in the nerves rather than in the wreckage of his brain.

He feels a hand on his head, running through his hair. He looks up at a young woman standing next to him. She is pretty, in her early twenties, maybe, with dark skin and bright blue eyes. Her hair is like fireworks. She is crying. He doesn't know her or recognize her. She puts her hand on his face. *Someone just did this, a minute ago,* he thinks. *But that was bad and this is nice.* The thought skitters away from him, and he focuses on the young woman. Along the inside of her forearm, there's an oblong scar that looks like a galaxy written onto her skin. He reaches up and touches it with two of his fingers. He knows it from somewhere.

"Did I hurt you?" he asks.

"No, Daddy," she says. "You didn't hurt me."

"I don't know you," he says. He looks at the gun. "Everything's gone. Can you fix me?"

"I can't," she says. "There are things that happen, and they always happen. There are things I can't fix."

He nods. "You should go," he says. "I have something I need to do. I don't think you should see it."

"I'll stay here with you, Daddy," she says. She kisses him on the forehead, above his eyebrow. Her hand presses against his face, then pulls away. She gives him a little nod.

He places the barrel of the gun under his chin and fires.

DEVICE

Fahima waits for Alyssa to get up before she starts fajr, finding things to keep herself busy as the sun climbs in the window. By the time Alyssa's out of bed, she's lost the best light, the kind that stabs from the horizon rather than above it. In dawn light, Fahima can imagine a god waking somewhere in Brooklyn and lighting the sun like a first morning cigarette. Alyssa watches from the counter, holding her coffee mug in both hands, taking in the view. They're both anxious about the apartment, both worried they'll have to flee the country. When things happen, there will be a window between when it becomes necessary to leave and when it's no longer possible. Every time they watch the news or go on the Internet, they add factors to this calculation. A young blond woman from the Kindred Network, one of Jefferson Hargrave's more palatable heirs, has been making the rounds on legitimate media, suggesting federal property seizure of Resonant-owned buildings and businesses. On *NightTalk*, Lakshmi Rameswaram, who Fahima considered an ally as much for her status as a fellow brown person as for actual demonstrated sympathies, listens, intrigued, as the porcelain-faced bigot outlines her proposal. The Overton window is shifting faster than Fahima imagined it might.

A humans first group that claims Jefferson Hargrave as its patron saint marches on North Avenue in Chicago and is turned back by Chicago police. Some of the cops share cigarettes and bottled water with the Resonants who live there. Others look longingly at the protesters, wishing they could disobey orders and join in. New York City cops are in front of Bishop every day. It's unclear whether they're protecting the students or keeping them in. A freshman congressman from Wyoming introduces an internment bill in the House that passes by two votes. Lowery says it will die in the Senate, barely. There are rumors. People gone missing. Militia groups with money building makeshift prison camps in the middle of nowhere. Patrick insists that he hasn't found anything, but he's not exactly Miss Marple.

Is it time to run? Is running possible?

They shower together, making the mundane intimate and important. Fahima lets her hand dwell on Alyssa's hip. She kisses her shoulder as Alyssa reaches for the conditioner. Excuses to touch. Alyssa talks about an operation scheduled that day, one she's told Fahima about already. Fahima listens like it's the first time.

"What about you?" Alyssa asks. "What's on your schedule?" She asks as if Fahima might tell her, although she must know that Fahima has been stonewalling for weeks.

"Death rays," Fahima says. "Death rays all day."

Fahima packs up the notes she brought home last night

and sits on the arm of the couch. She told Kimani nine, and it's a quarter past. Alyssa is ready to leave, but neither of them has gone yet. One secret of long-term cohabitation is the thrill of having the apartment to yourself, even for a few minutes. Alyssa and Fahima are locked in a standoff, but Alyssa relents. She grabs her bag and has her hand on the doorknob when Fahima calls her back.

"Lys?"

"What's up?"

"You know I don't care that you're not like me?" Fahima asks. "You know I couldn't love you any more if you could read minds or lift boulders or whatever?"

"Of course," says Alyssa. "And you know I'd love you even if you couldn't—"

"I know," Fahima says. *Except it won't be like that,* she thinks. Alyssa waits for her to say something else or to explain what's going on. Fahima nods and says, "Have a great day."

"You, too," Alyssa says.

Fahima calls Kimani, and the door appears immediately to take her to her lab.

"Can you make the door any bigger?" Fahima says as she drags a large box across the lab floor. Kimani obliges, and the door expands until it takes up most of the wall. Fahima planned this device in bite-size chunks, pieces she could carry. She knew she'd be doing this part herself.

"You're cleaning all this up," says Kimani, pushing an armchair against a wall to make more space. "You're not leaving any of this in here."

"You are standing in the way of progress," Fahima says,

grunting and nudging her aside. Slowly, the device takes shape, inscrutable to anyone but Fahima. Aesthetics have always been an afterthought. iPhones and sleek laptops, machines other people think of as beautiful, leave her cold. Give Fahima a steam engine with pistons jutting and boilers frothing. Give her the clicks and spinning wheels of a Turing Colossus, grinding the Nazi Enigma code into bits. Beauty is in function. The rest is a shell.

They break for lunch, pork belly banh mi from Num Pang in Union Square. Kimani's favorite. Any food in the world at her fingertips and Kimani chooses sandwiches from down the block. Between bites, she asks Fahima again what the device is, but Fahima shakes her off. The last piece she assembles is the one with an obvious purpose. It's a seat the rest of the machinery centers on. Anyone would assume that the apparatus feeds energy into it, an electric chair. They'd have it backward. The energy will come from the chair, from its occupant. Everything else is there to handle the energy when it comes.

Fahima goes into the Hive to find Patrick and Sarah. She puts out a call, pushing their names into the malleable substance of the place. Sarah answers first, followed by Patrick. They both look annoyed.

"This is a bad time," Patrick says. "I'm meeting with Senator Lowery before the Senate vote."

"How bad?" Fahima asks.

"He thinks it'll come down to one vote, maybe two," says Patrick. "The majority leader is supposed to call it to the floor within the hour."

"It's time," Fahima says.

Patrick considers this. "Give me twenty minutes," he says, then fades out.

"You have some little plan?" Sarah asks.

"I have one big plan," Fahima says.

"And the two of you are in cahoots?"

"I don't know anything," says Kimani.

"I'm telling you all now," Fahima says. "This next step we take together."

They leave the Hive, and Sarah enters through the door, Cortex along with her. Behind her, Fahima sees what she'll always think of as Bishop's library, although she supposes it's Sarah's now. One of the perks of the headmaster's job.

"How's Alyssa?" Sarah asks.

"She's good," Fahima says. "She's doing a big surgery today. Very excited."

"Good," says Sarah.

"Tell us what's going on," Kimani says.

"I wanted to wait for Patrick," Fahima says.

"Why do I think Patrick already knows?" Sarah asks.

"He knows some," says Fahima. "I haven't gotten into the technical parts."

"Keep it like that," Kimani says.

"So how are you fixing it?" Sarah asks. Cortex looks up at Fahima expectantly.

"We can't win," Fahima explains. "For all our abilities, for everything we can do. There are too many of them and not enough of us. More than that, there's the clear line. Us and them. What we need is to blur that line. We need to make them into us. Turn our enemies into allies." She looks at them to see if they get it, but they don't. "I got the idea from drugs," she adds.

"That fills me with confidence," says Sarah.

"Rez," Fahima says. "It gives users abilities for a little while. Nothing major, nothing world-breaking. And no Hive access. It pushes something latent in them to become actual. And if it can happen in a little way—"

"It can happen big," Kimani says. She opens the door for Patrick to come through.

"What did I miss?" he says.

"Blurring the line between us and them," says Sarah.

"I was also thinking about something you said," Fahima tells Kimani. "That Bishop built the Hive to keep our numbers regulated. Like a bottleneck. The Hive lets a fraction of the energy we use through into the real world. If there were more coming through, there'd be more of us."

"How many more?" Sarah asks.

Fahima shrugs. "We don't know how narrow of a bottleneck Bishop built. What percentage he thought was acceptable. Only way to find out is to break it open."

"And this does that?" Sarah asks, pointing at the chair and the devices that surround it.

"No," says Fahima. "This *lets* someone do that. I've got one more person I have to grab."

The dorm room is dark. Fahima hears Emmeline breathing into her pillow. There's something cruel about asking anything of the girl two days after her mother died. Fahima should go talk to her, tell Emmeline she knows what it's like to lose a parent. Or better, be there to listen. Instead, Fahima's recruiting her, using her. She tells herself there's no time left. She tells herself it has to be today, now.

"Hey, Em," she says. Sheets rustle as Emmeline rolls over. The light from Kimani's room shimmers in Emmeline's teary eyes.

"Did you bring my dad?"

"No, it's just me," Fahima says. "We can go find your dad. I'll help. There's just something we need to do first."

"The thing we've been working on?"

"The thing we've been working on." The lessons have been tense, none of the light back-and-forth they used to have. Every time Fahima takes the bracelet off Emmeline, she can feel the girl's body seize up. They both half expect Emmeline to explode.

"I don't think I can," Emmeline says.

"Em, the thing that happened to your mom and all those people?" says Fahima. "It puts all of us in trouble. We're not talking days. Hours. If we're going to do this, it needs to be now. Can you help me?"

There's a pause. Fahima thinks it would be better to be thrown into cells, into camps. Better for all of them be rounded up and shipped off to a desert island than to do this to Emmeline, to force her to help when she is so hurt. Before she can rush back through the door and close it behind her, Emmeline's hand slips into hers.

"Let's go," Emmeline says.

Sarah is on her feet the moment they step in. "No," she

says. "You are not putting one of my students in danger to—"

"I would never put her in any danger," says Fahima. It's a lie. What she means is *I'd rather it was me, but it has to be her.* What she means is *If she gets hurt, there is nothing you can do to me that'd be worse than what I'll do to myself.*

"It's okay," says Emmeline. "I'm ready."

She clambers up into the chair, which now seems outsized, a throne. She sets her hands on the armrests and leans her head back as Fahima affixes a series of wires. When she's done, when Emmeline is part of the machine, Fahima turns to the rest of them, her audience.

"It's going to look strange," she says. "She'll be here but not here. She may flicker."

She turns back to the device.

"That's it?" Sarah asks. "That's all you're going to tell us?"

"You'll *see*," says Fahima. The word isn't right. They'll feel. They'll register. Sight will be a component but not the most salient one. *You'll know,* she thinks.

Fahima gives Emmeline a nod. Emmeline takes off the bracelet and closes her eyes. She begins to flutter in and out of existence like the signal on an old television. Her eyes shoot open, icy blue, staring forward at something no one in the room can see. Emmeline is in the Hive and in the real world simultaneously. If Fahima is right, *simultaneously* is no longer a word that matters for Emmeline. Emmeline is everywhere at once.

"What do you see?" Fahima asks.

"I don't . . . see," Emmeline says. Her voice is curious, like a child exploring a new space. *Space* may not be a word that matters anymore either. The machines around her hum, soaking up the energy she's tapping into and dispersing it. They're an exhaust system, coolant rods for a nuclear reactor. "There is something deep. It's in me, and I'm in it. Is that what we're looking for?"

"Yes," says Fahima. She isn't sure. They are off the map.

"It's on the other side," she says. "Some of it is here, but there's more of it there. It comes through." She looks directly at Fahima, eyes unfocused. "There's some coming through already. It's in you, too." Emmeline's head turns the way a cat turns toward an imaginary sound. "Look over there."

"Emmeline, stay here with us," says Fahima. "Stay now."

"There's a candle in the desert," she says. "Mister Bishop is watching it from a hill. He's younger than my dad."

"Emmeline, come back here," Fahima says, sounding like a scolding mother. Emmeline ignores her, stretches out her hand, extends her finger. She gives it a little twitch like she's bopping a baby playfully on the nose. Her hand falls back onto the armrest.

"What is she doing?" Sarah asks. "I feel it in my head."

"Sarah, be quiet," Patrick says.

"Is she okay?" Kimani asks.

"Emmeline," says Fahima sternly.

"I'm sorry," Emmeline says. "It's hard to move here, but it's hard not to move, too. I'm flying through everything."

"Is there a wall, Em?" Fahima asks. "Something like a wall? A blockage?"

Emmeline laughs at her. "It's not like any of those things," she says. "But I know what you mean. It's part of the Hive.

It's what it's for. It's supposed to be there."

"I need you to get rid of it, Em," says Fahima.

Emmeline turns her head toward Fahima. Her open eyes search around Fahima, everywhere but her face.

"All right," Emmeline says.

The machines are in high gear. Fahima can feel heat coming off them. She doesn't know their upper limit. She doesn't know what an explosion of Hive energy inside Kimani's room, embedded in Hivespace, would do. It's possible she's killed them all.

Then it comes. A pulse, a rush. For Fahima, it is inspiration and communion. Her mind floods with a thousand immaculate gadgets. She can hear and touch everything with a wire or a circuit. For a heartbeat she is the god of machines, godlike in the sense of an embodiment, a form that contains all iterations of itself. It washes over her, a wave of infinite potential, crashes onto the shore, and disperses.

"What was that?" Sarah says. "I felt everybody."

Patrick's face has gone doughy, and he pushes it back into shape with his hands. At first he gets it wrong. It's sharp and sculpted but not his. Someone else's. Then he pulls together, looking amazed but afraid.

Emmeline's eyes return to focus, a little girl again, no longer a conduit, no longer the holder and shaper of unimaginable things.

When they manifest in the Hive, it's in the place where Emmeline was held captive once, years ago. Where Fahima got the first hint of what the girl was and what she potentially could do. If the Hive was built, it could be unbuilt. If it was a valve, letting some amount of energy into the world, that valve could be opened further, letting in more. From there, Fahima saw two possibilities. All of them, everyone with abilities, could become like gods. It was what she felt the moment after Emmeline opened the floodgates. It was terrifying. Fahima is relieved that it wasn't permanent. She couldn't stay like that forever. No one could. You'd go out of your fucking mind.

The other possibility was that the energy could be shared. Like a tuning fork struck against a piece of inert metal so that both ring. Only times a million. Times a hundred million. This ringing wouldn't die the quick death of the tuning fork's tone. It would resonate with a hundred million other ringings, form into one great note, the start of a song.

Fahima, Emmeline, Kimani, Patrick, and Sarah stand on a hill within the Hive and watch as people appear. They come faster and faster, crowding the infinite space.

"How many?" Patrick asks.

Fahima tilts her head to one side, then the other. "Two in three," she says. A guess. "I'd say somewhere from half to two thirds within the signal range."

"What's the range?"

"North America."

"I'll call Lowery," Patrick says. "Tell him they're going to need a bigger camp."

"Bet he already knows," Kimani says.

It doesn't stop. Fahima remembers a story. A flock of birds fly by. If there's a definite number of birds, God exists. If the number is indefinite, he doesn't. *There's no counting them*, Fahima thinks, watching the Hive crowd to overflowing, feeling like a creator god herself. In the Hive it lasts long enough that Fahima and her friends can recognize it for what it is. *A people become a nation*, Fahima thinks. *The wall between us and them torn down until there's just us.*

"What did I do?" asks Emmeline.

Fahima doesn't have a full answer. She has a suspicion about the candle Emmeline saw in a desert, the massive implications of Emmeline's tiny hand gesture. A notion of circular time. *You might have started everything*, Fahima thinks. *Alpha and omega.*

Patrick puts a hand on Emmeline's back. "I think you saved us."

THIS MUST BE THE PLACE

The biggest contributing factor to the day, the one she won't ever mention to Miquel, is that Carrie's lost all hope. Months have passed with no word, no response, and she's stopped expecting one. She's stopped looking at the fence line. She's started keeping her head down. *You have to make a life here or die*, she tells herself. Those are the options now.

Travis made the dress out of fabric Carrie helped smuggle in. It was teal and shiny, like the face of the ocean. Every fitting, Diane talked about what Travis *could have* done. "He could have dressed you in the true ocean," she said. "Glimmers of fish and the roil of waves. It would've been beautiful." Her hand traces the juddering seam lines of the dress, jagged like a cartoon shark's grin. Last fall, Mister Mosby cracked Travis in the back of the skull with a rifle stock for mouthing off in the commissary line. Carrie can see the bright red blood on pale green tile. The camp doctor, who reeks of gin and a faint whiff of piss, gave Travis a clean bill after a cursory exam with a penlight. Travis's hands still shake. Every time Carrie leaves the two of them, Diane rests her hands on his to steady them as he works.

"It will be beautiful," Travis said to her, kissing her on the cheek. Carrie and Miquel would never be a couple like this, united in a project, a craft that demanded its own language. She wished Miquel wanted to fight with her, but it wasn't something they shared. She looked at the dress and saw the Atlantic from Coney Island at night, Ferris wheel lights dancing in the surf. She worried that all that brought the two of them together was their past. She was trying to give weight and solidity to something that had already evaporated.

Miquel's suit is borrowed from Sidney in Hall B, who was wearing it when he was taken. The camp gets thrift store clothes, mostly tee shirts and sweaters. The suit doesn't fit well, although Travis did his best. *We'll do it again on the outside*, Carrie thinks. *We'll get everything right. On the outside* has a fairy tale ring to it. There's only this making do: borrowed suits and dresses that are not the true ocean but a memory of it superimposed onto bootlegged cloth.

The ceremony is held in the laundry. Mister Bailey guards the door for them, an armed usher. It's damp inside but cooler than the July desert night. The room is bright with the smell of mildew and bleach. It's perfect.

Felix, who cooks in the commissary, serves as the officiant. He was a minister once, in the last life. On the outside. It's good to remember that they were all something else before. The sermon is overprepared, more than they needed. It's as much for him as for them. *Maybe that's what weddings are like*, Carrie thinks, never having attended one as a guest. The way funerals are to remind the living they're alive, weddings call lovers back to the day when their love was worth celebrating. An infinite regression, new loves placing themselves in conversation and context with old so that one day they can be recalled, too.

All this overthinking as she stands facing Miquel, the one she loves, the one she's loved so long she can't remember a version of herself that didn't feel defined in relation to him. She has his hands in hers, the sleeves of his suit coat nearly covering them. He looks at her the way he did the first time they met, when he was the first one at Bishop to see her. A look that affirms that she is real and solid. He grounds her in the world when she feels most at risk of floating away.

There is a kiss that almost escapes her. She catches the end of it, returning to her body from her thoughts before their lips part. Their friends clap, and the sound caroms off the walls as if everyone they know is in attendance. Thinking of the people here as their friends is strange. Some of these friendships are old; some started in Topaz. They don't seem real. Bryce and Hayden, Jonathan and Rafa, who lost an eye while in custody. *An accident, of course.* These are the relics of their past life carried over into this one. Travis, Diane, Felix. All new to them but no less dear. Topaz has fused them all. If they ever get out of here, they'll be different from everyone else, everyone who's never been inside. She wonders what will happen to those friendships, then reminds herself that there's no point wondering.

"Waylon's going to be so pissed he wasn't here," Bryce

says to her, kissing her on the cheek. Tricia passes around paper cups of hard cider, mulled at the end of last fall and hidden in oak barrels through the winter. It's bitter and crisp. Rafa and Jonathan play quietly in the corner on an improvised drum kit and a guitar Hayden had smuggled in. The comforts of the real world, leaked into Topaz Lake.

"That's the thing with destination weddings," Bryce continues. "Not everybody's willing to travel for this shit."

"When you guys get married, I'll get arrested so I can be there," Carrie says. She immediately regrets it as his smile becomes brittle. She gets so caught up in her own unhappiness, she can't see how much worse it is for others. Bryce hasn't had any communication with Waylon in the year and a half they've been here. She wonders what's worse, the separation or the disappointment that Waylon hasn't managed to find him. Bryce holds out hope of rescue not because of the message in a bottle Siu threw into the Hive before Christmas but because he can't let himself think that Waylon would stop looking.

Hayden sings "I Found a Reason" by the Velvet Underground for their first dance. The words take on new meanings from the situation and their surroundings.

Something borrowed, something blue, Carrie thinks as she and Miquel sway and slowly turn. *Something old. Three out of four*.

The guests at the reception rotate in and out. Everyone wants to be here because of Miquel. For him. There are satellite receptions throughout the camp, and except for their close friends, guests leave to let others in, then come back, drunker, happier. Carrie imagines the other parties like lights on a string, connected but individual.

When the feeling comes over her, Carrie mistakes it for love. It's a pulse of warmth and strength, a rush. Like a chord sustained on a piano, it lands and holds. She's dancing with Miquel and feels like something has been lifted off her. Then she looks at his face and sees the shock there.

"Carrie, you're gone," he says. Carrie holds up her hand, which is wrapped in his. It's transparent. She looks out the small, high windows of the laundry, but the pale green of the inhibitor lights is glowing outside. This is something else. Carrie hardly has time to imagine what it could be when the door flies open. Mister Benavidez and Mister Herschel and Mister O'Keefe swagger in like gunslingers, hands on their hips. The whole contingent guarding the western fence in this sector. Miquel shoves Carrie behind him.

"I guess our invites got lost in the mail," Mister Benavidez says. "It's a good thing Mister Guzman let us know. It'd be a shame if we missed it. Congratulations, teach." He slaps Miquel on the shoulder. "Hey, Shakes, pour me a drink, huh?" Travis obeys. The cider sloshes in the paper cup as he hands it to Mister Benavidez.

"Did you know I'm a big reader, teach?" says Mister Benavidez. "I love reading history. Medieval times and shit? You know they used to have this thing called *prima nocta*. The lord of the castle, he had the right to fuck a man's wife on their wedding night. *Prima nocta*'s Latin for first fuck or some shit. So tell me, teach. Where's the bride?"

Mister Benavidez is looking right at Miquel and Carrie.

Carrie's eyes are locked on his, but he can't see her. He can't see her.

Carrie glances at Bryce and Hayden, who look like themselves again. She sees the glow in Jonathan's chest brighten. Carrie steps out from behind Miquel. She can feel her ability, like a radio signal muddled in static. But the volume's way up, and she can hear the song. They all can.

"I can see you're upset," Miquel says, patting the air between them with his hands. Warm waves come off him. Carrie rests her hand on the knife next to the cake. It's dull, useless. She eyes Mister Benavidez's gun, unclipped in the holster, his hand near it but not blocking it.

"You trying to put a whammy on me?" asks Mister Benavidez. He takes a threatening step toward Miquel. As he does, Carrie grabs the gun out of the holster. It hangs in the air, leveled at Mister Benavidez's head. He turns toward it and nearly has time to mutter *what the fuck* before Carrie shoots him in the forehead. Mister Herschel screams. Mister O'Keefe pulls his gun, but Bryce smashes him in the face with the thick branch of his arm. Blood sprays from Mister O'Keefe's nose and leaks from his eyes as he crumples to the ground. Edith Fowler, the nice old lady Miquel gave smuggled marmalade to, who just stopped by to say congratulations, gently pats Mister Herschel on the head, and he drops. The room is silent, the high whine of the gun's retort echoing in Carrie's ears.

"Is he dead?" Miquel asks, looking down at Mister Herschel, who could be sleeping.

"I'm afraid so," says Edith.

"We have to go," Carrie says. "I don't know what's going on, but they could figure out how to shut us back down in a minute. This is our chance."

"This is our wedding," Miquel says. He looks at her, in his ill-fitting suit, asking her to come back, stay. They are speaking different languages, and Carrie knows it. This path she's started on, toward making a life here, Miquel is far ahead of her.

"We have to go," Carrie says. Bryce and Hayden lead the others out the door. "We have to go now."

"We won't be able to get the kids out," Miquel says.

"We can't save everyone right now," says Carrie. "But if we can get out—"

"Go," he says. "Come back when you can save everyone. I'll stay here. We'll be ready."

Carrie wants to drag him along. She wants to explain that she can't go without him. She wants to say it, but she doesn't. She doesn't know what version of herself is waiting out there, what shape she'll be apart from him. But if it's impossible for her to stay, it's more impossible for him to leave.

She kisses him. This kiss she's present for; she tries to memorize it. *Not the last time*, she tells herself, but there's no conviction in the thought. She holds the hem of her wedding dress and takes off, over the hill. After a few steps, she stops and turns back, thinking she heard him call out. Miquel stands there, watching her go. Carrie realizes that he knew it would come to this. Even at Bishop, he knew that if they got together, she'd be the one to leave. He understood her love, the limits of it, better than she did. She wants to stay, if only to prove him wrong. But she hears metal strain as Bryce rips open the chain link. She hears shots fired along the eastern fence.

She'll go and bring help, fight her way back here. There must be a way to save all of them. She's insufficient to the task now. It calls for someone else, someone better. She can become that only if she gets out.

EIGHT

PUTTING OUT FIRES WITH GASOLINE

I hear in the middle of most wars anything
which swallows darkness is a blessing . . .
—HANIF ABDURRAQIB,
*"Genesis 9: A Suite for Those Declaring
Themselves to Heaven"*

PULSE

It takes place in a moment, a switch flipped. Across North America, 200 million people nod off like late-night drivers pushing too far in search of a welcoming rest stop, eyes drooping as their minds slip away for a blink. Within that blink, infinite space. A sex dream, a terror vision of a fiery crash. After the Pulse, people find themselves in the Hive for the first time. Startled, they look to people around them for answers. Some begin conversations, ask questions, before they wake up. They're in the Hive for minutes. In the real world, a fraction of a second passes.

They're changed, but not all the changes are immediate.

Ahmad Roche notices a patch of goose bumps on his forearm. He doesn't grow downy pinfeathers for a few more days.

Omar Wright wakes from his moment in the Hive with a splitting headache, a burning right in the center of his skull. He meets up with friends that night at one of Cleveland's divier bars, intending to self-medicate with tequila. In the morning, the headache is gone, replaced by a new one, more diffused through the entirety of his head. His mouth is dry and fuzzy. There's a man next to him in the bed, although he can't remember coming home with anyone. Omar gives him a prod in the ribs, and the man rolls over to face him. He's a perfect duplicate of Omar: every hair, every tattoo, even the pockmark above his left eyebrow where he'd picked off a chicken pox scab as a kid. Terrified, Omar scrambles backward, tangling himself in the sheets and toppling over the side of the bed. His double pauses breathing, then returns to gentle, undisturbed snores.

Jeneva Cheatham believes she ate something spoiled at lunch. She swears off clams the way she's sworn off hard liquor and guys who claim to be writers. That night she vomits up a sticky, opalescent black liquid that cools into glass in her hands.

Dorian Manzo feels a spring in his step. *Finally over him,* he thinks. He'd hoped his grief about the breakup would die this way, starved for the sunlight of his attention rather than picked apart in therapy. He doesn't notice that his feet are no longer touching the ground. Tomorrow he flies.

Barbara Stannis, single mother first, dental hygienist second, attributes the buzzing in her head to last night's third glass of red wine and gulps a handful of Tylenol when she gets home. The noise persists the next day and the next. It's a week before it resolves from a staticky distraction to a bell-clear running feed of her teenage son's contemptuous thoughts about her as he sits at the breakfast table, waiting for her to serve up eggs. Barbara doesn't last long in the brave new world. Before support services can emerge, she's overcome by the barrage of other people's honest, cruel thoughts. Pills and the most expensive bottle of vodka she's ever bought chase her into the quiet. She's not alone. The suicide rate in the United States skyrockets for six months. One in four newly minted psychics take their own lives before the year is out. It turns out that lying and concealment save lives.

Many of the affected are children, babies. Their abilities manifest in their early teens, in a changed world. They remember the Pulse as a time they felt safe. *I feel like a cell in an organism*, Rosa Nash tells Mr. Saunders, her sixth grade science teacher at Allentown Middle, who has grown stone-hearted to the intuitive insights of children. Years later, after the war, Rosa floats above Mr. Saunders's house, watching him load up his minivan so his family can join the parade of the displaced. She feels vindicated watching someone who pissed on her dreams crash hard against reality.

Some changes are immediate. In a marketing meeting, Lucie Arsenault bursts into flames. She's fine. Ronnie Eggleston, sitting next to her, is rushed to the hospital with second-degree burns on his arms. A polyester swath of his cheap suit fuses into his flesh, leaving him a houndstooth-patterned tattoo.

Syd Buckner breaks out in eyes, all over his skin. Each one pops open with a wet unsticking noise, flooding his visual cortex with information until he manages to get the bulk of them to shut.

Clay Weaver's boss is talking about the summer numbers, gesticulating enthusiastically, but the sound and his motions are slowed down. Clay feels as if he's watching a movie, and the film's become stuck in the projector, warping and melting.

In Central Park, a pregnant woman floats into the air. She

grabs at a lamppost to keep from drifting away.

On Main Street in San Jose, a teenage boy rips a mailbox out of the ground and holds it effortlessly over his head to impress a girl, grinning idiotically.

At a diner in Syracuse, a wife looks at her husband in horror and begins screaming curses at him. The words emerge from her mouth, streaming hot pink letters that crash into his face like the torrent of a fire hose.

In the common room of an Omaha nursing home, an elderly woman pets the luxuriously furred tail she's sprouted and invites others to do the same.

At North Fremont and Michigan in Portland, Oregon, a cop pulls a gun on her partner, aiming it at his face, which has the consistency of melted wax. Through drooping lips, he begs her not to shoot.

On Delta Airlines Flight 2377 from Los Angeles to Chicago, the passenger in seat 15F explodes in a burst of nothingness. Null. He turns up unharmed on the ground directly below, cradled in the piece of fuselage he took with him. The passenger in 12A, acting on instinct, unbuckles her seat belt, brushing aside the bright yellow mask dangling from the ceiling. She pushes through panicked passengers to the wound in the side of the plane and presses her hands toward it. A shimmering wall expands out, sealing the breach. When Flight 2377 lands, the passenger in 12A is taken into custody. The passenger manifests are scrubbed from Delta's computers. Of the 189 people on the flight, 103 are Resonants when they land. None say anything as the passenger is taken. Photos of the plane on the tarmac at O'Hare, gaping hole in the side, are drowned in the noise of that news day. The hero of Flight 2377 never resurfaces and is never named.

On the floor of the Senate, Senator Frank Adkins at the podium argues that although the Japanese internment was a mistake, we now face a clear and present threat. He looks down to see his hands, gripping the edges of the lectern in his fervor, are glowing blue. The minority leader, Stewart Quinn, can hear the thoughts of all the senators present, along with everyone in the gallery and the protesters outside. He bangs his gavel frantically to adjourn the session. Senator Lowery grasps what is happening and who's responsible. *Why didn't they tell me?* he thinks. *Why do they never trust me?* He reaches into the storm of Senator Adkins's mind. Frank's a bigot, yes, but also a colleague. Senator Lowery broadcasts ineffective words of calm.

Eleven members of the upper chamber gain abilities in the Pulse. This is statistically low compared with the general population. In the House of Representatives, the percentage affected is even lower. When enough time has passed to make jokes, a late-night host quips that whatever power intervened that day had no use for rich old white men. As the audience cracks up, a flicker of sadness crosses his face. He wasn't changed either.

Two hundred million change. Not only with the manifestation of their abilities but with a connection to one another. Their minds link together like their fates. The argument could be made that everyone is connected that way all the time, tied together in common cause. Someone is always around to spout off how the bell tolls for thee, all lives matter. But 200 million feel it, deep and visceral. It's a feeling not unlike love. It shares with love the potential to curdle, warp into its opposite.

For a moment, they are all together.

Fahima stares at the bedroom ceiling, Alyssa's arm draped over her. She should be at Bishop. She should always be at Bishop. A week has passed since the Pulse. Anything could happen at any second. But Fahima is late getting out of bed, waiting for Alyssa to wake up so they can be together a few moments more. *I've earned this,* she thinks, as if she's arguing with a world trying to take it away from her. Like a prayer answered with a no, Fahima's ears pop. Alyssa stirs next to her. Fahima scans the walls of their room for the door. Kimani opens it slowly and peers out.

"You got a second?" she asks.

"Hey, Kimani," Alyssa mumbles.

"Hey, A. I've got to steal your girl."

"Sharing her with the whole world," says Alyssa as she turns over and goes back to sleep.

"You couldn't call?" Fahima asks. She pulls a robe on over her nightshirt.

"They found him," Kimani says.

Fahima stops what she's doing. "Which *him*?"

"Both."

The day before, Chicago police had found the bodies of Avi Hirsch and Owen Curry in the attic of the Hirsches' house on Jarvis Avenue. Kimani got the call because she was listed as Avi's emergency contact, a demonstration of how few friends Avi had left that makes Kimani and Fahima both profoundly sad. The narrative is unclear, but the police think Owen Curry followed Avi from Powder Basin to his home and attacked him, severing Avi's arm with his ability before Avi shot him in the head. Then Avi shot himself. This last part, no one could quite parse. But they reasoned that Avi Hirsch had recently lost his wife. Add in a traumatic injury on top of an existing traumatic injury, and it wasn't a huge jump to get to suicide. The police said the bodies had been there several days before a neighbor found them.

"We should tell Emmeline as soon as we can," Kimani says. "It's not going to get any easier."

"Yeah," says Fahima. Her head plays a greatest hits compilation of every terrible thing she's ever said to Avi, with bonus tracks of things she thought but didn't find the opportunity to say. "It's good, though, that it was him. Avi." Her own voice sounds distant. "That he was the one to get Owen Curry. He must have been happy with himself." The thought fails to comfort her. How happy could he have been as he shot himself? Maybe he'd reached a place where he could finally stop.

"When I tell her, I'll say Curry killed him," Kimani says. "No need to tell her the other stuff."

"You're going to tell her by yourself?"

"Unless you want to—"

"No," says Fahima. "She trusts you. It'll be easiest coming from you." She's aware how badly she handled the death of Emmeline's mother, leaving the girl alone until she needed her, pulling Emmeline out of grief for her own purposes. She hasn't spoken to Emmeline since the Pulse, even to thank her. She's thought about Emmeline only when considering ways to replicate it. Fahima and Emmeline and the device on a European tour.

"She trusts you, too," Kimani says.

Maybe she shouldn't, Fahima thinks.

That afternoon, with the relish of a drunk settling in with a bottle of scotch, Fahima opens a folder of gas chromatography results on the black glass substance some of the new Resonants produce and manipulate, along with a comparative report on a sample of the silvery substance Isidra Gonzalez creates. Reading about chemical compounds while the world threatens to burn is a luxury she doesn't have time for, and a lot of the chemistry is lost on her. But the black glass is fascinating. It looks similar to the black flowers in the Hive, as if they've seeped into the real world. If they are the same substance, this is a gift, the meal Fahima's dreamed of appearing on her table. Imagine putting a cloud of dreamstuff through a gas chromatograph to see what it's made of. The building could be on fire and Fahima would be here at her desk with this report.

She makes it only far enough to see that unlike the substance Isidra produces, the black glass is nonmetallic when Emmeline knocks on the lab door.

"You have a minute?" Emmeline asks. Her voice is a small bird in the room.

"Yeah, Em," she says. "I was meaning to come see you."

"I was hoping you might want to go for a walk," Emmeline

says. "I need to get out of here a little."

The debt Fahima owes Emmeline goes unimaginably beyond an hour's walk and is past due. Fahima shuts her report and follows Emmeline to the elevator. On the way out, Shen puts a hand on Fahima's shoulder and whispers, "Be safe."

It's one of those days before New York dives into the swelter of full summer, before the air stagnates and curdles, when cool breezes blow through the streets and Manhattan feels like a city by the ocean. It's a different city than it was a week ago. Bike couriers race each other in the air overhead, no longer limited by the streets but by the canyon walls formed by the buildings on either side of Lexington Avenue. A boy with glowing eyes sits on his stoop calling *I can see your tits* at women as they pass by. On the corner of 58th and Fifth, a man leans over the edge of a fifty-gallon steel drum full of water, chatting with a news vendor in a thick Brooklyn accent. Occasionally he dunks back under to keep his shining new scales moist. People eyeball these new additions to the landscape, but doing so marks them as tourists. The locals and the city itself absorb all of it, accepting it as their new normal.

"I asked Viola to come," Emmeline says as they make their way toward Central Park. "She said she's tired."

"It wears on you," Fahima says, not sure what specific thing she's talking about. Leaving the building feels like an act of resistance. She has a feeling of her body as a thing at risk for what it is. It's a feeling she hasn't had since before she resonated. She associates it with childhood, the low thrum of fear she carried out into the world every day as someone recognizably other, Muslim for all to see. Bishop made that go away for a time. Not the academy but Kevin Bishop. His dopey confidence in the arc of history, even as he kept his students hidden from it, ready to rejoin the narrative of the world when it had better roles for them to play, safer spaces for their bodies to occupy. That fear returns, and Fahima remembers the positive aspects of it. She sees more, if maybe she feels less. Her consciousness doubles, looking at the world from inside herself and at herself from the outside. It's part of why she wears hijab, to keep herself other, to remind herself of what she is and how she's perceived. She can tell who feels the same, thinks the same, by the way they move among other people, other bodies. The ones with the fear are aware of how much space they take up, where they end and the world begins. They pass through crowds the way water seeps through packed gravel, finding gaps and filling them, pooling into empty spaces. At the end of the day, when they get to places they think of as protected, the surface of them burns from exposure to the world. They curl into themselves, exhausted, protecting their centers, their hearts.

"When I was little, there was a kid who got shot by the police. It was all over the news," says Emmeline. "He was twelve. My dad said he wasn't like me, because I don't look so black that someone could tell. He said it was messed up and unfair, but it would help keep me safe." Fahima hears the insufficiency of the word *help*. "He said I'd be safe because he and my mom would protect me, only I knew he was lying. That kid had parents who wanted to keep him safe. And he was dead." Fahima looks to see if Emmeline is crying, but her face is distant. She absently spins the inhibitor bracelet on her forearm. "Adults say they'll protect you, and you get hurt. I don't look like a Resonant. Not like Bryce or the other kids that came from the Commune. When I have my bracelet on, I hardly count as one. I pass as normal. Doesn't mean I'm safe."

"No one's ever safe," Fahima says. "You wake up and you go out in the world. You take care of the people you care about. You do your best."

Emmeline looks at Fahima like she's said something vapid, the kind of platitude Fahima can't stand. She keeps walking. She's nearly as tall as Fahima, mostly leg, and Fahima falls behind. Emmeline is lanky like her father. It might be temporary. She's at that point in adolescence when the body is buffeted with contradictory messages, arguing with itself over which set of genes it wants to express. It'll work out given time.

"Do I have to identify him?" Emmeline asks.

"That's only in the movies," Fahima says.

"If I was in a movie, I'd swear revenge," says Emmeline. "I'd dedicate my life to avenging my family, like Red Emma in the comic books. My mom used to like her." She turns to Fahima. "Have you ever killed anybody?"

Fahima thinks of her list. Everyone who died in Revere. Every accident that's followed the Pulse. Every new Resonant they didn't get to before someone got electrocuted or disintegrated or had her mind wiped like a chalkboard. Every suicide by a new Resonant Fahima created who couldn't handle what he was given.

"Owen Curry's dead," Fahima says, avoiding the question. "You'll have to find something other than revenge."

"What else is there?" Emmeline asks.

Life, Fahima wants to say. *Your whole life.* But it feels like a hollow answer, so the two of them walk a few blocks in silence. They stop on the path looking out on the lake near the Ladies Pavilion. The sun is weak and milky, but NYU students soak it up on the lawn. Girls roll up tee shirts to expose midriffs; boys pull off polo shirts to reveal carefully curated musculature. Fahima chuckles at how the whitest white girls aspire to brownness, pursue it until their skin goes leathery, but would never deign to date a brown girl. She misses Alyssa, and she scans the skyline for Mount Sinai Hospital, where Alyssa's working until late tonight.

A trio of Yemeni boys in their teens play in the patch of grass by the rocks. Fahima first saw them here the day after the Pulse. She spoke to them about the Bishop Academy, but they laughed her off. The youngest, close to Emmeline's age, raises a mound out of the dirt like a skateboarder's half ramp. The oldest runs up it, flying into the air. The middle boy tries to knock him down with a gust of wind. They talk trash to each other in Arabic and start it again. Parents herd their transfixed kids away as if it's obscene, but it isn't. It's beautiful, a pure thing.

"Hey, al'ukht alkubraa," the oldest one calls over to Fahima as he picks himself up from the ground. Fahima chafes at the boys' Arabic nickname for her, *older sister.* They also call her *the woman from that school.* "I didn't know you had a kid."

"She's not her kid," says the young one. "She's a student from that school."

"Is that right, al'ukht alsaghira?" the oldest says to Emmeline. "You have magic powers?"

"How's the food at that school?" the youngest asks. "They have fries?"

"Fries are okay," Emmeline calls, cupping her hands to amplify her voice. "Burgers are pretty good. It's no Shake Shack."

"Can I come have lunch with you sometime?" asks the youngest.

"Shut up, Dirar," the oldest says.

"What?" says the youngest.

"She doesn't want you to come to lunch at her school," the oldest says. "She said she likes Shake Shack."

"So what?"

"So ask her to Shake Shack, dipshit."

Dirar turns back toward Emmeline and Fahima as if they hadn't heard the last five seconds of conversation. "So you want to?" he calls.

Emmeline smiles shyly. She looks down and gives a barely perceptible shake of her head. Dirar shrugs and returns to his game. Fahima is struck by the prevailing power of normality, how the everyday shines through in crisis. The world collapses, and kids flirt clumsily. Siblings rag on siblings. People like Fahima feel the weight of everything on their shoulders, and others don't. Both ways are wrong. The best way to save the world may be to stay out of its way.

Behind the low mumble of the boys starting another

round of their game, Fahima hears the water lap onto the shore. The park has gone too quiet. The students tanning and grab-assing on the lawn have vanished. There are no families on the path. Four men in blue suits appear on the ridge behind the Yemeni boys. Three carry bulky inhibitors. The long tubes that focus the devices' signals rest on their shoulders like old-timey muskets.

"Emmeline, we have to go," she says.

Emmeline follows her stare. "Are they here for us?"

"No," says Fahima. The boys don't see the Homeland agents even as the lead agent closes within twenty feet of the youngest's back. They're absorbed in their game. A ramp rises from the dirt. A boy launches into the air. Another gathers wind in a ball, ready to toss it when his brother hits his apex. The lead agent points at the middle boy, singling him out as the most immediate threat.

"No," says Emmeline.

Fahima grabs her shoulder, but Emmeline is already moving toward the boys, down the hill to the grass.

"We have to go," Fahima calls after her. The agents unshoulder the inhibitors, training them on the boy.

Emmeline strips the bracelet off her forearm.

A ripple moves through the air, spreading out from Emmeline. It isn't only the air. It's everything. The ground and the water tremble. Fahima's insides quiver like a cage of birds. It passes over everything once and then is still. Two of the boys scramble backward in the grass, away from what's happened. Away from what Emmeline's done.

On the crest of the ridge, three agents unshoulder their

weapons and aim. Their weapons rest again on their shoulders. They unshoulder them and aim. Their weapons rest on their shoulders.

The group leader points, raises his hand, clenches it into a fist. Points. Raises. Clenches. Points.

A seagull makes a low, lazy half circle overhead, then jumps back to the beginning of its arc.

The youngest boy, Dirar, cranes his neck to watch the path of his brother's flight, although his brother is on the ground, backing away. Dirar grins. His lips part, about to say something. His face scoops upward again. Repeat. Loop.

Fahima runs down the hill and picks up the bracelet from where it's fallen in the grass. "Em, fix it," she says, holding it out to her.

"What did you do to him?" shouts the oldest boy.

"I can't," Emmeline says. She's in shock, transfixed by the sight in front of her.

"It's like before, with Viola," Fahima says, trying to calm her. "It's a loop. A little knot in time. You have to untie it."

"Fix him!" yells the oldest boy.

"I can't!" Emmeline screams, turning on Fahima. Fahima feels the tremor again. It's smaller this time, a warning.

"Hold still, Em," Fahima says. She slips the bracelet over Emmeline's forearm and clicks it shut. She feels it buzz against her hand before she looks up.

The agents unshoulder and aim their weapons. Point. Raise. Clench. The bird arcs, begins again. Dirar grins, lips parting to speak.

"You have to fix him!" sobs the oldest boy.

Fahima taps at the bracelet. It's working, but nothing is happening. Something has been permanently broken. Time is looped, a knot that can't be untied or sliced through.

"I'll come back," Fahima tells the boys. "I'll figure it out, and I'll come back and fix this." She knows she won't. The boys are the least of her worries. But Emmeline will need the assurance that this is fixable, even if it isn't.

The students and families that were hustled away from the conflict appear on the ridges and at the edge of the lawn. There is something about the scene that's physically hard to watch. The brain refuses to process it and pushes the horror into the body, landing it in the stomach. Fahima knows because she's seen it before. She turns to Emmeline.

"Em, we have to go."

LEGISLATION

Fahima checks connections while Sarah sits on a table in the old teachers' lounge, looking unimpressed. Sarah will never be impressed. The Gates are a big stupid attempt to wow Sarah with technology that bends and bruises the laws of physics.

"You're going to love these," Fahima says. She compensates for Sarah's lack of enthusiasm with an overabundance of her own. Cortex gives a bored whine.

Each of the three Gates is a freestanding doorway of exposed wire and coil. Fahima ordered chrome casings for them from a fabricator in the Bronx to make them look less janky, but they weren't ready. She wanted to mount them on the walls, but she can't figure out how Kimani's door manifests along a solid surface without disintegrating the matter of that surface. Small-scale tests turned pieces of drywall into so much fine dust. The Gates create a membrane, a physical interface between the real world and Hivespace. It turns out that the real world can't stand the strain.

Fahima flips the first Gate on. It's as loud as a jet engine, the other problem she hasn't been able to fix. *The best modes of travel should be deafening*, she tells herself. Cortex cowers under a chair, and Sarah is on her feet, mouthing something angry but inaudible. Fahima points at the empty space within the Gate. The round tables and empty vending machine waver like a heat mirage as another room superimposes itself on the space, becoming more solid until the only image there is the Gate room in the new Bishop school in Chicago. Karen Nowak, formerly a psychic defense teacher and now the headmaster of the Chicago school, is on the other side, hands clamped over her ears.

"Go through so we can turn it off," Fahima shouts to Sarah. She gestures in case she can't be heard.

Sarah, Fahima, and, begrudgingly, Cortex step through the Gate. Karen powers it down behind them, and the sound dwindles away to nothing.

"I'm working on that," Fahima says.

The Gate room is in the Chicago school's basement, the concrete walls sweating, thick air warm with heat pouring off the air-conditioning units, which are cranking to ward off the early onset of summer. The school is an old community center on North Avenue and Washtenaw, one of the churches that sprang up at the eve of the millennium and struggled through the decade after it before folding.

"I'm so glad you had time to be here to see how we're doing," Karen says. She's one of those white women whose skin is turning into porcelain as she eases into her sixties.

Sarah has spent every hour since the Pulse scrambling to set up three new schools. She and Patrick tapped their parents for cash to add to the endowment Bishop left. A network of old Resonant money emerged from the shadows, allowing Sarah to make cash buys of property in Chicago, Los Angeles, and Houston. None of the buildings are perfect. The building in LA is an old dance studio, and although the one in Houston once had been a school, it's been closed for years because of hurricane damage. Sarah drafted Bishop's teaching staff as administrators and called in alumni to pick up temporary teaching jobs at all four schools. Fahima and Sarah used to approach new Resonants who popped up in the Hive individually, laying out the philosophy and ethics of Bishop, extolling the academic benefits of the academy. Now Sarah can't hang a Bishop sign in front of a building without a queue forming.

"We have Kimani for this," Sarah says, waving dismissively at the Gate.

"Kimani is busy as fuck," Fahima says. "The Gates are locked paths between the schools. They fold the user through Hivespace."

"Fold?"

"It's not as bad as it sounds," Fahima says. "They're key-coded so only administration can activate them. I can upgrade that to biometrics if you want."

Sarah's face indicates that she doesn't care about biometrics. "How many are there?"

"Six. Each school connected to all the others. When you close on the place in Phoenix, I'll network it in with the rest." She's lying. Both doors of the Phoenix Gate are built. The Phoenix half is sitting in Fahima's lab, ready to be shipped to the former Sunkist Growers' Association Building that

Sarah is buying to serve as the site for the fifth school. When that goes live, it'll make sixteen Gates. Four only Fahima and Patrick know about. Two only Fahima knows about.

Trust is difficult for lots of people.

Fahima spends more time in the Hive now. She feels a sense of ownership she didn't before the Pulse. She walks among crowds of new Resonants like a mafia don walking down Main Street, bolstered by the sense that they all are indebted to her in ways they might not recognize but that are there nonetheless.

The walks are data-gathering missions. She has stacks of papers about the new applicants to the schools. Problem cases Patrick and Kimani deal with. She's been able to glean a few things from those reports. There are new ability sets, ones they haven't seen before or only rarely. There are the ones who can produce or manipulate the black glass. There are more Resonants exhibiting abilities like Owen Curry's, able to null out matter, though on a smaller scale. As reports pile up, statistics rise out of the anecdotes. But in the Hive, Fahima can observe the new herd and spot trends. She's convinced if she figures out who changed and who didn't, she can address it in subsequent machines. If machines are even the way to go. Maybe a change in approach is what's needed. She's been wondering again about Rez, the drug that's big around the North Avenue community in Chicago. Chemistry isn't her wheelhouse, but it might be worth exploring.

Since the Pulse, Fahima's Hivebody feels more solid, but the Hive itself feels like more of a physical presence. When she feels the tug at the back of her brain as James Lowery gently reminds her that she's keeping twelve senators and twenty-six members of the House of Representatives waiting, Fahima tries to move through the Hive in the all-at-once way she used to. It doesn't come as easily as it should, and that worries her. The Gates are built to exploit the transspatial properties of the Hive. If those properties are shifting, Fahima needs to know. She makes a mental note to ask Kimani if she's noticed a difference. Fahima rises out of the Hive and manifests again back in the designated meeting spot.

Senator Lowery set this up, which Fahima imagines was no mean feat. None of the newly resonant members of Congress have made a public statement since the Pulse, even Senator Adkins, whose hands glowed blue on C-SPAN before they cut the feed. Fahima manifests in the middle of the collection of congressmen. All eyes are on her, not entirely because she's the new arrival. Fahima is also the only woman here. It's James Lowery and a gaggle of white men, mostly elderly, who regard her warily. Fahima has a flashback to her oral exams at MIT.

"Gentlemen, this is Fahima Deeb," says Lowery, throwing Fahima an impatient glance. "Ms. Deeb is my liaison with the Bishop organization and has offered to advise us." The group grumbles hello. Fahima looks around to see who she can recognize. She spots Stewart Quinn, the Senate minority leader, who has the poise and presence of a yacht club member even after the life-changing events of the last few days. Lowery says Quinn's a passable reader but can't project anything beyond garble. Keith Williams, whose career in tech Fahima paid some attention to before he threw it away for a California House seat. Of all of them, Williams was the one Fahima expected to go public, but he's kept to the closet. And Frank Adkins, the sweaty little bigot who was in the middle of introducing an internment bill when the Pulse hit. Fahima's seen pictures of him with his arm draped around the late Jefferson Hargrave. She's heard him on the Kindred Network, offering defenses of violent anti-Resonant hate groups. She can't help feeling smug satisfaction seeing him here, his Hivebody barely sustained, flickering in and out like a lightbulb on the fritz. *I did this to you, you hateful fuck*, she thinks. *I made you into exactly what you're afraid of.*

"I know we come from both sides of the aisle," says Lowery, "but I think it's important that we discuss among ourselves what the new world might look like and the ways we might shape it at a policy level."

"How the fuck can you talk about policy?" asks one of the men, whose Hivebody looks like a russet potato in an off-the-rack suit. "Everything I touch is trying to tell me where it's been. Do you know what my assistant's been doing with my pens, Jim? He's been sticking them up his ass after I go home and setting them out for me to use in the morning. Every fucking one of them. I pick one up to sign a donor letter, I can feel the pen sliding right up his ass."

"It's called telemetry," Fahima says. "Psychic impressions off objects via touch. You could try wearing gloves until you can control it a little better." Lowery glares at her as if she's failed to give the correct answer. "And I'm sorry. About the ass thing."

"My pens hate me," he mutters. "All my pens."

"We're all grappling with personal situations, Tom," says Lowery. "But the nation is grappling, too. And we've pledged ourselves to serve." It's hokey, but it strikes a chord. The men stand up straighter, prouder. Even Tom the potato man becomes a little less amorphous. The shoulders of his cheap suit fill in; the lumps that make up his face smooth themselves out. It's the first time Fahima sees potential in Lowery. His earnestness is a virtue. There are people who speak it as their native tongue. Those who don't, like Fahima, can hear it and can wish it were their first language. Lowery might be something people could aspire to. This man might be their model minority.

He's going to be president, Fahima thinks. When it happens, Fahima will share some of the credit. She's created a constituency for him. Of those here, Lowery will be the quickest to grasp that. *He's the reason they've all kept quiet about what they've become*, Fahima thinks. *He wants to be the first to come out.*

Lowery outlines the proposal package he and Fahima worked on, although her name is absent in his discussions. Federal funding for Resonant schools, overseen by the Bishop organization. Emergency and disaster relief funding to deal with accidents like the blackout in San Jose and the earthquakes in Cleveland. A legislative committee and a civil rights committee. Ideas spark with certain members of the group. Lowery crafted the package this way, shaped the ideas she gave him into individual pet projects. The whole thing takes hours. The men drift into cliques and knots, ignoring Lowery once he's moved on from whatever aspect of the plan appeals to them.

"There will be specific issues related to criminality," Lowery says. "Not every new Resonant is going to be an angel." He turns to Frank Adkins, who has been left out until now. "Frank, I was thinking that with your background as a prosecutor, you'd be uniquely suited to address—"

"I am no part of your bullshit, Jim," Adkins says. His Hivebody, a slow strobe a moment ago, solidifies. His face sets into a hard mask. It's the look that separates true believers like Adkins from opportunists like Jefferson Hargrave. Hargrave saw hatred as something he could market and brand. Adkins has hate in his heart, a seed he cultivates. There are shows of civility required of a man in his position; his hatred has to lie quiet in him. But she can see it in his pained smile when he has to disclaim his hatred publicly and in his dead-eyed glare when he finally can let it come to light.

"We're abominations. Damned things," Adkins says. "You want me to address 'issues related to criminality'? You are, each one of you, a crime against God. I am, too."

He flickers out again, and Fahima understands where she's been wrong. He doesn't lack the control to maintain his Hivebody. He's going back and forth, conscious in the real world and dropping in on this meeting. He's *there* while they're all here.

"What did you do?" she asks.

Adkins ignores her. He puffs up his chest. "Gentlemen," he says. The word drips with contempt. "You map out the stars and build castles in the clouds. I've been doing my goddamn job. I asked the president to call a special session of both houses to introduce my internment bill. The Adkins Act for the Protection of Human Life. It passed the House right around when your towelhead friend here showed up. Passed the Senate just now. One of my pages is going to run it all the way to the president's desk. Our *human* colleagues understand the threat. They have shown the bravery to act."

"Jesus, Frank," Quinn says. "You set us up?"

"I hope each of you will submit yourselves to the proper authorities as an example to your fellow citizens," Adkins continues. "I've read about the enactment of Executive Order 9066. The resolve of our Japanese citizens to quietly accede to the demands of their government in a time of war gives me hope and strength. We are in a time of war. We should do no less."

"Who the fuck are you speechifying to?" Fahima asks, grabbing his arm. It burns her hand, and she pulls it back.

"Don't you fucking touch me." He smooths the lapels of the suit his Hivebody wears as if it is actual cloth. "I've given your names to the Department of Homeland Security," he says to the other men. "They will be tasked with implementing the Adkins Act. You should each expect a visit soon."

"Did you out yourself, too?" Lowery asks. "They know what you are, Frank. They saw you on television."

"I know what I am," Adkins says, baring his teeth like a cornered animal. "And I'd rather be nothing than be this." His skin glows blue like the cone flame of a Bunsen burner, and thin wisps of smoke snake from his cuffs and collar. The other congressmen gape, unsure what's happening.

Even Fahima isn't convinced she could be seeing what she's seeing, a Hivebody representing what's happening to its owner's physical body. Frank Adkins's face takes on an expression of religious ecstasy as he lets his newborn ability loose, immolating himself in a blaze of azure heat.

Within the hour, there are leaked photos on the Internet of the scorched desk chair in Adkins's office. A pale pile of ash flecked with the charred remains of bones and teeth rests on the burned leather. It spills onto the floor around the chair, tracing pale runes on the seared Turkish rug.

DEFENSE

When Fahima came to Bishop as a fifteen-year-old, she was impressed by the liveliness of the place. It felt like a community, vibrant and engaged. There were cliques and social castes as there are in any high school, but the boundary lines weren't as thickly drawn. They were permeable. At a level above all of that was an understanding that in this place, they were all on the same side. This is the power of a common enemy.

This morning as she makes her way through the halls, Fahima has the sense that as the threat from the outside grows more concrete, the unity within the academy is breaking down. The students retreat into themselves. They regard one another warily even though the danger won't come from their classmates. It may be temporary; the shock of the internment law is new, the implications barely understood. The news reports roundups across the country. Facilities were waiting for occupants, equipped with supplies and racks of inhibitor lights. Secure in the rightness of its action, the government released the names of the camps. Topaz Lake in Nevada. Holiday Home in Wisconsin. Alta Mons in Virginia. Half

Moon in Massachusetts. Camp Wakpominee upstate. The names sound so innocent. But Dachau and Treblinka were just towns before they became part of a language of genocide. In a hundred years, Resonant kids may hear Holiday Home in a history class and shudder at its implications. If there are any Resonant kids in schools in a hundred years.

And there are camps they don't talk about. Ones without names.

Even Fahima, who understands her government's capacity for cruelty because she's seen it firsthand, held on to a belief that this wouldn't happen, that it would be stopped either by her efforts or through a grace she was fairly sure didn't exist. She hopes the students don't give in to fear and despair, that the individual protective clenched fists will ease open and an instinct toward solidarity will kick in. She's not convinced they'll survive if it doesn't.

The gym doors are locked, and she can hear Patrick's voice inside, berating the student he's tutoring. He's been burning it at both ends, and it's turning him meaner than usual. He and Kimani dart across the country, trying to help new Resonants whose abilities present a danger to themselves or others. It's not a matter of ill intent, although there are those problems. It's a matter of control. Fahima's made a dozen more inhibitor bracelets for the worst cases. It's a stopgap. When things calm down, Patrick will help ease these people into their new selves, teach them to rein in what they can now do. But if putting the clamp on some kids' powers for a couple weeks keeps them from going full Owen Curry, well, there are forms of oppression Fahima's made herself comfortable with.

There have been accidents. Fahima keeps a list, names of the dead. *These are mine*, she thinks to herself. *These are on my tab*. She wonders if Alyssa keeps the same list. She knew immediately that the Pulse was Fahima's fault. Fahima came home that day to find her drunk and sobbing.

"Why didn't I change?" Alyssa asked her. "Why didn't you change me?"

"It's not who you are," Fahima said, half sad and half relieved. It was a good question, though, and one Fahima would want an answer to. Why some and not others? And could she make it happen for the others, too? Could Fahima change everyone? As she patted Alyssa's shoulder, performing the mechanics of comfort, her mind wandered into permutations of machines, drug treatments, and Emmeline Hirsch.

In addition to trying to keep new Resonants from blowing their fool selves up, Patrick meets individually with students whose abilities have "offensive potential." Sarah is unhappy about it. Some of the teachers have lodged protests, saying it's counter to academy philosophy, whatever that means, and that it reeks of paramilitary training. Sarah's had no time to deal with it. They all have more than they can handle. The point being, no one has stopped him.

The gym doors open, and Viola, Emmeline's roommate, emerges, flushed, hair dry and frizzed. Patches of sweat bloom at her armpits and sternum. She rubs the butt of her hand against her temple.

Fahima waves, but the girl walks by her, vacant stare directed down the empty hallway.

"Viola looks broken," Fahima says. Patrick's white dress

shirt is singed at the shoulder and along his right side. The latter burn is smoking.

"I'm trying to prepare them," he says. "They're soft. They're too kind to do anyone any damage."

"You can't think of them like that," Fahima says. "They're kids."

"You sound like Sarah," Patrick says.

"Funny you mention our headmistress," says Fahima. She picks up a medicine ball that's half scorched, leaving a crescent moon leaking metal pellets onto the gym floor. "We've been called upstairs."

"I don't have time," Patrick says. He sounds petulant. "I have an hour per student, and even that's more time than I can spare. A hundred students on my list and I've barely met with a third of them."

Fahima is impressed that he's had time even for that. "You want to get a fresh shirt? You look like shit." It's not the shirt that's the problem. Patrick's eyes are sunken, and his skin looks jaundiced, its usual lily white a thin layer of paint over something sick. She suspects he isn't sleeping. But then, neither is she. The few hours she spends in bed, Fahima lays awake next to Alyssa and sinks into the Hive, admiring her handiwork.

"Headaches," he says, tapping his temple. He pokes at the scorched cloth on his shoulder, and it flakes into ash. "My sister will have to tolerate me looking like shit."

When Fahima and Patrick arrive, Sarah is sitting at Bishop's antique oak desk with Cortex asleep at her feet.

She's trying to look as much like the headmaster of the Bishop Academy as she can. Patrick and Fahima have been in this room enough times that the desk will always be Bishop's, waiting for him to come back and take it. The once and future headmaster. Sarah looks like a little kid behind daddy's desk.

"We need to give ourselves up," Sarah says.

"What the fuck?" Fahima says. She's been expecting this for a few days, but it hurts to hear that Sarah's ready to capitulate.

"I've been in touch with Louis Hoffman at Homeland." Sarah once confessed to Fahima that she found Louis Hoffman attractive in a way. She said there was a sad sense of duty in him, creating one of those moments when Fahima felt she would never understand straight people. "He says the facilities in the Northeast are the best. Yuppie summer camps, like the ones we went to as kids. They're actually using Half Moon in Great Barrington. Do you remember that summer?" Cortex stirs, and Sarah rests her bare foot on his back, rocking gently. "We canoed. You capsized us in Lake Buel."

"It's not sleepaway camp, Sarah," says Patrick.

"He says they're pouring money in to get them ready for colder weather," Sarah says. "Insulation, new heating systems. It'll be better than here. I haven't had a hot shower all week."

"Gilded cage is still a cage," Fahima says.

"What are we in now?" Sarah asks. "We're at triple capacity. I can barely staff the cafeteria, much less the classrooms. Today we can go outside. Who knows about tomorrow? If we don't go, they're going to keep us holed up in here, and the academy is not equipped—"

"We need to fight this," Patrick says. "We hide the students who are too young or whose abilities aren't useful, put them somewhere safe, and the rest of us line up and fight."

"We'd be wiped out," Fahima says. "We're not ready."

"We have our abilities, and we have the numbers."

"We have kids," says Sarah.

"I'd rather die here than in my old bunk at fucking Camp Half Moon," Patrick says.

"It'd be temporary," says Sarah. "The ACLU has filed a dozen suits."

"They filed suits in Revere," Fahima says.

"And people died because they didn't wait for the results," says Sarah. "How is this different?"

"This is our home," Fahima says. Sarah's shoulders slump. Cortex lets out an exasperated huff. Technically this is her decision to make, but she won't override them. Bishop would have. He would have listened to their opinions calmly and done whatever the fuck he wanted. But Sarah isn't Bishop. "We use our time to get ready," Fahima says.

"How long would that take?"

"If I had another week," Patrick says, "I'd have enough—" He stops as his phone buzzes in his pocket.

"Patrick, leave that," says Sarah.

Patrick looks at the screen. "It's Mom."

"Why is she calling *you*?" Sarah asks. She stands up, leaning toward the phone as if she might hear.

"Calm down, I can't understand you," says Patrick. He puts his hand over the phone. "Sarah, turn on the news."

CNN runs a split screen. On the left, Senator James

Lowery leaves his office in handcuffs. His shoulders hunch when they duck him into the back of a white van. On the right side is a long shot from a view Fahima recognizes. It's the ridge above Oceanside Way, the enclave in Maine where Sarah and Patrick's parents live. Homeland vans line the street. Inhibitor lights are rigged to the streetlights, casting a green pallor over the entire street, a miasma that bends the Maine summer sun. Front doors open, and Oceanside Way's residents are marched out of their homes with their hands on their heads.

"I see it, Mom," Patrick says. "Call the lawyer right— Well, then Dad's doing the right thing. He won't be able to. The lights. Your abilities won't— Mom? Mom. We're going to fight this. For now, I need you to open the door for them and give yourselves up. Don't do anything stupid. I love you. Sarah and I are going to fix this."

"Why would they start with them?" Sarah asks after he's hung up. "It's a retirement community. None of those people are a threat."

"They help fund the school. Cut off the money," Patrick says. "I expect our accounts are being frozen. They'll try to starve us out."

It's not the money that worries Fahima. The fact the cameras are there has meaning: Homeland called it in. They wanted an audience. They have no interest in doing this quietly. Fahima wonders if the thought of footage of dead kids in the Bishop lobby will be enough of a deterrent to keep Homeland from breaking down the doors.

"We're next," says Sarah.

"We don't know when next is," Fahima says.

"I need a week," Patrick says.

"Start relocating the younger students to the other schools," says Sarah, issuing orders to neither of them in particular. "I'm not letting our kids get killed."

"There're some we should keep around," Patrick says. "I have a list." He turns to Fahima. "I can't help thinking Emmeline Hirsch could be an asset."

"By asset you mean weapon," Fahima says.

"Yes, Fahima, that *is* what I mean," he says coldly. Something about the faux casualness of his suggestion puts her off. It sounds like he's been thinking about Emmeline's strategic potential for a while. He looks hungry at the prospect of conscripting her.

"I'll go talk to her," Fahima says. "She may not be in the best mental state for battle."

"None of us are," Patrick says.

When Kimani's door opens on the lab wall, Fahima holds out two six-packs of expensive West Coast IPA like an offering.

"Someone needs a favor," Kimani says, taking the beer and inviting her in.

"I've been keeping these in the fridge for just that," says Fahima. "I didn't think I'd have to use them both at once."

Kimani sets the beers on the table where the silver sculpture used to be and cracks one open.

"I need you to take Emmeline and hide," Fahima says, collapsing into the plush chair she thinks of as hers. "Just bring her in here, pull the door in behind you, and sit still for a couple days."

"Fahima—"

"I'm probably wrong," she says. "But I'd rather be paranoid than be right and . . ."

"And what?"

"A couple days," Fahima says. "Don't move or someone might spot you in the Hive."

"We're not talking about Homeland."

"I'm probably wrong," Fahima says again.

Kimani takes a long sip of beer. She looks around the room, assessing its size, its potential to house two people for an undetermined string of days. "She's going to think she's being punished," Kimani says.

"She's being protected."

"She won't see it that way."

"Make her see it that way," says Fahima, too loud, too sharp. Kimani, never one to be yelled at, glares at her. "*Help* her see it that way." Fahima's struck by how feeble the word *help* can sound.

"She needs more than me right now," Kimani says. "She's hurt. She needs all of us."

"I know," Fahima says. So much comes down to what Fahima's willing to do, who she's willing to hurt. At the end, afterward, she can tell them all it was for their own good. At the end, she won't need to be forgiven.

"You're going to want me here if shit goes south," Kimani says. "I could drop her somewhere and come right back. Put her somewhere safe."

"I don't want her to be alone," Fahima says, because this is the limit. Emmeline will have someone with her even if that puts everyone else at risk. Emmeline's done enough.

"You need a back door," Kimani says. "You need a way out."

"We won't," Fahima says. "One way or another, we walk out the front door."

SIEGE

The dorm rooms at Bishop are packed with new students, especially on the first- and second-year floors. Rooms on the sixth and seventh floors house four or five kids each in bunks and on cots. They've barely settled in and need to be relocated to schools that don't yet have their feet under them. It's a challenge, but Sarah is loved and feared by those she's installed as the heads of the other schools. They scramble to make arrangements, to keep her happy. The teachers at Bishop line the youngest students up outside the old faculty lounge, and Sarah fires up the Gates. The students walk through in single file to the schools in Chicago and Houston and LA, where teachers they've never met are waiting for them. The students' protests are drowned out by the jet engine roar of the Gates. All the Bishop facilities are one massive school now, hallways linked by Gates that can jump a student across the country in a blink. But the academy is on its own, the flashpoint for whatever comes. The Gates can be shut down with the flick of a switch and will be the second Homeland comes through the front door.

The minute a dorm room is emptied, Patrick has people there to fill it. Sarah's developed a network of teachers and administrators. Patrick's built a pyramid of fighters and trainers. It's apparent he's been at this a long time. His wilderness years were not all about hunting Owen Curry. They've adopted the name of the first group of resisters in Revere, calling themselves the Black Rose Faction. Patrick laughs the first time Fahima salutes and calls him "Commandant Davenport," but as more of Patrick's soldiers flood the school by the hour, the joke stops being funny. She's not thrilled that the first group to goose-step through a Gate is lead by Ji Yeon Kim dressed in a Pussy Riot tee shirt and flanked by others who had survived Revere, but Fahima swallows her pride and says, "It's good to see you. I'm glad you're here."

Ji Yeon blanks Fahima, her eyes already sizing up the academy for entry and exit points, strategic details. While working on other things, Fahima watches Ji Yeon operate, determined to figure out what she doesn't like about the girl. When they first met, Fahima fiercely *wanted* to like her. There's a cyclic split between generations of leftists and rebels. Every younger generation thinks the one before didn't go far enough, and every older generation thinks the younger one's tactics are desperate and irrational. With Ji Yeon, Fahima felt herself on the elder side of that divide for the first time. Ji Yeon made revolution look sexy and fun, and Fahima was outside with practical concerns about survival, pressing her nose up against the glass while the kids sang Crass songs about eating the rich.

Now Ji Yeon lacks that self-righteous spark. Her efficiency looks plodding, passion replaced by dull resolve. She has the long look you see in deployed soldiers and suicide bombers, the look of someone who's accepted her own death as a possible consequence of her actions. It's antithetical to everything the Bishop Academy is supposed to be. They're supposed to be on the side of life.

Within the Faction, there are a number of new Resonants Ji Yeon calls obsidianists, who produce and manipulate black glass. Ji Yeon tasks them with building a wall along the academy's front facade. Ji Yeon has names for every type of Resonant, sorting them by ability. Sparks. Metalurges. Voiders. At the bottom of the ranks are the noncoms, those whose abilities are noncombative. The useless, like Fahima.

Fahima watches the obsidianists draw black glass up from the ground or puke it out of their guts. The ones who create it can't shape it and the ones who shape it can't create it, so they work in pairs. They layer sheets of the substance into a wall that stretches to the building's fifth floor, protecting the windows and sealing the building off from the outside. When it's done, it looks perfect, seamless. It makes Fahima miss the ramshackle quality of the Revere barricade, the everything and the kitchen sink approach to resistance. But the last element in the Revere barricade, the final thing thrown in, had been bodies. If perfection avoids that, Fahima will take perfection.

As she had at Revere, Ji Yeon sets up supply and requisitions systems. They outstrip the existing ones at the academy. The cafeterias, not to mention the hot water heaters and sewer lines, had been overtaxed by the influx of new students, but Ji Yeon has engineers on the issues immediately, along with food brought in through the Gates. The first night of the siege, 600 students are treated to Texas-style barbecue delivered through the Houston Gate by Faction members. After weeks of frozen pizza, the students are ecstatic.

The Faction members make a point of bringing too much. The leftovers, the greasy wreckage of the meal, are a sign of the Faction's generosity but also its power. The next morning, after a round of scalding hot showers, students sport makeshift black armbands, and Fahima sees sign-up sheets for a Junior Faction in the halls. Fahima remembers her father telling her about how Hamas came to power in Lebanon when he was growing up. "They fixed the sewage lines," he said. "People will fall in love with you if you keep them from drowning in their own shit."

Homeland shows up in the afternoon. Fahima is upstairs in the headmaster's quarters with Sarah when she takes the call. Sarah puts it on speaker. The two of them watch out the window as military vehicles amass on the cordoned-off block of 57th outside the academy entrance. Cortex stands on his back paws to catch a glimpse.

"Sarah," says Louis Hoffman, "you don't want to do it like this."

"I don't want to do it at all," Sarah says. "We have kids in here."

"Send the kids out," Louis says. "Come out with them. We want to keep everyone safe."

"You have tanks on our porch, motherfucker," Fahima shouts.

There's a pause. "Hello, Fahima," Louis says. He sounds less than thrilled.

"We had a deal," Fahima says. Sarah turns to her, confused. Cortex gives a curious whine.

"That deal did not include a city in Wyoming getting wiped off the map," Louis says. "That deal did not include four agents and a little kid in Central Park skipping like an old record."

"That was an accident," Fahima says too quietly for the phone to pick up.

"And it most definitely did not include turning half the U.S. population into freaks."

"Two thirds," Fahima says.

"Open the doors, Sarah," Louis says.

"Didn't you see? There aren't any doors," Sarah says, and hangs up, her eyes still on Fahima. "You had a deal?"

"I gave him some tech," she says. "In exchange for staying away from the school."

"Did you give them the inhibitors?"

"They would have come up with them on their own." It's not true. No one had the biological research on Resonants to shut them off. Inhibitor tech would have been decades off for anyone but Fahima.

"But they didn't have to," Sarah says.

"I bought us time."

Sarah jerks her thumb at the window. "Time's up." The high whine of an industrial saw interrupts them from the street. "We're not done talking about this," Sarah says as she steps to the window. Below, Homeland agents press the blade of a massive circular saw to the surface of the black glass. "Can they cut through it?"

"Fuck if I know," Fahima says. She and Sarah spend the first night of the siege manning the window as if it were a watchtower. After blunting three saw blades, Homeland switches to acetelyne torches. Sparks bounce futilely off the wall below. A new agent rotates in every time a torch dies. Sarah and Fahima take turns napping on the couch, but Cortex keeps a constant vigil. Fahima's on her shift, idly stroking the top of Cortex's head, when her phone rings.

"You're on the news," Alyssa says.

Fahima smiles. "Can you see the top-floor windows?" She waves enthusiastically, forearm like a windshield wiper, like a kid on the back of a boat as it pulls away from shore.

"Why didn't you tell me?" Alyssa asks.

"Tell you what?"

"You left for work this morning knowing this could happen."

"I leave for work every morning knowing this could happen," says Fahima. It's funny how little of the situation Alyssa understands. Maybe it's a failure on Fahima's part, an inability to communicate the threat. She hasn't had the time or the energy to hold Alyssa's hand and slow-walk her through it. Or maybe it's something you can grasp only from the inside.

"I can come there," Alyssa says. "Kimani can get me, and I can—"

"Lys, there's no reason for you to be here," Fahima says. "I'll be home soon."

She says it knowing it isn't true. She's resigned to never

seeing their apartment again. But Alyssa believes her and after an exchange of "I love you"s hangs up.

By morning, Homeland has made no visible progress. Faction obsidianists work their way up, sheathing the building in black glass. By noon of the second day, the windows on the top floor, the headmaster's quarters, are covered. The Bishop Academy is encased, an onyx tower in the middle of Manhattan, surrounded by armored vehicles.

The Faction turns the gym into a command center. Schematics of the building are spread on tables. A remote viewer sits cross-legged on the wooden floor, casting her consciousness out over 57th to reconnoiter the street while someone records her every word. As Faction members bustle in and out, students awaiting relocation stand outside, hoping to overhear what's happening or be tapped to join up. Fahima is permitted to come and go as she wants. She isn't sure who among the faculty isn't allowed access. She suspects Sarah's on the list of excluded.

The second night, Patrick calls Fahima in for a strategy session with Ji Yeon. There are others in the gym, but they keep their distance, working on whatever they've been tasked with while the generals make decisions. Patrick seems to be able to pull them close or hold them at a distance without saying anything.

"What are our options for getting out?" Patrick asks.

"We can get to the other schools," says Fahima, "but Homeland is rolling up on Houston and LA, too."

"What about Chicago?"

"Chicago's going down different," says Ji Yeon. "The

mayor sent police to keep Homeland off North Avenue."

"Chicago's on our side?" Patrick asks with the barest hint of a smile.

"Having the police on our side and having police *officers* on our side are two different things," says Ji Yeon. "I wouldn't count on a blue wall to hold."

"If we run, we end up in the same situation somewhere else," Fahima says.

"Worse," says Ji Yeon. "We're fortified here." The black glass walls have been up only a few hours, but they already feel more like enclosure than defense.

"What are our options if we fight?" Patrick asks.

Ji Yeon shrugs. "They've got inhibitor rigs set up. Unless we take them out, we're dead out the door. If we open up windows at the top and send fliers down on them—"

"You want people to throw their bodies on the lights?" Patrick asks.

"Unless you have a better idea."

"I might," says Fahima. She's relieved that Sarah and Kimani aren't in the room. She can hold on to her secret a little longer. "If their inhibitor rigs are anything like the ones I designed, there's a flaw. A weak point."

"Is it the thermal exhaust port?" asks Ji Yeon, smirking. This is the girl Fahima met in Revere. Whip smart and funny, the kind of girl who drops a *Star Wars* reference into a war council.

"I can short them out," Fahima says.

"Okay, then what?" Patrick asks, turning to Ji Yeon. The light that flickered on behind her eyes goes cold again. She points to the schematic of the building, the windows on the sixth floor.

"Obsidianists pull back the wall and we send out fliers," she says. "They carry sparks and metalurges. Take out the heavy weapons. While they're looking up, we open the front doors and hit them low. Disorient them with psychics, throw physical kids at them."

"What's the goal?" Fahima asks.

"We get them off our lawn," Ji Yeon says.

"They'll send more," says Fahima.

"Then we kill more."

Fahima looks to Patrick. She knows this isn't going to stop but holds out hope that it will. Either way, the decision falls to him. He nods. "Now what?"

"We wait till morning, closer to noon," Ji Yeon says. "They've got the lights on us now, but if the sun's high, it'll mask—"

The gym doors bust open. Sarah drags Viola in by the arm. Cortex is at Sarah's heel, teeth bared. One of the Faction members takes a step to restrain her. Sarah puts her palm on his face, and he crumples to the ground. His partner steps back, holding his hands up defensively. Sensing the opportunity to see behind the curtain, students file in behind Sarah. Fahima sees Maya Patel and Jovan Markovic, both in their last year. She sees Alma Mason and Boyd Scott and Mona Lamb. *How many students have I taught?* Fahima thinks. *What percentage of the original Resonant population, before the Pulse, passed through the Bishop Academy?* These are statistics she could find, numbers she could summon up. Then there's the unquantifiable corollary: *How much good have we done?*

"What did you do to her, Patrick?" Sarah asks, shoving Viola in front of him, presenting her as evidence. Sarah's hands rest on her shoulders, holding her still. Viola glows with heat, and Sarah jerks her hands back. Viola stands with her arms crossed, smirking knowingly at Patrick. It's not a face Fahima's ever seen Viola make.

"What did you put in this girl's head?"

Now that the question is out there, Fahima realizes her own stupidity at not asking it. She's seen enough to know something's been wrong. The blank expression on Viola. The cold, dark look that passes over Ji Yeon's face, over the faces of all the Faction members. It was all in front of her, but Fahima hadn't wanted to see it. She needed not to see.

"Sarah," says Patrick. "I need you to calm down. I can explain." He stretches his arm to sweep Viola protectively to the side. Ji Yeon steps in front of the girl, arms crossed, face mirroring Viola's.

"She burned her name into Daniel's arm," Sarah says. "This sweet little girl *branded* Daniel Ramos like it was nothing."

"Sarah—"

"I looked in her head, Patrick," says Sarah. Cortex is tense on the ground, looking from Patrick to Ji Yeon, assessing threats to Sarah. "I saw you. A little piece of you in the middle of her mind. How could that be, Patrick? What did you do to her?"

"Sarah, this is me," Patrick says. "You know me."

"If you won't just tell me—" Sarah reaches out to touch him, to go into his head and find the truth. She could do it without contact, but something in her needs the physical connection. She'd doubt what she saw without it, and she needs to be sure.

Her hand falls on his bare arm, and Patrick's face blurs. His features sink into a pool of skin and become indistinct.

He yanks his arm out of Sarah's grip and backhands her hard across the face, knocking her backward. Sarah is registering the shock of it when Cortex leaps at Patrick and bites into his arm. Patrick screams, but Cortex holds fast, dangling from his flailing arm as Sarah scrambles to her feet. Fahima stoops to help her. She sees Ji Yeon produce a shining needle, a foot long and menacing, from her right hand. It rests on her palm a moment, then she grips it like a spear and plunges it into Cortex's belly. The dog yelps in pain but keeps his jaw clamped on Patrick's arm. Ji Yeon produces another spike, thicker than the first. This one she drives through Cortex's eye. He yelps, shudders like he's shaking water from his fur, and drops in a heap at Patrick's feet. Sarah screams like she's being torn in half and sits down cross-legged on the floor. Ji Yeon smiles, and the same smile flickers across Patrick's face before it's replaced by proper horror at what's happened.

"Sarah," Fahima says, kneeling down next to her. "Sarah, are you okay?"

Sarah looks at her blankly. "Hey, Fahima," she says. Her voice is high and light, like a child's. "Have you seen my dog?"

Maya Patel, one of Sarah's prize students, charges at Ji Yeon. All around her are images of weapons: a twirling mace, a collection of flying swords. None of them are real. Ji Yeon pierces Maya in the shoulder with a spike, and one of the other Faction members, pimple-faced and balding, lights the little girl up with a bolt of electricity from across the room, tossing her back against the padded wall. Maya slumps to the floor, body twitching.

Jovan Markovic, who carried a crush for Maya since their first year, throws himself at her second attacker, jumping on the pimple-faced boy and grabbing the sides of his head. The pimple-faced boy goes slick with sweat as Jovan draws the water out of his body, pulling every bit of moisture through his skin. The pimple-faced boy goes into seizure, but a bulky Faction member grabs Jovan off him by the back of the head and slams him into the hardwood of the gym floor again and again. The first few strikes are accompanied by wet, cracking sounds that deteriorate into noises that remind Fahima of her father's hands hitting ground lamb in the kebab stand when she was a child. Dull, meaty thuds.

The rest of the Faction members watch, grinning. They eye the students who crowded into the gym the way wolves eye prey, licking their teeth. Fahima hears screams from out in the hallway. Whatever is happening is happening everywhere. The whole academy.

"Patrick, stop this," Fahima says. She takes a step toward him, but Ji Yeon stands between them.

"I don't know what this is," he says. *Something in him wants this*, Fahima thinks. "This isn't my fault," he pleads. But he's lying. He might not understand it, but part of him knows.

"I don't care whose fault it is, Patrick," she says. It feels important to say his name, to establish a connection to who he is. Fahima doesn't have enough data to understand everything, but there are things she intuits, a collection of impossibles and improbables, several of which must be true. Ji Yeon produces another spike and spins it on the tip of her finger like a witch brandishing a cursed spindle. She smiles at Fahima. Fahima glares at her to back her off, but Ji Yeon can spot a bluff. "Stop this, Patrick."

Patrick's features drown in a mask of skin, leaving his face an eerie blank. "Fine," he says. The voice comes from somewhere behind the caul, a voice made of white noise and wasps' nests, buzzing and multivalent as if it's not one voice but thousands, coalescing from everywhere and emerging from inside Patrick.

The Faction members stop what they're doing as if someone has hit a pause button. They return to themselves, a soft flood of consciousness sluicing over them. They look confused. Some wake confronted with immediate horrors, atrocities committed while they slept. Ji Yeon drops to her knees, cradling Cortex in her arms, weeping. The bulky Faction member who pummeled Jovan into the floor nudges the boy's body with his foot, as if trying to rouse him from sleep.

Patrick Davenport, face restored, looks over what he's done. He kneels next to Sarah, and his arms extend until they coil around her like snakes. "Sarah, it's me, Patrick," he says. "Your brother. Sarah, you remember me, don't you? Sarah?"

She looks confused but not worried. Without Cortex, she doesn't have the memories of what's happened. She lacks the context to be properly terrified.

AFTERMATH

There is no place in the Bishop Academy set up to be used as a morgue, and so the bodies are carried down to Fahima's lab. Faction members serve as pallbearers, looking suitably penitent. Fahima wonders if guilt will evaporate from them or if they will stow it away, letting it haunt them in the days to come, after whatever horrors are next.

The bodies are laid out on tables under sheets. There're only five. In the scope of how many people Fahima has killed, this is nothing. But those are names on a list, and these are bodies, tangible. She lays hands on the sheets that cover them. They seem so small. Not one is quite full-size.

"O Allah, forgive Tiesha Ibarra," she whispers. "And elevate her station among those who are guided. Send her along the path of those who came before and forgive us and her, O Lord of the worlds. Enlarge for her her grave and shed light upon her in it."

She says *duas* for each one, pulling back the sheets and making sure their eyes are closed, a final separation from this world. Except for Jovan Markovic. A glimpse under the sheet tells Fahima that there's not enough left of his face for her to do him this last kindness.

She takes the elevator up to the fourth floor, where the nurse's office and the classrooms on either side of it have been converted into a triage unit. Nurse Burgess, who's been here since Fahima was a student, patches and bandages while healers she's decided are capable work their abilities on wounds and breaks. Nurse Burgess lays students down and elevates their feet, covering them with blankets against the chill of shock. When she pauses, leaning heavily against the teacher's desk to get her breath, Fahima approaches her.

"Do I need to make room for more downstairs?" Fahima asks.

Nurse Burgess glares at her, a look she's deployed to chastise a generation of students for drug use, promiscuity, and general lack of self-preservation. "You won't if you let me do my job," she says. Fahima takes the hint and clears out.

The gym doors hang off broken hinges. Otherwise order has been restored. Ji Yeon and Patrick are in the same corner, conferencing. Whoever was responsible for cleaning up did a poor job. Pink ghosts of Cortex's blood streak the floor, and there's a divot where Jovan Markovic's skull was crushed. Patrick turns away from Ji Yeon when he sees Fahima come in.

"How is Sarah?" he asks with genuine concern. Fahima can't look at him without remembering the blankness that passed over his face.

"She's destroyed, Patrick," she says. "I don't know if I can bring her back."

"I should go see her," he says, breaking eye contact, examining his hands. He's always been a shit liar. "How many are there?" he asks. "How many dead?"

"Five," says Fahima. "Jovan Markovic. Ozella Libron. Tiesha Ibarra. Martin Danner. Emmeline Hirsch." It's an unconscious substitution, replacing Dashiel Rowling, downstairs with his chest cavity blown open, with Emmeline, safe somewhere in Kimani's room. Fahima erases Dashiel from today's tragedy to protect Emmeline and Kimani.

Hearing Emmeline's name brings a change to Patrick's face, a chill flicker of disappointment. It's gone in a second, and Fahima sees her friend again, not the person Patrick is shaping himself into but the person she went to school with, the one she ragged on and counted on. His guilt is real, but there's something in him that doesn't share it. A part of Patrick doesn't give a single fuck for the dead. That part is waxing inside him, pushing her friend to the margins of himself.

"I lost control of them," he says. "It was like—"

"Why were you controlling them to begin with, Patrick?"

"I wasn't," he says, looking away. Another lie. "It was a communication system. I thought it would be a way to coordinate. Like the Hive, only we could use it without going under."

There's more she needs to know about the mechanism, the method of communication. Maybe it was intended as harmless and went awry. Maybe it was never meant to be harmless. Sometimes a bug is a feature. Regardless of intent, Fahima will need to have Sarah's question answered. She'll need to know exactly what it is Patrick did to people like Ji Yeon and Viola. Those answers will have to wait.

"I need you to promise me you won't do it anymore,"

Fahima says. "Whatever you did to those kids, you undo it."

"I already did," he says, looking directly at her to convince her but overshooting the mark. *Shit liar since we were kids,* Fahima thinks. *Sarah always used to say so.*

"I need to trust you, Patrick," Fahima says.

Patrick looks afraid. He leans in close to Fahima's ear, and the Faction members watch, straining to hear him, as if they're worried that Patrick might conspire against himself. "There's something wrong," he whispers. "I don't think I'm a good person anymore. I need you here to watch me. Keep me good. Tell me when I'm going too far."

"We'll get through this," Fahima says loudly enough for those who are close to hear. She forces herself to look relaxed, and he smiles at her. She slaps him on the back like an old drinking buddy, and his face slackens back into the mask she now realizes he's been wearing for years.

It seems to work. Ji Yeon returns to her schematics. The remote viewer closes her eyes and resumes her reports on the army amassing outside. Fahima keeps her pace as she walks out of the room.

Preparations for war continue.

EPILOGUE

IN OUR RAGS OF LIGHT

Go, go, go, said the bird: human kind
Cannot bear very much reality.
—T. S. ELIOT, *"Four Quartets"*

The entire academy is on lockdown except for troop movements. The students who haven't been shipped through the Gates wait in their rooms for orders. They wouldn't be out in the halls anyway. They've gone to ground in small groups for comfort.

Fahima takes a last tour of the halls. The moment is closing in on her now, her options narrowing. She ducks into an empty classroom, the black box theater where Sarah used to teach her art students. She pulls out her phone and calls Alyssa, who picks up but doesn't speak.

Fahima takes a deep breath. "There's something I need you to do," she says. "And there can't be any questions. I need you to just do it right away."

One more piece in its proper place, Fahima walks to the elevator at the end of the third-floor hall. A Faction guard stands in front, sucking down bottled water, blocking her. He's the pimple-faced boy who knocked Maya Patel out of the air. Maya is one floor above, hooked up to a breathing apparatus. Fahima takes her left index finger and pokes it at the bunched fingers of her right hand. It's a gesture her uncle used to make at annoying customers' backs that roughly means *You have five fathers.* It's an illegible act of rebellion, but it makes Fahima feel better. The pimple-faced boy takes it as some kind of secret salute and steps aside, letting her in.

The elevator makes its slow climb to the top floor. *A regenerative drive to capture the friction heat from braking and channel it back into the grid,* Fahima thinks. *A shaft of variable gravity.* She makes promises to herself. She lists the people she needs to protect. Emmeline and Sarah. Alyssa and Kimani. They can never ask her what she's done or why. There are decisions coming that will be terrible but necessary, and in the end she won't apologize. She'll make them to ward off further horrors and to stop Patrick if it comes to the point where he needs to be stopped.

The library of the headmaster's quarters is dim and quiet. The black glass lets in the barest light. There are moving boxes shoved into the corners, empty shelves where Bishop's first editions have been relocated to the student library on the seventh floor. Fahima wonders if Sarah ever would have settled in here, made it her own. Bishop's ghost fills the space, haunting it with questions Fahima never got around to asking him or he never saw fit to answer. She's searched the bookshelves and desk drawers for a diary or journal with no luck. Bishop's past was swallowed up in his death as surely as if Owen Curry had gulped it down into whatever nowhere now held the town of Powder Basin and its residents. Some things are simply gone.

Through an open door, Fahima sees Sarah on the edge of the bed in the headmaster's bedroom. Her blond hair is in a windblown tussle, and her sharp business attire is askew, making her look as if she's wandered away from an explosion. It isn't far from the truth. Sarah stares out a window sheeted over with black glass. Her hand trails at her side. Her fingers search. One of the Faction members must have led her up here from the infirmary and forgotten about her, unware that Sarah has barely used the bedroom in weeks. She's been sleeping on the couch in the main office downstairs most nights. Fahima knows because she's checked on Sarah before sneaking in here at night to work, to install. Crisis can afford one opportunities. She bends down and takes Sarah's hand in her own.

"Sarah," she says.

"Fahima," says Sarah. Her face lights up with recognition. "I was with you earlier. Something is wrong." *She's not entirely gone*, Fahima thinks. Cortex was like an external hard drive for Sarah's memories, but there has to be information stored inside the system. Parts of her are here.

"Sarah, do you remember what happened?" Fahima asks. "What happened to Cortex?"

It takes Sarah a moment to place the name. When she does, her hand pulls free of Fahima's and gropes the air at her side, seeking her companion. Her hand closes into a loose fist. "He wanders off sometimes," she says, bringing her hand to her chest and holding it in the other. "He's not a bad dog. He'll come back in a minute." She turns back to the window. Fahima puts her hand on Sarah's shoulder, and she startles. She examines Fahima's reflection in the black glass, confused. She smiles and turns around.

"Fahima," she says. "I was with you earlier. Something is wrong."

"It is," Fahima says. "I'm working on it." She doesn't have a plan to fix it yet, but she has a plan to buy herself time. Bury the ones she wants to keep. Hide them deep in the earth to keep them safe. Fahima pulls a footstool over to the doorway. She stands on tiptoe and removes the wooden corner piece on the top right side of the door frame, revealing a panel of buttons. She's proud of her work. The dark wood molding around the door perfectly covers the machinery of the Gate Fahima built into the frame. She enters a code, and the Gate ramps up.

"Fahima, what's that sound?" Sarah asks, yelling to be heard. Fahima climbs down, holding on to the jamb for balance. Her hand feels like it's resting on the hood of an old car. The wood is alive with the working of the machinery underneath. The library on the other side of the door shimmers like a heat mirage. Another room swims into view. Fahima sees Alyssa waiting for them in her OR scrubs. Her features are out of focus, but Fahima would know her anywhere.

"I've got a place for you to stay," Fahima says. "Somewhere you'll be safe."

Fahima takes Sarah's hand and leads her through the door.

ACKNOWLEDGMENTS

I wouldn't have even attempted this book without the encouragement and support of my agent, Seth Fishman. This book started from a "you could do something like that" conversation over beers when my first book was still new in the world, and I cannot thank him enough for the times between then and now when his enthusiasm has managed to overwhelm my doubts.

At some point, a book needs someone to see something in it that isn't quite there yet. Thank you to Sarah Peed at Del Rey for seeing what this book could be and helping to get it there. Thanks as well to Andrea Schulz at Viking, whose early reads on it helped me rein in my natural impulse toward sprawl and turn what was a guided tour of a world into a focused story.

Thank you to my incredibly talented writing group, Melanie Conroy-Goldman Hamilton and Jennifer Savran Kelly, for their willingness to speed through large chunks of novel, guided only by breathless summaries of what's come before or which draft we were on, or what characters had been changed, replaced, or cut entirely. Thank you to

Mariam Quraishi and Khaled Malas for advice when asked, correction when required.

This book owes an obvious debt to a half century or more of X-Men comics. There's not enough room to list every writer and artist whose work on those books I admire, but I'd be remiss in failing to acknowledge the impact of Chris Claremont's writing on me as a kid, and still as an adult. Thanks also to Jay Edidin and Miles Stokes, and Ramzi Fawaz, whose loving and critical assessment of those comics has shaped the way I think about them.

This book also has Octavia Butler's Patternmaster series deep in its DNA, and now that you are (presumably) at the end of this one, I urge you to go pick those books up, if you haven't already.

A lot of the thinking and approach of this book comes from the discipline of disability studies. *Enforcing Normalcy* by Leonard Davis, *The Minority Body: A Theory of Disability* by Elizabeth Barnes, and *Deaf President Now!: The 1988 Revolution at Gallaudet University* by John B. Christiansen and Sharon N. Barnartt were touchstone texts as I was writing, as were Wesley Lowery's *They Can't Kill Us All* and Keeanga-Yamahtta Taylor's *From #BlackLivesMatter to Black Liberation*, and, from another vector entirely, Andrew Solomon's *Far from the Tree.*

I started writing this book late in 2016, and the ghosts of David Bowie, Prince, and Leonard Cohen haunt the text. The book evolved while watching resistance movements forming around the country in response to what was happening at a national level. I began from a point of despair, convinced America was unsalvageable or, worse, not worth saving. It was a long path back from there, and this book and the next trace that arc. The way has been lit by the efforts of amazing, impassioned people who manage to imagine a utopia when dystopia seems alarmingly close. This book is a sort of long, elliptical thank-you note to all who fight, who strive, who resist.

And thank you, always, to Heather, for suffering through the emotional and economic swings of my particular form of employment. It's difficult to float away in one's head all day without knowing you have a safe place to come back to, and you're mine.

ABOUT THE AUTHOR

Bob proehl is the author of *A Hundred Thousand Worlds*, a *Booklist* Best Book of the Year. He has worked as a bookseller and programming director for Buffalo Street Books in Ithaca, New York, a deejay, a record-store owner, and a bartender. He was a New York Foundation for the Arts Fellow in Fiction and a resident at the Saltonstall Arts Colony. His work has appeared on *Salon*, as part of the 331/3 book series, and in *American Short Fiction*.

bobproehl.com
Twitter: @bobproehl

EMBERS OF WAR
GARETH L. POWELL

From award-winning author Gareth L. Powell, the first book in the critically acclaimed Embers of War space opera series.

The warship Trouble Dog was built and bred for calculating violence, yet following a brutal war, she finds herself disgusted by conflict and her role in a possible war crime. Seeking to atone, she joins the House of Reclamation, an organisation dedicated to rescuing ships in distress. But, stripped of her weaponry and emptied of her officers, she struggles in the new role she's chosen for herself.

"Fast, exhilarating space opera, imaginative and full of life."
Adrian Tchaikovsky, author of *Children of Time*

"Powerful, classy and mind-expanding SF, in the tradition of Ann Leckie and Iain M. Banks."
Paul Cornell, author of *London Falling*

RE-COIL
J.T. NICHOLAS

The Expanse meets *Altered Carbon* in this breakneck science fiction thriller where immortality is theoretically achievable, yet identity, gender and selfhood are very much in jeopardy...

Out on a salvage mission Carter Langston is murdered by animated corpses left behind on the target ship. Yet in this future, a consciousness backup can be safely downloaded into a brand-new body, losing only the memories of what happened between your last backup and your death. But when Langston wakes in his new body he is immediately attacked in the medbay and has to fight once again for his life—and his immortality.

"A vividly written action-adventure."
Elizabeth Moon

"Perfect for fans of *Altered Carbon*"
Gareth L. Powell, award-winning author of the Embers of War series

For more fantastic fiction, author events,
exclusive excerpts, competitions, limited editions and more

VISIT OUR WEBSITE
titanbooks.com

LIKE US ON FACEBOOK
facebook.com/titanbooks

FOLLOW US ON TWITTER AND INSTAGRAM
@TitanBooks

EMAIL US
readerfeedback@titanemail.com

CENTRAL 18-11-2020